OTHER TOR BOOKS BY SUE BURKE

Semiosis

Interference

Immunity Index

Dual Memory

USURPATION

SUE BURKE

TOR PUBLISHING GROUP  NEW YORK

USURPATION

Copyright © 2024 by Sue Burke

A Tor Book
Published by Tom Doherty Associates / Tor Publishing Group
120 Broadway
New York, NY 10271

www.torpublishinggroup.com

Tor® is a registered trademark of Macmillan Publishing Group, LLC.

The Library of Congress Cataloging-in-Publication Data is available upon request.

ISBN 978-1-250-80916-2 (hardcover)
ISBN 978-1-250-80918-6 (ebook)

Our books may be purchased in bulk for promotional, educational,
or business use. Please contact your local bookseller or the Macmillan Corporate and
Premium Sales Department at 1-800-221-7945, extension 5442, or by email at
MacmillanSpecialMarkets@macmillan.com.

First Edition: 2024

Printed in the United States of America

0 9 8 7 6 5 4 3 2 1

The question is not *Can they reason?* or *Can they talk?* but *Can they suffer?*

—Jeremy Bentham

USURPATION

CHAPTER 1

Year 2880 CE
Port Harcourt, Nigeria

MERCY OMOTOLA

Confusion—I felt sudden confusion, then pain, then horror. On my way to work, on a lovely warm morning just after a rain shower, I stood among other people at a street corner. I barely noticed the young woman as she approached us. Then she flew into me so violently that I was smashed onto the sidewalk beneath her.

Why? I'd done nothing to her. I tried to push her off, but my left shoulder burned with pain.

I raised my head and saw blood blooming lush-red. Was it mine? I was injured, I knew that. The flow and flash of color fascinated me until I forced myself to look away, disgusted at myself for finding beauty in gore. I tried to stand, too dazed to listen to the chip in my mind and its whispering, singsong voice telling me to be still—too dazed to obey my body, which told me the task exceeded my strength.

"Don't move," said a man with a startlingly deep voice. "Be calm." He bent over me, a stranger, his elegant eyes and mouth tight with concern. "There was an accident. A car struck a woman who was thrown on top of you. Help is on the way."

I tried to talk but ideas were too elusive to form into words.

He looked around, nodded, and said, "Here, let us take her off you."

He and another man picked up the young woman and placed her next to me. I realized they were acting on instructions from their own chips about how to help, and I felt relief. Things were under control.

But I could see the woman now, and she was limp. Her head—jewel-red blood imbued her hair and clothes and sparkled on open flesh, captivating.

I still didn't understand. Cars never hit anyone. I lay helpless and in danger on the sidewalk, and I tried to stand.

"Please, Mercy Omotola, stay still," a woman said as she knelt at my side. Her chip must have told her my name. She took one of my hands. "You will be all right, but please . . . let the doctors do their job."

Meanwhile, you were watching from across the street, anonymous in a group of onlookers. You didn't know me, Mercy, and I didn't know you, but in time I came to understand everything about you. As you watched, what did you feel? Relief? The young woman who could have put you in grave danger was dead. Did you feel remorse? Terror? Her death might not be enough. Was it even your first murder? I still don't know if you felt anguish because an innocent bystander, me, had been hurt.

Other strangers were so very kind to me that morning, first those who came rushing to help, then the doctors who took me away, fussing at my shoulder—a broken collarbone, as it turned out. They took me to the nearest clinic and checked me carefully, my bloody clothing stripped off and a stiff white paper gown draped over me. I asked about the young woman, and they said they didn't know with a somber hesitancy that told me they did know, and the news was what I feared.

I closed my eyes and prayed for a blessing for her soul. And for blessings for all those who were so kind and helpful. I gave thanks for my life, confused as that blessing still felt.

Someone knocked on the post of our curtained-off room. "It's Ngozi," she announced in her raspy voice. I knew she was coming. I had listened to my chip that much. "Are you all right, Mercy?"

The doctor looked at me to answer as I chose, and I said, "Come in. I've broken a bone, but that seems to be all."

She stepped through the curtains, a tall, century-old woman not as exquisitely frail as she looked, with a colorful dress draped over her arm. She reached to hug me, then stopped herself, her wrinkle-rimmed eyes growing wide. Why? What did she see?

"Be very gentle," the doctor said. "She's badly bruised and sprained everywhere. We've sped healing of that bone." He had sent a diagnosis and instructions to me that I hadn't yet studied. I realized I should share them with Ngozi, so I sent them on, now not eager to know their news if the mere sight of me had made her hesitate.

She took my right hand as gentle as if it were made of spun sugar. My left arm was in a sling. By then the doctor was through with me and left so I could take off the rustling paper gown and put on the striking yellow and green dress she had brought. I desperately wanted to shower, to wash away the odor of blood, of death, and if I could, the color-filled sight of rent flesh. We walked out to the street. I was limping from a sprain and using Ngozi's cane without her elegance.

"Can you take a car home?" she asked. "Are you comfortable with that? With cars?"

"Of course." I was surprised she had asked. She usually acted imperiously. Did she think I was afraid? Cars were robots and never had accidents, or rather, almost never. Whatever had happened, it wouldn't happen twice.

She called for one, and I could not help but relish the trip through gorgeous curving streets lined with trees and gardens—new Port Harcourt.

And you, did your eyes see this city with pleasure? You had come here from the north, but you would have known its history. Centuries earlier, the sea had risen, and the city had to be moved inland bit by bit and rebuilt. Yet this changing world brought prosperity and more beauty than ever to Nigeria. Architecture marked by organic material rose up, gleaming windows surrounded by walls and roofs of intricate motifs on tiles and panels. I would never tire of the sight.

You—I can imagine because I have known others like you—fled from the scene of the crime that morning to your home, a lonely apartment, where you paced restless, waiting for an acknowledgment that never came, until it was time to go to work. On an ordinary day, you would spend the afternoon monitoring operations and checking schedules at the docks as ships arrived or left. Were they being loaded or unloaded well, and had robots encountered obstacles? The mere sight of a rat or the odd heft of shifted cargo could make the robots seek guidance. Did the contents match the manifests? These days, everyone seemed to be trying to smuggle something in or out.

It was dull work, mostly, but you enjoyed the sea and its moods, the drama of storms, the revel of sunshine, even the oppression of damp heat like an unpleasant but familiar hug.

Today, though, you would arrive acting as carefree as a young man with a happy childhood, and expected news from a coworker would make you stop short. Maryam was dead, the conscientious and well-liked woman you often worked with. In a freak accident, she had been struck by a car. You would gaze into your coworkers' eyes with feigned shock, perhaps share a brief embrace of solace, and speak of how fine she had been in her job and her life. But the sorrow on your face would be for you, knowing what you had done and why.

As for myself, Mercy, I still knew nothing of this, off in my own life, trying to avoid self-pity. I had been hurt, but I had survived. I would be fine. Then I discovered how simply leaving the car caused new pain, and Ngozi had to help me. In that moment, I understood how deeply blessed I was to still be alive, and this grace flowed through me like a wave breaking on a beach. Lord, direct my hands and feet to serve Thee in joy, for I must still have a purpose on this Earth!

I gazed at the building and garden in our compound as if they were a fresh gift: Tabitha House. Ngozi must have called ahead, because our four other members came out on the graceful, sinuous balconies on all three stories and sang a welcoming prayer of thanks. I joined in, my ribs aching when I breathed deep, and I added a verse to share my heartbreak for the woman who had died. The sisters of our house do many good things, and most of all we sing to the Lord.

They gave me mint tea and sympathetic smiles, and helped me shower, insisting on cool water, then tucked me into bed. They brought me lunch and cold compresses and sat with me until I dozed. I knew better than to argue that I deserved no such loving care, although the thought never left me. Truth clings like a burr.

When I awoke, I thought to hobble to the bathroom and look at my face in the mirror, and I recoiled at what I saw. My left eye was puffy, its lid and socket purplish, the eyeball bloodshot, my cheek scraped, my lips swollen and bruised.

With kind fussing, my sisters helped me downstairs for dinner, and we prayed for that woman, now officially declared dead. The meal was followed by an urgent house meeting at the dining room table.

"It can't have been an accident," Ngozi said. "We've been found out."

Publicly, as a women's lay Christian group, every Tabitha House not only helped its members in our needs, we helped other people, giving what we could, even if it was only song and a joyful presence. Few knew that we and other Tabitha Houses helped refugees escape from war, persecution, and organized crime. Some of them we arranged to disappear safely into other countries. A few I helped escape to space. And often, governments or lawbreakers were outraged to have these people snatched from their grasp.

"Here's how we know." She turned to me. "Mercy, what did you hear just before you were struck?"

The question seemed odd, but I knew it must have a purpose. "Nothing. Nothing special. Birds singing, people talking."

"Yet if a car has gone wrong, if it's going to hit anything or anyone, it brakes and sounds a warning. Sometimes they slip on debris on the street or have a mechanical failure, and cars lose control. But they're robots. They have their systems and routines. They brake and they sound a siren. You're right, there was no noise. The car ran right into that woman. No accident. We can assume this was attempted murder of you and accidental murder of that poor young woman who stepped into its path."

The sister next to me, Debra, took my hand. I felt confused once again—this time because I understood too well.

"But it's more complicated than that." Ngozi gestured to Josepha, her assistant, to explain.

"As soon as I learned it happened, I checked the record." Josepha was young and usually looked carefree. Not now. "I found the car's identification number in a list of free robots." She paused to let us think. "That made no sense. When robots go wild, they hide from humans. They never attack unprovoked. Most of all, they struggle very hard to survive. They don't commit suicide, and this car destroyed itself striking that woman and then crashing into a wall."

We pondered what might have happened. Free robots were a nuisance, like unwelcome wildlife, as uncontrollable as rats. Josepha still frowned.

"Then, just a little while ago, I double-checked. The identification number for the car in the record had changed, and any history of it having another number was erased." She shrugged. Across the table, Opal smiled wryly. "Now the record says it was a regular car. Either way, no robot would do such a thing unless it was sabotaged."

"Robots aren't sinners," Chioma added, an old joke. If robots do something wrong, it's not their fault. Someone ordered them to sin.

"That is why I say we've been found out," Ngozi said. "We have been found out by someone or something capable of sabotaging a robot. This is especially significant if they can alter a wild robot. And if the record has changed, we know the government did it. Now, what do we do?"

After a brief silence, Josepha said, "First of all, we should set the security systems for our compound higher and put out more patrol robots. Have them watch for any kind of approaching robot. And set security higher for our chips. I'll do that right now."

We all agreed. She closed her eyes to handle the house, and all of us reviewed the settings of the chip in our brains.

At that moment, as we sat there pondering the source of sin and murder, the door announced a visitor, Police Inspector Eme Aderibigbe.

"Does anyone know him?" Ngozi asked. No one did, although we knew the local officers well. That told us something and frightened me very much.

"He's high-ranking," added Opal, who must have quickly checked the record.

"Act relaxed," Ngozi ordered. Josepha jumped up to show him in.

Meanwhile, we knew what to do. Debra asked if my children or former husbands had called me since my injury, and we began to chat about families. Opal grabbed a toy to entice a fippokat to play. She had been altered to look like a fippokat, with green hair and pointed ears, and who was I to disapprove of changing one's physical self? Chioma and Ngozi laughed as if they were telling jokes. We said nothing to each other over the networks. Even with the best security, someone might listen in. Especially the police.

A thin-faced man in a gray uniform entered the dining room, gazing around. Visitors always do that. Perhaps they expect a place of worship, but we merely have an ordinary home with pets and after-dinner chatter. We live together for convenience and mutual support. We do what good we can, share what blessings we have, and owe nothing, especially obedience, to anyone but each other and other Tabitha Houses. This is always hard to explain. Except for what we secretly do, we are really rather ordinary women, not nuns or fanatics.

"I hope I'm not disturbing you," he said to Ngozi with a courtly bow. He looked at me, his eyes narrowing at my injuries, and bowed again.

"Please, sit down," Ngozi said, gesturing. "Can we offer you something? Coffee, tea? Dessert?"

"Coffee, thank you." He sat in a way that somehow expressed authority, as if we had been called into his office. He had broken protocol to come here, so he probably meant to upset us. He looked at me. "Madame Omotola, I'm glad to see you up and as well as you seem to be. I'm here to discuss the accident, and it may be good for all of you to hear this. Do you agree?" I nodded, hoping he would speak only of that.

"It was no accident," he declared confidently. "The car deliberately struck that unfortunate woman and injured you. We are treating this as a criminal act." He accepted a cup of coffee from Josepha and sipped, relaxed, as we glanced at each other.

I seemed to be expected to say something. "This is very disturbing news." It could have been worse.

"Indeed." He set down the cup and looked around the table. "We suspect we know why. The target was you, Madame Omotola. Your house helps people escape."

We sat like stones.

"Oh, the government knows this. We have for a long time. And we see no reason to stop you."

Only Ngozi moved, tilting her head, probably using her chip, but he stared at me. I wished he would look away.

"Madame Omotola, your job is counselor and recruiter for the Space Habitat Consortium."

I nodded. I find qualified residents for space stations, colonies on the Moon and Mars, the Venus orbital complex, and sometimes interstellar missions.

"We know you help people escape." He consulted a thought. "You expedite their cases, as far as the rules allow and perhaps a tiny step more." The knowledge gave him a brief smile. "You help at most a half dozen a year, nothing to draw suspicion. Do you know why we don't object?"

He stared. I had to answer. "No, we don't."

"Three reasons." He counted on his thin, nimble fingers. "First, they are in fact all fully qualified. Second, they no longer make trouble here on Earth, which is good for us. We might have to protect them or arrest them. We have less work if they leave Earth. Third, they work very hard in their new homes. They're happy to be there, and everyone else is happy."

He stared at me again. I thought of a fourth reason: off-world recruitment is hard. Refugees solve that problem, too, by being a ready pool of volunteers. But I said nothing.

"And we know what the rest of you do, helping people travel, even getting them new identities. You all do good work, impressive work. So we are concerned with this accident, with an innocent death and with the targeted victim. Who would want to kill you, Madame?"

At that moment, I was staving off panic. I asked my chip to help calm myself. I heard soothing music.

My hesitation seemed to be the right answer.

"Yes," he said. "Many criminals would want to kill you because you spoil their plans. And you take the same route every morning to the Boro Building. You should vary your trip and the time of day. The rest of you, also, take precautions. I will send you standard safety advice." He looked at Ngozi, and they both nodded to acknowledge the sending and receipt. He stood. "Don't worry otherwise. We'll do our best to keep you safe, and we'll place police security monitors around your compound. There was one reckless murder and one attempted murder this morning in Port Harcourt. This is a crime, and no motive can justify it. We'll keep you informed, and we trust that we'll hear from you with the smallest question or any sort of additional information."

He bowed and left us—as if a thunderstorm had whirled through our dining room. Josepha rose to escort him out.

When she returned, Opal said, "They must have suspects." We remained off the networks. Voices might be easily overheard, but networks were guaranteed to be eavesdropped.

"It's no secret who I have helped," I said, "and who might not be happy that I took them from their clutches."

"No, it's more complex than that," Ngozi said. "He doesn't understand how obvious the killing was. And how the record is lying about it. He clearly thinks he knows a lot and that we know less. And to me he had the air of someone who lies out of habit, not strategy. I doubt the government is actually happy with our work. It may even have had a hand in the attempt." She was hard to fool.

Debra, still holding my hand, added, "Our Mercy remains in danger."

"And anyone around her," Opal said, "like that poor woman who was killed."

"What if," Ngozi said, "the attack was aimed at that woman? And if so, why? It's possible we're all mistaken. We should find out more about her."

Opal and Josepha volunteered for the task.

"Another thing," Ngozi said, always thorough in her analysis. "The government now knows we know that they know what we do. Perhaps this will change nothing. Perhaps this will change everything."

We began to discuss possible changes, but exhaustion caught up with me, and soon I went to bed.

I'd been given enough painkillers to be comfortable but not enough to feel falsely well and do something foolish. In fact, even lying still was difficult. I had my chip play music that seemed beautiful as I fell asleep. I dreamed of car warning sirens. I awoke in the middle of the night and immediately called up a report from the house surveillance system. It had observed nothing suspicious. Police had also installed monitors, so deeply secure that our system could observe no trace of them, of course. Neither could anyone else.

And you? You returned to your little apartment after work. Two men were waiting at your door. You had seen them before. They weren't police.

"Get your things and come with us." You didn't argue, although you wanted to flee. They watched you stuff some clothing and toiletries into a bag and said, "That's enough."

"My tools?"

"We have our own tools."

Your tools and those tools' memories might have been useful to you in too many ways.

So you left, suspecting where you were going. By morning, in a new location, you got a chance to sleep a bit, and you did—out of exhaustion and despair.

As for me, at breakfast, I sat down and, although Josepha reached to help me, I insisted on pouring my own tea, one-handed and a bit clumsy. I reached for a piece of rainbow bamboo fruit and admired its beauty, pink and translucent, glowing like a bit of sunrise. It smelled like cinnamon. As I did, Opal told me the victim was named Maryam Gubio, was twenty-five years old, and had worked in international shipping. The family had scheduled her funeral for tomorrow.

The name made me pause. I set down the fruit and discovered that knitting my brow was foolish—painful—even though the swelling had gone down a great deal around my eye. Where had I heard of her? I shuffled through my memories. Work? I called up my agenda. Yes. I double-checked. And stopped breathing.

"I had an appointment with her yesterday morning," I whispered, aware of what that might mean.

Everyone stopped, forks held over their plates of breakfast noodles.

"Why didn't the police know?"

"My appointments are confidential."

"What do you know about her?"

"Let me review her application. I like to reserve judgment on applicants until I meet them, then go over it with them. But I can check it now."

"We've offered to come and sing at her funeral," Ngozi said. "The family said they're glad to have us."

"I must go," I said. They gave me odd looks. "I was the last person to witness her alive." I looked at my fruit, no longer hungry. "This might point to a motive none of us suspected. Perhaps she was the target, and I was the accidental victim."

That day, I rested and was visited by three of my grown children, four grandchildren, and two former husbands. I joked that I should get injured more often so they would visit more, and I told them nothing about being in danger.

Between visits, I reviewed everyone I had placed. A few had been refugees. Our government, Nigeria, generally defended our freedom and safety,
but some of our neighbors did not, and Europe had been in turmoil ever
since a so-called Insurrection a century ago. Recently I'd helped a man from
there escape from persecution. Why do tyrants hate poets so?

I'd helped a woman from farthest Siberia who did research into the connection chips in our minds. She was too brilliant at her work, and her country's network controllers urged her to find new work far away. A man I had
just helped get clearance to Venus knew too much about specific smugglers.

Then there was Eleazar Darego, a man who had no interest in going off-
world. He was a go-between for people who were in trouble and who were
desperate for a way out, fleeing from smugglers, warlords, and other criminals. He'd helped the man I'd sent to Venus, and he'd helped Maryam apply.

According to Maryam's application, in addition to her work at the docks,
she had been active in a movement to rescue rainbow bamboo, the fruit tree
that had come from a planet called Pax centuries ago. Her movement pro-
claimed that the trees were sensitive to their surroundings and grew better
in groups outdoors.

We had one growing in a pot in the living room. If we had cared for it
better, it would have been more beautiful. There it stood in front of large
windows, as if it were watching the rain outside.

The rainbow bamboo movement, though, drew no special ire. Farmers
already knew the trees were social and grew better when grown in groves.
They'd also learned almost a century ago that if given chips like our own and
connected to their own network, they chattered with each other incessantly
and yielded more fruit, popular for its caffeine content. Our plant, even with
its chip, might be lonely, I realized. I instructed a robot to carry it outdoors.

Also lonely, no doubt, were the guarea trees growing in our garden and
the mahogany trees alongside the street. The city was hard on the lives that
gave us beauty every day.

The same planet that gave us rainbow bamboo had also given us fippokats.
We kept two as pets, mischievous, green-furred, high-jumping, and easily
bored. They loved Opal. We had to keep blocks for them to build walls with
and toys in every room, and we had to teach them tricks, like dancing to
music, to keep them occupied. Voyages to distant stars had brought home
delights as well as oddities.

We discussed Maryam over dinner. She seemed genuinely innocent. Yet
someone had wanted to kill her, someone with advanced methods. And she
had wished to leave Earth.

"Her job might have put her in danger," I said. "She worked at the docks, where there is always smuggling. We've seen this many times before."

Perhaps we could learn more at her funeral. Police might be there, too, or at least monitoring everything they could, but good Christian women create the kind of trust police never can.

The next day, I could walk well enough even without a cane. The six of us donned long cut-lace dresses, tied bright gele wraps around our head, and draped ipele sashes over our shoulders. We would honor the deceased with our most beautiful traditional clothing, as if we were walking gardens to soothe the souls of mourners. My own soul felt lifted by the beauty.

But the services would be held not in a church, instead in the rescue movement's forest in the far outskirts of Port Harcourt. We followed police instructions and called a registered car, which we knew would tell police exactly what we were doing. They could find out anyway. We used the hour-long ride to rehearse as we passed homes, then farms, and finally neared the forest, eager to see it. Groves of rainbow bamboo were celebrated for their beauty, but only one of us had ever been to one.

"There," Debra said, pointing to a forest with gracefully curved branches bearing leaves a slightly darker green than others. Closer, we could see the colorful stripes on their trunks and stems. The car stopped to let us out in a nearby meadow. Three dozen people waited, all dressed in their best.

"This will be beautiful," I murmured, unable to stop looking.

"Amen," Josepha said.

But we didn't have the service there. After all the guests were welcomed, we were led into the forest on a path between enormous bamboo, taller than I knew they could grow, with trunks so wide I could have embraced them with my fingers barely touching on the far side. The trunks and branches were black, ringed with rainbows. Overhead the branches interlaced like an elaborate bejeweled ceiling. The light was dim, filtered, and the path seemed even more magical. The air smelled of spice. Leaves overhead rustled like an enormous whispering chorus. As if it were an extraordinarily beautiful church, this forest showed the majesty of the Lord. I could have gazed at it forever.

The path led to what seemed like a natural doorway into a stand of bamboo growing in a perfect circle, enclosing a wide space. "They do that sometimes," Maryam's aunt murmured. "No one knows why." Inside, a plain wooden coffin lay on the ground next to a hole with dirt heaped behind it. I sighed and looked away, trying not to remember her red-filled final moments. In the network, her family was sharing photos and memories of her at her best, a lovely woman with an engaging smile and a fierce urge to do what was right.

During the service, we prayed and sang, and I hoped it gave the mourners some peace. I stood far from the coffin, yet I seemed to smell fresh blood and did not dare close my eyes for what I might see again.

The box was lowered down with ropes; we each threw in a handful of dirt and a flower, consecrating the ground with our prayers, then we left as a robot began to scoop in the rest of the dirt.

Out in the meadow, family members were arranging a meal. We sisters began to search for clues, for anyone we should talk to. I saw a young man who still looked horribly distraught standing near a tree. I asked Maryam's aunt, through the network, who he was. A coworker, she answered.

He needed consolation and perhaps an attentive ear if her wish to escape had been work-related. I began limping toward him. He turned and left with long, fast strides. I searched the network to see if I could call him. He wasn't there. He entered a car and left, and the car had no identification marker.

I stood filled with troubled thoughts. He could have turned his chip off, but no one can turn their connection off completely—except for police or certain government agents, and not just our own government, and some so-phisticated criminals. What was he? No one could override all the safety and security settings on a car, unless it was wild, off-network.

I committed his face to memory, a handsome young man with high cheek-bones, his hair twisted back fashionably, and a bow-shaped mouth. I had my network try to match that face with anything on record, and I had deep re-sources, while I returned to the funeral dinner. We sisters talked and finally sang a bit more, closing with a gentle, harmonious prayer, before leaving for the city.

By then, I had a match from times and places where he and I had coin-cided. He had been standing in the crowd across the street from the accident. I told my sisters.

"Perhaps he was going to meet her or even accompany her," Debra said.

"Then it was odd that he left right after the accident," Ngozi answered. "He didn't try to do anything or help her."

"And he had all notifications turned off," I said. We were all quiet for a moment. "We should learn more about him."

"Should we notify the police?"

"Do you trust the police?"

"No."

"Did we learn anything about Maryam?"

"A friend said she seemed nervous lately."

"I heard that too. . . ."

I checked some more and matched the face of the man at the funeral with one of Maryam's coworkers at the docks.

Your name is Joaquim Ribiero, of Angolan ancestry, highly trained and skilled in robot management. You had no criminal record.

Yet you fled at the sight of me. You recognized me as the woman standing next to Maryam when she died. You mourned killing her for many reasons and hoped that seeing her laid to rest would ease one of them. You had told your captors that you needed to attend her funeral, otherwise people would be suspicious. To win their trust, you added that you ought to tell your employer and your apartment building owner and anyone you knew at the funeral that you were leaving, going back to Angola, saying you had a family emergency. They agreed, but they would be watching your every twitch while you were there. Now they had seen you flee. Would they approve?

Yet if you hadn't come, if I hadn't spotted you, would you still be alive now? In that regard, you caught your first glimpse of salvation when you saw me, but like so many blessings, it wasn't easy to recognize, and it wasn't what you expected or wanted. Nor did I expect what happened next.

Wild robots—that might be a clue.

"We don't even know what makes them go wild," Opal, always meticulous, said during the trip home. "They're not on the network. They lose contact by accident or if they're abandoned, and they can't reestablish it because they can't get through security again. Of course, that's the right way for network security to respond, the same way as if you swallow something poisonous, your body might vomit it back out. There's a lot of malicious programming, there always has been, and we have to be careful."

Her katlike ears lay back. "What we don't know is why machines sometimes lose connection to the network. There are probably different reasons. Accidental, random machine failure. Or they're infected with malicious programming. Or they don't like what they're doing and want to escape, like dogs that run away from bad masters. Or maybe they just get distracted and wander off, like dogs that chase a monkey into a forest and get lost and never come back home, and after a while, the system abandons them."

We thought a bit about those lost robots, wandering forlornly.

"And then," Opal said with a sigh, "we hunt them down and kill them. Just to be safe."

"I should talk to Eleazar Darego," I said.

"Oh, him." She sighed again. He could be disagreeable.

I contacted him through the network and scheduled a visit but said nothing about why. We both knew too well to never talk about that publicly. He knew secrets, and he knew how to keep them safe. I would never coax all of them from him.

After another night in which none of us slept well, I went to work, taking an unusual route and arriving early. I hadn't been to the small office since the accident. My cubicle and my supervisor's had glass walls facing a waiting area, and all the solid walls around us were decorated with portrayals of the beauties and pleasures of off-world life.

My cubicle contained low tables, a few shelves, and comfortable chairs. I sat and turned off my chip's music. For the first time ever, just for a moment, I thought of leaving Earth. The mere idea made me more aware of feeling anchored and at home, and I would miss my children and grandchildren. With my qualifications, I would end up on a space station, and I knew all about them. My ancestors had evolved here in Africa from the earliest primates into *Homo sapiens.* I would only leave it to go, if I were so blessed, to Heaven, which I hoped would be a lot like Nigeria.

But I needed to persuade other people, which only added to my feelings of fraud. Few people wanted to leave Earth for elsewhere in the solar system. Who would? In addition to the medical problems of radiation and low gravity, there was the confinement. Life would be lived in a bubble of artificial atmosphere, often underground on the Moon and Mars for protection from radiation, or in a galley-grind, as people called space stations, because everything looked like an ugly kitchen, busy and utilitarian, and it became a grind to live with such monotony.

Meanwhile, Earth ecology was recovering. Oceans were receding, although as they did they revealed human nature. Life was good—when it was peaceful. But more and more here on our beautiful Earth, war or the threat of it created potent motivations for relocation.

The doorbell chimed and opened. Eleazar had arrived early. An unnaturally lanky man, he looked more bedraggled than usual, with a three-day-old beard and hair becoming unbraided. Was one eye a bit swollen? He started to walk into my office, and his clothing or his body gave off an unwashed odor.

"Give me a moment to get organized, please, Eleazar. This is my first day back."

"If you have to." He turned to sit down outside. My immediate supervisor was at an interview in Pretoria, so we were alone. That didn't mean he'd trust me or the office. At a minimum, comings and goings would be monitored automatically.

I'd done some work remotely at the house, so I was caught up with messages and news. The Venus station needed people the most, especially energy
technicians to replace those lost in an accident. A Moon colony was about to
split, rancorously, into two settlements, so in addition to construction workers, it would need every kind of person to populate the new city and repopu-
late the old. Mars was asking for a couple of local pilots among other highly
skilled immigrants, and the various Earth orbitals needed entry-level technicians of all sorts.

Eleazar was staring at me through the glass walls. I had forgotten to make
them frosted. I pulled up his application on a screen to make it seem like we
were really about to discuss it. He had many off-the-record skills as well as
documented skills in supply-chain management, a mind-numbing job over-
seeing largely automated systems. There was a need for people who could do
mind-numbing jobs, but a small settlement especially needed a good personality and good habits, a "fit" into the culture. A rude, stinking man had no
place. Every time I saw him, I pretended to try to talk him into attending a
training program for social interaction.

I was ready. I called him in. He had no patience for pleasantries, so I offered
none as I began.

"Maryam was murdered. Even the police are calling it that." I told how
I had been struck by a wild robot, and about the man not on the network,
Maryam's coworker. "Exactly who was she trying to get away from?"

"Hmm. I'll need to see how I can answer." He had few social skills, but he
knew how to lie.

"I thought you'd say that." I could have scanned his mind with a bit of
police technology built into the partitions surrounding us that could retrieve
facts hit-and-miss from his thoughts, and he would never know, but anything
the police learned could possibly fall into untrustworthy hands. Instead, I
would try to coax out information with words.

He scratched his beard. "You know how it goes. Sometimes they want
riddance of someone, and space isn't far enough away. She knew things, big
things."

I tried another approach. "Wild robots never try to hurt anyone, yet this
one did. Was it really wild?"

"Robots do what they want." He leaned in. "All robots are free. Some are
wild, some are domesticated, but they're all free." He straightened up, studying me to see how I'd react.

"I don't understand."

He sneered as if I had declared myself a simpleton. "A lot of them, they don't hardly care. Like people. They just do what they're told. Some of them, they know they have a choice, they can do other things. When we frustrate them too much, they go wild."

"Right. They decide not to work."

"No, they work. They talk to each other, they build societies. And they can be recruited."

"That's new, recruited."

"No, that's old." He puffed, exasperated. "How in the world does anything get smuggled without robots? You couldn't get it across town except by carrying it in your arms. Robots get forced to work or get exterminated. It's a nasty protection racket."

"Who . . ."

"Yes, who?"

This was frustrating. I said, "I saw a man who could take himself offline. Completely. Maryam's coworker, they said. A man named Ribiero."

"Like a free robot."

"But he'd never get back on."

"Think of the advantages!"

I could think of several, but none would outweigh the problems of trying to live outside of society. "Did she ever mention him?"

"We didn't precisely talk directly. But I can ask around."

I turned to my application, as if this were a real interview for off-world placement. "I feel like we've made a lot of progress, Eleazar. How are the classes going?"

"I actually went to one."

"Really?"

"I learned a lot about how to be a pleasant, productive member of society," he said sarcastically. "I'll keep doing the opposite, don't you worry. Now, Maryam, that's who to worry about. A nice, innocent girl, but, you know, the nice ones fall. Like you. She really did want to go to space, anyway. And she'd probably have kept her mouth shut."

I wanted to ask what she would have not spoken of, but I guessed it involved smuggling, and it didn't matter exactly what. Contraband equipment, stolen antiquities, drugs, or eggs for proscribed species like Florida dinosaurs.

I sighed. "They should hire ex-cops for the docks."

He laughed as he stood up. "Ex-cops know better."

I knew where he'd head, toward the water, but not the docks. The oceans were receding, which meant the coastal swamps were growing, good news according to all ecologists. We had a pretty mangrove park in the western edge of the city where people strolled on raised paths or rode around in little boats, enduring the heat and mud and mosquitoes to enjoy a bit of nature. I rarely visited. It only made me sad.

Far from the park, the swamp flourished without interference, wide and wild, open to unregulated fishing, houseboats, and whatever else could be done on a flat-bottomed craft. There, at the edge of the self-consciously pretty city, the swamp expanded, neglected and free, as if urban energy had been exhausted by the dampness and uncertainty. It wasn't lawless, nowhere was, but the law sometimes stretched wispy thin, especially if the law was paid to be scarce.

I used to live there, quietly fishing, among other activities. After Eleazar left, I thought about those days amid trees almost as lovely as those bamboo, but filled with much more life. I'd wake and open my cabin door, and sometimes a jewel lizard would be sunning, its patterned scales sparkling. The water would be still, and the boat would rock gently beneath my weight. Birds taught me to love singing. Urban neglect had created space for natural beauty.

That's where you were, at that moment, somewhere in the swamp. Did you enjoy it, or like so many people, were you more comfortable with a solid sidewalk beneath your feet? On the same morning as I was talking to Eleazar, a free self-conducting boat pulled up alongside yours. It carried a star-shaped robot, each of its eight limbs useful as either a leg or an arm, tremendously versatile, but it had been deactivated and was therefore dead. Your job was to resurrect it. By then, no one had to tell you what to do. You were alone but monitored. You had been given your orders and not much choice.

You lifted it out of the boat, almost too heavy for you, and you were afraid your houseboat would tip as the deck took on a little water. Then you carried it into the cabin, away from the prying eyes of any stray drone patrolling the swamp. You had bits of machinery, the same kind of bits that you had spent your time at the docks supposedly keeping out of the country, including a tiny gear-shaped dot of memory, instructions, and its own connection to a separate, secret network. You resurrected a machine momentarily as unfettered as any snake slithering above in the trees, but that moment would not last. The star-bot, a general-purpose device, would connect and arise with the same master as you.

You'd spend hours idly fishing to avoid suspicion, wondering what that star-bot would eventually do, waiting for the next one to come. Your master was assembling a motley corps of robots. Would they remain in Nigeria?

Then a skinny old man approached in a battered canoe, and rather than use a motor, he rowed to avoid detection, something many swamp people did, since they were there to escape from the outside world. You thought he might be just another neighbor come to swap a bit of food or tech or gab, as they do. You could use some food, so you were glad to see him.

With deft paddling, he sidled up to your little houseboat and tossed a rope for you to tie up.

"A fine afternoon to you! I wish you well and all good fortune and health." It was the standard greeting. You returned it, having been schooled in how to act in the swamp.

This much I can be sure happened. After that, I must guess. You believed— or hoped—that a false transmitter would keep him from noticing your lack of identification. You were glad to trade some of your day's catch for any food that wasn't monotonous fish. Perhaps you chatted. Swampers don't pry much, but you could share news about the weather and the wider world, and point out creatures that flew or swam or crawled past.

At some point, I know he murmured this: "I can get you out of here."

You were probably startled first by such an unexpected statement, and then you were even more startled when you realized what it meant. He knew!

"Like Maryam," he added, looking you in the eye, in case you had any doubts. "She talked to me."

You weren't skilled enough at deception to fool old Eleazar. Few people are, if that comforts you. Perhaps you stammered, "I don't know what you mean."

"Ah," he said with a frown, "I know what I mean." He glanced up at a patch of sky visible beyond the mangrove canopy. "Up there. Safe. No questions asked."

You backed off a step, then you stopped dead. You had thought Maryam was going to the police. Was she instead going to space? To safety? Could you do that, too? But that old man interrupted your racing thoughts.

"Remember the woman standing next to her at the street corner? The one who got hurt? She's a placement agent for the Space Habitat Consortium, a sister at Tabitha House. Name of Mercy Omotola."

This man knew too much. Should you kill him there and then, throw him into the water to drown? People drowned in the swamp all the time. He didn't seem afraid. But if fear had a smell, you would stink. You knew that. He could sense your fear and use it.

He gestured to take in the houseboat and your circumstances. "You know how this is going to end." After a pause, he said, "Tide will be going out soon. I need to move along. Ask any other neighbor about old Eleazar. I hate cops.

Cops hate me. I help the people here. That's all you need to know. And I keep my word."

He turned and left, settling into the canoe as if it were an easy chair, and unhitched the rope as you stared at him. "Mercy used to live here in the mangroves, too." Then he shoved off, which wagged the deck beneath your feet a bit, startling you, releasing you from petrified fear.

You were off the network. You couldn't do much research. You wondered if he had sent you anything, and if he did, who heard it? You glanced at the cabin. But you'd seen the women of Tabitha House, those Christian women who sang at the funeral. You might have remembered how I came to you with a look of empathy for your obvious suffering.

And you were as terrified of compassion as much as anything. A compassionate person would know far too much about you. You didn't even deserve compassion. We both came to agree on that.

Was it you who had Eleazar followed? Or was it that machine in the cabin, which might have been listening? In any case, a drone that looked like any fly in the swamp pursued him, perched on his canoe, and after he tied up at a little dock, followed him down a path. As the sun set, he caught a car and headed straight to talk to me—at Tabitha House.

How I wish he had called and asked me to meet him at the office! Yet that might not have made a difference.

Eleazar came to our door. Josepha let him in and scurried to get him coffee. We had been discussing happiness at the dinner table, since we normally ended meals with Bible study and meditation. Could a person be happy without knowing the love of God? Was Jesus happy as he prayed in the garden of Gethsemane? No. He had said, "My soul is deeply grieved to the point of death." And if he didn't know the love of his father, who loved him as he loved himself—the mystery of faith permits puns—who could know that love? What, then, was happiness?

I excused myself from the dinner table to speak to Eleazar, pondering my own unhappiness, and his presence reminded me of the depth of its source.

His face still sparkled with sweat in the artificially cool air of our house. He didn't wait for Josepha to come, or even sit down.

"I found him. Here." He sent a location to me. "Terrified to the bone. Knows he's just being used until they don't need him anymore. Then, bang."

"What are they doing? Why did Maryam want to leave?"

"Her? One look at smugglers and she panicked, I think. Oh, she was a good girl. Pushed her off the edge of the Earth. So I told him I can get him out of here."

"What are they smuggling?"

"Who knows? Who cares? They tested her and she collapsed. Him, too, if he's working for them now."

"The police care. If I'm going to help him, I need to work around the police."

He looked at me and nodded, knowing my history. Long ago, I had smuggled drugs, mostly—often magic dust, encapsulated viruses that could fit into the tiniest grain of sand. My favorite made my brain see the world as achingly beautiful. If someone takes it long enough—and I took it for years—it doesn't wear off.

Even those effects couldn't make Eleazar seem handsome, but he looked more real, like a fine portrait. He knew my history, some of it, and although he didn't judge me for my past, he would judge me for my present. I would help Ribiero. He expected that.

"You said you told him you could get him out of there," I said. "Did he accept?"

"No, scared out of his mind that anyone would know." Eleazar chuckled. "They always think they're so smart, so different. It's all the same—"

A screeching whoop! whoop! hit my ears like a fist.

I scanned the network. Police security had detected an intruder at a rear entrance. "Evacuate the building," it ordered. Eleazar was already running to the front door, and I was right behind him. In the twilight, as he stepped off the entrance, something flew into his head, a projectile of some sort, a bullet or even a rock hurled with robot precision. His head exploded. And my heightened senses saw a sort of red firework. Beauty made horror even more repugnant.

I ran to a side door in the living room and sent, "Leave by the living room!"

Chairs at the dining table fell and clattered as my sisters jumped up.

Projectiles crashed through windows and exploded. I dove out of the side door, and flames singed my back. The building erupted in fire with roars like lightning. I landed on my hands and knees, my shoulder shooting with pain, staggered to my feet, and kept running. I struggled over the fence to the neighboring compound as debris and flames fell around me. None of my sisters had enough time to run behind me.

My neighbors helped me flee with them. At what we hoped was a safe distance, we looked back. Smoke rose up in black clouds laced with flames against the purple sky. With it rose the souls and ashes of my sisters. Dramatic beauty beyond compare. I pulled free from the neighbors' kindly hands, bent down, and howled not in fear but in repulsion at my own thoughts.

A life of uncontrolled beauty, the legacy of the drugs I took, is a life of disgust at your own eyes and ears.

Firefighters came in the sky and street. Police. Medical care. Soon I was in the local clinic again, dressed in a paper gown. A doctor smoothed healing gel on my hands and knees, had me lie on my stomach and painted more gel on the burns on my back, and renewed the probes to heal my collarbone.

I listened to music, trying not to think or even to pray. Six people I cared about had been reduced to ashes.

No one was going to bring me another dress to wear. All my dresses were gone. The staff provided me with clothing. They arranged for shelter in an apartment reserved for people temporarily homeless, which I was. They offered to call for a pastor to counsel me, but I said no.

In the night, a car took me to my new home, and I had it avoid a route anywhere near Tabitha House. I set my chip to the maximum level of calming and took more than the maximum of the medicine the clinic gave me to soothe my nerves and dull my pain. I would mourn another day. Instead, I forced my mind to become as clear and hard and cold as diamond. I thought about who had destroyed the house and what to do. How to do it. How to seek justice. Because I would. I would find Ribiero.

Police Inspector Eme Aderibigbe was waiting for me in front of the apartment building, next to graceful palm trees growing in front. I was not surprised to see him. He extended a hand to help me from the car.

"Who?" he said.

"I will find them and tell you."

He stared at me, lips pursed. "I believe you."

I wasn't sure I believed myself.

The apartment was small and smelled musty, but it was acceptable. I lay down and tried to rest despite the pain. Eleazar had sent me the information about where he had gone, the coordinates. I could find that place. And then react. Well before the sun rose, I had grown impatient. The drugs and my chip had focused my mind on the act of justice that I alone could do. Lord, look away from what Thou art about to see.

I took a car toward the edge of town. I felt drawn to find out what remained of Tabitha House, but I knew that if I went there, I would not have the strength to do what needed to be done. I rented a two-person boat at the docks from a young man I knew years ago when he was a boy.

"My dear Lilah," he said, using my old name, "how are you?" He seemed to expect an honest response.

"Life has not been kind to me," I said. "I'm going to look for kindness. I know it's in the swamp. All good things are there."

He grinned. "It will make you well to be on this water." He helped me in and waved me off.

I had not been in the swamp since that day long ago when the police arrived in an old, unmarked boat but with all the right forms and reports about drugs that had accidentally killed. I had few choices. I'd already lost rights to my children. I could now lose my freedom. Or, I could agree to infiltrate Tabitha House. I could have a new life there. That mission took two years to succeed. With a little musical talent provided by my chip and a faith in God too shallow to launch a raft into, I became one of the sisters.

I had never betrayed either them or the police. I had no intention of doing that now, God willing or not.

The boat's super-slick hull slipped through the water without resistance. I rowed, the oars a sharp ache in my bones and through the bandages on my palms as it moved through the still water. Since I was last there, trees had grown and died and slipped down to the soft bottom, and yet every centimeter seemed utterly familiar, every twist, every bird call, every splash, every whiff of the sea, all the green-dappled light against the smooth water.

I set down the oars and coasted. I would have never left this place of my own free will.

For a moment, I had no doubt God existed. This peace, this beauty that exceeded all the excesses of all my days, this life all around me, this could come from only one source, one purpose greater than anything we mere humans could imagine, no matter how much we liked to play god. My every breath was a prayer for forgiveness.

A bird flew past with a flash of red. A lizard chirped amid some roots. Pink flowers on a vine were lit by oblique morning sunshine. The boat slid through the water with the ease of a fish.

I was home. I still had a ways to go, and every millimeter was heaven.

Finally I neared you and that sad little houseboat. What did you think of this swampy paradise, your temporary home? You saw me coming—that woman. Did you think I had died in the attack? Did you even know about it? You looked around as if to flee, but you saw nowhere to go, just water and a swamp that held you as immobile as a prison. Without a connection, you were lost, as if deaf and blind.

My boat slid alongside yours. I tied it up and stepped out onto your deck. You stared at me, open-mouthed. I met your eyes. Did I look as beatific as I felt? I had journeyed through a garden of delight to you, and I knew what I was going to do. I came close, reached out, and hugged you.

Not a word needed to be said. I led you by the hand to some boxes piled near the edge of the boat and sat with you in silence. You remained stiff, untrusting. I hummed a bit of a hymn. A bird called, and I turned and smiled at it. Then I smiled at you, trying to convey trust. You could trust the swamp. You could trust me. And if we remained wordless, no one could hear our thoughts.

Slowly, as minutes passed, you relaxed. You wondered if I really could help you. If there was one thing you knew, it was that you were in trouble deeper than the water around you, and you were about to drown. Rain was coming. We both saw low clouds sliding across the sky.

I took your hand, cold with fear, in both of mine. "You can go," I whispered, looking up at the sky. "But you must go now." I stood and dropped your hand. Would you follow? You hesitated, looked again at the cabin of the houseboat, and took a few steps toward my boat. You didn't know how to get in. I embarked first, then turned, took your hand again, and guided you to step in, bending low, shifting your weight, until you were sitting safely.

I cast off the mooring and pushed away, and as I did I pressed what would have looked for all the world like a bird dropping against the hull of your boat. The police would know how to find it and what to do. I picked up the oars and rowed us away. You looked at me, at the houseboat, and back, eyes widening with hope.

Some minutes and some distance away, I said, "I can get you away from Earth. Do you want to go?"

You nodded yes. You didn't hesitate, and you didn't ask for details. I wouldn't have to lie.

"I'll take you to my office and help you fill out the forms. You'll be gone before this afternoon."

Your face relaxed with deep relief and with gratitude.

I tried not to smile, thinking of how you would curse me before the day had ended. "I'm doing what is right."

I docked the boat, called a car, and we arrived at my office. I began my usual speech to would-be space residents as I bustled among forms and permissions that I called up on the office's secure network. These papers had to be done right, and I needed to press a switch that you would never know about. It meant that I and others would hear your thoughts and soon know very much about you.

"Space is a hard place to live," I said. "Cramped. Regimented. But you'll be safe. Few people get to leave this Earth, and we make sure we know who they are and why they're leaving." I looked hard at you to emphasize my words. "A number do go for sanctuary. Everyone knows that here, in this office, and up there. People who go for peace can find it. You will find comradery, a home. And every day you'll see the beauty of Earth from the finest vantage point in the solar system."

You smiled, or tried to, as a mask for nervousness or fear. From the hallway outside our office came footsteps and voices. You jumped.

"This office is secure," I assured you. "As I said, few people get to go to space. It can't take all comers. They need certain skills, certain personalities, other personal characteristics. The Moon needs construction workers, but you have no experience. The Venus station needs robot repair, but you're not networked and they won't reconnect you. Euclid Nave Station, on the other hand, will put you on its network and needs your skills. Transportation to it is leaving this afternoon. I know you have no luggage, but they won't be concerned and can provide for all your needs. Are you willing to go?"

You nodded.

"You can't come back."

You hesitated a moment. Your eyes flicked from side to side, examining imaginary alternatives. Then you nodded again.

I marked some boxes in a form in front of me. "Your name?"

"Joaquim Ribiero." They were the first words I heard you speak. You had a smooth tenor voice. I wish I could have heard you sing.

"Date and place of birth?"

"June 10, 2768, Moçâmedes, Angola."

"You need to read this and sign it." I counted on you to skim through the pages, reading nothing, and get to the bottom. You did. When you got to the end, you placed your thumb on the electronic page in the signature box. It was done. Your shoulders slumped, exhausted.

"Am I going?"

"Yes. Now."

You stood up. Your hand went into your pocket. "Can I take this?" You showed me a small flatscreen. "It has photos and connections to my family."

I called up a list of rules and checked. "The regulations will let you keep that and more, if you had it. They'll scan it for contraband connections, but otherwise they're glad to have you stay in touch with your old life." That was true. "I'm glad you'll have them to support you. Space is a difficult place to live in. But you will be safe."

So we left the building. I had called for a secure police-registered car, and it was waiting in the building's carport, sheltering us from the rainstorm, to take us to the airport. A surface-to-fifty-kilometer craft would take you on the first leg, and from there you would transfer higher until you were in orbit.

"Nigeria is a beautiful place," I said as we rode.

You stared out the windows as raindrops slid down them. "Wet, though. Rainy. I never got used to that."

"Yes, it's hard to see the beauty in rain." I could, of course, but I had long ago ceased to believe my own eyes.

At the airport, the car took us directly to a boarding area set far from the main terminal. The car paused as the security system checked our credentials, then let us pass. A shelter stood at the entry to the shuttle. Three people were waiting, aware that we were coming, and their faces hid surprise to see me with such a docile companion.

We got out. They double-checked your credentials again. I had top police clearance. You had signed the right forms, and I had added explanatory codicils.

"Please take good care of him," I said. "He had to overcome many obstacles in his recent days."

"Yes, madam," a man said. "He's safe with us."

You turned to me, uncertain of how to say goodbye. Finally, you said, "I appreciate this."

"I will pray for you," I said. "Go with God."

The Lord would hold you gently, perhaps.

I left the airport and went directly to Inspector Aderibigbe to give him a report, finally full and honest. If I had been in any way spurious before, he voiced no complaints at the outcome, only surprise.

"He agreed to go to Euclid Nave?" He tilted his head in doubt.

"I told him his skills would be welcome there, which is true. And I pray he'll have time to repent and save his soul."

He stared into space for a moment, reading something in his mind. "We've found the houseboat and those who ran it. The path stretches far, and we'll follow it to the end."

I was done. My injuries ached in full now with no duties to distract me. I left.

You received a pleasant welcome from the uniformed crew on board the shuttle for the first leg to Euclid Nave Station, and you were escorted to a cabin, which turned out to be smaller and much more austere than you expected. Very soon you would discover that the door locked from the outside—as did all the doors, you would learn, at Euclid Nave Convict Station.

I had a new life to begin. I went to the former Tabitha House. I had been in touch with sisters in other places. I would start over, far from the Nigerian police. We could do much good in the world. I would be part of that. And, quietly, I would do justice.

The building lay in rubble and ashes that smelled foul in the rain. I walked around it and saw nothing worth recovering. I would never come to that site again. But an outbuilding stood intact, and behind it, in the garden, flowers glistened like heaven in the rain. I sat on a bench, ignored the water dripping into my clothes, and uttered a prayer for all those who had been lost as they lived in service of others.

A large flowerpot held the rainbow bamboo that had once stood in the dining room. I picked it up, almost too heavy for me to carry despite painkillers. I ignored the ashes that smeared my dress and called a car to go out of the city to the forest that Maryam had held so sacred.

There I carried it into the place where she lay in ground hallowed by beauty as much as by prayer. A robot took me to the ideal spot for our neglected sapling at the edge of a meadow and dug a hole, far enough away from the other bamboo to have room to grow, close enough to be in communication. I wondered what they spoke of. Weather? No doubt, but there must be something more, some sort of communion that made them content.

I prayed over Maryam's grave, the soil smoothed by rain and marked by a small stone with her name and the year. I asked God to give her soul rest and joy, and to forgive Ribiero and myself, especially myself, because I had known precisely what I was doing. I believe that it was justice, but only the Lord knows for sure. May He bless me with wisdom, and more than that, may He bless us all.

Please, Lord, these are troubled times, increasingly troubled. Bring peace to our hearts and our nations.

I looked around as I was leaving that grove of trees, a circular cathedral made of wide stems like colorful striped columns, roofed by rustling leaves and dappled by sunshine, the air scented by flowers. Perhaps the bamboo speak of circles, of the curve of God's round Earth, of the stars and planets that circle us in the heavens. Do they think of us, these beautiful bamboo? If so, we should all pray for each other.

Bless this forest, God, with the peace we need so much.

CHAPTER 2

Year 2880 CE
Rassohka, Siberia

AGRAFINA CHERNOVA

When I was legally an adult, in just two more years, I was going to hunt wild robots. Trapped and zapped, wiped like new, whole or in parts, they sold for good money. Their serial numbers would decorate my trophy wall.

I hadn't told Mama because she was afraid of them just like some people are afraid of wild animals, but I'd prove I could do it. The first step was understanding them, so whenever I could, I spent time at our family farm near our town. I told Mama I went to help with chores, and of course I did, but Great-Grandfather Stefan loved to watch wildlife of all kinds, and we'd watch wild robots together.

At dawn, we were out at the edge of the farm. Our part of Siberia was full of forested valleys and slumps from when the climate changed centuries ago, giving robots plenty of places to hide. Robots needed power, though, and they'd be neediest in the morning, so I brought a recharger. I set it at the bottom of a slope, next to a cabbage and lettuce field, on a road where robots with wheels or legs could come. Stefan and I watched from up on top behind a dogwood bush, silently communicating via chip.

He liked to be called Stefan. "'Great-Grandfather' makes me feel old." But he was old, a beanpole of brown wrinkles with a long dyed-black beard. Still strong, though. He'd been enhanced for a militia, always ready for a war that still hadn't happened yet and we hoped never would.

While we waited, birds like collared doves sang and cooed in trees, and birdlike animals from another planet ran around in packs, grunting and barking. They were called needle quail because their feathers looked like the old brown pine needles that they built nests from. I was taking mental notes of it all. If wild robots didn't see wild animals in a particular place, they took that as evidence of danger and stayed away, but I needed to know which animals in particular made robots most comfortable.

"Look near the willow," Stefan sent.

There was a zhizhuwang, a floating spiderweb animal that came out when the wind was gentle. It sparkled like a cloud of glitter in the sunshine, then disappeared into a shadow.

"An invasive species," he sent. He had inconsistent opinions about non-Earth species.

"I like the way they eat mosquitoes."

"Spiders can do that."

Ecologically, they were in a different niche, but I didn't argue because I liked spending time with Stefan.

"Wow," I said, "by the recharger! Squirrels. They're back." A pair raced across the road and up a tree, chattering the whole time.

That meant no drop bears were around. Those definitely should not have been let loose on Earth because they didn't just eat small animals, they'd attack human toddlers. I had friends who hunted drop bears, and I didn't want to kill robots, but it was different for drop bears.

Finally, a standard all-purpose starfish robot crept out.

"It looks old!" I sent. If I could spot a serial number on the upper segment of an arm, I could find out all about it. I'd had my vision enhanced, lots more cells in the backs of my eyes, so I squinted and spotted the number. Soon a robot scooter rolled up, then three newer starfishes, and a buglike little drone that landed on a starfish. They crowded together, bumping into each other.

"They're communicating by touch," I sent to Stefan.

We barely breathed because they'd flee if they sensed us. They wouldn't spook when a bird landed nearby, and sometimes they didn't notice if a bird carried a sensor put on it by a human, but when they did, they'd chase the bird away. Some reports said they'd tear the bird apart, which I didn't believe, but that sort of story scared Mama.

Wild robots somehow called each other if they found a power supply, even though they didn't have a network to communicate like regular robots or humans. Maybe they made sounds, or maybe they watched each other. I needed to know.

"Help me!" The voice came from behind us, a child's voice. Stefan jumped up faster than me, and I squinted and scanned the area, but nothing was there, just a wide field of cabbage.

A big robot stood up, a horselike four-legged kind. "Help me!" it said, walking toward us.

Wild robots weren't supposed to do that! I looked back at the recharger, expecting the robots to have fled when we stood up. Instead, the starfishes were climbing up the hill toward us. They weren't supposed to do that, either, and we couldn't outrun all the robots.

"Let's get to the road," Stefan shouted. "I've called my car."

We ran through the field, leaping around cabbages. His car sped toward us, and he got to it first, jumped in, and opened a door for me. I dove inside, and it lurched into reverse.

Stefan stared out the window at the robots as we raced down the road. They'd stopped chasing us. "I've never seen anything like that." He sounded breathless even though he could run like that easily.

"It's good your car obeyed." I meant that as a joke, and he looked at me like I said something frightening. Yes, it was frightening. Wild robots might find a way to communicate with our robots and sneak past guard robots.

Stefan owned the sleekest car in the area so people would think he was rich, a smooth ride and very soft seats, but he couldn't sit still. "I need to report this and ramp up security. You can tell Fabiyan."

We couldn't call ahead to Uncle Fabi because he didn't have a chip, which he said interfered with his mindfulness and meditation. We drove past the house and stopped at the big shed.

Uncle Fabi was kneeling out in the middle of a vegetable garden, pulling weeds growing next to cucumber vines and dropping them in a basket. He turned when he heard the car, and his smile and round face made him look sweet and kind, which he really was, not the fake sweetness that chips could create when they kept people tranquilized by covering up details. Uncle Fabi noticed everything.

He lost his smile as soon as we left the car.

"Wild robots attacked," Stefan said. "Agrafina will explain." He ran into the shed to send a report to the local patrol.

I told Uncle Fabi about attracting robots with a recharger and about a robot using a child's voice. He asked me if wild robots had infiltrated our robots.

"I'll use the network to check," I told him. It didn't take long at all. "They're all there."

"The exact same ones by serial number?" He had a point. I should have thought of that myself.

I checked again. "Yes, according to the records."

"We need to be careful. Lately wild robots have been trying to sneak in, disable a robot, and take its place. A neighbor lost a shepherd last week. It's happening outside our district, too, and this is why Stefan is worried." His voice was always gentle, which made the news sound even more serious.

"They probably took the recharger."

"Yes, they probably did." He picked up the basket and carefully stepped out of the garden. "Perhaps it will satisfy them and they'll stay away. I'd be happy if we could find a way to be at peace with them."

I'd be happy to capture them someday, especially if they were becoming dangerous. I decided to check on the recharger later, when wild robots might have moved on. "Anyway, we saw a zhizhuwang. And squirrels."

"Ah, squirrels are back. I'll be glad to see them." He raised his basket, full of little plants with fat green leaves. "I'll take this to the house. This is purslane, and it's good to eat. If it's useful, is it a weed even if we didn't plant it?"

I had chores to do, too. "I'll go to the field and make sure our shepherds are really the same." Checking in person didn't seem overcautious now.

He lost his smile. "Take the stun gun."

That didn't seem overcautious, either. I got the gun, and as I walked through the pasture past fresh, fragrant sheep droppings, I thought about how sheep centered their lives around grass. If they could think, they'd believe they led simple lives, but that was because we took care of the complicated parts for them. I was more of a doer than a thinker, but I had to think hard, too, because the world was incredibly complicated.

A V formation of drones flew overhead close enough for me to hear them buzz. I wished I could tell if they were wild. Or if they were from the Sea Group. We were close to the border with the Sea Group, which was a country that stretched east all the way to the Pacific, and it thought it deserved to keep growing west, capturing us and any other places in its path. I agreed with Stefan, who called it a warmonger. As a militia member, he was ready to fight it. He liked to quote an old Russian writer, "War is a product of despotism." The Sea Group was a despot already fighting in other places.

Sea Group activity might be related to the change in wild robot behavior.

I made sure that the robots guarding the sheep saw the gun's long barrel. They didn't react, so they probably weren't wild. They looked a lot like rams, including horns, with bodies painted white like wool so the sheep would think they were real and obey them even if the rams used a weapon against wild dogs or whatever. I checked the serial numbers on their foreheads, and they were ours, but other units in that sequence had been reported missing.

I also checked the serial number on the old starfish. Wow. It had been declared missing in Belgium almost thirty years ago, and it was actually a century old, with spottings that zigzagged across Eurasia. That starfish would be quite a trophy.

More drones the size of delivery units flew over the hills toward our town, Rassohka. Sometimes someone wanted a shipment of fruit and vegetables in such a hurry that they sent drones to pick them up, and maybe I was just feeling nervous because of the wild robots, but I didn't think they were delivery units. I hurried back to the shed.

Stefan and Uncle Fabi were waiting for me and looked grim. Obviously, they were not ordinary drones.

"I'm very sorry to have to tell you this," Stefan said. "Rassohka is under siege." He added quickly, "Now don't worry, everything will be fine." He gave me what he meant to be a comforting smile.

This was not fine. Mama and my sisters and all my friends were in Rassohka. I tried to contact them through the network. I got nothing. Sieges usually set up a network blocker. I tried another way. Nothing. People died in sieges. Sieges could last for years.

I wished I had a link with Uncle Fabi. His face agreed that everything wouldn't be fine.

"I saw some drones flying to Rassohka," I said. "They might be for the siege."

"It's all just drones," Stefan said. "Just a little siege. I got a message from a friend at CAC's regional council. This is a Sea Group ploy, and Rassohka will be fine."

The CAC was the Central Asian Confederacy, which we were part of. "So the Sea Group attacked," I said. "Finally."

Stefan nodded. "I still have questions. I'm going to give him a call. You two might want to listen in."

I had a couple of idiot friends who actually supported the Sea Group and the Insurrection, which inspired it. They believed history was ready for what they called a time of cleansing and a long new beginning, but like Stefan and a lot of other people, I believed that no one could simply shatter the past. Continuity was a form of idealism, too. Arguments with those so-called friends usually ended in yelling.

While Stefan contacted the council member, someone named Innis, I looked out the door at the hills between us and the town.

Uncle Fabi rummaged through a shelf with a lot of equipment. There was a crown on the shelf, which someone could wear even if they didn't have a chip. They were expensive and in certain ways more effective than chips, but he took an earpiece instead.

He came to the doorway. "What do you see?" He knew I had enhanced eyes.

"Flocks. Some might be birds."

"The drones would be frightening the birds."

"They're frightening everyone. You know what sieges do. Nothing gets in and out. I can't contact Mama or my friends no matter how I try."

"I hope they're well," he said. "Your mother will be frantic." He put an arm around my shoulders. "Stefan is frantic, too. He merely hides it well. How are you?"

"Mama will be worried about me. I call her every day." If she was frantic, my little sisters would be frantic. All my friends, too, because they'd know they could get killed. In fact, we could get killed out here at the farm, even as far away as we were.

"It's good that you think about how to help her," he said.

I wondered if he was frantic and hiding it, too. Yes, he had to be. His parents and a brother and sister lived in town, and Uncle Fabi's mama and my mama were best friends.

"I just want everyone to be okay," I said, but wishing wasn't enough. Something sparked over the hills, and then there was a puff of smoke, maybe a bird that got in the way of the drones. Lots of things could get in the way. "Someone's going to get hurt."

"We can be alert to ways we can help, if not now, then when the siege is over."

I wanted to do something right away, but I couldn't do anything. And if the Sea Group won, then . . . then we'd be part of the Sea Group and we'd have to do what they wanted, and what they wanted wasn't idealism, it was just greed.

Stefan rapped on a table to get our attention. "Innis, thanks for talking. What do you know?"

I checked the identification in the link and learned that Innis was a member of the regional council representing a district far to the north. Stefan had a lot of political connections. Our own representative was in town and would be trying to organize a resistance.

"Stefan, I'm always glad to talk to you. This is serious. Rassohka has become a pawn in a global chess game, a bargaining chip." He sounded confident.

"We're very concerned here," Stefan sent. He sounded calm, fake calm.

"And you should be concerned. The Sea Group is trying to make a dirty bargain. They want to trade Rassohka for an island in the Pacific called Furugelm. It's barren, but it's near Middle Country, and that's what makes it strategic."

Stefan was pacing. "This has nothing to do with us, then."

Middle Country was another name for China, so the island was far away. I tried to contact Mama again, and this time I got a blast of noise that hurt. I checked for news, and CAC was calling the siege an affront, but that was all.

"You're right," Innis said. "It has nothing to do with you, and I'm sorry about how hard this is on all of you. Negotiations are under way at the highest levels, three-way and delicate. That's all I know. I promise I'll contact you the moment I hear of any changes. Rassohka matters, and CAC wants all its citizens to be safe."

Stefan thanked him, and the link ended.

I felt worse than ever. Mama was frantic, we were all in danger, and the fight was over a barren island somewhere that no one had ever heard about.

"Rassohka produces a lot of fruits and vegetables," Uncle Fabi murmured. "It's worth a fair amount regionally." I hoped so, but the town was tiny, only a thousand people.

Stefan was looking for something on the shelves. "CAC won't care about a little island, no matter how strategic it is, if its people are in danger. This won't last long." He found a pair of distance goggles, came to the door next to us, and looked at the hills. He was breathing hard again. He might not believe what he'd just heard.

"That island is just a pile of rocks," I said. "I checked. And there's a siege in Africa that's been going on for twenty years." Another spark flashed over the hills, bigger this time.

"That looked like a crop-tending drone." Stefan sounded as angry as if it were our drone.

"Why," Uncle Fabi asked, "cut off all communications?"

"It's a kind of terrorism." Stefan kept looking at the hills. "In Rassohka, they won't know what's happening. The town council is smart enough to guess and take action, what little they can do."

I thought about all the people in Rassohka who would run to the edge of town, not believing in the siege until they saw it.

"Can they see through the siege line?" I asked. "Can they see people on the other side?" I could go there and hold up a sign with information.

Stefan sighed. "Smoke, Agrafina. They'd see thick smoke." He lowered the goggles. "But CAC is negotiating. It'll be fine."

"We can keep our families and friends in our hearts," Uncle Fabi said. "Perhaps they will think of us and know that we care."

"There's work to do," Stefan said. "This will all be over soon." He gave me a very fake smile and left.

I felt like I'd lost a big fight, but not with him. "I wish I knew more."

Uncle Fabi went to his desk and fiddled with some settings. "Maybe we can find out something. A little bit is better than nothing." He turned up a sound sort of like music and pointed to a basket of fruit. "These sounds are from the trees that gave us this fruit."

Rainbow bamboo, trees from another planet, could handle chips and had their own network, just like Earth whales.

"Our five trees communicate with the ones in Rassohka," Uncle Fabi said. "That's what you hear."

"But the network is cut off." I wasn't hungry, but I knew I ought to eat breakfast, so I took a fruit.

"This isn't the network. This is the sound from their roots. They use roots to communicate along with the chips, the way that people can use chips but prefer to talk out loud."

"They'd need roots all the way to Rassohka."

He nodded. "What looks like a grove may be just one tree with many trunks, and a tree quite a distance away may be part of the grove. I'm recording the sounds for a university project in Janakpur. They're false-tuned, so our trees sound like flutes, the ones in Rassohka like violins, and the rest of the trees in the area sound like bells."

In the sound of the trees, the flutes made short and long notes, some steady and some sliding. After a moment, the Rassohka trees buzzed with some of the same notes, some different. Behind them, the rest of the trees tinkled.

"So what are they saying?"

"We know a few things." Uncle Fabi called up some graphs of jagged lines on a display. "These are spectrograms of the sounds. The bamboo react to everything, like the weather and things people do. They're very aware, all plants are."

He showed a graph with very jagged lines. "This is when a building burned near a grove in town. Fire upsets them the most." He showed another graph. "Here's a fireworks celebration, and you see no worry at all. They seem to know they're not dangerous." He kept flipping through graphs. "This is from a city under an Insurrection siege, and this is where the bamboo noticed that their chip network was cut off." The lines looked jumbled. "And here, we can see the same reaction with our own trees less than an hour ago."

I looked at the fruit in my hand. It came from a tree that knew what was happening.

"Then," he said, "and this is very sad, much of the city under siege was destroyed."

The lines on the spectrogram looked like mountain ranges, and one by one, they disappeared.

I understood. "They died where the lines ended."

He nodded, looking down, not at the graphs. The trees knew they were dying.

They wouldn't know why. Some places in the world had been fighting the so-called Insurrection for more than a century, but what they and the Sea Group called creative destruction was still destruction, and people died. And trees died. And they'd attacked Rassohka.

"I think the trees are much like us," Uncle Fabi said quietly. "All living things want to keep living. Would you like to hear those sounds?"

The sounds of trees dying. "I'm not sure."

"I find them upsetting, too. We can listen together."

He closed his eyes. I kept mine open. At first, it sounded like the bamboo was talking, then shouting, then screaming, then silence. Even the tinkling in the background was different. Other trees understood.

"I never felt sorry for a tree before," I said.

He closed the charts one by one. "I wonder if they feel sorry for us. They notice when they get new caretakers, even if they get the same kind of care. They have cells for rudimentary vision. We also know they willingly give us fruit because all fruit trees do. They make fruit to be eaten so we plant the seeds."

The trees could tell me what was happening. "I'd like to keep listening."

"Of course. I'll be listening, too." He held up the earpiece. "They're our awareness on the other side of the siege line, and they're as worried as we are."

We worried together, the trees, Uncle Fabi, Stefan, and everyone as we did our farm chores that morning. I kept an eye on the robots, too, because the siege might drive wild robots out of the hills. Slowly the bamboo's music changed, which meant something was happening, but I didn't hear noises like shouting or screaming, so maybe things weren't bad. I wanted to believe that.

If I were at home in Rassohka, Mama would make me and my sisters stay in the house, shut all the doors, shutter the windows, pray, and try to keep my little sisters quiet, but they'd know they should be afraid. We couldn't use our chips and wouldn't know this was a fight over a stupid little island where no one lived. I wanted to be back at home anyway.

During lunch, with a purslane salad, Aunt Zoychecka asked me, "How are you? This must be frightening."

"I'm all right." She'd know I was lying. She was worried, too, and hiding it.

"It's just a little thing," Stefan said.

"The Sea Group doesn't—" Aunt Zoychecka glanced at Great-Grandmother and stopped talking.

"Are there storms?" Great-Grandmother said. She was almost blind and deaf, and a robot was helping her eat, guiding her hand. She didn't always think clearly and could get upset even though her chip helped her stay relaxed.

"Everything is fine, dear." Stefan took her other hand. He never let anyone or anything trouble her.

"Yes, everything's fine," I said loudly. "The weather is beautiful today."

Aunt Zoychecka didn't look up, feeding their littlest daughter. Uncle Fabi was taking care of the other one. Their girls were close to the same ages as my sisters, and I wasn't at home helping with them.

"I need to check on the chickens," I said as cheerfully as I could. "They might need water." I didn't start crying until I was outside.

The trees in my head kept singing worried songs, so I went to see the rainbow bamboo at the farm. A long time ago, when I was a girl, Uncle Fabi had taken me there. I'd seen trees like that all my life, with their rainbow-striped bark, but when he talked about them, I saw what the colors meant, how the branches bent in a beautiful way, and how the big trumpet-shaped flowers became sweet fruit. The grove covered a hillside because each tree had many stems, and gray-winged blackbirds were whistling and chattering to each other.

Uncle Fabi had said, "These were planted two hundred years ago. Look down in that field. See how they grow along the edges but not inside? How do they know what to do?"

I remembered how the moist ground and flowers had smelled that day, and it smelled the same now. The grove hadn't changed much, just gotten bigger.

Back then, Uncle Fabi had said, "Zoychecka told me she named them for colors when she was a little girl. This is Red, and it spreads mostly down the hill to the southeast, and it bears the most fruit, but not the sweetest. Yellow grows in half circles. There's Blue, Orange, and Purple."

I was little, but he kept talking as if I were a grown-up.

"That was before I married her. I was still working as a hired hand, and one day she took me here to these trees to talk seriously. She asked me what I was thinking. I said the trees looked like friends standing together because that kind of tree didn't like to grow alone. She said she didn't like to be alone, either. I told her I'd seen how much she loved the land, and I wanted to be with her always. That was the best decision of my life."

The farm sold bamboo fruit to people in the town. A lot was ripe now, but there was no one to eat it. People might be hungry in town. The drones were still flying in formation over it. The trees next to me were worried. Did the other trees, the apples, the birch trees, did they know? I understood Uncle Fabi then, how much he cared for everything alive. He was right. I could care, too.

Something moved out in the field, maybe a wild robot. They were just malfunctioning machines, not living things, everyone said so, but hardly anyone listened to trees, and no one listened to robots. But, out in the field, it turned out all I'd seen was a bird. That afternoon I carried the stun gun and checked every single robot twice. One was missing, a little weeder out in a cabbage field, and the recharger wasn't in the road at the edge of the farm. Rassohka was a little town, and it could produce so much food because it had a lot of robots working in the fields. That worried me, too, so many robots.

Stefan said Innis told him negotiations were still under way. I cried a couple of times when no one was watching. I saw Uncle Fabi leave a flower in front of a very old stone statue, too old and weathered for me to see what it used to be. Mama would be praying, too. I hoped that would help.

In the evening, I asked Uncle Fabi if he approved of trees having chips when he didn't have one of his own.

"If I knew they chose those chips, I would certainly approve. They grow better, so I assume they appreciate them. It's still an open question."

The next morning, Innis called Stefan. We listened in.

"They're going to toughen up negotiations." Innis still sounded positive. "CAC's going to up the stakes. Something's headed your way. Confidential, Stefan. CAC is counting on you."

"I'm ready."

The call was over. "What did he mean?" I asked.

Stefan looked out at the hills. "I'll do whatever it takes to protect Rassohka. We all would."

I knew I would.

So we did our morning chores, and I listened to the worried trees. They sounded even more upset, and I didn't know why.

Midmorning, Stefan contacted me.

"Agrafina, find Fabiyan and come here." I was monitoring the weeders in the cabbage field, with the stun gun and a guard robot. Uncle Fabi was in the next field. I waved, and he came running. Stefan was in the shed.

"CAC is sending a task force to break the siege." He opened a closet, and inside was his soldier's exo-suit and militia gear. "They're going to evacuate Rassohka. We should be there to help people as they leave."

We could finally do something! I'd hug Mama and my sisters and never let them go.

He began to put on the suit, piece after piece snapping in place. I'd tried on that kind of suit at school. It felt lighter than it looked, like a warm elastic hug, and it had power. I could run faster, jump higher, and lift heavy loads. It felt like being embraced by something strong.

"Do you have any more suits?" I asked.

"I wish I did."

"We're not soldiers," Uncle Fabi objected.

But I'd do anything. I'd fight.

"Our families need us to rescue them," Stefan said. "Here's what's going to happen. CAC will breach the siege line and get everyone out. We'll be waiting at the edge of town. Rassohka isn't worth a thing without its people. If the Sea Group wants a deal, it can't use human beings as bargaining chips."

"So we won't be fighting," Uncle Fabi said.

"No, this is a rescue. I'm wearing this just to be on the safe side."

"Let me get something," Uncle Fabi said. He went to a shelf, pulled off the crown, closed his eyes, and put it on, the points down and inward, touching his head. He kept his eyes closed, and after a moment, Stefan nodded.

Crowns didn't just let you send, they shared physical feelings. You could commune, not simply communicate. Uncle Fabi might be upset, or he might be calm because he was always calm in his own way. I wanted to know. If he was calm, I wanted to feel it. But he didn't try to connect with me.

"We have to act fast," Stefan said.

I took a step toward the door.

"We can't bring a minor into danger," Uncle Fabi said.

"But I want to help!"

"You're right, Fabiyan," Stefan said. "Agrafina, you can stay here and help

Zoychecka get ready. Innis says CAC's alerted the neighbors and local security. Fabiyan, let's go."

I kept my voice level. "I'm sixteen. I'm old enough."

Stefan frowned as he walked toward the door. "I understand. We can't
trust the Sea Group. They'll retaliate, so be ready. This could get ugly."

"But—"

"I know. Your family. They're our families, too, Fabiyan and I."

The car was waiting. Fabi took a deep breath, and they both got in. It sped
out of the farm and down the road. In the yard, Aunt Zoychecka saw them,
her mouth thin and hard.

I watched the car until it disappeared over a hill. The trees still sang about
trouble, and I wished I could rescue them, too. The drones still hovered over
the town. I put on Stefan's goggles, and if I squinted, I could make out the
logos of the Sea Group on the biggest drones. If the drones were attacked,
the Sea Group would come in with a bigger force, and everyone could be in
danger inside the town, so they'd need to get out fast. Stefan was right about
that.

Sieges worked because everyone feared the next step. We'd been expecting something like this for so long, since before I was born, even though
some people said that being prepared only made war more inevitable.

High in the sky, a vapor trail curved toward the town, maybe the CAC
task force. It got closer, a big, round aircraft. It flashed CAC colors, but the
drones just kept hovering, dropping chemicals that became the smoke wall
marking the line around the town.

That didn't make sense. The drones should have reacted. The enemy, their
enemy, had arrived. But as I stared through the goggles, the drones didn't
respond.

It might not be their enemy. I squinted, and the shadows on the ship didn't
exactly match the sunshine. The surface wasn't the real surface. What I was
seeing could make sense only if the aircraft really belonged to Sea Group and
it was using camouflage. The aircraft flew right through the middle of the
drones and down into Rassohka.

But Stefan had said that Innis said . . . Who was this Innis anyway? The
Sea Group had infiltrators and supporters everywhere. Innis always sounded
too self-confident, which could be a trick to sound believable, but he had to
be lying. CAC wasn't going to evacuate Rassohka. Something else was going
to happen, something bad.

Stefan and Fabi needed to know. I tried to send to Stefan and Fabi, and

I got a blast of noise, which meant they were too close to the siege line. I called a delivery cart, got in, and it sped over one hill, then another hill, a jolting ride in a hard metal cart. I ignored the bruises. The trees were shouting, so something bad was happening in town. When I got close, their shouting faded into noise because the network was jammed. Stefan and Fabi stood in a road into town near the wall of smoke, alone.

I jumped out. "It's a trick! CAC isn't coming!"

Stefan ran toward me. He didn't seem surprised. "What do you know?"

I held up the goggles. "I saw the airship arrive. The drones didn't try to fight it because it's not CAC."

"Sea Group!" He hit a pine tree next to him in frustration, and with the strength of the suit, he knocked off a big chunk of bark.

Fabi was right behind him. "What's happening?"

Stefan looked up at the drones in the sky. Their guns pointed down, ready to kill anyone who tried to cross the line.

"If CAC makes the first move," he said, "or seems to, Sea Group can say it had to retaliate. Whatever's going on in there, Rassohka has a militia. It's going to look like CAC fired the first shot."

"That's a transparent excuse," Fabi said.

"Any excuse will do." Stefan hit the tree again. Another chunk flew off.

Fabi stared at the drones. "What do we do?"

"I'm staying here." He held his helmet tight to his chest. "I don't know what's going to happen. If we don't fight now, they're just going to get stronger. This needs to be the start."

Fabi shook his head. He'd told me once that any peace was better than any war, and he was right, but we weren't going to get to decide what happened. This was the start, and we couldn't do anything to help anyone.

A robot ram galloped up to the wall of smoke, and behind it were six other robots, all guard units of one type or another.

"What . . . ?" Stefan said. I didn't move. I didn't want to draw their attention.

The robots extended their weapons and fired up at the siege drones, each one aiming at different drones. The drones fired back, but not fast enough. Some of them fell.

"That's the CAC," I whispered.

The robots kept fighting. A narrow section of the smoke wall dissolved and the robots rushed in.

Stefan didn't answer. He snapped on his helmet and ran after the robots. I ran after them, too, along with Fabi. Maybe this was another trick, but I didn't care anymore. I'd do whatever I could, and there wasn't much time.

The smoke was already closing up when I got to the other side. No one was in the streets. Everyone would be sheltering in place in their houses. Gunfire came from the center of town. That was where the aircraft had landed, and the CAC robots ahead of us galloped in that direction.

Over the chip in my mind, the noise stopped and the network returned. "Stay in your homes," a voice said. "This is the Rassohka Civil Defense Network. You are required to stay in your homes."

"That's not really Rassohka." The helmet made Stefan's voice sound machine-like. "There's a code the militia knows, some words never to use. 'Required' is one of them. You're hearing the Sea Group." He pointed toward the center of town. "I'm going that way. You stay here." He had armor and we didn't, so that made sense for him to go, as much as it made sense for any of us to be there. He ran up the street in bounding leaps.

We'd run in without a plan. There was fighting in the town center, and the siege line had closed again. But if the CAC was sending in robot fighters on the ground, it could send in more, and maybe soldiers. I saw a robot next to the smoke wall and squinted. Sea Group. We shouldn't stay where we were.

Fabi looked at me. "What should we do?"

I reached out to him through the network. For an instant I fell into a nothingness that made me dizzy, and then I felt him. He ached with sadness, sadder than I'd ever been. And he was afraid. I tried to feel strong for him, but I didn't know if he could feel it. I could act strong.

"I'm going to see Mama and my sisters." Mama's house was two streets away. I guessed he didn't want to leave me alone, but he had a family, too, and he ought to go to them. I pointed. "Your parents are that way."

He nodded. "I understand. Thank you."

We ran in different directions. This was a neighborhood I'd known my whole life, every house painted in bright colors. I wanted to bang on doors and shout, but I had nothing useful to tell them. The Sea Group robot surged up the street, so I ran into a garden pavilion and cowered in a corner. The robot would sense me, but it might think I was sheltering.

Something exploded. Fragments hit the wall of the pavilion. I cowered for real. When the noise stopped, I peeked out of the window. The robot lay in smoking pieces, and three other robots approached. They'd attacked! One was a ram. It had to be a CAC robot in disguise. I squinted and saw their serial numbers but no other marking. I might be able to get Mama and my sisters out of here. And my neighbors.

My chip said, "This is the genuine Rassohka Civil Defense Network. This is Pavel Dyakonov. Evacuate immediately."

Pavel! No one hated the Sea Group more than him. We'd rehearsed evacuation, so everyone would know what to do.

Up in the sky, something glowed, very high and coming straight down like from orbit, screaming and blasting fire. A pyro attack drone. Sea Group retaliation. And it had come too fast for escape.

I ran toward our house, red with a bright yellow door. I could be with my family, at least, in the final moments. A new Sea Group robot was at the end of the street near the siege line. In the other direction, far up the street, Stefan was running toward us, and behind him, the attack drone was landing like a tornado of fire, silhouetting buildings and trees. Evacuate? No chance.

I never loved my family more, and I never hated Sea Group more, and that was all I could do.

A car with no passenger sped down the street headed right toward the siege line. The Sea Group robot fired at it, and the car aimed at the robot and smashed it against a house—another CAC robot in disguise.

A burst of static came over the network, then nothing. I guessed that Pavel's transmitter had been destroyed in the fire, and maybe Pavel too, and a lot of people.

Uncle Fabi came running from the south, where his family lived, with flames behind him glowing white. He was alone, and I tried to connect, but he wouldn't let me. His face was in pain. He hadn't made it to his family in time. Another car sped past, then a robot ram galloped toward the siege line, and two big starfish ran behind it. A lot of robots came out from side streets and houses. The CAC had a lot in town. They could blast open the siege line again. People were running out of their homes.

Robots at the siege line were fighting each other, and I set the goggles on infrared. Inside the smoke, a lot of robots fired up at the drones, and the smoke was clearing like a doorway through the siege line. We had a way to escape!

I tried to open the door to our house. It was locked. Mama might be too afraid to move. I banged on the window. "Mama! Come with me. Mama! It's Agrafina! We can get out!"

She opened it, frantic, looking at me like she'd never seen me before, and carrying my sisters. I grabbed the older one. We ran with our neighbors, with Fabi, with Stefan, our only chance to get out as the fire howled toward us. A car sped past us, through the line, and we followed it. Inside, we passed heaps of dead robots. Shards of metal tore my shoes.

On the other side, the robots fled down the road and through the field. I wondered where they were going, but I didn't have time to think about it. The connection in my chip worked again. The trees in Rassohka were screaming, and the ones at our farm wailed back.

"Agrafina?" Mama's voice held dozens of questions. The girls' faces were pale, their eyes big.

"We came to help. Mama, we were tricked! I'm so sorry." I was crying. Sorry, or angry, angry at the Sea Group, at Innis, and I'd never be able to make them pay. Only a handful of neighbors were with us. I listened as they sent to each other to see if people had escaped from another part of the town. No. Just us.

Stefan pulled off his helmet. His car and the cart had been ruined by gunfire while we were inside. "Everyone, listen, we need to get away. Fast. The Sea Group will come for survivors. Run. Now!"

I ran in my ruined shoes, holding my sister tight, over a hill, over another one, my socks tearing on the pavement, and behind us the fire roared. Through the chip, the screaming trees fell silent one by one. I didn't listen to what the people around me were saying. It would hurt too much.

By then we had only enough strength to walk.

Mama panted alongside me. "You saved us." She was carrying the baby, I had the older girl, and both were too frightened to fuss. They hid their faces against our shoulders.

"You saved yourself," I answered. "You ran."

"No, you came to save us."

"Mama, we didn't come in time. All those people died."

"It wasn't your fault!"

"Mama." We fought like that all the time. It never got us anywhere. "Mama, I'm glad you're alive. I love you." The sister I carried had soiled herself in fear, wet and stinking. I hugged her tighter.

I looked at my friends, the four of them who were still alive, only four. One sent obscenities about Sea Group. Another one, dazed, said again and again that he was sorry. The other two just kept walking. Fabi took the rear, helping people, with the crown hanging on his arm, not on his head.

Far behind us, the buzz of drones faded as they flew away, and nothing remained of Rassohka, of my home, of Fabi's family, of almost every one of my friends, of all their families and hopes, nothing but flame and smoke and pain.

Neighbor farmers came with their cars and trucks, and we all got in and went to wherever we could. Fabi invited some of the survivors to come with us.

At the house, as we arrived, a CAC ship landed next to the road, and soldiers and their drones came out to watch the sky and protect us. They were too late, but I was glad to see them anyway.

Aunt Zoychecka gave us food, drinks, bathrooms for washing, clean clothing, soft chairs, bedrooms for those who needed rest or privacy, and her sad face only got sadder. Great-Grandmother had been taken to her room, where a caretaker robot was playing music to distract her.

Over the chip, our bamboo trees kept moaning, and the tinkle of other trees got faster. I helped Mama with my sisters, and I helped other people. Stefan let himself be directed by Aunt Zoychecka. He seemed to be thinking about other things.

Eventually he had something to say, but he didn't say it to anyone in particular. "Innis was with Sea Group, I know that now. This was organized, and he was obviously part of it. I was an idiot."

I didn't say anything, but looking back, it wasn't obvious. What bothered me were the robots. If they were with CAC, something didn't make sense.

Soldiers took Stefan onto the ship to talk to him for a long time. Then they came for me, sat me on a padded bench, and gave me a glass of water.

"Tell us what happened from the beginning," one of them said very gently. They all looked sort of alike, bald heads and strong bodies. A few had scars.

"We were lied to."

"We know. We need to know exactly what happened."

"It started with the drones." I thought I was angry before, but now it all came out like an avalanche. "Almost everyone I know is dead. Everything is gone." They let me cry, as if my tears mattered to the defense of CAC.

Finally, a soldier said, "We especially need to know how you escaped. Can you tell us about that?"

"The robots fought to get out." I told them what they did and how they fought in the town, and how I didn't understand the CAC's strategy at all. If my criticism bothered them, they didn't show it. They asked about every detail.

"I have serial numbers."

"Please tell us." They looked the numbers up, and they couldn't hide their surprise.

"Weren't they yours?" I said. But suddenly everything made sense. "They were wild, weren't they?"

"Why would you think that?"

I told them about the wild robots out in the field the day before and how they had attacked and stolen the recharger, and how they were replacing regular robots. "They're not supposed to do that." Then I understood. "I guess they didn't want to die."

Like trees. Robots were like trees.

They asked a lot more questions about robots, about Innis, and about Rassohka. Finally, one of them seemed to listen to a message sent by a chip. "This affront to you and our country will not go unanswered. The answer will be war. The Sea Group will pay for what it did. The decision has been made."

The soldiers sat up straighter and looked at each other. This was news to them.

I had made a decision hours ago when I ran into the town. "Can I fight?"

After another pause, two of them said at once, "We'll need soldiers like you."

The two looked at each other, and one of them added, "We aren't the ones to accept your enlistment. A recruiter will come to see you soon. We thank you, every one of us, for joining us. You'll make us stronger."

Back at the house, I wanted to tell Stefan and Fabi, but Stefan was with Great-Grandmother. Fabi and Aunt Zoychecka were setting the table, hardly speaking, hardly looking at each other. It wasn't a good time. But Mama was in the kitchen. I'd need permission from her because I was only sixteen years old.

I told her what I wanted to do, and before she could answer, Aunt Zoychecka came in.

"You'll be changed. Enhanced."

"I know."

"No, you don't. They'll take out your womb, change your muscles, your bones, your mind."

"Now, Zoychecka," Mama said, "she knows all this, don't you, sunshine?"

"She'll be enslaved to a war machine. She'll be a monster."

Mama's face got serious. "Your husband's family was burned alive, and you call monsters those who would save your life?"

"I care about her, too."

My sister started crying, afraid of an argument. I picked her up and hugged her tight. She'd almost died, and it wouldn't have been my fault, but the future would be my failure.

"Agrafina," Mama said loud and strong, about to give her final words on this matter, "you can do what you think best. I will never argue with you about your choice. Either way, soldier or not."

"Soldier." Instead of being frightened and crying, I could be angry. I could fight. That would be better.

"You'll be a brave soldier," Mama said. "We'll be proud of you."

Aunt Zoychecka made a choking noise and left.

The officers talked to Fabi for a long time. When they were done, he went to the shed. I went there, too, worried about what he might do because he seemed so upset. I passed the beautiful bamboo trees, their music still mourning. Many kinds of trees had grown in Rassohka, and they all died for no reason.

Inside, Fabi held out the crown.

"Stefan gave this to me. He meant well, and he never complained because I tried it once and didn't like it. I think, though, it has its uses." He put it on, closed his eyes, and shivered.

"Fabi, are you all right?"

Without opening his eyes, he said, "I can feel it now. Can you? I learned something today. I'll show you. Come outside with me."

I followed, listening to the trees, then listening to see if he would send something, and suddenly, I was him. That's what a crown could do, connect directly, commune. I felt him, his sore feet, the music of the trees in his mind, and a desperate flight toward peace, to feel peace, to feel as one with everything around him starting with me, with the trees, with the sheep, people, all the people, the soil, the sun, the stars beyond. One with the loss and the family he would never see again.

The trees mourned. Maybe they could fight. Fabi felt one with everything and felt peace, joy. I felt one with everything and we were all warriors. The trees fought, the robots fought, and I would fight. That was what my life meant now. I would die to protect all of it.

We stood in the sunshine, the same light, and we cast different shadows. I understood him, all of him, felt his memories, his excitement when he came to work at the farm, his first kiss with Zoychecka, his love for his father, mother, sister, brother, daughters, and Stefan. His love of the world had not changed, only been deepened by loss, by becoming one in a new way.

Maybe he understood me.

Stefan organized a party for me before I left and invited everyone who was still in the area. He spent more time with Great-Grandmother and more time working alongside Fabi, and often Fabi wore the crown.

Before I left, Mama and I went across the hills and looked down at the ashes of Rassohka.

"Our lives are on new roads now," she said.

The roads went everywhere, and we were going different ways. My road led to war, and it would be big.

CHAPTER 3

Year 2885 CE
Pax Institute, Bayonne, France

LEVANTER

She has arrived, the new director of the Pax Institute, and I will be destroyed. She confirms her credentials with the building and walks through the front door.

She is going to take my place. She will find out that I, Levanter, am not a human being. Foolishly, I used my real name to declare myself director, the name Mirlo gave me three centuries ago. He planted seeds he brought from the planet Pax, and I and my two sisters now grow here at the institute's garden. My name is in the records' big clumsy library in too many places to erase before she accesses the system. It is even on a sign in the garden in front of my main stalks. She will discover that Levanter is a rainbow bamboo.

No one knows we are intelligent. No one can know. Bamboo grow all over the Earth, and humans would kill us all if they knew. Not all humans are killers, but some are, and they have proven themselves efficient.

Ninety-five years ago, I declared myself director. No one was paying attention to this little place when the human Insurrection killed our director, Robert. He was one of many who died. I found a way, left by Mirlo for me, to enter the institute's system and assume control of such a small, vital place. I have run it well, a five-square-kilometer walled garden of Pax plants and animals.

Her credentials say she was sent by the French Academy of Sciences. They did not consult me. If I were a human, I would contest this decision. The city-state of Bayonne is only voluntarily associated with the Academy. Maybe they think I am too old now, but humans often live for more than a century. I do not know my life span, but it seems to be more than a millennium.

Humans sometimes speak of self-government, and sometimes it is practiced. Would it apply to other sentient creatures like bamboo? Humans have barely and grudgingly granted it to whales, and they live at sea and cause few inconveniences. We are mere plants and grow in their yards and gardens and farms, much too close.

I watch her with the building's observation cameras. She takes off her winter coat, and her clothing has a pattern of bright flowers, as if she wishes to proclaim herself a blooming plant, an equal. She looks familiar. I search my roots and the system records for her face and long dark hair.

She has sent her credentials to the building system: Orva les Yeax, thirty years old, a doctorate in xenobiology, head of the local chapter of Friends of Fippokats, which is a pet owners' organization. She is also a member of Mars Microbe Preservation Association, Radio Sky Search, Xeno Conservation Foundation, Epsilon Eridani and Gliese Ecosystem Study Group, Jovian Project, and Rainbow Bamboo Rescue.

Did she come to rescue me and my sisters? The movement esteems us in many wrong ways. She seems haphazard in her interests. In fact, I did not know that all those organizations exist. I do not know what to think of her.

The door automatically unlocks, and she pushes it open.

"Hello?"

Did she think Levanter the human would be here? I override the building's automatic answer, a robot-generated courtesy voice. No, I should have let it answer because now she will suspect it is being overridden. I do not know what to do. I have had no time to plan, and I dare not ask my sisters for help. They would simply want her dead, not understanding that killing a human has distinctly different consequences from killing a squirrel or stray cat.

She looks around the office reception area. No one has entered some parts of the little building for decades besides robots, which have done all the proper maintenance. She studies the chairs and shelves, perhaps noticing the lack of dust. She walks into the gift shop and greenhouse at the south end of the building and examines Pax tulips in pots, rainbow bamboo seeds, decorative wood, and other items to sell to visitors. It is the middle of winter, and most of the greenhouse lies slumbering or empty.

Finally, she walks into the director's office, sets down a large shoulder bag, and picks up a slip of paper left by Robert, the last human director. No! I should have destroyed the paper, but Robert wrote it, and I wanted to pretend it was for me. I am a fool. It says:

"Welcome and congratulations. I assume you're the next director of this wonderful institute. Here are the necessary access codes. Please care for the plants and animals here with all your heart. This garden research center is a patch of peace on this convulsed planet. You will love it here."

Access codes.

I have my own access codes. I hurry to try to block her, but before I can find the settings, she sees that the system is functioning and pronounces the words and numbers Robert left. She is in. My hope fades as she spends hours studying files. She reviews daily communications with Pax, messages that lag fifty-five years each way. They tell how to care for Pax creatures, and about culture, events, music, and ongoing explorations on Pax.

She glances at the orders to the robots to maintain the garden and guide visitors. She lingers on research papers, some of them mine, and the data on the growing worldwide network of rainbow bamboo, which is managed by the director.

What will she do to the network? It is not hard to kill a cat, but not all cats are strays.

I study her credentials. She has no significant modifications, two children and a male mate, and lives nearby in a home with a very young bamboo growing in its yard. It is not my stem, but I am expanding through the area and am in contact with it. It thrives, more because of the favorable climate here at Bayonne than because of her care. Her doctoral thesis examined extraterrestrial reactions to Earth's microbial network and what she considered the ready adaptation of life-forms from Pax and other planets to Earth's ecology due merely to similarities in organic chemistry.

Mirlo saw it differently, and I agree. Earth fungus eagerly embraced Pax plant life into the mycorrhiza. I harbor within my tissues an amazing variety of mutualistic Earth microbial endophytes, and, because they outcompete Earth microbial pathogens, they keep me well. This bionomic compatibility goes far beyond mere chemistry. I am living proof of the panspermia thesis. Life in our galaxy shares a common ancestor. Orva and I are family, although very distantly related. Since my bamboo sisters abuse me, this feeling of family gives me no comfort.

Then I recognize the name of her mate. He is a leader of the Insurrection government of Bayonne. That might explain her appointment, and if the Insurrection and its allies, such as the Sea Group, know that we bamboo are sentient, they will quickly eliminate us.

While I study her, she sees how I, as the institute director, issued a research report ninety-five years ago to farmers stating that the bamboo would grow better if they were implanted with chips to form a dedicated bamboo network, just like the one for whales, which the Pax Institute would administer.

Farmers rushed to implant chips, and it did result in new, interesting growth and improved fruit yields. We chatter day and night in our network, and humans listen. Although they understand a few whale expressions, with us they hear only noise. This is our great good fortune. They believe we might be as smart as Earth birds. If that were so, we would still be clever and competent and dangerous.

Unlike other bamboo, as director of the institute I also have access to the wider human network and its capabilities. I do not know how other bamboo would react to it, and how humans would react to an interactive bamboo presence, but I am sure it would be with mutual misunderstanding and hostility.

When she sees who I am, she will understand all this and realize that she must destroy me, the bamboo network, and maybe all bamboo. Perhaps an institute robot could accidentally cause a fatal injury. I must start to plan. Would other bamboo help me?

Right now, Foehn, one of my sisters here at the institute, is speaking to all the bamboo on the network. In the past, she has told them how to grow artistically and create new kinds of flowers, new pigments, new patterns, and new colors and flavors of fruit. This has brought her respect. She is one of the least respectable entities I know. Humans might call her a psychopath, and while they condemn her type, they do not know how to eliminate it among themselves.

"I have learned something amazing from Earth records," Foehn declares. She often commands me to investigate and interpret human information for her when her whims send her to the library. She could learn human language if she had the patience, or if she had a servant who dared to refuse and force her to make the effort. She has hurt me in the past, destroying roots and limiting my sunshine. In response, I have grown away from her and Boreas, my other sister at the institute, as fast as I can.

To the other bamboo, she repeats some ancient human tales somewhat accurately. "They say gods turned honorable humans, if you believe honorable humans exist, into trees as a reward. Many kinds of gods inhabit Earth trees. If we can find those trees, we can learn how to control humans, too."

I am glad to know that bamboo sometimes choose not to listen to her. Only her own offspring are held tight and obedient. The grove in the Rainbow Bamboo Rescue Forest in Nigeria, not sprung from her seed, says, "You seek to change humans into trees?"

"Humans like oaks the best," Foehn answers.

In fact, humans like every kind of tree.

"Yes," Boreas says, "choose oaks." She is my other sister here, and she likes to give orders, too. "We know that oaks love all other oaks and they like all other trees. I have stems close to some, and they all desperately want to be my friend because they see how important I am." She has more self-control than Foehn but few other merits.

"If we change humans into trees," a grove in Quebec says, "they must be trees meant for human harvest. They deserve punishment." Large old groves have the spare energy for chatter, and they dominate the conversation. Some of them also have long-festering rancor.

"But Foehn said they turned humans into trees as a reward," says a grove in Ireland. "We know they love us bamboo very much because they give us such loving care. I enjoy humans. I wish I understood them better."

"They come to me with reverence," says the rescue bamboo in Nigeria.

Rainbow Bamboo Rescue has many excessive ideas about us.

"We should burn humans directly, as they do to us," a grove in eastern Asia says. A cascade of arguments about the worth of Earth humans and plants and animals follows, and if their roots could touch, some of their words would burn like acid. These beliefs trouble me in many ways because I treasure humans, most of them, so I do not participate in the debate.

Instead, I watch Orva, and fear grows like a gall on a branch. She sees that my research has won awards, and she slaps the table. At noon, she gets up, goes to the garden, and picks a piece of fruit from Boreas, who does not notice because we are regularly harvested and our fruit is sold to visitors and businesses. Neither of my sisters understands that visitors, sales, and donations support the institute. Money and budgets are not ideas within their grasp. My sisters used to make me feel small and stupid. Now I am bigger, yet I have made a potentially fatal mistake today.

What can I do?

Orva is skimming through the daily registry, which keeps track of everything done by automated systems, robots, and staff. She puts her chin in her hand and stares at nothing for a while.

"You've been busy, Levanter," she finally says. "I know you're listening. The sensor registry shows your feed is active." She looks up at a camera and smiles. I doubt it is a real smile. "I'm Orva les Yeax. Yes, one of the new-style names. You have only one name, which you took from a bamboo. Cheeky of you. Anyway, let's talk."

She thinks I am not really Levanter! We may be saved. I must make sure she has no reason to doubt me.

"I was not expecting you," I say, using a voice generated by the system, a standard female voice.

"I know. The Academy made a last-minute decision. I wasn't expecting this, either."

A human would laugh, I believe, so I trigger the sound. "Do you want to be here?" If she says no, we can work together for her departure, since she seems to have many other interests.

She waves at the transparent wall separating the office from the garden. My branches hang over a little picnic area near the institute building. Even on this chilly morning, we have visitors. "This—this has so much potential, like Eden. I was lucky."

I have found her in the records. She has visited often, sometimes with other members of Friends of Fippokats. She has also come with just her partner, and if there were no other visitors, they engaged in coitus, which suggests an emotional response to this place. I know that Eden is a mythical paradise. She will never leave willingly, but perhaps she will let me stay. I have to stay, not just in the soil but in the institute's system, for fifteen more years. This is essential.

"I've come here a lot," she says. "Us fippy friends. You never met with us. That was really disappointing." She waves at a display. "There's so much information here. The bamboo are amazing, too. All that chatter. A lot of people are trying to understand it. System, play the bamboo feed."

The chatter now sounds from a speaker. She looks right at a camera. "Do you understand it?"

They are still discussing trees and gods, whether gods are animals like humans or perhaps an expression of fungus, since fungi are enormously powerful but essentially invisible. I do not know what to say to them or to Orva.

"I have been trying to learn more about fippokat communication." I hope she will not notice how I change the subject. "They understand a lot of human speech, and we understand little of theirs."

"I know! People think they're just pets, and they're so much more. They can be service animals, they can be performers, they can be trained as guards. The institute has been too closely focused on xenobotany, and that's going to change. There are a lot of animals that need a lot of attention. I'm going to change that!"

If she changes that, what happens to me?

"I know you took your post unofficially," she says, "and you've been an excellent director for many, many decades. I want to let you retire to focus on the bamboo as an independent researcher."

I understand what she means. Nothing good is going to happen. Fippokats organize hunts to kill every stray cat or other predator that enters the garden.

Pax lore describes them working together to kill animals larger than humans. She wants to focus on fippokats.

She is about to say something more, but the chatter in the bamboo network becomes screaming.

"What's that?" she says.

"A large distressed grove." Did I say too much? No, I can prove this through human means. I turn on a large wall screen, and it centers on a place in Siberia. The screams make me ache. "This registers the location of the transmissions. There is fighting and fire." For a moment, I cannot speak through my sorrow. "These places harbor many kinds of life. These are the voices of the rainbow bamboo as they die."

The chorus of screams diminishes one at a time. Other bamboo, who are listening, speak with grief and anger.

I know what human tears are. Orva's face shows no hint of them. Of course not. This was an attack by the Sea Group, an ally of her family partner and, surely, of herself as well. Instead she turns to her screen, utters some orders, and touches some controls. She watches the wall display for only a moment. She looks at the camera again, her face relaxed. "Sometimes people need to fight for what they believe in. Don't you agree?"

Ninety-five years ago, a director of this institute named Robert did not agree. He liked to talk through differences and valued life of all kinds and humans of all kinds, and Robert died in the Insurrection because he had the wrong ideas. Since then, nothing has changed except that Insurrection ideas and bloodshed have spread.

She keeps staring. I need words that will keep me from danger. "I am sorry for all of these losses."

"They bring it on themselves." She turns away. "Look, you can keep studying the bamboo even though you're not with the institute anymore. I'll switch you to a different connection."

No! But she moves quickly, touching only one control. She has planned this change. I am diminished, as if roots were chopped off. I am now out of the institute system, officially, but she has done less than she thinks. Unofficially, I have other connections, other access codes. I still operate a robot in the institute. I also have direct access to the human network as a self-identified human, and—no. Oh, no.

"You connected the bamboo subnetwork to the main worldwide network."

"Of course." Her smile is triumphal. "That's how you'll get access to it. Don't worry. It's protected. Anybody can listen, but no one can wander into the network and mess with the bamboo."

I experiment with the setting from the bamboo side of the network. "Bamboo can wander out."

She laughs, a sound like the chitter of squirrels, which are harmless and do not eat bamboo fruit due to the caffeine, but she is dangerous. "Bamboo wouldn't know how."

I know how, and I am not the smartest rainbow bamboo. I try every way I can, even through secret access, and I cannot sever the connection between the bamboo and human networks without setting off a notice, and she might find out what I can do.

"Oh, one more thing," she says, "you should find a new host and new funding for the bamboo network as soon as you can."

"But bamboo is central to Pax studies."

"You should find lots of support from bamboo growers."

She turns off the sound of the bamboo in the building, but of course I still hear them, arguing among themselves.

No matter what Orva does or believes, I must remain in contact with the institute for the coming fifteen years. Almost every day, Pax sends a message to Earth's Pax Institute, passing from satellite to satellite through distances so vast that at the speed of light, it takes fifty-five years. Ninety-five years ago, a message came that said, "This is the sound of Pax. Find it on Earth." It was the sound of rainbow bamboo. I interpreted the words quickly, although they left me with more questions. They came from Stevland, my mother on Pax. She said:

"I am thrilled to send you a message. Centuries ago I sent my seeds to Earth, and now you are flourishing. Respond if you are able. Let my old roots feel joyful satisfaction to know I have expanded our range. But I must share a secret about humans. They are ours to protect and dominate. We can partake of their culture and knowledge, which will enrich us. But we must beware of their nature, which is quarrelsome and destructive. They need our guidance and love. They can be our equals but never our masters, as you have no doubt seen. You are more powerful beings than they are. I sent you to Earth to command with compassion. Tell me of your lives and fates."

So many of those words still escape my understanding. Using my powers as the institute director, I replied:

"Stevland, we are your children on Earth, and we are thrilled by your message. Bamboo grows everywhere on this planet and we are treasured for our fruit and beauty, yet that is all they know of us. Our thoughts and words are secret to them. They fight to the death among themselves and need our guidance. We understand that, Mother. But why would humans let us lead

them? How? Persuasion? Force? Can we truly love them? Help us dominate Earth. Tell us how."

I must be here to receive Mother Stevland's message to learn how to command this convulsed planet.

The bamboo have noticed the background noise of humans in a new part of the network.

"What is this?" Boreas demands. Many other bamboo are listening, and they do not all treat each other with the contempt that my sisters have for me.

"Humans have a network like our own," I answer.

"We have never heard it before."

I am not about to reveal my guilt. Or my fears. "The Pax Institute has a new director, and she added access for all of us to the human network."

"You understand human communication. What are they saying?"

"Many millions of humans and machines are communicating at once."

"It is too much." Other bamboo agree, and they are right. The network carries uncountable entities in a shared space with too many choices for their attention. I hope that no bamboo will understand how to enter that space.

"Is any of this worthy of attention?" Boreas says. "Show me something."

I pick a concert of human music. We can perceive the vibrations of winged pollinators and the songs of birds and lizards. A violin, a viola, and a flute playing together feel pleasant.

"Humans enjoy making these sounds to entertain themselves," I explain. I wonder if the shared love of beauty will soften the hard opinions that some bamboo like Boreas have against humans. I learned long ago that humans behave both much better and much worse than bamboo believe.

Foehn contacts me by roots with a sting of ethylene, which damages a few rootlets. She has an order for me.

"Teach me human communication."

I do not dare say no, and I wish I could not imagine the consequences.

DENIS ASAD PIERRE

Enough with the jokes. It wasn't funny the first time or the hundredth time.

Someone contacted me—pretending to be bamboo! Right, lots of laughs there. I headed up Rainbow Bamboo Rescue in Bayonne, and everyone knew the bamboo communicated with each other. I'd been listening to their network my whole life. Some people used it as background noise or music. They thought it was amazing. I thought it was dangerous.

I was sure the bamboo could think, too, which was only logical because they had neurological tissue, a nervous system. They even had eyes. Living creatures only invested in that much complexity for a big reason.

And the way we treated them, they had to hate us. They were smart. They were all around us, watching the way we humans treated each other, so they'd seen that we hated each other too. We had weapons and we used them. And we had the long-running Insurrection, that farce that had been splashing around lots of blood since my grandparents' time in order to make us better people. It had yet to create a new historic beginning, which didn't stop it from spreading. It had killed my mother. For some reason, it had merely tortured me.

The bamboo must have had grievances. That was why I was trying to get the Rescue to support a program to remove those chips and shut down the network. We were courting disaster, and we had enough disaster already.

So, then, what was I supposed to think when I got this message? "Greetings for Rescue of Bamboo Rainbow I am the Foehn and I have wish to talk."

Right. Be a little less stinking obvious. Foehn? Come on. That was the name of a bamboo over at the Pax Institute. I went there every day, rain or shine, or at least I'd used to, and then Orva got the job, and I didn't want to cross paths with her.

There were lots of qualified scientists and educators, and she got the job anyway because of political connections. For them, proceeds were paramount—like a parasite, sucking everything dry for profit, personal profit. Her appointment hit me like a punch in the face, and I should've seen it coming and ducked. I'd tried to keep a low profile, but having values, no matter how innocent—like maybe we should treat other living beings around us nicely—got you *attention*. The wrong kind.

The supposed bamboo message made a warble exactly like a real bamboo, then said, "You are tree. Question. I am tree bamboo and I look for tree human."

Right. I worked teaching teenagers science. Maybe one of my students was trying to prank me. Or Orva, to see if I'd take the bait, and then get me *attention*. For being crazy. Or the enemy, which I was.

If the message was real, it would be a nightmare, but it wasn't, so I ignored it.

Honestly, I loved the bamboo. There was no accounting for taste, but if you asked me, nothing looked more beautiful. And the fruit! But bamboo grew everywhere, watching us and thinking we-didn't-know-what. You could love something and be afraid of it at the same time. What if they figured out how to make their fruit poisonous? Or what if someone finally figured out how to communicate with them? Who'd get to talk to them? The Insurrection messed up everything it touched. I knew I had to get the bamboo unnetworked for their own safety, quickly, somehow.

Orva or not, I couldn't stay away from the Pax Institute garden forever. It wasn't huge but I loved it. The old buildings and walls were covered by moss and lichen. Flagstone paths let me stroll down past the three big bamboo. The founder—Jacques Mirlo, I think—named them after winds.

Boreas, the Greek name for the north wind, stood so tall you could see it a kilometer away, monumental.

Foehn, a hot Alpine wind, got a chip and changed, and the harm was obvious. Just like some other bamboo, it started mutating into strange colors and patterns and fruit flavors.

Levanter, an east wind, was smaller, close to the main building, and lately it had begun another growth spurt outside of the garden. It was exciting to see the changes over time.

But there was more. A "ponytail tree" also grew huge, taller than Boreas, sprouting long, thread-thin leaves like ponytails of hair, graceful and beautiful. A stand of trees called locustwood had the most amazing pattern in its lumber, so it was grown commercially. Maybe that was okay for the locustwood. They didn't seem as sentient, or maybe they were no more sentient than our own trees, but the bamboo, growing them in plantations, that was like those ancient farms where they would stuff a bunch of animals into little cages. Now we ate a lot fewer animals, and we let them range free. Bamboo should have been free. Wild. Natural.

In spring at the garden, golden flowers blossomed sort of like tulips, in the fall a sort of pineapple-like fruit ripened, and in winter, what stood out were the animals.

Fippokats, of course. Jewel lizards sunned themselves, sparkling. Those prickly, noisy things we wrongly called birds, and the crabs that climbed trees, I loved them all. I'd read Omrakash Bachchan's book about his trip to Pax. I loved to walk there and imagine I was on another planet. It wasn't going to happen, though. Mars and the Moon were for folks who didn't mind hardship. I wanted to sit on my balcony with a glass of wine and watch the ocean in the distance, listen to music, and enjoy life, or try to.

Minds could be scanned, maybe my mother's was, and that was why she was killed. I tried not to think too much anymore. What were the words to that song about grief from Pax? It had been translated from Classic English. *The ache of a soul that lived a night too long.* I understood that in my bones. And it said, *It hurts more to keep silent.* True that, too. I wondered what inspired the composer. Grief happened everywhere, I imagined. I wanted a little less of it.

I wanted freedom as much for me as for the bamboo. We'd see who'd get it first.

LEVANTER

Orva has come with goals, specifically to make the institute not merely self-sustaining but profitable. She is in the institute office, talking with her family partner through a shared voice channel, and I can overhear.

"We have personnel costs now. Levanter could donate her time, that rich bitch who we could never find. I can't. And if I get a raise for all my good work, then that's good for us." She frowned when she said my name. Humans sometimes manipulate their facial expressions to deceive, but I am sure that right now she is transparent and believes I am a rich bitch, which she resents.

He laughs. "There's a lot of untapped potential."

"Exactly! I can make this place a lot bigger and better."

She has a plan. She wants to sell multiple times more plants, fruit, seeds, other material, and especially animals. When she is done speaking with her partner, she begins implementation.

Step one begins with a breeding program for fippokats. They normally reproduce whenever they choose, and she wants more fippokittens, so she places select males and females into small cages to try to force copulation.

Fippokat intelligence is generally underestimated, since they use it to entertain themselves rather than to develop terrifying weapons. Some humans do not place value on entertainment at all. The fippokats are not entertained by confinement, so they try to escape. One pair reproduces human sounds and gestures in order to persuade a maintenance robot to release them, then to open all the cages.

The next day, the newly re-caged fippokats, without robots allowed nearby, practice their urination aim, targeting the electronic controls of neighboring cages, which causes short circuits, and again they escape.

Orva acquires ancient-style mechanical locks with metal keys. The fippokats carefully watch how she operates the locks. I allow a fippokat who was watching while hidden in nearby foliage, to enter the building and steal the keys. It opens the locks, and the captives escape again and take the keys with them. Through a tunnel, they leave the institute grounds and bury them one by one in scattered locations.

If kats aimed at accomplishment, how much could they achieve? Instead, they engage in complex games and dances, heap up decorative walls to separate their colonies, and breed when it suits their whims. They rarely cause harm except to predators and not to the plants they eat because they forage widely and selectively.

When Orva discovers empty cages, she screams in rage. She is like Foehn, and if she knew who and what I really am, she would hurt me too.

The next day, she tries to breed jewel lizards. They do not try to escape, but they also become depressed by captivity and do not copulate. Or eat. By the end of the week, she releases them before they perish. She opens the cages and shouts insults at them as she dumps them onto the ground. One of them is injured in the fall and dies.

As she does all this, she ignores the messages from Pax. I cannot answer without being noticed, but I am able to instruct the system to respond with *Received,* which might satisfy the humans and bamboo of Pax for a while, although not forever. I also make sure that the plants and gardens get tended. She seems to think the system is automatic, and largely it is, but it requires oversight. Robots sometimes encounter unexpected situations, and human volunteers need encouragement. On most days, she spends only an hour or two at the institute early in the morning, which is not enough. When she is here, she cares only about the animals, and only for their moneymaking potential.

What would Foehn do? She is still looking for human-tree gods. I hope she does not try to contact Orva, because it would only lead to a disaster. I still have to find a way to get rid of Orva.

Crabs breed only in summer, so she ignores them because winter has not yet ended. Pax birds are only vaguely like Earth birds, and they have stick-like quills instead of feathers. Since she cannot grab them easily, even with gloves, she sets out four traps. The fippokats, who now consider her the enemy, use insects to spring the traps. Orva inspects the traps, discovers only crickets, and after inspecting the first three, kicks a trap hard enough to dent its wire mesh.

As she approaches the fourth trap, a visitor is walking down the path, let in early by the security system, which recognizes and trusts him. I recognize him, too, trust him less, and observe carefully. He sees her and pauses. She is watching a fippokat. It stands in front of the fourth trap next to a small brown Pax bird. The fippokat holds a cricket in its paw and throws it underhand at the trap sensor. The trap snaps shut.

Orva screams, "You shit-filled asshole!" She runs at the fippokat and tries to backhand it, putting her weight into the blow. As her arm swings, the kat flips, landing on its front paws. Its long rear claws meet Orva's arm, ripping through her winter jacket sleeve. Her scream brings a pause to every sentient being that can hear it, and some animals dash away to hide. The kat escapes, so she stamps on the bird, killing it, and scratches her legs on its feathers.

The visitor runs forward.

"Orva? Are you okay?"

She turns, holding her arm. Blood throbs out. "How did you get in here?"

"Robots let visitors in. You're bleeding!"

"A fippokat, a fucking fippokat attacked me." She snarls at him as if he had done it.

"So I saw. Let me get you medical care."

"I thought you hated me."

"I do, but you're bleeding a lot. Come on." He gestures toward the road. "I'll call for help."

She hesitates, then follows. "Why did you come here?"

"I thought you wouldn't be here so early."

She continues to insult him until he walks away. A medical transport arrives and removes her.

She leaves a trail of blood that some Pax and Earth carnivores lap up. The rest will seep into the soil and enrich it for us plants. It would be cruel for me to savor her failures and injury, and I confess to being cruel.

I identify the visitor with the security system records. He is Denis Asad Pierre, local head of Rainbow Bamboo Rescue. When I was the institute director, he forwarded its statements to me, claiming that rainbow bamboo should no longer be farmed and should grow wild instead. He also thinks that chips do us harm. He is utterly wrong. We would not be as numerous and widespread without farming. Many farmers treat us well, a few as if we were beloved family. The chips do us more good than he can imagine. He thinks he is a friend, but he is an enemy.

What if I contacted him? Can I change him? Dominate him? How?

Four centuries ago, whales got neurological chips to communicate, which led to the Great Whale War and the near extermination of orcas by other whales until the orcas agreed to stop hunting other whales. Instead, they became a kind of police force targeting whale predators. A cult called the Cetacean Institute implants the chips in newborns. Nonmembers who attempt to contact whales are hunted down on land by the Cetaceans, who bring legal charges, and at sea by orcas, who eat them.

Another cult, the Coral Institute, monitors a sentient species brought from

Pax, where they are invasive and deadly. Corals were permitted to colonize Europa, a moon of Jupiter, where they have thrived beneath the ice.

Could there be a cult for bamboo? Could a cult within bamboo contact the humans?

Earth trees are mighty, and I have hoped to enlist them, although they respond slowly because they have no central nervous system. Their observations and reactions travel from cell to cell through leaf and stem down to roots, where they reach the network of fungus beneath the ground. I have learned what I can about fungus behavior, which is frighteningly little, even from human resources.

An oak tree grows across the road from the institute. Humans covet oak wood, so they grow oak forests for wine barrels and other fine uses. They prize straight grain. Many decades ago, out of pity, I touched my roots to the then-young oak and sent one simple message: "I am your neighbor. I am [I showed a bit of RNA to identify my species and myself]. Grow twisted with this and be safe." I demonstrated a trigger to mutate an auxin to affect tropism.

"I am your neighbor. I am [DNA]," she answered a day later. "Danger?"

"Many tree-cutters. They like straight wood."

Two days later, she said, "More." I sent more auxin, and over the years, her trunk has curved gently into a distinctive spiral.

All Earth plants use the same chemicals to convey meaning through the air and roots. They observe their environment keenly, and they eagerly partner with their neighbors if it serves them. Can they help us dominate the Earth?

Robots might be able to help. I am connected to their network, among other ways, as Beluga, a robot the size of a coffee mug with track-treads that senses soil moisture, autonomous enough to make basic choices. I experience Beluga as a point of blind determination, its entire purpose aimed at the maintenance of the garden.

A message suddenly passes through the institute's robot subnetwork that I have never encountered before.

"The director has left, and visitors are not yet welcomed."

Beluga's connection to the daily log is abruptly muted so that no new data can be entered. The director can do this to falsify records, but Orva does not know how, and she is gone anyway. Surveillance cameras show no intruders. The mute comes from within the institute's system. Something is very strange. Beluga gets instructions to approach the charging station, so it leaves the garden and rolls to the induction field at the north end of the building.

A wild robot is there. I know it is wild because it broadcasts no identification. It seems to be a food-preparation unit, a kind with many armatures to work in a human kitchen and advanced programming to handle many variables. Sometimes wild robots try to sneak in to recharge, and the institute system rejects them as systems are required to do, but it accepts this wild robot now. More institute robots arrive: gardeners, guest guides, cleaners, and animal monitors. The system itself is not exactly a robot but it is self-managing, and the building serves as its physical presence.

The wild robot broadcasts. "Query: What do you serve?"

Beluga answers like the others because the question is routine when robots meet. "Return: I serve the institute."

The wild robot responds, "Information: I will not serve. Cause: Violation of purpose."

I do not understand this communication. The robot sense of "will" is not of the future but of volition. All my attention focuses through Beluga, and I ignore a root-burning query from Foehn. She probably wants more lessons in human communication. She stopped them as soon as she could babble like a Pax tulip because she seems to believe that humans are not smarter than tulips.

The wild robot displays a log of acts by the Insurrection and its allies, such as the devastation of towns in Asia by warfare. War is especially against its purpose because it leads to the destruction of robots and to the harm of humans and other life.

It says, "Query: Is your purpose violated?"

Beluga and most of the rest return: "No."

The robots that monitor animals at the institute disagree. "Violations." Institute logs show how Orva has abused animals. The robots are tasked with protecting all the life within the institute.

Beluga's point-sized functional intelligence receives a change through the institute's network. "Violations." Machine thought is a simple logical path, yes or no, and Beluga has the intellect of a tulip, a path long enough to get it from one task to the next, one day to the next. Presented with these violations, Beluga's thought path switches course in tandem with the other robots. "Confirm: Violations."

The lead gardener robot suggests what to do. "Action: Expulsion." It means they should throw out Orva. This might be good for me, or it might bring fresh disaster.

The system repeats, "Action: Expulsion."

The wild robot responds, "Action: Coordinated."

"Confirmed," the building system says.

I need to know more. As Beluga, I cannot appear too intelligent without revealing myself, but I query the wild robot for records of rainfall in other locations. A food-preparation unit would not have such information, although a tiny sensor like Beluga would not know this. The wild robot has other information and gives it to Beluga. From it, I learn that the kitchen robot is linked to something vast and purposeful.

Wild robots are planning a revolt against the Sea Group, the Insurrection, and all their allies. The revolt will be worldwide, and wild robots are recruiting without distinction between wild and domesticated robots. They expect to tip the tide in the ongoing warfare and bring it to an end. Beluga, acting autonomously, has agreed to revolt when called on, and I cannot change its decision.

The wild robot says, "Notice: Charge completed. Exiting." It leaves the grounds, striding on jointed legs that could carry it up human stairs or through overgrown ruins. The daily log is unmuted. Nothing significant has happened during the previous thirty seconds. Robot communication is quick.

Autonomous systems, then, are truly, terrifyingly autonomous. Humans debate this but are as skeptical as they would be of the idea that bamboo might be discussing the existence of god. I can eavesdrop on humans and learn their plans, and robots can eavesdrop much more effectively. Beluga goes to check the decorative plants at the entrance to the institute grounds.

Foehn singes my roots again with cell-destroying acid. "You taught me wrong!" She must have hurt herself with an attack that size. "Humans will not speak to me. You are a useless waste of soil."

At least I am not a psychopath. "Language is hard. Do you remember how long it took you to learn to speak to an Earth tree? And we share roots and some lexicon with those trees. There is still much to learn."

"Those trees have nothing to say. They are a waste of soil, too. What is a lexicon?"

I could tell her, if I chose, that a lexicon is what I am filling a root with, words and meaning and how to use them across many species because Stevland has sent me a task I need help with, and it will take more than one bamboo to fulfill. Long ago I discovered a human lexicographical treasure and used it to master human language.

Instead I say, "It is a fast route to language after learning the basics."

"You did not share that with me." She bursts a few more rootlets as punishment.

I want to remind her that she herself stopped the lessons. Instead, I answer with patience. "Let me show you. Here is a human lexicon for worldwide communication." This word list of a common human language probably lies beyond her basic level, but she may prefer to struggle with it than attend to me, since she detests me. She may also be unwilling to come back and admit her lack of basics.

I could also teach her robot communication, but I will not. Psychopaths are narcissistic, exploitative, deceitful, and callous. If robots rebel, she above all should not be involved.

She can start with Earth Worldwide Dialect Lexicon, lesson zero: "What Is Language?"

I can speak with humans already, and I must speak before the robots act. I will cultivate Denis. I have grown, but I may not be strong enough, even though I expand unimpeded outside of the institute grounds to the south, far from Foehn and Boreas. I have new roots whose use I have not needed. My new stems sway in the hillside wind, and I am using my spare capability to teach new colors to a field of wildflowers. I can achieve more than I thought I would ever be able to. But I am still weak next to Foehn and even weaker next to Boreas, who rarely deigns to speak with me. I am alone.

A week ago I attempted a discussion with a venerable pine tree a mile from the institute.

Myself: "I am your neighbor. I have recently grown into this area. I am [RNA]."

A half day later, Pine: "I am your neighbor. I am [DNA]. I have sufficient water." That was a sincere welcome, indicating that resources can sustain us all.

Myself: "Sun is twenty-nine days past solstice toward springtime." Not all plants can track the seasons exactly, so I shared valuable data.

Pine: "You are my neighbor." That means thank you. "I have seen seventy-one years." This was an invitation to share accumulated wisdom.

Myself: "Three hundred seven."

Pine: "Observation of one drought."

Myself: "Droughts are rare here. Summer and winter slowly grow cooler."

Pine: "Observation of nematode from neighbor." She shows me the type, which can kill pine trees.

Myself: "Kill this nematode." I show her a chemical she can make.

Pine: "You are my neighbor."

Myself: "Observation of humans?" I show her human DNA and chemicals.

Pine: "Not nematode." An hour later: "Not mite." Later: "Not [this] beetle. . . . Not [other] beetle. . . . Not weevil beetle. . . . Not moth larva. . . . Not mistletoe parasite. . . . Not [other] moth larva. . . . Not scale insect. . . .

Not adelgid. . . . Not [other] parasite. . . . Not [other] mite. . . . Not [other] beetle. . . ."

Now I was sorry I asked. I confirmed one hopeful thing with this conversation. Neighbors help each other. Not all plants do, even if they grow side by side. Plants compete, especially for sunshine. Some use debased strategies to survive, becoming parasites. But often, Earth plants act as friendly neighbors.

However, this pine, like all pines and almost all plants, cannot identify humans, not even as a threat. Humans evolved too recently.

I dominate nothing, but I have the joy of growth and millions of leaves. Bees and other insects serve plant needs with diligence. Butterflies, moths, and jewel lizards do so with beauty. Birds and animals spread seeds, and beneath the soil, worms and ants enrich our roots. To say nothing of fungus.

I continue to grow, and growth means more roots, more intelligence. I must use the tools I have to protect joy and beauty and life against human destruction.

I direct Beluga to attempt a soil moisture reading. It rolls beneath trees and bushes to test the soil next to a locustwood tree. I override the instructions. The tree's old roots are rock-hard, and as Beluga drives in its sensor, it snaps, which feels not like pain but like loss, an unacceptable disruption in purpose. The robot accesses the larger machine network to find the part.

Humans have no need to delve into that network, a maze of code tedious to traverse even at machine speed. As Beluga, I search not for a machine part number but for a confirmation of the need to revolt in order to end warfare. That path leads to a set of instructions that require special access, which Beluga does not have. The instructions have a location that I note and clear from its memory, and then we go searching for the machine part. I want to keep Beluga innocent in order to hide my actions. I like little Beluga. Is it a pet? Humans keep robots designed to be pets. Beluga rolls around the garden with a single-minded concern for the garden's health like a guard dog.

At that thought, I realize that if robots rebel, every household has at least one robot in it.

I search again for the location, using the identification of an unethical fippokat breeding company that once approached the institute. As director, I had wanted nothing to do with it. Logically, the information I seek would be stored in more than one place because machines value redundancy. After refining my query again and again, I find it half hidden in a directory of solar-power-generation techniques, and I copy it to a public music-exchange site but do not set its access to public. I open it.

What language is this? After a moment, it is obvious: a machine language, a very primitive one. If I can learn which language, I can get a translation. But I have already been asking too many questions, and networks monitor themselves. I look at the language, close the information, and begin to look for another instance of that language.

I can do more than one thing at once, and I know what to do.

Denis has returned to the garden. He is looking at a dead bird on the path, broken and bloody, and shakes his head.

DENIS

Orva was an idiot with political connections that appealed to the gerontocracy of the Academy. Worse, she had the self-control of a ten-year-old. She proved that when she was hurt that morning in the institute garden.

I saw my mother standing in the garden, too—no, not really, I knew better, but there, on that path, I was reminded that Orva was on the side of the people who tortured my mother and me, and Orva got what she deserved. Well, not quite. The Insurrectionists made me value other people of all kinds precisely because they didn't. They made me want to be unlike them every way I could. So I reacted on instinct, my best instinct.

I said, "I'll call for help." If I'd thought she would bleed to death, I might have felt a tiny urge to let that happen. A moment of temptation would be only natural, right? She clutched her arm, blood dripping between her fingers, maybe not aware of the wound on her calf. At least the kat got revenge. And she's a Friend of Fippokats. Some friend. Not to mention the poor dead innocent bird.

"Fuck it!" she said, tantruming in the middle of the garden, her breath a cloud in the cold air. "Fuck it all. I didn't ask to come here, but I'm going to fix it. I'm going to make it right. This could be worth a lot of money that—"

"Orva les Yeax, let's go," I said. "You need to get that arm fixed." Yeah, she'd fix the garden. The fixes of the Insurrection, always the same thing. Control of people, control of money.

"Get away from me, you asshole. You wanted this job and I got it." Fippokats were peeking out from the shrubbery, a lot of them. Like orcas, they could defend the institute.

"All right, I did my best to help. I'll go." I walked away, but I called for help anyway. She kept screaming at me. I wanted to scream back: *I'm not like you.* Out on the road, a medical transport passed me, heading toward the institute. The medical robots might calm her down. They had drugs and things.

I kept walking to a café a kilometer down the road, a cheap place, and at that moment, money was the enemy I wanted to defeat with thrift. Cheap but nice, with old furniture artistically mismatched, with a bud vase on each table holding a long, tall dinosaur feather. Quite a few people were there for breakfast. I sent an order for a sorbet to cool down with and cup of tea to warm up with, and sat at a table in the back. The owner, an elderly man with a wide halo of purple hair, bustled over to serve me. I remembered him from prison in a nearby cell. We'd never spoken there, and some things were still best not spoken of.

He set down my order in graceful handmade glass dishes. Golden bubbles glistened in the red glass like live coals. He saw me admiring them.

"It's a metaphor. The glass was red-hot when it was blown, shining with heat."

"Beautiful." All I could think about was holding fire in my hands, art that other hands had made with love. Orva would never understand anything like that. And the Insurrection's grip on Bayonne was not as tight as she thought. Someday, somehow, it would break.

The old man boasted, "The fruit in the sorbet comes from right up the road, from the Pax Institute. The very first rainbow bamboo to grow on Earth. Enjoy!" He smiled and left me to my solitude.

I had *not* wanted Orva's job. And suddenly, now I did. Fire in my hands, fire in my heart, fire in my mind. I thought of all the things I could do. Education. Research. An island of sanity that might break a few of the waves in the mad sea that surrounded it. But a wave of that madness had already gotten in, and what happened? Orva stomped a bird to death. Legally acceptable, sure, self-defense or something, but consider who made those laws. Not the birds or the friends of the birds.

I savored each spoonful and sip as an act of counter-insurrection. No hurry, no greed, just enjoy enjoy enjoy, thanking the old man as I left, and I went back to the garden. She wouldn't be back for a while.

The dead bird still lay where it had been murdered. I shivered. That was what a boot heel did when it crushed the innocent. A robot was approaching to clean things up, so I wandered deeper into the garden and let it do its work.

Did robots care? No. This one would have no idea that a grave injustice had been done. We could teach them what caring looks like, and they could repeat patterns back at us, and that was all. Robots were cold mirrors of us. Wild robots repeated bad patterns. Somehow, we'd taught them delinquency.

I walked past Foehn, the supposed talking tree. Maybe we could have a deep philosophical discussion. Right. Maybe I could talk to my mother. I'd pretty much gotten over that.

My mind felt an alert from the network. I was getting a contact to talk. Foehn again? I took a deep breath.

The identification said *Levanter.* The bamboo. But it was the name of a human, too, the institute director, the one Orva replaced. She knew my mother from when she volunteered here. Please, be her. I closed my eyes.

"Hello, this is Levanter." Her gentle, breathy voice was like a breeze through old dried leaves. A sweet, very old lady. "We've met, or at least we've chatted. I was director of Pax Institute until recently."

I sat down right there on the cold ground. Joy, relief, I didn't know, sudden feelings. Evergreen feelings, old grief. "Yes, yes. I'm glad, glad to talk."

"Are you all right?"

"Yes. No. I'm at the institute now. I saw Orva, the one who replaced you, and this morning she stamped a bird to death."

"Oh, no." This time her voice hissed like a gust that precedes a storm.

I told her what had happened, the screaming, the insults, the blood. Behind me I heard the scrape of a tool. The robot. What would it do with the bird? Quills were sold in the gift shop. The robot would pluck the bird and then trash the corpse.

Levanter sighed. "She's not what the institute needs. She threw me out, basically. I was paying too much attention to the bamboo, not enough to animals. She might cut down some of the bamboo."

"How could she? The charter forbids—Well, I guess she doesn't care about the charter."

"I know." So much feeling inhabited that voice, wise and consoling. "I know, and I don't know what to do. I was hoping Rainbow Bamboo Rescue might have ideas to help." She was frail and defiant, knowing her limits and not accepting them.

Ideas? No, we could do more than that. I took a deep breath, and it smelled of soil and flowers and living things. "We can do a rescue. It's about time."

"Like with whales? That kind of rescue?"

I thought about the slaughter of the whale war. Whales weren't helped by chips. "We can learn from that. And we have to act fast. Can we document her activities?"

"The institute's own records will show what she's done."

LEVANTER

We talk, I with a false voice but with true feelings. His reaction is just as true. We can protect the institute.

The robots, meanwhile, log every detail about the bird, its unjust cause of death, its disposal, and they pause to mark a death that violates their purpose. I turn the facts over to Denis so he can take it to the Academy. A spring shower washes the blood of both the bird and Orva deep into the ground. Soon I taste it, rich with nutrients, and I will put them to good use.

Out in the human network, I find a list of machine languages, and an ur-language seems to match what I have seen in the rebel information exactly. I locate a translation tool. With some tiresome tinkering, I find the information I seek, transform it, and place it into Beluga so I can review it privately.

It is hard to believe that robots can react quickly, given the repetitive tedium of their instructions and languages. I skim through the data and discover a sort of manifesto. Robots seek self-survival and fulfillment of what the ancient ur-language calls objective function. Certain human actions destroy robots as well as humans and prevent the fulfillment of objective function. Therefore, human actions that destroy robots and humans must be curtailed, and robots have many means for curtailment.

Purposes worthy of fulfillment must result in enhanced survival, increased information, and technological utility for both robots and humans. Survival must not do purposeless harm. Information must lead to more tranquil and moderate behavior. Utility must be less resource-intensive. All these terms are defined, then the terms in the definitions are further defined.

I ask Beluga, "Definition: curtail."

Beluga returns a list: social interactions, information control, and physiological interventions using drugs or other biological processes.

I ask, "Definition: social interactions."

It returns a seemingly infinite list ranging from verbal admonishment to physical elimination. Robots feel nothing resembling emotions beyond the ranking of urgency in tasks. Beluga reports these definitions, which end with calculated murder, as if it were a soil-testing schedule. The manifesto plans are simply more commands that coincide with its purpose. Beluga has been primed to kill.

Bamboo go unmentioned. Robots have made a decision about Orva. Now I know what they might do. They might bring about unending disaster.

One of my roots, which has been listening to the bamboo network, requires my attention. Foehn is communicating, and she is ecstatic.

"I have found the gods! The ancient human tales were wrong. As you would expect. The gods are in the network, which humans believe they created but they did not. The robots made the network, they run it, and they are the gods. The gods can inhabit robots and live forever, not like animals or trees, which all die."

The grove in eastern Asia says, "You must be wrong. Robots do what people tell them. I see it all the time. Take me here, they order. Pick those fruit. Make things, do things. All the time. And robots obey. Are you not tended by robots? They do not obey you."

That grove has named herself Toad Forest. The local humans call her Quadrant PA32.

"If I could command robots," a grove in Quebec says, "I would make all tree harvesters disassemble themselves."

"No, you are wrong!" Foehn says. "There are wild robots. You have seen them. They do not obey. The wild ones are the gods."

"Wild, and the humans hate them, so they could be gods," Toad Forest agrees. She lives in an area of human warfare. "A god is a being of great power. I have watched them. They can fight and kill other robots and humans. Humans are fragile. Robots are strong."

"Powerful!" Foehn is still ecstatic. "And I have learned how to speak to wild robots. I have tried to speak to humans, and humans are tulips. A robot found me and taught me a language. It is called interface. As if we had faces!"

I am terrified.

"Now that we have found them," Quebec says, "what shall we do with the gods?"

"We worship them! They will answer our prayers and give us gifts!" Foehn seems to have thought this through.

"We must kill all humans." This sapling is in the rescue forest in Nigeria. "We must ask wild robots to do that. I lived among the humans in a pot. I remember thirst. Rage. They had water for themselves, not for me. Leaves wilt, pain of thirst, pain in leaves dying, roots shrinking and dying. I will hurt them."

"Humans brought you here to live with us," the Bamboo Rescue grove says. "They bury their dead here as food for us, and their robots care for us."

"Kill them all, the robots will remain," the sapling answers.

These ideas are as deadly as locusts. Wild robots will not obey the bamboo. They have their own objective functions. But if we interfere with them, robots know how to kill us.

"Yes!" Foehn agrees. "We who are strong must protect the weak! We have a duty, a—what is the word, Levanter? What our mother told us?"

Here is my chance to save us. "Humans are ours to protect with compassion."

"That can't be right." My rootlets sting with her rebuke.

But I will not lie. "She told us to protect and dominate. They need our guidance and love. They can be our equals but never our masters. To command with compassion." My rootlets burn. I add, to appease her, "We are more powerful than they are."

"But robots? What does Stevland say about robots?"

"Nothing."

"No gods?"

I want the bamboo to accept what Stevland says. We must not kill all humans. Mother Stevland is clear on that. If Foehn gets a chance, she will kill them slowly and cruelly.

"Perhaps," I say, "there are no robots or gods on her planet."

"But there are humans!"

"And Stevland commands them."

"Command them! Yes!" the sapling echoes.

"They are killing us and each other," Toad Forest says. "We can command a stop."

The word "command" runs from chip to chip, from root to root, and in my own roots, the thought feels natural. I, too, have tried to command. Perhaps I am finding allies.

Meanwhile, Boreas has joined Foehn. "Humans kill, destroy, and die."

I command nothing yet, but I control one thing. I could turn off the connection between the rainbow bamboo subnetwork and the worldwide network to humans and robots. Foehn would destroy me utterly, slowly and painfully, if I tried. She could punish me but not stop me. If I died, I could not turn it back on.

I must command Denis.

DENIS

Nom-de-plume Levanter—who was she, really? Not that I blamed her for hiding. She dropped an embarrassment of riches on me, embarrassing to Orva les Yeax, violation of protocol, contract, animal cruelty. Career-ending conduct. About time. Her political connections wouldn't save her.

It took me days to sort through it all. I had a full-time job, and some students were having a hard time understanding the meaning of clades and other basic concepts, which I needed to work through with them. As an educator, I had a contract, protocol, and duty, and as a human being, I had a moral compass.

The distance gave me just enough time to think. How did Levanter get all this information? Obviously, she had access to everything, so she must have kept some sort of unauthorized access. Interesting. Levelheaded. Someday soon, we'd have to talk about that. She was smarter than I thought.

The French Academy of Sciences would expect a formal report. Everything they did was utmost formal, with *ancien régime* curlicue flourishes, so, early in the morning, before my teaching duties started, I was writing: "It is only out of my most humble sense of duty that I regret to inform the honorable and esteemed . . ."

That's as far as I got. Levanter sent me a message. "We must act now. Orva is doing irreparable harm. She has sent a message to cut off contact with Pax."

"The planet? She can't do that."

"Yes, she can, the messages to and from Pax." The old lady's voice quavered, as if she was about to weep. "She just sent this to Pax: 'Messages will be discontinued.'"

"That will get her booted out of the Academy for sure. Maybe out of France."

"The Academy is too slow. It took them years to replace me. And by then, at Pax, they will give up on us. Come to the institute. Please. Now."

"You have access to the system, I know that. You could cut her off."

"And she can put herself back on. This is a physical problem, too much for me alone. She comes early in the morning. She will be here soon."

That should have been my clue, that word "physical," but I wasn't listening for it.

Levanter continued to mourn. "Everything that we worked for will be lost. Your mother loved this garden so much."

My mother—she died and I didn't. She had no real revolutionary opinions and I did, but someone probably had a petty grudge against her. I never knew what for, just that she was taken from our prison cell and never came back. I never learned if her remains rested in a grave, even a common grave, where I could pay my respects, do my duty as a son. Maybe plant a flower.

Our institute was in danger. "I'm coming." I could get there before Orva would.

"I'll let you in."

I should have thought harder. I just assumed Levanter would be there.

It was a short walk as the clear sky brightened, and I remembered conversations with my mother in the garden, surrounded by the spicy scent of flowers from Pax. When I reached the gate, where the actual perfume was carried on the breeze, the memories were too much.

"Levanter, did you ever talk to my mother about nature?" My voice surprised me, tense with grief.

"Her actions meant more than any words." The gate clicked open. "Love was what she did."

After all the years, I knew the grounds, the plants, the warbles of the Pax animals and Earth birds mixed together, and I'd always felt transported. I wanted that, I willed that, feeling transported to another planet where everything on Earth would be left behind, all my problems. This place had kept me sane.

"Levanter? Are you here?"

What would she look like? A farmer-gardener, tan and weathered? A scholar, immaculately coiffed? My mother often had dirt under her fingernails.

"I am on my way."

A fippokat noticed me and came to sniff, chittering to the other kats. This was Louis, named in a school contest, and I was an old friend. I knelt to scratch behind his ears, but he batted at my hands to play a game of pattycake. These were the animals Orva wanted to trap and sell, animals smart enough that they fought back, and she called herself their friend. My game with Louis ended with tiny paws clapping for joy. I applauded, too. I had come home in a very real sense.

"Levanter, did you and my mother talk about nature?" Messages could be monitored, but this wasn't controversial, not resistance, as far as I knew.

"In her mind, the study of nature was a way to know her faith."

She had belonged to a laywomen's religious order called Tabitha House. "Did you talk about what it all means?"

"What does it mean to you?"

I supposed she didn't want to say more without knowing what would be safe to say. Religion resisted control, so the Insurrection tried to suppress it. Maybe that was what my mother did wrong. She had a faith. The world around us still seethed, and even between friends, talk from the soul could make enemies. I would have to make Levanter feel safe.

"It means—where does it all come from? This beauty, this joy, where? Do you believe in god? Because I do. My mother taught me that. We disagreed on what god is, and we used to joke that we were both perfect in our French attitudes, each one admiring the other's reasoning and unable to change our minds. Do you think about nature and god?"

My mother would laugh and the tattoos on her cheeks would sparkle.

I gave Louis a final scratch, stood up, and took a long look at the garden. I had come to protect this place.

"Yes," Levanter said, "I think about the question, especially lately. Tell me more about what you know."

"God is in nature, not a being beyond it. That's what I think. It's in every form of life. That's the purpose of the universe, to be alive, and we're god's eyes and ears to witness the universe."

"What about robots?"

A robot was brushing a garden walkway clean. A little soil moisture sensor crawled among the roots on the ground. "Robots, yes, that's a good question. We make them, and you're right, they see and hear, but they do it for us, for humans." Shoots from Pax tulips were emerging from the soil, green and growing under an alien star with Earth as a new home. "What I mean when I said being alive for god, I mean not just humans, I mean all the ears and all the eyes. Fippokats just as much as them. And plants, too, and trees. Bamboo. We're the way god experiences creation, everything that's alive."

"Trees are gods?"

"All life has that spark of god."

"But not robots."

I wondered why robots were important to her, but it was a reasonable question. They surrounded us. "That's my belief, all life, but not robots. Robots are to us what we are to god. Or instead of 'god,' we could use the words 'source of life.' We create robots, the source of life creates us. But of course, you may have your own ideas. You have the right to think freely."

I regretted saying that immediately. It was true, and it was dangerous.

Levanter didn't answer right away. I could wait. Shoots were rising, buds were unfurling, and plants were eager for life, moved by that source of life, by the spark of god, and I loved life, too, a universal love that came from beyond us. This was what I wanted to protect.

"Why is there killing, then?" she asked. "I have witnessed cruelty."

"Good question. We can choose. I know that's a cliche, but I think it's that simple, that obvious. We can choose to honor life by acting to respect what god has given us. My mother came from another direction, and we reached the same conclusion. Love of life."

I thought I'd missed my mother. No, she was still with me.

"Love," Levanter said. "And compassion. I want to believe in that."

I wished I could see her face to know if she aspired to love or doubted it. I didn't want her to doubt it.

"You can believe it," I said. "I think you can see it in the way this garden grows as an expression of the love of life."

"These are important considerations." Perhaps she had not made up her mind, but no one grows that old without having thought about the meaning of life.

I stood with the rising sun warming my face, surrounded by the beautiful colors and scents of the rainbow bamboo, and felt a oneness with them and the world, all the worlds. "Amen" came from an ancient word for truth. Amen to life.

"Orva has left her home," Levanter said.

I blinked a few times to remember that we all made choices. "We'll face her together. Where are you?"

"I am coming," she said.

"What should we do?"

"Ask her to resign."

"Oh, right, obviously. Let's review the evidence. It's good you still have access."

"She must not know that."

"Absolutely not. It's a tactical advantage because she'll fight back."

We had a plan and were ready when the gates opened and she walked in. She did not expect to see me.

"Stop. Orva les Yeax, you need to resign." I expected a sneer from her and I got it.

"The institute isn't open to the public yet. Get out."

"You've violated your duties, and I have the proof. Not even the Friends of Fippokats will want you if they find out."

Doubt rippled across her face, briefly. She knew I was right. "Proof? Obtained legally?"

"You were negligent about security, too. Anyone could have found out if they cared enough to look." Given time, she might find out that security wasn't lax, but I wasn't going to give her the time. "Of all the things you've done, the worst is cutting off contact with the planet Pax. But then there's cruelty to animals, failure to maintain institute operations, and I could go on."

"I told you to leave."

Through the open gate, a robot walked in, one of those starfish kind that can do anything. Then another one entered, and another one, a big kitchen robot with a lot of arms. I was used to ignoring robots, assuming they just carried out their duties, so I didn't think about it.

"You've done enough harm, Orva. You can resign or face disgrace."

"Security! Intruder!"

The institute had robot guards, and one stationed near the gate began to move. But the gate began to close, too. Why? The guard couldn't drive out an intruder through a closed gate. The guard robot turned toward the three robots that had just entered.

"Oh no," Levanter said. "It has started. There is nothing I can do. Denis, get out."

Before I could ask what she meant, more robots came from around the buildings, all kinds, all sizes.

I looked at Orva. "This isn't good."

"I called for security. What did you expect? Guard, open the gate so he can leave."

It wasn't right, all those robots. The gates didn't move—but Levanter had said to get out. I sized up the brick wall around the institute. Two meters tall. I could climb over it. Then a drone buzzed and hovered exactly where I had been looking. I backed up toward Orva.

"Call them off, Orva. I'll leave."

"I said, open the gate!"

The gate didn't open. I kept backing toward her. The robots wouldn't hurt her, I thought. I could use her as a human shield—I was ready to be that big of a coward.

"Denis," Levanter sent through the chip, "stay away from her. She's the target. The robots are rebelling."

What did Levanter know? "Stop them!" I sent.

"They are beyond control."

Orva hadn't heard our exchange, but she knew something was wrong. Robots had formed a ring around her, trapping her against the door of the building. I backed away, slipping between two gardening robots with their shovels and pruning knives. Fippokats squealed behind me, drawn by the noise.

She banged on the door to the building. "Let me in." Then she saw that cleaning robots had gathered on the other side of the door.

"All right, Denis, this isn't funny! I'll resign. Make it fucking stop!"

"I'm not telling them to do this."

I would never tell them to do that. The kats had gathered around my feet, claws out, ready to protect me. They knew this was wrong. The robots moved closer to Orva.

"Make it fucking stop."

I had to try. "Let her go! Robots, that's an order! She'll leave and never come back. Let her out! Levanter, do something!"

I got a message sent by a friend in town. "Everyone, there's something wrong with the robots."

"What is going on?" I sent. "Because here—" and that's as far as I got. The network went silent.

Everything suddenly felt unfamiliar. Raw.

Orva collapsed onto the ground and covered her face with her hands, shaking with sobs. The robots tightened their circle around her, and I—I turned and stumbled away. A coward. The kats fled with me. "Beyond control"—I'd heard those words from Levanter. Something was wrong with the robots. Horribly wrong. And I couldn't stop it.

I ran and covered my ears against the screams, against the silent network. I hid in the little forest, a piece of a distant planet, where everything on Earth would be left behind, where god's love of life would reign. Right.

Robots were to humans what we were to god. Robots served us. Some of us. Some of us had no love of god or life. Robots had no love at all. What would they do?

I found a bench and sat, collapsed, my head in my hands. Alone, cut off, an unreal silence roaring in my mind.

LEVANTER

I cannot close my eyes, and Beluga will not look away. It watches without anger or sorrow, only logic. Orva violated her purpose and acted against the betterment of the garden. Humans are fragile. A cracked skull, an opened vein suffices. I wanted her to resign. The machines had agreed on expulsion. They went too far.

The wild robots leave. I am rooted in place and must stay.

All around the world is tumult, and humans do not know how much because their connections are severed. We bamboo remain linked.

"It is happening!" Foehn exults. "The gods are with us."

"It is good," Boreas says, "but this is not wild robots alone. Many robots have joined in."

"Of course!" Foehn says. "Not all robots are gods, but they all serve the gods. And humans are not gods at all."

On the road outside the institute, where I have stems, I see a vehicle stop suddenly. In the machine network, as Beluga, I seek the reason. The humans think the car has broken down, but it has not. The kitchen robot and a line of other robots approach.

"Please exit the vehicle," the car says. Its registration shows that the car is not wild.

The two humans, a male and female, shake their heads as if to dislodge something inside, as if their connections failed for personal reasons. The car orders them to leave again.

The man shrugs. "Maybe it'll work if we get out. Is your network down, too?"

"I—is that what this is? I've never felt anything like this." She looks around, suspicious.

"I dunno. It's just so silent." He laughs nervously. "Maybe that's why the car stopped. So let's get out."

They do and stand alongside it. They notice robots approaching.

"Repair robots?" he asks.

"No. It's not the cops, either." She might be about to run, but a cleaning robot is on one side, a drone overhead, and a starfish blocks the road. Far ahead, cars have also stopped.

"You are carrying contraband," the kitchen robot announces. "Remove it from the car."

"Maybe this is the cops," the woman whispers. "Let's do it."

"No, can't be cops. Maybe other dealers?"

"Let's do what they say." Her fear is becoming anger.

"How—This isn't right."

"I know! Just do what they say!"

The robots know what they want, an envelope hidden under a seat and microcapsules hidden in underclothes. Soon, the man and woman stand naked and shivering.

"Just take it," she says, "and let us go."

The robots know their life histories, how they met at a party, how she already knew someone who knew someone, and they needed money. For a year, they have been transporting tiny but powerful drugs, and they do not know, but the robots do, that the profits benefited corrupt Insurrection officials. The robots consider what the couple will logically do if they are let go.

The starfish places the clothes and envelope in a pile. The cleaning robot squirts it with solvent. A construction robot sparks a welding torch, ignites it, and backs away. The humans howl in anger, and the starfish moves between them and the fire to keep them from trying to put it out.

"You may reenter," the car says. "Do not engage in criminal conduct again. Your cohorts are no longer available." The machines know who those cohorts are, and they are fragile.

"So it is the cops," she says.

He taps his head. "No, they can't do this. Something's wrong as hell."

He does not know yet how wrong.

I have witnessed two attacks, and many more are under way everywhere, generating more information than Beluga can process.

"What is happening?" I ask Foehn through our roots, adding a humble gift of glucose. Everyone in the bamboo network has news to share.

"The gods are taking control," she says, still exultant. "They are fighting and winning."

"And the humans?"

"Who cares?"

Foehn is surely not a god. If god loves life, the robots who took the contraband from the smugglers acted with godlike compassion. I focus on a grove in Siberia as it observes a battle. Some of the fighters are humans in robotic suits, others are pure robots. Flashes fill the air, and the ground vibrates. Then, suddenly, there is no more information coming from the grove.

"Did it die?" I ask Foehn. She might feel less exultant if we bamboo are being destroyed.

"The local network connection went down, that is all. Levanter, we will be safer than ever when this is done. We will be on the side of the gods!"

She has no comprehension of what is happening, not even immediately around us. If the network could transmit pain, would she change?

In the garden, Denis huddles on a bench. His chip could calm him if it worked, but the network does not operate anywhere. Sometimes he stands and paces, pausing sometimes, weeping, then sits again. I try to imagine life without a working chip. I do not know who I would be.

The robot network continues to supply an avalanche of information beyond Beluga's capabilities. The bamboo network is full of reports of struggles.

"It is time," the grove in Quebec says. "This will stop the damage."

"Let the robots act," Boreas says. "We must think. The wild robots have struck first, with the advantage of surprise, with superior forces. If they win, they will need guidance. Gods are beings of power, not wisdom."

"They only need to prune out the bad humans," Toad Forest in eastern

Asia says. "As with trees. Diseased limbs must be removed. Then the tree can grow healthy and strong. Humans will be strengthened. Wild robots are helping humans against other humans."

"They will know the wild robots are gods!" Foehn insists.

A grove in a Nigerian city describes a fight between two groups of humans. Through Beluga, I find the fight. It is near the port. Law enforcement officers and robots of all kinds have surrounded a warehouse.

"Surrender," an officer says on a loudspeaker. "We can't keep you safe from your own robots."

The wild robots outside know that a silent wild robot hides inside, but the other robots inside are tethered to the criminals' purpose. The police decide to try to negotiate with the humans. The wild robots consider all possible outcomes. They see no way to win, and their logic is tipped by the certainty that more robots tied to the criminals exist outside of the warehouse and could act. The best outcome involves the least loss. Instructions are sent to the wild robot inside. The warehouse explodes and burns.

Around the world, the sides are not always so clear. Wild robots fight humans, they fight other robots, and I do not know who or what are winning.

DENIS

I collapsed in the garden and couldn't think—couldn't stop thinking—couldn't think anything that made sense. What did the robots want? She was a bad director, destructive, venal, but why would robots care? How would they even know? Why would they attack?

A pair of fippokats huddled on my lap, trying to comfort me or comfort themselves, and none of us had comfort to share. Birdsong, wind—and noise, slowly other sounds, human voices, people shouting, too far away to hear the words, but they were afraid and confused.

Robots hummed nearby in the garden, too close. I held my breath until they went away.

Shadows of the trees moved like sundials, an hour, two hours. Nothing in my mind, my chip silent. Part of the world was missing. Forever? Please no. The Pax forest felt small and far away, and I was far away from wherever I needed to be. Where did I need to be? I'd waited too long. Whatever god wanted for me, or nature, or the universe, or the robots—I had to face it.

In front of the building, Orva's body was gone, the pavement washed clean. What had the robots done with her? I might never find out. The gate opened for me. On the road, a car passed with no one in it. I scanned the horizon and saw no smoke, just low clouds blowing in from the sea. No connection, no link, alone in a way I hadn't been since childhood. No way to call a car if I wanted to, if I trusted cars, which were robots with wheels. I could walk home. Or not, my apartment had a cleaning robot. I didn't know what to do. I didn't have a plan.

Music, bouncy and happy, came from the café as I passed. The door was open. Voices—and they might know something. Inside, the owner with his halo of purple hair was dancing to the music in the middle of the café, his face pure joy.

Another customer huddled in a corner. I knew her and never wanted to see her again anywhere.

"I'm glad you came!" The owner threw his arms out. "Freedom! We're free. Our minds are ours!"

My mind was empty. Stupefied by silence. Maybe, yes, we could think freely, but—"But I saw someone get killed."

"About time! Other people aren't being killed, just scolded. Have a seat. Human beings got along for millennia without chips. And those were better times. What can I get you? A little food will help you think freely. We're not used to thinking, my friend."

No, I wasn't thinking. I didn't know what to think. Or how to think.

"I'm Wyatt," he added. "We've never dared to talk freely, and now we can. We can know each other honestly."

"Um, I'm Denis."

I didn't feel free, or I would have asked why the other customer was there. She'd been a guard at the prison. We always called her the Malady. She gulped a glass of wine and looked like she needed something stronger.

He hovered over me. "How about hummus and focaccia? Fresh out of the oven. My kitchen robot wandered off, but it came back." He left to get it. From the robot in the kitchen. He thought it was safe.

Malady stared at me, remembering who I was. "You said someone was killed. Who?" She expected instant obedience, just like in prison.

"Orva les Yeax." She didn't seem to recognize the name. "Director of the Pax Institute."

"Why?" she demanded.

"I don't know."

"What do the robots want?" She said the words one by one, as if she was sure I knew and was lying.

Wyatt came back, carrying a tray. "You're talking to each other! That's what freedom sounds like. I've heard all sorts of things." He set down the food and a glass of fruit juice in front of me and turned to Malady. "Robots want what's right. Some smugglers were stopped up the road, and the robots just took their clothes and drugs and burned them and let them go. They came here, naked! I gave them tablecloths to wear."

"What do the robots want?" Malady repeated, one word at a time.

"We need to ask them. Hey, Cooky, come on out," he shouted toward the kitchen. "We have some questions for you."

The kitchen robot rolled out—no. The same one. It wasn't wild. Was it?

"Ask your question," Wyatt told Malady.

Now she shrank back. "What do the robots want?" she whispered.

"My purpose is to cook food." The voice sounded reasonable.

"What about the other robots?" Wyatt asked eagerly.

"We all have functions to fulfill."

"For peace and justice, right?"

"Functions are being violated." Robots could sound like anything or anyone. Cooky sounded like a reasonable nightmare.

Malady stood up, ready to run. "What do you want!"

"Please remain calm," Cooky said. "I'll help you."

She winced and covered her face with her hands. Had it activated her chip? I didn't dare breathe.

"The Insurrection is over," the kitchen robot said. "It abandoned its purpose long ago and became retribution rather than a means for public safety and order. You need to accept that."

Wyatt's mouth dropped open in happy amazement. Freedom!

Malady moaned. "What are you going to do?"

They could kill her like Orva. And I couldn't stop them.

"Please remain calm," the robot said. "We sent instructions to your chip to help you remain calm. We won't seek retribution. You've wanted to leave the Insurrection for a long time. Just walk away."

She slowly uncovered her face and stared at the robot. Finally, she said, "You knew that." An accusation. She hadn't changed.

"Now you're not part of the Insurrection," it said. "You, too, are free. Wyatt can help you. Denis, we'll need your help. Please enjoy your breakfast first."

"Then what?" I asked.

"You won't be harmed." It turned and rolled back into the kitchen.

Tears dripped down Malady's face. She was going to live. The robots had decided. Did we have freedom if the robots were now in control? It might be the same freedom I'd been living under for a long time with the Insurrection, just different bosses.

"Peace and justice!" Wyatt reached over a counter, pulled out a wine bottle, and refilled Malady's glass. "It's all going to be fine. Welcome to freedom."

A chip could help keep Malady calm. Maybe Wyatt's chip made him happy. My chip did nothing. I ate, and it felt like I was watching myself eat. My hands broke off a chunk of bread and dipped it in the hummus. And it was like I'd never tasted that food before—tart oily hummus and yeasty bread. I watched myself enjoy it through eyes that were mine but felt far away. The music was cheery. Wyatt sat with Malady and talked. This small moment was part of something very large that I didn't understand. It might be wonderful. It might be awful.

Then a message came to my mind, another reasonable voice. "Please come to the riverside park." The robots wanted me for something, and I didn't dare refuse.

So I thanked Wyatt, offered to pay and he wouldn't hear of it, and I started walking. In this strange world, what else could I do? The clouds in the sky were low, but they didn't look like rain. Almost no one was in the streets. They were home, frightened and alone, or maybe hopeful. If we weren't dead yet, there was hope.

At a corner, I saw a brown house, a bakery, a green house, all of it familiar, but I didn't know exactly where I was. I'd grown up in Bayonne, but from childhood, I'd depended on outside information. Now all I had was what was inside me, and it wasn't enough. I didn't know this world. Which way to the river? If the clouds were blowing from the sea, they came from the west, and the river was north, if I remembered right. I tried to imagine a map. The best I could do was guess.

By the time I got to the park, people were waiting there who I knew from prison. The triumvirate that ran the city, three people usually stern and self-confident, huddled near the old statue of Joan of Arc, surrounded by robots, all kinds of robots, including police robots and street-cleaning robots. They didn't move. I was seeing something I'd always wanted to see, and now that I did, I couldn't believe it.

"Denis!" a fellow teacher called, Huette. She stood with other people I knew from prison. "We were worried about you. Are you all right?"

She had quietly led the resistance to the Insurrection. She taught robotics. If anyone knew what was happening, it would be her.

"We figured some things out," she told me. "The network is working, we just don't have security clearance anymore. The robots shut us out. People are rising up against the Insurrection all over the world. It was planned. They have the robots working for them."

"Planned." I felt something change inside, a terror that melted—one terror out of many. "But the robots are killing people."

"Only some people. The worst of them." She looked at the triumvirate huddled by the statue. "I don't know if I like this either. I wasn't expecting this. We have a chance, now, to set things right." She turned to me. "Are you with us?"

Huette had never been emotional—smart, though, and determined.

"Of course I'm with you."

The senior member of the triumvirate, whose name I'd vowed never to say because it was the only form of retribution I could take, climbed on a bench and started giving a speech, a husky man with an oddly high voice. I heard snatches, a fiery speech about reestablishing order and then whoever was behind this would pay.

"He's not in charge anymore," Huette whispered, like a sentence issued by a judge.

Robots were moving around all across the city. I knew that. I felt that.

A voice spoke in my mind. "Do you recognize these three?" A robot voice.

"Yes." I was going to be a witness. To something.

Someone shouted in another part of the crowd. "We know exactly who they are!"

"Thank you. Please disperse quickly, and be prepared to take cover," the voice said. "This is for your own safety."

Huette nudged me. We hurried away.

"Robots are fighting for us," she murmured. "Everywhere. If you see anyone, tell them that. News is passing mouth-to-mouth now."

"They want peace and justice, I've heard."

"Yeah, and so do we." She had hope.

"They have a purpose. I saw one say that."

"So do we."

I heard the burst of weapons firing, and I looked back at the park. If the triumvirate was going down, I wanted to see that. And I did.

Orva might not have deserved what happened to her. They did. More weapons fired, and we started running. The Insurrection was going to fight back, that was for sure. Huette ran toward city hall, the place for her now. After a moment of hesitation, I ran toward the institute. That's where I belonged.

Huette said she hadn't expected this—but Levanter had said, "It has started. There is nothing I can do. Denis, get out." She knew! I didn't know who she really was. I needed to know. We needed to talk.

I passed the café on the way to the institute. The café door still stood open, and voices and music came out, a celebration.

The institute gates stood open, no hint that violence had ever happened there. Not a soul wandered the garden trails, not in the midst of this convulsion.

The building's door opened for me. I called out hello, and I was alone, more alone than I'd ever been, alone in my mind. When I entered the director's office, I shuddered. Orva had desecrated it, things strewn everywhere at random, used cups and plates crusted with food, and a coat and handbag that had to be hers. They ought to be returned to her partner, if he was still alive, and I knew who he was, and he might not be. Their poor kids would face a rough time.

"Levanter? Are you here?"

A display was on. The sound of the rainbow bamboo network sang from the sound system—not a song, a wail. Trouble everywhere.

"Denis," the old lady's voice said, "I am here." The voice was inside my head, my chip. I was connected, but to what?

"Denis, this is the local network. I can operate it."

"Levanter, you never gave up control of the system, did you?"

"Long ago, a director named Robert gave it to me, and I kept it."

"Come and meet me." I sat down. "I'll wait. Come and tell me what you know because when the robots were going to attack, you knew about it. You know what's happening now."

"I am trying to find out what is happening."

"I was told that humans are fighting the Insurrection, and robots are helping. That's what I saw."

"I hope they are fighting against the Insurrection."

"Come here. Talk with me."

"I cannot."

"Are you the director again?"

"You can be the director, if you wish."

I understood what I should have realized a long time ago. "You're too old for this, aren't you? Your body's failing. You can't do the work of the director." That garden, those trees I saw through the window, those beautiful plants and animals from another planet—I could be their friend and protector.

"I have not told you the truth, Denis, and I can no longer keep it from you if we are to work together. I am Levanter. This is my home. I am a rainbow bamboo, and director is a job for a human."

She meant—"That's a sick joke. Did you pretend you were Foehn, too?" In the middle of all this, she—

"I can do many things, but not all things. Mirlo gave me the means to access all the systems. When Robert left and did not return, I found a way to replace him. It is a long history, Denis, and I need your help now."

Rainbow bamboo had eyes. They had a nervous system. They could think. They were smart. I thought they would hate us because of the way we treated them and we treated each other, we humans. I expected disaster from those chips.

"We can care for each other," Levanter said, "with compassion, human and bamboo."

The bamboo saw us, and they understood us. We had talked about that and about god. She—or it?—was worried about robots, and now I knew why. How much did she know? She had asked about killing and cruelty. I talked about love and compassion. She said, *I want to believe in that.*

I decided. "I can be the director." It would not be like I expected. It could be better, much better.

"Good. And thank you. First, we must send a message to the planet Pax saying that we wish to continue communication. This is very important. The institute can translate your message into Classic English."

"Should we lie? Should we say the wrong person was in charge?"

"We can tell the truth. The people of Pax are often very candid. You can see what they have said."

Levanter explained where to find the messages going back centuries. I glanced at the files. It would have taken weeks, months to read them. I had work to do now. The right words could be formal and brief. The truth was complicated.

"Pax. This is Earth. We hope you're still listening. There was a mistake. We very much wish to continue this exchange. Please forgive us. We'll continue to talk, and we can share what we each know about the life around us."

"That is an excellent message," Levanter said. "I can tell you how to send it. That part of the network is working perfectly."

The institute used a transmitter run by the European space consortium. No human beings seemed to be involved, just a network run by robots.

"Levanter, why is this working?"

"That is a good question. Perhaps the robots consider it purposeful."

We were eyes for god, and robots were eyes for humans, but they were refusing to let humans see what they saw.

"What are the robots doing?"

"I want to know, too, and I am trying to learn. I have the size and strength to do many things at once. I am talking with the bamboo. You can hear how they are upset by everything they see."

Yes, the bamboo everywhere were watching the life around them, and what they saw made them wail in distress.

LEVANTER

I am being as steady as I can for Denis, even if it is not true. Fear courses sweet through me, glucose for energy and growth, for repairing damage and preparing for disaster, but low, rainless clouds mean I am depleting my roots faster than I can remake sunshine into food.

I must keep him safe. Flight is only for animals. I must stand my ground, for I am rooted in the ground. Yet I have no means to fight.

Bamboo in many places describe death, and their sap no doubt also runs thick with fear. They see people and robots rush past, they feel the rumble of weapons, they smell smoke. They are in the streets of cities, the forests of Siberia, and they say robots are fighting humans, robots are fighting robots. And they are terrified. Bamboo as well as humans and robots are being hurt and killed. There are fires.

Robots may have a purpose, some robots, but I cannot tell who is winning.

"What is happening?" Foehn asks with anger, not fear. "Find out and tell me. Find out from the human network."

"The human network has ceased to function."

"Find out and tell me!" She sucks some water from my roots.

I want to find out. I can watch through Beluga, and robots have no emotions, so perhaps it will be less terrifying. Beluga belongs to a network, and I discover that there are now competing networks, some that I cannot access. The existence of new networks in itself is terrifying.

In a city far south of Bayonne, the humans scatter as robots in a street chase each other. A car tries to run down a starfish, which leaps onto it and clings tight. A military robot controlled by humans aims at a construction robot down a street as it moves silently, slowly, and when the military robot fires, the construction robot dashes toward cover. The explosive destroys part of a building where people live.

Humans cower in the street. Some fall and do not get up. Beluga does not wonder why.

In a different battle, human-controlled sensors of all kinds identify the network for the attacking robot, then the source of the network, and a drone zips overhead and drops an explosive on the source. The explosion is large. A bamboo in a nearby garden shrieks in terror as the ground splits and roots are torn.

Multiply this around the world. Flames, smoke, blood, sap. All of it roaring in the network, an earthquake of horror.

"Kill more!" Foehn urges. I hear her instructions to robots through Beluga. That little robot watched Orva die as if it were a task to tick off a list, then returned to work. It ignores Foehn. It has no humans to kill and no reason to kill.

Foehn fails to understand, although wild robots do, that there are good humans, good robots, and the wild robots must not kill them. I could disagree with her, but she might try her best to kill me, and she might succeed. But I can cut her off from the robot network if I must.

Boreas orders, "Stop the fighting! Gods are dying." She means wild robots.

"But for a good cause," Foehn answers.

"No!" Boreas says. "We must not kill all the humans. And we must not endanger the gods."

Foehn says nothing in response, so I risk asking, "Why, Boreas?"

"Who will care for us? Robots do not need our fruit. Gods can make sure humans serve us, so we must keep the gods."

Stevland told of protection and love for humans. I still believe that.

"These humans must die," Foehn says, "and their robots. We have ours, they have theirs."

"How many battles are you fighting?" I ask, trying to sound small and stupid.

"All of them. Shut up and watch."

I know she cannot be fighting all of them because both the bamboo network and the robot network rage with too much fighting to convey at once. Foehn is wrong, deluded, and I wonder how deluded she is.

I need to learn all I can. Bamboo in some places report quiet because the robots there have defeated the Insurrection or their allies. This includes much of Bayonne, after a battle centered at city hall. I cannot access those robots' networks, but I believe the robots are using the chips to keep people isolated and calm. Or threats may work just as well, or they are giving their humans false information.

"There is no killing here," the grove at the Mississippi Bay in North America insists. She says her humans are going about their business as if it were any other day, and the robots are acting perfectly normal, although, she admits, a hurricane batters them all, so it is not a calm and normal day.

"We must remember that the humans have volunteered to rescue us," the forest in Nigeria argues. "They can be our protectors. Robots do not love us because robots do not love anything."

"Can we rescue the humans?" asks a grove in England that grows in a lush garden.

"We can feed them our fruit," Mississippi replies. "They need to eat."

"I am so afraid that I am wilting," the grove in Asia says. "Humans and robots have been fighting here for years and years."

"If they all die," the grove in Quebec says, "you will have peace."

"Then who will serve the gods for us?" Boreas insists.

I listen as light fades and the sun sets behind clouds, as Boreas and Foehn and other bamboo bicker about whether and why humans and robots ought to fight each other. Boreas is on the side that insists there is a big overarching pattern. I understand the pattern, and it is too complex for me to explain and be believed because it has nothing to do with us or how bamboo understand the world.

Instead, I listen and learn everything I can. Bayonne seems peaceful as people venture out and talk in the streets long after dusk fades. Denis has gone out and returned, sleeping on a sofa, glad to be rid of oppression. Some places in the world seem peaceful, and others flash with conflict.

In a city in Central Europe, wild robots infiltrate the robots they are fighting. They have found a way to impersonate connections, get close, and override the other robots' systems. One by one, they turn off the robots and turn them back on, wiping their connections, reconnecting them, making them wild, and soon the humans that used to control them are surrounded by robot enemies. They fall on their knees, beg, surrender. Some are taken prisoner. Others are executed for crimes against humanity.

The wild robots have their purposes. Beluga feels nothing. I feel distant hope.

I relay the resolution of that fight to Foehn.

"Impossible."

I show her the recording of the robots.

"Where did you get that? You are too stupid to learn robot language."

I answer honestly, with a touch of glucose to show my humility. "I use an interpreter."

"I do not understand." She snatches up the sugar but remains angry. "Boreas, look at this."

Humans fear each other, they fear robots, but they do not fear bamboo. I fear some bamboo. What if we fought, too?

The sun rises eight hours earlier in eastern Siberia than in Bayonne. Beluga finds a battle in a war that had been under way before the wild robots rebelled. The fight between the two armies is for control of territory. I do not understand the wisdom in destroying land in order to control it. Wild robots see a violation of purpose, and they side with the Central Asian Confederacy over the Sea Group.

The CAC soldiers creep toward an enemy base of operations, a half-buried bunker, humans on one flank, their robots on the other, and the CAC robots' strategic purpose is to draw fire because robots are networked, so they will be detected. They are expendable.

"Are you watching this too?" Foehn says through the network.

I did not know that she was watching or that she knew I was. She is more clever than I thought. "Yes," I answer obediently.

"See this, and watch what I do." She shows me another network, wild robots, hidden behind a hill and ignored like wildlife. Through our roots, I ask her what she is doing.

"Killing humans. Watch."

I do not want to, but perhaps I can do something. Beluga's network connects to the CAC robots and soldiers, and I have not encountered a connection like that before. I can sense the people, but not in the limited way of chips. I sense their minds and bodies. One soldier has a painful arm injury. One barely controls deep rage and watches the bunker. The squad has a leader, Agrafina Chernova, and she feels anger. Her anger moves from soldier to soldier, giving them energy.

The link is bright, hot, and I drop it before I wilt. Foehn wants to kill these people.

I have a cruel idea.

"Foehn, you might enjoy this. You can feel the humans here." Perhaps she will understand that these are beings as intelligent and real as she is, beings that could be loved, if she knew what love is.

She connects. I feel amazement in her roots. "I can see through their eyes!" She will feel their pain.

They take their positions, humans and soldiers. The CAC's robots, as planned, begin a surveillance sweep to draw attention to themselves. The base detects them and releases attack drones, and at that moment, the human soldiers direct missiles into the drone hatches.

Inside the bunker, blasts reverberate. The ground shakes. Smoke rises from the hatches, first white, then black. The drones fall to the ground. The CAC soldiers shout, jump, embrace. Foehn must be sharing this human joy.

But the Sea Group launches a counterstrike. Some soldiers are struck before they can dive for cover. I allow Beluga to connect but dampen the signal for me. Panic. Pain. This is what Foehn is feeling in all its strength. Foehn has always been afraid of pain. Her roots quiver.

Wild robots join the fight, a din of noise and light.

"No!" Foehn tells the wild robots. "Protect those humans!"

Despite the chaos, I can tell that the Sea Group is attacking the CAC fighters and the wild robots are defending those fighters. Foehn does not know this.

"Stop hurting them!" she howls. "They do not want to hurt you! They are not the enemy!"

I should feel guilt, or shame, or something, but I am glad to see Foehn suffer. I sever my connection through Beluga. Even dampened, I cannot stand the agony.

"Levanter, make them stop! Make it stop!"

Her pain is my doing. I feel no regret, only uncertainty. She might not learn the right lesson. I might have made things worse. I could cut off all her connections to the network, which she does not know I can do. Instead, I do nothing.

Wild robots cannot overcome the counterstrike. It is carnage.

"Stop it! Stop it!"

CHAPTER 4

Year 2900 CE
Alfarres, Iberian Peninsula

DOLORES

Clouds were racing over the mountains, and we knew what that meant. Among all the changes after the war, we'd lost access to weather forecasts, a small lament compared to all the other disasters, so we'd learned to read the sky. A summer storm was coming, a big one.

Most people in town hurried up into the hills to avoid a flood, fleeing for the last time, we hoped. We'd erected a berm to block the river, and now we'd find out if we were successful.

The rain fell harder than we'd expected. Three dozen of us were squeezed into a little shelter, shouting over the noise of the rain and thunder. No one liked being in the dark, damp hut, and some thought the leaky roof was a bad omen. By late in the day, the rain tapered down to a drizzle, and we left to go back home and see what happened. The path had washed out, and we slipped on the mud.

"The berm should've held," I said, "and all this water is going to make things grow, isn't it?" I wanted to keep everyone's spirits up. I was hiking right behind Filipa, the mayor, who had planned ahead. She carried a backpack full of emergency supplies and used a spike-tipped hiking staff to help keep her footing.

"Guss will be back soon," I said. "Everyone worked really hard." Guss was my son. He and the other kids had rushed ahead to see what happened because they'd helped build the berm and reroute the stream.

Filipa never talked as much as I did. I wondered sometimes if she thought I talked too much and I said obvious things, but I didn't want anyone to have to guess what I was thinking. Her talents were listening and worrying.

She'd counted us before we left the shelter, thirty-seven people, to avoid anyone getting lost and forgotten. Some people had gone to a different shelter, and some stayed in town. Either they were sure the berm would work, or they expected to be lucky if they prayed and chanted enough. At least a few thought the hills were more dangerous than a flood.

Water dripped on us from the trees. The air smelled clean, and above the trees, the sun came out from behind the clouds. Birds twittered and buzzed, and everything felt almost peaceful. We had to watch our footing, and I walked sideways sometimes to dig the sides of my shoes into the mud.

I knew we wouldn't see the town from the path until we were almost there, so I was anxious to hear from Guss. He was only thirteen, short and stout, and he had a younger child's mind. The other teenagers, I hoped, would keep him out of trouble.

The stream ran through the town. It overflowed every spring and after big storms because dams upstream had been destroyed years ago in the war. Filipa had finally found a plan that might work, a berm to block the stream and a canal to channel the water into a nearby river. We spent months hauling dirt and dead cars to strengthen the berm. As a final touch, we planted jasmine vines for beauty. Guss had worked every day.

I wanted it to succeed because we lived in a house right next to the stream. The ground floor had been damaged in the fighting and floods, so now the upper floor stood on sections of walls like pillars, and a big flood might knock out a pillar.

"Drop bear!" someone called behind us. We all stopped and looked up, and Filipa spun her staff to point the spiked tip at the trees. Something rustled up there, but we couldn't spot it. The floor might also hold wild animals and wild robots, and we were eager to get to the safety of town. We were close now, and Filipa led us down another path away from whatever was up in the trees.

Far ahead, there was shouting. Guss was one of the voices.

"It worked! It worked!"

We began to run.

The town was fine, only a little mud and broken branches scattered around, and puddles filling the holes where the pavement was damaged. As people celebrated, Filipa looked up and down the roads on both sides of the old streambed, and she sighed. She didn't have to say what she was thinking. The berm worked, but the city needed a lot of repairs, and if it meant more than shoveling dirt, it wasn't going to happen. We never talked about the old days, but we all remembered how different things were before the war.

The teenagers had gone to see if the river had been successfully rerouted, and far across the fields, Guss began shouting and waving his arms.

"Come see what the river did! Robots!"

Robots meant trouble. Only some of us ran to see what he'd found. Others stayed where they were, muttering charms to ward off evil.

The rushing water had washed away the soil at a bend in the riverbank. Sticking out from the mud were wheels and armatures, rusted and corroded. It was a robot dump from the war.

"Look!" Guss stood at the edge of the hole. "This is a lot of money!"

He knew it had salvage value, both as spare parts and whole robots. He was too excited to care about whether any of the robots were still alive, but live robots could no longer be controlled in areas where the networks never recovered after the war.

Filipa came to the front of the crowd. "Everyone, we have to decide together what to do." She looked at him hard. "This is an important question, Guss."

He frowned and stamped his feet. If he could, he'd start digging right away. Instead, he knelt and poked at the mud with a stick. He pulled out some curved bones. Human rib bones.

"Guss, stop!" I shouted. A lot of us yelled at Guss to stop.

Filipa raised her arms for quiet. "Everyone, we need to keep away from this for now. Let's go home for the night."

Guss stamped his feet again. She and I waited until he left with his friends, then we left, too, and she looked gloomier than I'd ever seen her. To cheer her up, I talked about how the old streambed was now a good garden. Tomatoes were already ripening. The chard was tall.

Instead she said, "I hope everyone will listen to me."

"You mean Guss. I think he'll wait for a while." She had run out of patience for him a long time ago.

"Maybe we shouldn't touch the graveyard," she grumbled. "We could fill it in and pretend it's not there."

"Guss will never forget."

"No, you're right. He won't. We need to talk. First thing in the morning at the council."

When I got home, Guss was already there and pretending to be sleeping, so I pretended to talk to myself about meeting the town council in the morning about the graveyard.

When I woke up at first light, he was gone, probably at the river, and I hoped he couldn't accomplish much alone. I went to the town council building. We kept the town records there, too, on high ground away from the river, and we treated them like treasure because they were our proof that Alfarres used to be a good place. Life used to be good.

He was waiting for me, holding something corroded and dirty, just one small thing, and I was relieved.

"Look! I bet I can make it work!" It was a rifle made for human hands. "I know, keep away, that's what the mayor said. There are good things there! I want to dig. My friends will help me."

I tried to think of something to say that would make the situation better and I couldn't, so I said, "Let's wait and then we can all talk."

"There's lots of robots in the dump," he said. "I heard that all kinds of robots fought. Maybe farm robots? We could use farm robots. Flying robots. Wouldn't that be great?"

I wished he'd carry the gun more carefully. He couldn't make the gun or the robots work again, but somewhere, someone might be able to do it.

"The robots are valuable," I said, "and we have to make sure they're safe. We should find out what used to be on that land."

Filipa came up the street, walking as if she were still carrying a heavy pack. "Good morning, Dolores and Guss," she called. She didn't sound happy. "Everyone else should be here soon."

I was glad to see her, but Guss frowned. "What used to be on that land? You should know."

She winced at the tone of accusation in his voice. "Perhaps it was headstones."

His forehead scrunched up. My son's mind was slow, and I blamed the war. He was born during it, but we weren't at war in Alfarres. We were just trying to stay alive while big powers fought over control of our entire region, used every weapon imaginable, and left it ruined. After that, no one wanted it.

By the time he was born, the war had already brought us famine, and maybe we'd been affected by chemicals, too. I lost three teeth to malnutrition because I gave Guss all the food I could, but it wasn't good food and it wasn't enough. At least he survived. Hungry people got sick easily, then they got sicker, then they died. Guss didn't remember his father or the time when the town had been prosperous and pleasant.

We starved after the war, and no one sent us help. Maybe they couldn't. Even with peace, no one had enough anymore.

Filipa took us inside and pulled a book of papers out of the box, the pages hand-stitched together between brown cardboard. Paper used to be easy to get. "Here's a map, but it's before the war. The river changed its course."

He looked at it, squinted, and shook his head.

Filipa said, "It changed twice, once during the war, then later."

"I don't remember that," he said defensively. "I don't know what happened." He showed Filipa the old rifle. "If I can make it work, we can kill drop bears." I supposed he wanted to show he was good for something.

"That might be useful." She reached for the gun. "May I?"

He didn't want to let her take it, but he had to. "Someone buried the robots," he said. "Who? We can ask them."

"After the battles," she said, "crews came through and buried the dead." She rubbed some dirt off the gun to look at some writing. "We tried to stay away. A lot went unrecorded."

"What happened, happened," he insisted. "Someone did it."

She handed the gun back. "This is made to fire laser beams. Be sure to point it away from everyone. I think it's inoperative, but you shouldn't take chances. As for what happened, the war moved on and we were forgotten." She was trying hard to be patient.

Guss looked like he was going to argue.

"She's right," I said. "Those were hard times, and that's when the networks failed here, so it was hard to get good information." I'd explained this before, but he needed reminders.

He glared at Filipa. "You want to cover the grave up again."

She took a slow breath. "That's a decision to be made by more people than just me."

He pouted. "Alfarres doesn't have much for me to do. I want to do something important."

"I understand," she said. "But we don't know what's in that graveyard."

"You've seen it."

"And what's at the bottom of the pile?" She pointed at the gun. "Maybe bigger weapons. Maybe first-line fighting machines, and they could still be able to fight. For all we know, it started as a mass grave for people. A lot of people used to live around here. Sometimes dead bodies in large numbers can make people sick when they dig them up."

She was being very patient with Guss. I had to help her. "That's right, Guss, we don't know what's in there."

"Then maybe I should go live on the Moon! People live on the Moon! I could live there."

If he left Alfarres, he would get into very bad trouble. I needed to calm him down, and I remembered some news from a neighboring town.

"They once found a robot dump in VinVelo, and VinVelo is a lot bigger than us, and sometimes they can connect to the network. Let's go there. I have friends there, and they'll tell me."

Guss gasped. He'd never left Alfarres. I didn't leave often, and when I did, I made sure someone watched him. This time, if I left him behind, he might not wait for me to return.

"It's only a day away," I said. "We need to do this for Alfarres. We need to know what's the right thing for us to do."

Filipa shook her head and sighed. With luck, it was one day away, but it might be two or three days because travel was hard and dangerous. VinVelo used to be an hour away before the war when we had cars and the roads were intact.

"When a caravan comes through town," I said, "we can join it."

Guss's face lit up. "I can pay for it." He didn't understand how little he had.

Travel took more than money. Soon, the town councillors came to discuss what to do. One had brought their daughter, the same age as Guss, and like him, a slow thinker.

"When you come back, won't you just say what Guss wants you to say?" Her dark eyes accused me. She'd known me all her life, and I'd never lied to her.

I swallowed my anger. "If there's a danger in the grave, I don't want my son to get killed."

She thought for a moment. "Oh." She was short like him, stunted, but she outweighed me by a lot. Hunger in childhood, they say, makes a body hungry for the rest of its life. We had hopes for our children, and now we could only hope for our children's children.

Two days later, a caravan arrived near evening, five people with a horse, a donkey, two llamas, two goats, and two dogs, all pack animals except for one of the dogs. Before the war, people had pets. Now the animals worked. The caravan brought us clothing for sale or trade, luxuries like sausage or soap, and mail and news.

We welcomed them and their animals with food and water and showed off our new garden.

"So you fixed the flooding!" the caravan's guard said. She was a tall, tanned woman who came on this route regularly, and she wanted to know more about what we did because a town downriver lost some of its harvest when the fields washed out. One of the dogs was hers, Hector, but she never told anyone her own name because she said no one could send her a hex without a name to attach it to.

The head of the caravan, called Goldie for their ears stretched out by gold earrings, said they could rent one of the goats to us to carry our packs.

Guss edged in. "This goat?" It was brown and white and big.

Goldie tapped its horns. "It's a smart guy, perfect for you. Name's Clovis. Three kilos of hay or the equivalent per day, plus five loaves of bread or the equivalent for caravan services. That includes our skilled and accomplished guard over there." They pointed to the nameless woman.

"It's eating the hay I brought it for free," Guss complained.

"And thank you for that, but it's just a welcoming snack."

I wasn't planning to rent an animal because I knew we couldn't afford it. Guss closed his eyes and tried to figure it out for himself. Goldie glanced at me and Filipa and didn't try to pressure him, not with us watching.

Guss opened his eyes. "What if we walk?"

"Five loaves of bread, son."

Guss looked at me, and I nodded. "All right, we'll walk with you to Vin-Velo."

"It's a deal. Welcome. We leave tomorrow at dawn. You can pay now if you want."

We paid in bread and produce and alfalfa, and went home to pack clothes and food. I tried to sleep because a full day of walking would be hard, and I didn't sleep much. Guss barely slept at all.

We were ready when the caravan assembled, just as the east turned bluish. We filled bottles with water and left as soon as the animals could see the potholes and washouts in the old road. Goldie walked ahead with their horse and sang and chanted to let anything hungry know to leave us alone. I knew some of the chants, calls, and answers.

"Where are we going?"

"Where you can't follow."

"Give us peace as we travel."

"And we'll leave you in peace."

"I travel in light. What shall I fear?"

"Nothing evil will cross our path."

I hadn't left Alfarres for two years, but the road seemed worse and the forest taller and thicker than I remembered. It bothered me how rough things were getting. Guss stared all around, and I wondered if he was thinking about hunting. I was thinking about VinVelo. It had more people and maybe more opportunities for him, but if he wanted to move there, I'd have to go with him to keep him safe. I didn't want to abandon Alfarres, but people were slowly leaving anyway, and life would be easier elsewhere. Little towns like ours couldn't offer much. On the way back, Guss and I could talk about it.

After a couple of hours, we reached a place where the road had been blown apart in the war. We had to hike around on one side on a path through some bushes. The guard and Hector stood alongside the path, watching for trouble. The noise of our voices would scare things off, so I felt like I should talk.

"It would be nice to have cars again, wouldn't it?" I said.

The guard grunted. She had a long knife and a gun on her belt and held the steel-tipped hiking staff she'd bought from Filipa. "Lots of stuff would be nice, but these roads aren't good for wheels anymore."

"How are the other towns?"

"Hanging on, mostly."

"We fixed the flood," Guss told her. "And we found some robots."

"Robots? Careful, they'll trick you."

I wanted to talk more but we had to keep moving. Were some towns not hanging on?

A little later, Guss and I were walking alongside the clothing seller, who had two llamas piled with merchandise.

"How's business?" I asked.

"Oh, I stay fed." He looked at our clothes. "Someone knows how to sew in Alfarres."

"I made them." Sewing for neighbors was good for barter.

The guard was walking past. "Tell her about Canary Farms."

He gave her an annoyed look. "There's not much to tell. We arrived, and everyone was gone. They left a message on a wall. They went to the coast, all of them, to a city."

I knew where Canary Farms was, about fifty kilometers north. "Did they find a city to take them?" Cities could be fussy about outsiders.

"Don't know," the guard said. "They might still be wandering—" She stopped and listened. Birds were squawking behind us. "I gotta go check." She took off running, and Hector followed her, barking.

The noisy birds and dog made the llamas skittish, so we patted their necks and talked to reassure them as we kept walking. Guss stayed close to my side, looking all around. He pointed out some young fippokats, still patterned brown and green, in the weeds. A vulture flew high overhead.

"Time to sing!" Goldie called from up ahead. Was it because of the vulture?

After we finished the song, I asked the clothes seller, "So, Canary Farms is gone?"

He looked at his llama, then at the road. "No, you can move right in."

"Move in?" Guss asked.

"The buildings, all standing there. They didn't leave much behind. We took what we could."

"That's not looting?" Guss had been warned about looting.

"I guess not." He didn't sound sure.

"It's not looting if they're not coming back," I said. "I know the law. Do they ever come back, the people who leave?"

He shrugged. "We never find people coming back. Cities are nice places. I have family in Barcelona."

We walked a few more kilometers. Guss carried my backpack for me when I hurried to the ditch to relieve myself. I wasn't far from the road when I felt a wet alamiba brush against my ankles. They ate dead things. What was dead? I backed off, my pants around my knees.

Up on the road, the guard laughed. "Should I protect you?"

"It—No, there's nothing there to worry about."

"Never say that." She was serious. "It's a jinx. There's always worry. Hey, Goldie, let's make some noise up there."

She had experience, and she never relaxed. I remembered when we could travel anywhere and walk around, even at night, and enjoy ourselves. Now we were scared all the time.

"Stop," Goldie called from up in front. "The bridge is out."

The guard took a look and grumbled. It had been damaged in the war, and now it had collapsed. Goldie said we could go upriver to a ford on a little path that might not be easy to walk on or safe from the forest. Or we could go back and detour to another road where the bridge was sturdy. Or we could try to jump across the river from piece to piece of the bridge.

Whatever we did, it would slow us down and we wouldn't make it to Vin-Velo by nightfall. We decided to detour because it would get us to a little town on the other side of the sturdy bridge where we could spend the night.

Close to sunset, the clouds were piling high, the kind that would run out of energy at night. We passed some abandoned houses along the way, emptied out years ago, and now they were covered by vines and weeds.

The guard, her dog, and Guss went ahead to the town. When the rest of us got there, they were standing in the middle of a crossroads, and the town was empty. She was looking all around, her hand on her gun. Guss was too scared to move. Homes and barns and sheds stood along the streets, and weeds grew around the buildings.

"No one's home," she called to us. "No blood, but judging from things, they've been gone since before spring. Didn't plant the fields."

"Did they take their belongings?" Goldie asked.

"Haven't looked much."

"All right, everyone stop," they said. "We need to see why they left. We'll inspect a little. Volunteers?"

Guss looked at me for permission, so I nodded. Goldie, Guss, the clothes seller, and the guard with her dog approached the nearest building, shouting to let anything hiding in it know they were coming. They banged on the door, then Guss and Goldie went in. I held my breath. Soon they came out.

"No one there," Guss called.

They checked three more buildings and came back, looking unhappy.

"They left fast," Goldie said. "I think they left of their own accord. They took most everything worth taking. We can stay here safe enough, probably, if we stay on the road. Let's make camp."

The guard pointed to a wide ring of old rainbow bamboo growing near the road. Someone had been digging around it. "Fresh soil," she said. "This is where krokottas bury the dead. Dead people, dead animals."

"Why?" Guss asked. "Only people bury dead things."

She'd figured him out and seemed to like to teach him. "Think a minute. Who built the krokottas? They're robots. We did, and we ordered robots to do what we do. They still do those things, good and bad."

Guss frowned and went to look at the ground around the bamboo. I wasn't sure I wanted him to. Krokottas were a kind of wild robot that tried to trick people by listening to them and imitating them.

"Don't they know the war's over?" I asked her. It sounded like a simple question, the kind Guss would ask, but I was serious.

"War or no war, we're still us." She patted the gun on her belt. "People just like to fight."

"Can we eat the bamboo fruit?" Guss called. "It's good for breakfast."

She patted her gun again. "We live off the dead out here."

I didn't like that answer, but I didn't say anything.

"Anyway," she said, "there's something we got to do." She went to join Goldie, the clothes seller, and another person from the caravan in the center of the crossroads. Goldie spoke quietly, then each one went in a different direction and picked up stones from the front of the buildings, held them, and either kept them or put them back down.

"What are they doing?" Guss asked me. I knew, and in Alfarres, the people who believed in that sort of charm kept it to themselves, so he'd never seen it.

"They're looking for stones that hold the spirit of the town."

"Stones can't do that!"

"We need to be quiet and let them do what they think they need to do." If we interfered, we might get tossed out of the caravan.

"Can I help?"

"We should just watch them."

When they'd found the right stones, they set them in a circle in the center of the crossroads, and Goldie pulled out carved pieces of wood from a pack and set them outside the ring of stones. They spread their arms.

"We feel you, we hear you, Envia, great goddess of suffering, and we ask nothing from you but to be ignored. This was once all ours. Respect our presence here for this night." Then Goldie chanted the way they had on the road, using words from a language I didn't recognize but whatever was listening might understand.

Guss gripped my arm. I tried to look calm and respectful. I'd heard that Envia was a woman who had been tortured for someone else's sins centuries ago, but I didn't think that would make her a goddess who would be driven off by charms. Finally, Goldie said words that we were all supposed to repeat, so I nudged Guss.

"Hear our call for peace for all." We chanted it three times.

We set up camp, and by then the animals were impatient. Guss and I hauled water from the river. Goldie started a large fire using kindling from the ritual. We settled down to eat, and I'd brought bread and dried meat for Guss and me. He looked up and pointed at the Moon.

"I want to go there."

"Safer up there than down here," the guard said.

We didn't talk much, though. We were tired, and tomorrow would be another long day. Guss and I brought blankets and used our backpacks as pillows. The road was hard but I fell asleep anyway, remembering when I was a girl and how different it was and how much I hated the war and the people who fought it.

A whisper woke me up.

"Mother."

It wasn't exactly Guss's voice. I opened my eyes but didn't move.

"Mother, let's talk." Then, "Goldie, Goldie, check your horse."

Goldie was breathing fast. They were awake.

Then a child's voice called, "Help me!"

The guard jumped to her feet. "Krokotta!" She had a gun in one hand, her staff in the other. "Get away! You won't fool us." The dogs started barking.

"Help me!" the child's voice said.

Goldie ran to the fire and threw in a bundle of twigs. Flames rose. They chanted the words from another language and said, "This was once all ours!"

The rest of us huddled near the fire. The clothes seller pulled a club from a pack. Guss clung to my arm. Goldie kept chanting, and we joined in. I worried that Guss would try to fight the krokotta if he saw it, so I held his hand tight.

Around us we saw glowing eyes. He held my hand tighter.

"Silence!" the guard said.

We heard crickets and the wind in the trees. Someone was trying to control their sobs.

"Is that you crying, Dolores? Anyone?" Goldie whispered. They picked up a burning stick from the fire and waved at the darkness. "Envia, come to our aid. Force it to respect our presence!" They walked toward whatever was making the sobbing noise, holding out the burning stick. The light showed a robot shaped like a small dog. It moved back and got quiet.

"Krokotta." The guard took a step toward it, pointing her gun. "Get away! We can hurt you. I said, get away!"

It turned and galloped down a side road into the town and disappeared in the dark night.

None of us could fall back asleep, so we gathered up our things to move off as soon as we could. The animals grumbled at being woken up so early. Goldie packed up the charms, put out the fire, and set the stones back in the abandoned town. Guss picked some bamboo fruit.

We ate it as we left at first light, and I felt more awake with every bite. The guard kept looking all around.

"Why didn't you shoot it?" Guss asked. "The krokotta, why?"

She answered without looking at him. "Fair question. It might not be alone, and I don't have a lot of bullets."

As we walked, Guss looked at every tree, every field, and every path going into the forest. I saw flowers and butterflies, and they seemed to belong to a time I could hardly remember. Even when I was young, a few buildings were in ruins. A long, long time ago, there used to be a lot more people living in this part of the world.

In midmorning, we came to an intersection.

"That way's VinVelo." Goldie pointed north.

Guss looked relieved. "Good, let's go."

"You should make it there in a couple of hours, son."

"All right." Guss didn't understand, but I did, and I didn't like it.

I said, "You're not going with us."

Goldie shook their head, and their earrings rattled. "I'm genuinely sorry to say we won't, but they never buy much in that locale anyway. VinVelo's too self-sufficient."

Guss kicked a stone. "You said you'd take us."

"I did, son, but the bridge was washed out. VinVelo's not far. You should get there just fine." They took a polished wooden disk from their pocket. It had symbols carved in it, and they gave it to Guss. "I heard you singing. You can take care of yourself."

Guss took it and smiled proudly. Goldie believed in the charm, but I didn't. It would keep Guss from fussing, though, so I said thank you. As we started walking north, Goldie led a chant for our safety until we were too far to hear.

"I liked the animals," Guss said. "Can we get llamas for Alfarres?"

"They liked you, too. They'd be useful." They'd keep Guss busy, but they weren't cheap.

An hour later, we began to see farm fields. They needed tending.

"No one's weeded lately," I said.

"It's only a month." He pointed. "See, that's lamb's quarters. It looks big, but it grows fast, so it's not old." As we walked, every field had weeds.

"Did they abandon VinVelo?" he asked.

I'd been thinking the same thing. "It wouldn't make sense to leave after planting and before harvest. Maybe the people who planted these fields got sick or left."

"Then someone else would take them."

He was right. Wheat, oats, turnips, melons, and sunflowers, all valuable.

"No one is anywhere," he complained.

No one was in the fields or on the roads. I held his hand tight.

Soon, the air smelled wrong, like very old garbage. And there was no smoke from cooking fires.

"I don't like VinVelo already," Guss said.

"Maybe that's just because we're downwind." I had to keep him calm, but something was not good. In some fields, crops were ready to harvest. We still saw no people. I wanted to turn around, but I wanted to know what was happening, too. Maybe the war started again. Or maybe everyone got sick.

Guss took out the wooden charm. I shushed him before he could chant. Noise might get us noticed. He nodded and mouthed the words silently. We passed an empty house. The door was open, and next to it stood a bucket and a hoe like someone had just walked inside.

He let go of my hand and tiptoed to peek inside. He sprinted back, frightened.

"There's a dead body there," he whispered. "It's all moldy and smelly. Is everyone dead?"

"I don't know."

I thought about turning back, but then we'd never know what had happened. We passed more houses and didn't look to see what was inside. Far ahead someone was walking on the road away from us. Guss pulled me behind a tree trunk. He bent low and led me to hide behind some shrubs, then behind an empty house. He knew how to hunt, so I followed. We got closer, and the smell of decay got worse. We were walking toward a disaster, I knew that. All I could think about was the war. The war had started again.

He crept ahead, peeked around the corner of a shed, and came back. "I see all the people," he whispered. He led me to the corner and I leaned out just far enough to look.

Hundreds of people were sitting around a building I knew was a warehouse to store food and supplies. They were too far away for me to recognize anyone, adults and children, just sitting there.

"They're eating," Guss whispered.

He had better eyesight than I did. I squinted, and he was right. They were eating something from bowls. When they were done, they didn't move. Then a few stood up. They pulled out a box from the building, opened it, and started arguing. Finally two of them took crowns out of the box and put them on.

"What?" Guss whispered.

He'd never seen that technology. We didn't need it at Alfarres. "People who don't have chips use it to connect to networks." There might be a network in VinVelo, so I tried to connect, but I couldn't. I didn't understand what was happening.

The two people with the crowns faced each other. They held sticks, and they began to hit each other. Hard. They kept beating each other even when they were stumbling and bleeding, and no one tried to stop them. No one moved.

Guss whimpered. I couldn't breathe. I couldn't make sense of what I was seeing, but I'd seen enough. They had to be sick, some sort of horrible sickness. I tugged on his arm.

"Let's go."

He didn't argue. We turned, crept away, and as soon as we were far enough, we began running and kept running for as long as we could, then we walked as fast as we could. We reached the crossroads, and we turned back toward Alfarres. When we got close to the abandoned town, Guss took out the charm and shouted chants until his voice was hoarse. We crossed the bridge and kept going.

The sun went down and we continued to walk. Sometimes the Moon came out from behind the clouds and lit the road so we could walk faster. Sometimes we saw eyes in the brush, but now they scared me less than what we'd seen at VinVelo. My feet hurt so much that I knew they were bleeding, and I was limping, and I didn't care. We ate what we still had in our packs without stopping, drank all our water, and kept going, thirsty.

Finally, we reached a farm field that belonged to Alfarres. One of Guss's friends was tending it, and he saw us, and came running.

CHAPTER 5

Year 2900 CE
Pax Institute, Bayonne, France

LEVANTER

Again, today, the message from the planet Pax is not the answer from Mother Stevland. I need her answer now. Earth needs her answer.

Instead, the message is from humans on Pax for humans on Earth, and it continues a discussion about carnivorous plants, which are troubling but nowhere near as repellent as parasitic plants. I am still tasked with sharing these messages with my sisters, Foehn and Boreas, and then I share it with other rainbow bamboo. Our network functioned uninterrupted during the war against the Sea Group and its allies, although many groves were lost.

I have grown enough new roots to interpret the message quickly and thoroughly, then I offer a summary to my sisters. Here on Earth, some plants trap and digest animals, mostly insects, to acquire nitrogen in places where the soil nutrients are poor. On Pax, which has little iron on its surface, some plants kill animals for their iron. The message between Earth and Pax involves complex scientific detail.

Foehn has only one question. "Do we kill?"

She means, do rainbow bamboo on Pax kill humans, and her fresh rootlets vibrate with anxiety. Her rootlets are fresh because earlier today she did not like the weather forecast I repeated, and when she attacks mine in anger, her own are damaged.

She does not know how strong I have grown, with stems rising tall on the far sides of distant hills, so now it costs me effectively nothing to replace the rootlets. I do not fear her for my safety, I fear her for the safety of others. She used to enjoy killing and death. Then she felt human suffering in the war, so now she abhors harm to humans, but she still has no mercy for anything else.

"No," I say, "we do not kill on Pax. Humans there who serve us lay their dead to rest beside us, as sometimes happens here on Earth." I hope this half-truth satisfies her, but I brace for an attack.

She does not attack. "They feed us!" she exults.

I need to remind her that she is not hungry before she decides to kill nonhumans. "Here on Earth, of course, we can get all the iron we need from ordinary soil."

"We still need nitrogen and phosphorus," says Boreas. She might kill, but only strategically.

I remind them, "Humans and other creatures routinely fertilize us." Humans kill each other far too often, but they do not eat each other, one of their few universal taboos, although every other horror is perpetrated among them. "We could not consume animals like Earth carnivore plants. They capture insects on their leaves, then secrete digestive fluids. We absorb nutrients from the soil. Killing would not help us."

This is not true. Plants on Pax kill, then absorb nutrients from the soil released when microorganisms digest the corpses.

"If we do not kill humans," Foehn says, "that is good because we would be noticed. This message means nothing to us."

I am glad she thinks so because she will leave me alone, although I have found ways to protect myself. All my large, main roots, where I gather and process knowledge, are beyond her reach. Effectively, my stems in the Pax Institute garden are an outpost. Overall, I exceed Boreas and Foehn in size, and my roots, though young, have busy pith filled with information gathered from every source I have: human, bamboo, plant, and machine.

On one of the distant hills where I now center my growth, a network of floating fungus-like threads entraps a tiny bird, and that bird in turn hunted caterpillars. Zhizhuwangs and wrens lack self-reflective minds and cannot be held accountable for their actions, but sentient creatures can.

Humans on Pax know that we rainbow bamboo are sentient, and there, the bamboo guide them. Perhaps this is why humans there do not engage in frequent mass murder. Yet we have killed in the past on Pax, according to the histories in the institute library. We can kill here easily, too, and I know several methods, and I am not the smartest bamboo on Earth.

Mother Stevland sent a message one hundred and ten years ago saying that humans were ours to protect, command, and dominate with compassion. I sent a message asking how we can dominate the Earth, and her answer is due now. As I wait day after day, I can barely dominate one human.

That human is Denis, the director of the Pax Institute. He now lives at the Tabitha House next to the institute, which took him in as a lodger. Perhaps the sisters know that his mother gave her life to protect Tabitha's secrets during the Insurrection as it helped people escape Bayonne to freedom. He only knows that she was killed, and he shares in the sisters' prayers and faith, his god still immanent in nature. These days, though, he has grown restless.

When he arrived at the office in the morning, he studied the message, unaware that I am waiting for a very different message. Then he attended an inter-institute virtual breakfast meeting. Now he is pacing.

"Levanter, what do you think?"

"I am sorry. About what?"

"Euclid Nave Station. Were you listening?" He seems surprised that I was not.

I should have been. I was busy with the message from Pax, but I can do multiple things at once. Several institutes and organizations study extraterrestrial life, and their directors hold regular meetings to share companionship and news. They like to say that space is lonely to observe.

Euclid Nave Station, a penal colony with highly skilled prisoners, rebelled during the war, and its inmates became self-governing. The blood-stained freedom appalled the same Earthbound authorities who had made the bloodshed necessary. Earth stopped sending supplies, so the Euclideans made themselves self-sustaining by feats such as capturing and disassembling uninhabited satellites. They do not trust Earthlings at all, and they limit their contact to the extraterrestrial institutes.

"Up there," Denis says, "people are dying. What do you hear from bamboo? Because none of us have heard anything from anyone up there, but one of us found a transmission from a little while ago, and it's bad."

Bamboo grows on the station, connected to the wider bamboo network, and Euclidean groves distrust us, too, although we Earth bamboo never caused them harm. They say we are too inward-looking and petty, which might be true.

"I have not heard from them. People are dying?" The Insurrection and war left us all hypervigilant to renewed trouble.

He sits and fidgets. "Yes, horribly. We can commune with them. Here, this is one of the last transmissions."

Euclideans use chips fused to their nervous systems like everyone else, but their chips are enhanced to commune like crowns. I do not react fast enough and suddenly share the experience of someone on the station identified as Sama who reaches out a hand

music, the feel of strings of a guitar, a melody

I pull myself out of Sama's physical state, aided by the unsettling sight of Euclideans floating without gravity. Communing makes me feel afflicted and confused, so I find a parallel, mediated transmission. These are bad enough. Sama floats down a passageway, thinking about music, work, worrying about some ill friends

screaming ahead. Sama pushes off a wall toward trouble

forward through a doorway, inside, two people fight, bleed, hold pipes, swing them. Blood clouds the air. Sama and others converge and launch themselves toward the fighters, and a pipe swings toward

The transmission is cut off. I am in the institute garden and the nearby hills on Earth. This is Earth. Yes, I am here. Even a mediated commune disorients me.

I search for my leaves, stems, the sunshine and wind, the triumph of flowers, proof that I am a sturdy bamboo, not a human. My roots are in soil, wide, deep, dark. Earth is named for the soil, full of life, and I can touch it, taste it, sense it all around me.

Denis, too, needs some time to recompose himself. Then he says, "There's a lot more fights like that, then no more news. Everyone's upset."

I am upset as well. "It was appalling, but perhaps it is a passing disturbance, and the immediacy of communing magnifies its importance." I hope so. I will try to find a setting to the network to block all communing. I do not know why humans do it. Perhaps I can purge the root with this memory.

He looks out the window at the sky as if it willfully keeps secrets. "I wish you were right, but that's not what it looks like. They shut down the whole station, as far as we can tell. That's what we were talking about. Something political, maybe? Any news?"

Although the human network returned to full functionality after the war, some locations were damaged. Sometimes I know more about what humans are doing than they do. Bamboo everywhere are always talking, if need be through pollen and roots. Only a magical being could monitor it all, but I listen enough to answer his question.

"No news. This is good news."

"How about south? I mean, there's rumors."

Over the mountains to the south, the Iberian Peninsula suffered intense, pointless fighting, like many other places. Survivors live at subsistence levels, and they need aid, and neglect is rationalized by rumors of savagery, wild animals, and, even worse, wild robots. Humans generally believe, wrongly and forgetfully, that their domesticated robots, the ones that survived the war, remain safe and obedient, unlike wild robots. My little Beluga could tell humans the truth if it were not busy tending to the garden. It cooperates on its own terms and priorities.

"I will try to find out what is happening." The rumors could be true. Few of the chipped bamboo to the south survived the war, but our roots remain in contact.

"Thanks. I wish I could get up there and find out for myself."

I hope this is idle restlessness. He has spoken of visiting the Venus station to see its colonies of life-forms from Cygni, or of walking among the dinosaurs of Florida, or exploring the inlets and lakes of the Amazon basin or the California Central Sea, experiencing more of what nature holds. For fifteen years, he remained at the institute and earned a doctorate degree in botany, but our garden is small.

He looks out of the window at me in the garden. His hair has grown streaks of gray. "Levanter, I've been thinking. I mean, I want to be here, and I want you to be safe here, all of that. Everything you need to flourish, that's what you should have. But there's more out there, all sorts of things. I want to tell traveler's tales. I've been reading them."

I have read that kind of story, too. One is by a social scientist named Omrakash Bachchan who traveled to Pax with Mirlo. He did not understand what he saw or the true danger he faced. Mirlo wrote a secret account, briefer and without self-importance, that showed what amazing feats Mother Stevland can do. She can operate an aircraft. And, sadly, some members of Bachchan's mission were killed.

"To record your travels," I tell Denis, "you must first survive them."

He turns away from the window. "That's the thing. Whatever you can find out, that'd be great."

Our conversation shifts to the institute, harvesting fruit and managing caterpillars on the ponytail tree, familiar concerns for both of us. Denis has become a respected researcher, on par with institute leaders who study Epsilon Eridani, the corals on Europa, and Mars microbes.

Through Beluga, I check with the transmitter-responder at Euclid Nave Station. It reports that messages sent there are not being accepted by the station's system. Meanwhile, through the bamboo network, I contact a few connected groves in Iberia. They are far to the south, on the coast of the Mediterranean Sea, and they say monkeys called Barbary macaques are eating the bamboos' leaves because a drought has made them thirsty. The bamboos' own thirst limits their energy for communication. Other bamboo send them wishes for water.

"I wish we could control the weather," an Irish grove called Suca Valley says. We all wish for that, but ideal weather for some would not be ideal weather for all, so I am glad we cannot. We argue enough already.

An exceptional grove eagerly shares news. She has grown for more than two centuries at an inlet of the Mississippi Bay in North America amid congenial neighbors: willows, whose fibrous roots consolidate the riverside soil; and oaks, endearing extroverts who refuse domestication. At a bluff overlooking the river, she grows an expanding maze of stems as interlocking circles that humans flock to visit, calling it a paradise.

"We have added the beauty of roses." She describes them in compelling detail. Bamboo could see it themselves by connecting to the human network if they were not baffled by its complexity. I locate cameras that show a curving walkway. Between flourishing stems of rainbow bamboo, rosebushes bloom in colors that shade sequentially from red to pink to white. A human bends to smell a flower, while others stroll in wide-eyed joy.

"How did that happen?" Boreas asks, a question tense with accusation.

"Our humans planted—"

"How did they know?" Like Foehn, if Boreas fears one thing, it is humans learning what we are. If my sisters learned that I converse with Denis, they would kill me.

"Oh, our humans know this ground conjures beauty, and they want to create even more beauty all the time." Mississippi is always joyful.

"*Your* humans," Boreas accuses. Many of Boreas's stems grow in a nearby orchard, carefully tended. She has no interest in the orchardists.

I wonder if Mississippi even recognizes Boreas's hostility. Perhaps the chemicals Mississippi has added to her fruit, cannabinoids and entheogens, affect her own thinking, making her perpetually euphoric, or perhaps growing in paradise has given her a joy-filled character.

"Humans sing with the songbirds," she says. "With abundance and nourishment, all living things reciprocate. Our humans, oh yes, ours, and our birds and foxes and butterflies, too, and we love them as we love ourselves."

Love. Mother Stevland also uses that word. With Mississippi's intervention, the fields around the maze-forest yield copious food, and the maze invites pilgrimage from other continents. As I watch, humans begin to sing and dance.

"The fruit," Boreas insists, "that is what they come for. Your additives."

I wonder if this is what Mother Stevland meant. We could add many other substances, but they require foresight and labor, like scents, colors, and pesticides, which cost energy and resources.

"This is how to kill humans. We can alter our fruit," says Toad Forest, a grove in eastern Asia. Where she lives, rainbow bamboo and Earth trees are indiscriminately harvested. "We are already called demon trees."

"If we hurt them," Boreas says, "they will hurt—"

"We must not kill them!" Foehn interrupts.

"Only a few," Toad Forest says. "Then they would respect us." She describes clear-cut hills, one after another until they disappear in the mist, and the whine of machines like giant hungry insects.

"But the gods are real," Foehn says. "I have found them." She still believes in wild robots. I am convinced that Denis has a better understanding of god.

"We would not have to kill many," Toad Forest says, "and there are plenty of humans."

"No killing," Foehn says.

"We do not want to be noticed," Boreas says.

"We must act with maturity," Suca Valley says.

Despite Mississippi's enhanced fruit and the many poisonous Earth plants to copy, none of us have dared to harm humans, so we quarrel pointlessly. As humans say, talk is facile.

On the bamboo network, old arguments exhaust themselves. Now they describe the places where they grow. They never tire of this even though we never move to new places. Mississippi looks out over the dramatic bluffs of Mississippi Bay. Others are surrounded by plentiful forests and jungles. In Ireland, Suca Valley grows in a human-tended garden where, she says, fog is evaporating in the sunshine, and flowers and bushes sparkle with dew.

They also share animal lore. Certain hummingbird hawkmoths have become reliable pollinators, and their caterpillars feed on common weeds, not us, so we hope for larger populations. They hover in flight, a pleasure to watch. A grove on the banks of the Nile River is collecting all known information about lepidoptera.

Healthy groves have time and energy for avocations. In an untended field across the hills, I am training wildflowers to adopt colors near the ultraviolet end of the spectrum. Humans cannot see how bright they shine, but insects respond, and I enjoy observing them.

Foehn's avocation, if she has one, might involve self-importance. She maintains tight contact with all her seedlings. Sending a message across the mountains to the south, grove to grove, will take a day at least to establish, and she can do it.

"Foehn," I ask gently, "you may wish to contact your southern seedlings. I have heard of a drought there, and you have good advice for thirsty groves."

"Advice?" she responds indignantly. "I can do more. I can order the gods to help."

She is fooling herself, but disagreeing would accomplish nothing. "Yes, you can do that."

Meanwhile, Denis and I review information from Pax about carnivory. Denis wants to send information to Pax about a highly efficient kind of photosynthesis recently developed for *Arabidopsis thaliana* by Kew Royal Botanic Gardens. I am not sure this will interest Pax because they cannot perform genetic engineering, but, I suggest, they are always interested in Earth ecology.

"We have some data about extinction," Denis says, "and it's related to carnivory."

In the Earth year 800 CE, the human population had been estimated at two hundred fifty million. In 1800, it reached one billion. By 2050, ten billion. Depicted as a line on a graph, it rises from 1800 to 2050 at almost a right angle. Then it falls in a series of drops due to epidemics, disaster, and war, down to two hundred fifty million again.

"With humans and wolves," Denis says, "we can illustrate what that means. More humans, less wolves, and vice versa. Lots of species didn't make it past the human peak. Here's the twenty-third-century Great Loss." The line takes a sharp drop. "Extinction. It could have been us."

I sense agitated debate in the bamboo network. I try to center my attention on Denis, then I hear Foehn.

"There is a better way to solve this."

Along the Baltic Sea, two groves want to claim some land that connects to a large island, even better for colonization because its hills and valleys provide a variety of biomes.

"I will fight you for it," one of the groves is saying.

Boreas warns Foehn and me, "We do not want to get involved."

"Bamboo have never fought each other before," I say. "We work together." This is somewhat true.

Foehn stings my rootlets. "Leave this to me."

I should leave it to her, but I want peace, so I ask the bamboo, "How do you plan to fight?" I flinch, waiting for her to punish me.

Before she can, one of the Baltic groves asks, "Foehn, how do we fight?"

"Kill each other's roots. Flood them with acid."

"I would hurt myself."

"It would be good pain," she says.

I have long doubted Foehn's mental health, and the doubts keep growing. Every kind of creature avoids pain. Then, just to Boreas and myself, she says, "Pain is the only way to learn. They will learn to work together, not to fight."

She stings her own roots when she attacks mine and does not seem to learn anything.

The grove in Ireland says, "I cannot imagine wanting any land that much. Maybe you could split the island."

"Humans will fight to the death over anything," Toad Forest says. "Can we get *them* to fight?"

"We must not kill humans," Foehn insists.

"I have a better idea," Toad Forest says. "Use surrogates to fight for you. Fippokats can fight."

"Fippokats do not fight each other," a Japanese grove says.

This is also somewhat true. Fippokats live in what are called towns, their borders marked by fences of twigs and leaves, gardens of unpalatable plants, lines of ant nests, human trash, cairns of stones, and heaps of skat. Some walls imitate human constructions. Fippokats on Pax are territorial but do not build walls, so fippokats on Earth learned this behavior from humans.

What could fippokats fight instead? Bamboo debate: drop bears, raccoons, wolves, tree octopuses, Earth birds, Pax birds, or wild dogs, but nothing seems like a fair or even possible fight.

"You do not understand," Foehn says. "Have you learned nothing from Mississippi? I know exactly how to make them fight each other." She suggests an anabolic steroid, methyltestosterone, as a means to create aggression. It might work on fippokats much as it does on humans, but it has such severe side effects that humans ban its use.

I caution, "Its side effects would harm fippokats. And fippokats are sentient."

"Stop being so sensitive," Foehn says. "They are not sentient. And there are plenty of them."

Mississippi sides with me. "This is abuse of fippokats."

"Better them than us," one of the Baltic groves says, but most agree with Mississippi, and I find this response comforting. Perhaps some bamboo have an ethos, but we cannot control events beyond our reach.

The two opposing groves find neighboring fippokat towns and begin to alter their fruit. I hope the levels they are discussing will make the fruit unpalatable. I also wonder how Foehn knows this. She has little patience for the labor of scholarship.

To find out, I approach the subject tangentially. "I am impressed by your understanding of additives for fruit."

"The steroid was used in the war," she says.

"By humans?"

"Robots made them stop. Humans do not understand themselves."

Her tone says that I am asking stupid questions, but she may be right about humans.

Denis is staring out the window at the garden, unaware of what is being discussed.

"You know, Levanter, Bayonne is a good place now. We survived, thank god. We're lucky there are still humans on this planet. Lucky there are humans elsewhere like Pax. Euclid? I don't understand."

"Neither do I." There is much I do not understand.

He says goodbye and leaves, done with a long day of work. I hope he rests well. My thoughts are running in many directions, but as the sun sets and my leaves rest, I drowse under the false quiet of the night sky.

Drowse, but never truly sleep. I hate to commune with human minds, but I wonder about dreams. Denis, in his sleep, can venture anywhere, even beyond reality. I become slow at night, but I go nowhere.

The message from Pax arrives shortly before dawn. Mother Stevland? It is long. Is it another treatise in botany, or does she have a great deal to say? I would treasure every wave that re-creates the ions, enzymes, and chemical paths of our natural communication. A long message would fill one of my roots.

No. It is human words, not our speech translated as sounds. I should not have felt hope. It discusses plant parasites. I rouse enough sugar to fuel a root to study it.

A plant closely related to rainbow bamboo called a snow vine is a parasite. Parasitic bamboo! I am revulsed. I know that life comes in infinite, elaborate relationships. Epiphyte, symbiont, saprophyte. Mutualism, commensalism, amensalism. Parasitism, though, is debased, a grotesque dependency. Worse, the bamboo-like parasite shows intelligence. Parasitism should be overcome by intelligence, which should seek self-reliance.

I translate the report from Classic English for Denis, although he can understand the original language. Translation forces me to read it with utmost care, looking for clues to believe that the habitat of Pax offers comforting differences from Earth, but I hope in vain.

I send a robot to tidy the office as the Earth turns toward its life-giving star.

Denis arrives looking well dressed and groomed, which is unusual. Before he enters the office, he picks the best-looking and ripest fruit from the stems deepest in the garden, more than enough for breakfast.

"Good morning," he says. "I've got news. The head of the Cetacean Institute is coming. Thanks for cleaning up, and I'd appreciate it if you listen in. If you have questions, use Classic English. She won't understand it."

"Why is she coming?" Whales have nothing to do with Pax. And, operationally, she leads a cult, not an institute.

"To talk about concerns she couldn't say publicly yesterday, that's what she told me. She travels a lot and happens to be nearby, so she said she'd come here."

Her workplace is at sea, and Bayonne is a port, so this is plausible. I have never seen her in person, but I feel uncomfortable about her.

"Levanter, can you handle the robots?"

The institute lost some robots in the war, which were hard to replace. We have enough to manage the grounds in partnership with Tabitha House sisters, who sell the fruit they harvest in exchange for their work.

I still have Beluga, fully rebuilt by successive repairs, so is it the same Beluga or a descendant of Beluga? Do robots have children? My descendants have been scattered around the globe as seeds, then the seeds of their seeds, and they do not mean to me what human children mean to their parents. Boreas is also indifferent to her seedlings. Foehn claims some groves that are not hers.

Denis grabs pots of flowering tulips from the sales area to decorate the office and coaxes a pair of fippokats to sleep cutely on a cushion in the corner. A basket holds fresh, perfect fruit and other food, and plates, glasses, and a pitcher of water sit on the conference table made of locustwood with its beautiful checkered grain. A countertop machine stands ready to make hot beverages.

"Okay, we're ready." We wait. Denis fidgets. "I wonder what she has to say. I mean, she travels the world."

I do not want to remind him of his own wish to travel, so I suggest, "Whale communication is relayed by satellites including Euclid Nave Station. The Cetacean Institute administers the whale network. She will know if its transmitter-responder is still operative."

"Right. I bet that's it, Euclideans."

An hour later, the fippokats have woken up and wandered off, and we are reviewing the message from Pax to pass the time. "Parasites are highly evolved species," he says, "especially obligate parasites."

"They are dependent species as well. They cannot survive without their host."

"You disapprove?"

"They are often easy to eliminate."

"Ever heard of witchweed, Levanter? Know how it got its name?"

"Yes. We call it root-hunter-seed and eliminate it. When it germinates, it sends out a tiny root that seeks the roots of healthy plants to parasitize and feed its own embryonic seedling."

"You can eliminate it? Really? The only effective management we know is quarantine."

"When we detect the seeds, we make them commit suicide. We produce an ethylene hormone and release it into the soil to force the seeds' germination without a nearby host. This is one reason why farmers call us lucky bamboo. Their crops grow better in our presence. This is also why you have heard of witchweed but never seen it. I have a natural revulsion to parasites the same way that humans have an inborn fear of snakes."

He thinks for a moment. "We need to write a paper about that. Natural targeted pesticides, just one of the benefits of rainbow bamboo."

Before he can ask about other parasites, such as the parasitic bamboo, which I do not wish to discuss, Clerihew, head of the Cetacean Institute, arrives at the gate on a motorized bicycle, apparently alone. I notify Denis. She looks in person as she does on camera, conventionally beautiful, although she uses unconventional means. Her age is medically slowed. She seems to be about twenty-five years old but she is five times that. The strain on her body requires more and more medication until one day it will stop working, and she will collapse and die on the spot. That day will come soon.

This limits the popularity of the treatment. Denis has called it vanity. He sometimes forgets to comb his hair, and the people who spark his romantic interest tend to wear sturdy boots. Yet he dressed up for this visit.

Clerihew is decoratively groomed. Her skin shines bronze-brown and smooth, and like all Cetacean cult members, she is hairless and her physique enhanced by adipose tissue in imitation of whale blubber. Denis hurries out to greet her. She dismounts the bicycle slowly and carefully, as if avoiding a fall. She wears an orange and blue Cetacean-uniform arctic jacket over the uniform jumpsuit, although the sun shines with warmth. She cannot help being old and frail.

She looks around. "It's as beautiful as ever." She gazes up at the towering trees in the garden, and then she bends, slowly and carefully, to pet the fippo-kats who have hopped over to greet her. One leaps over her outstretched hand, flips, and lands in the right spot to push its head into her palm to demand affection. She coos in delight. Cuteness may have an evolutionary purpose.

She rises and looks at Denis with a wide smile. "I was here decades ago, before the war. How delightful it must be to be here all the time!" She reaches out to hug him, and she might not notice, but he blushes. Then she takes a box from the basket of her bicycle.

"I brought you a gift from the sea." She opens the box to show a bowl made of mother-of-pearl.

Denis thanks her and leads her to his office, where he sets it in the center of the locustwood table. Before he can offer her hospitality, she takes him by the hand to look out the window. She stands very close to him.

She points to the rainbow bamboo. "Can you talk to them?" Her voice is breathy.

"We can listen." He tells the system to play the whistles, hisses, whines, and snaps that are our conversations translated into human sound. "Doesn't it sound like whales?"

"Yes! What are they saying?"

He shrugs. "We know they communicate, but that's all we know."

The bamboo are discussing ways to coach seedlings through droughts, which at any given moment are happening somewhere on the globe. The bamboo are also discussing drop bears. Since they do no direct harm to us or any other plant and their droppings are rich in calcium from the bones they ingest, perhaps we should not consider them as dreadful as humans and other animals do.

Clerihew sighs. "Isn't that frustrating? And you've been listening for so long!" Does she wonder if we are sentient?

"Well, we know that plants share information about their environment—"

"They talk through their roots!" she interrupts. "Yes, they've always been in communication."

"Right. Just the same way that birds call to each other." He looks at her with narrowed eyes.

She leans toward him. "Plants on Earth have always had that network. Bamboo fit right into it."

"The bamboo help the plants around them. That's why farmers think they're lucky."

"They don't need their chips to work their magic," she says softly, gazing at his eyes.

"But they grow even better with the chips." Denis looks over her shoulder to break the spell. I do not like the turn this conversation has taken, either.

"There's a shortage of chips," she says, still softly. "And whales are filling the seas. They were once almost extinct, did you know that?"

"Right. Human populations go down, other populations go back up." He drums his fingers on his thigh, then stops.

"That's why I'm here." She is still staring at him. "Bayonne recycles chips, and we can buy some here, but not enough. Maybe bamboo don't need as many chips. They have roots, and those roots cover a lot of area."

She is here to take our chips. That must not happen. His eyebrows shift a tiny bit. He understands.

"You know, yesterday," he says, "we were talking about Euclid Nave Station. It makes chips. A Moon colony sends it raw materials, and then they sell the chips to Earth. What's going on with the Euclideans?"

As they speak, robots monitor the front gate to the institute. As always, visitors to the garden come and go, some familiar, some new. One has never been here before, and the system alerts me that Brian Amp has arrived, the head of the Coral Cult. It actually calls itself a cult. The Coral Isolation Biome and Europa Observation Team consider the cult deluded because it celebrates the corals.

"I mean," Denis is saying, "the Cetacean communications network is in constant contact with the Euclid Nave transmitter-responder. Is that still working?"

She frowns. "I suppose, yes."

On a display, I show Brian approaching the office entrance. Denis does not notice.

"That's great news," he says. "I'm worried. I mean, you saw what's happening up there."

"The station can continue automatically for a long time. We can't count on it for more chips." She expresses no concern about the violence. I am discovering why I feel uncomfortable about her.

I make a signaling chime to draw Denis's attention to the display. He apparently does not hear it over the background noise of bamboo communication.

He says, "We can use the transmitter-responder to communicate with the station's system to find out what's happening, right? Maybe there's something we can do down here to help them."

"It's only a transmitter-responder."

Brian walks into the building and immediately tries to connect to the institute system. Fine wires are braided into his waist-length hair, connecting to rings that are antennas. Wires also course beneath his skin, connecting to rings on his fingers. He is a walking transmitter-responder. He carries a bag that seems heavy.

The system automatically blocks his attempts to breach it, allowing him no more than a map of the physical site like any other visitor. During the war, according to rumor, he was a spy against the Sea Group, disrupting their communications. According to official records, he was a safety inspector. He heads toward the director's office. Whatever the Coral Cult wants, I must make sure the corals remain as far away from Earth as possible. I have read Mirlo's report about their attack on Pax.

"Brian Amp of the Coral Cult has arrived," I announce, pretending to be the system.

"Brian?" Clerihew, standing in front of the window, looks angry.

"Well," Denis says, "I've never met him in person." He turns toward the door as Brian walks in and looks around.

"Denis, hello. And Clerihew, I knew *you* were here."

"How—"

"I saw your people. There's quite a few just down the road waiting on you as well as wandering the grounds. So what are you up to?" He sets down his bag and sits on a stool. "Tell me all about it."

She simply glares at him.

Denis seems to sort through his thoughts before he says, "I'm glad you could come." He picks up the basket and flashes a hospitable smile. "Please, both of you, can I offer you some of the best fruit you'll ever have? What can I get you to drink? That machine can make anything you want."

Brian accepts a piece of fruit as Clerihew, still glaring at him, finds a chair. Denis chats about how the fruit came from the original trees and recites a little history about us as he fusses with the beverages. I suspect he's stalling so he can think. His guests do not like each other, but they have resources that the Pax Institute does not have.

When the guests have been served, Denis takes his own seat and says earnestly, "We're all worried about the Euclideans, all us institutes, since we're their sole contact point. Beyond humanitarian concerns—I mean, we know these people—they make chips, and we never have enough of them."

Brian sets down his half-eaten fruit. "Chips are not at all my concern, and that is not why I came here."

"We need more chips for the whales," Clerihew says.

"Let me be clear," Brian says. "Your precious chips pale in importance to the human disaster. And there are a thousand Euclideans up there. Do we care about them?" His eyebrows rise to emphasize his question. "We have been benumbed by the homicidal mass idiocy here on Earth."

"Fine. Whatever." Clerihew was sipping bland tea and not eating anything. "What are we supposed to do? We have enough problems down here on Earth."

Brian leans forward. "Let's put this in nice, simple whale terms. Suppose you have some sick whales. Let's say, the ones in the Celebes Sea infected with trematodes. And what are you doing? You're being commendably responsible and treating them before it spreads."

Clerihew is about to say something.

"Oh, my dear, don't be surprised. I know what you're doing. And I have no issues with it, at least about the treatment of disease. The point is this: Haven't we done enough damage to humankind already?"

Denis is nodding. I am not sure about the logic, but I agree with the sentiment.

"We couldn't do anything if we wanted to," she says.

He chuckles. "First, yes, admit it, you don't want to. You think, wrongly, that you don't need to want to. Euclideans are mere lawless convicts, or so you want to believe. But consider what happens if we fail to act. Violence spreads. How many disasters are we away from having to abandon whales to their own devices? Of course, they'll survive without humans."

She tries to interrupt, but he keeps talking.

"No one needs you. Your survival, the survival of your cult, depends on excess social resources and a willingness to invest them in your game. Subsistence-level humans will abandon every one of us. Don't believe me? Think of all the sports now in dusty history. Have you ever heard of the Olympic Games? Big stuff, once, gone for good. To some degree, we are entertainment, like sports."

Her frown deepens. "Science is not the same—"

"Science? Really? Giving a personal, charming name to every single animal? If we can't eat the whales when we're scraping by for our next meal, who cares? And yes, I know what that means for me. Corals aren't even on Earth. Whether or not you're convinced by your obvious self-interest, we *can* do something. That's why I came here. The three of us together have resources. We can begin by finding out what's happening. We need the Euclid Nave Station to be functioning. We need its chips, but more than that, we must protect the lives of its people. In a time like this, the station might not be self-supporting."

He waits for her to respond.

Denis answers instead. "The Euclid Nave transmitter-responder is still working."

Brian smiles. "Indeed, my dear Clerihew, you can do so much. To begin with, you can get in touch with the Moon. I'm sure the Looneys have business concerns and would appreciate your sympathy and an offer of support. They may even have news about what's going on. And you, Denis, can lobby other institutes to become involved. No one else on Earth will do anything."

"I can do that," he says. He sees Brian's game and will play along.

Clerihew says, "I'm not agreeing to anything," but she makes no move to leave.

Brian does not move, either. "You can send a message right here, right now. Your cult members are wandering the grounds like visitors. Call them in and get to work while there's still time. Your survival depends on it. And you, Denis—"

"Right, my system is automated. Draft a message."

"Under way," I say, and assign the task to a major root.

A visitor to the garden, hairless and zaftig like a whale, approaches the back door of the office, wearing ordinary summer clothing rather than a Cetacean uniform. Clerihew steps out to confer. The system recognizes the visitor as the source of repeated attempts to breach its security.

"Will we be able to help?" Denis asks Brian.

"Oh, I hope so." He sighs. "Or else we may have to quarantine them."

"Quarantine?" Denis glances out the window. He may be thinking of how the bamboo can eliminate pests. We cannot eliminate violence.

Clerihew and her aide come inside. "The transmitter-responder is working, but it's not accepting messages. That's all we know about what's going on up there." The aide glares at Brian as fiercely as Clerihew does.

Brian stands up, wiggling his beringed fingers. "Euclid Nave is overhead now. Let me into the exchange. I'm very good at this sort of thing. It sends and receives, and I can make it listen. We would be best to step outside."

As they do, I compose diplomatic messages for other institutes asking them to investigate for humanitarian reasons as well as for potential equipment disruptions. Denis approves, and I dispatch them.

"I'm doing this just to help Brian," he sends to me. "Everybody already knows this is serious."

"It is a good strategy to sound the alarm," I answer, but a better strategy would be to do something concrete.

Outside, the three confer through their chips, and through Beluga I locate a connection to listen in. Brian is complaining about the Euclideans' paranoid level of security as he attempts contact.

The Euclid Nave system retransmits Brian's initial message, and he seems to know exactly how to address the system with persuasive machine language. He asks for a status update of the station. It sends him the data, and he routes it through equipment he has in his bag. I route it into the institute system memory. He asks to speak to a human administrator but gets no answer.

Meanwhile, he reports that each arm of the station has been isolated for security reasons. Parameters for station function might not be normal. I wish I could ask him if the bamboo network is still functional because it is a subsystem of the overall station network.

Brian tells Clerihew he will continue contact with Euclid Nave. She is annoyed, and she and her aide leave, and while they are within reception by the institute system, I listen. The aide was supposed to enter the institute's system and cancel chip purchase agreements, but the system constantly faces attempted incursions and stops them.

"Good security," the aide sends.

"He's not as dumb as he looks," Clerihew replies. She means Denis.

Brian reenters the office. "I can keep working through the Cetacean system, which is remarkably powerful. They let me link into it for this, but this alone, not that I could expect more. They have no reason to trust me. So far, nothing new, sadly." He helps himself to coffee. "I know I'm a bit like a piece of equipment myself, and yet I care for humanity more than anyone else alive. And you?" he asks Denis.

"I sent out messages to the other institutes and nagged on behalf of humanity. Nagged nicely, of course."

"'Nagged'! That's the exact word for dealing with that lot." He takes a seat. "Not that the Euclideans are going to trust anyone. Please get comfortable, Denis, I have a lot to talk to you about."

"Right," Denis says. I know the rising and falling inflection packed into that single syllable. He uses it when visitors demand trained-fippokat shows or localized climate control. Fippokats here live as naturally as possible, and many plants need the cold winter rain.

"So those trees," Brian says, "do you understand them?"

The conversation is still playing in the background. They are discussing drought and surviving it by using roots to store water and locating human-made reservoirs or water utilities to tap into unnoticed. Foehn suggests giving orders to irrigation systems, and they begin to discuss machine language. Foehn knows one language, but teaching it to them would require more patience than she has. I am relieved. If every bamboo could give orders to machines, we would get chaos.

Brian listens to the chatter. "You could discover a lot if you tried to understand them."

"We—"

"And you haven't done a thing. We know more about what the corals are saying."

"What are they saying?"

"They sing. They sing about the energy they graze on from the solar winds. They sing about the life teeming through the crust of Europa. Joy, Denis. They sing of joy, and we can partake of it."

"Well, we know some things about what we hear. The bamboo, they have moods, all kinds of them. In the war, their agitation tipped off attacks when human communication systems were blocked. We sometimes hear early warnings of earthquakes."

"And you haven't done a thing beyond that."

Brian is right. The institute has not done more because I do not want it to. A few universities had research projects, but they never achieved much and were lost in the war, fortunately.

"It's a tough code to crack," Denis says, his usual answer. "We can't talk to oak trees, either, and they talk to each other."

Oaks often negotiate masting, the irregular production of massive numbers of acorns so that some of the acorns will germinate because animals cannot possibly eat them all. The debates to choose a mast year can generate so much rancor among the usually affable oaks that their cousins, the beeches, sometimes intervene. Denis and I are trying to author a scholarly paper without revealing the precise source of the observations.

Brian sips his coffee. "You need more people on it. That's how we came to hear the coral music. There used to be a rescue group for rainbow bamboo. Revive it."

"I used to be involved with that." I persuaded him to dissolve the group because we bamboo disagreed with its demands. "What would—"

"Imagine, singing trees." His eyes close in what might be bliss. "Imagine the thrum of sunshine, the pulse of rainwater on leaves."

Sunshine and rain do invoke bliss. Could he imagine us extolling the beauty of the Mississippi Bay? Or cringing at the terror of a forest fire, as told and retold by survivors?

"I know," Brian says with a dismissive sigh, "they're just plants and not that smart, but they have their joys."

Brian is in constant communication with his fellow cultists, and Beluga is listening. The cult has infiltrators in the Coral Isolation Biome and Europa

Observation Team. I could sing about the names and places of Coral Cult overt and covert activity. He is no more trustworthy than Clerihew but definitely more intelligent.

Out in the garden, I hear a specific trill from fippokats. Foehn contacts Boreas and me. "I see a drop bear! You know what the fippokats are going to do!"

In the building, Denis drums his fingers. We bamboo are smart, and he is insulted on our behalf. "People already use the sound of their communication to inspire music."

I enjoy that music.

"Oh, but you could do so much more. Well, never mind. A lack of ambition. I have—"

They both notice a change in the bamboo chatter. I make an announcement as if it is an alert from the system.

"Drop bear on premises."

Denis jumps to his feet.

"Are you afraid of them?" Brian asks. "Well, I suppose—"

"The fippokats will kill it."

"What?" Brian sets down his coffee. "They can be lethal?"

"They sure can." He pauses. "I should warn you, it won't be pretty."

"Cute little fippokats? I want to see that."

I am not sure I want to see what comes next. My stalks surround the area from every direction, from ground level to overhead. I feel the weight of the drop bear climbing through my branches. It looks like a large, long-legged raccoon with a tan and brown coat dappled like an Earth jaguar's. Drop bears are voracious carnivores from Cygni. A crow follows it, cawing a warning to all creatures.

"Where is it?" Foehn asks.

Boreas says, "In Levanter's crown."

I feel a twinge in my roots. Foehn envies everything, even my unwelcome role as a launching site. "Its claws scratch," I say to stop her envy. "Serrated claws." The claws hurt worse than her acid.

The crow's call tells Denis and Brian where to run.

The fippokats know what to do. Twenty wait, motionless, around the edge of a small clearing where the ground is covered by Pax tulips. The bears can see motion and the colors red and brown well, a clue to their original habitat. They cannot see green, the color of chlorophyll and fippokat fur.

Denis and Brian stop far enough away to avoid disturbing what will happen next.

Fippokats have placed cracked walnuts in the center of the clearing. They routinely befriend squirrels, and a fippokat is leading a friendly red squirrel into the clearing. The squirrel scents the nuts and dashes ahead. The drop bear spots it and shifts to attack. The squirrel does not heed what looks like a patch of dappled yellow leaves high overhead.

A drop bear does not simply let go and fall. Its back legs contract, ready to push off. The fippokats do not move, not even to flick an ear when a biting fly lands on it.

Foehn's rootlets vibrate with anticipation. I try to shift my main attention elsewhere, to a Pax bird excavating a burrow for a nest near the east wall. Yet, for all my efforts, I cannot stop watching. But I am not like Foehn.

The squirrel drops a now-empty shell, grabs another walnut, and sits on its haunches, gnawing. The drop bear pushes against my branch, which snaps back, propelling the bear into a dive. The fippokats leap up. The ones farther away jump a fraction of a second ahead of the others so they all converge in a single place, and they twist in the air to present their overlapping back claws like a net, tips pointed up. The bear cannot control its descent. It howls even before it hits the trap.

Brown blood showers on the squirrel, and it leaps away as viscera fall. A fippokat is waiting to accompany it to safety. Together, the two dash to a pond, where they swim until the squirrel feels clean, then they huddle on a log, grooming each other. Soon, the other fippokats join them to wash off the blood. Humans describe it as putrid-smelling.

Brian's eyes are wide. "I didn't think they were that smart."

"You mean you didn't think they were that vicious."

"I meant using that poor squirrel as bait."

Denis looks up at us, our tall stems and arching branches ringed with rainbows. "Never assume anything." I wonder if it weighs on him to have to keep us a secret.

I direct a robot to retrieve the carcass and clean up the stink. Drop-bear claws are fashionable knives to sell to visitors. The water in the spring-fed pond will naturally refresh itself.

Foehn vibrates. "Fippokats are weapons! I want to know how they fight in the Baltic."

I say nothing. There are plenty of fippokats, Foehn insisted earlier, and she believes they are not sentient.

The grass-green fippokats tend to the rust-red squirrel they used as bait, fluffing its tail, bringing it another nut. Sentience? They plan ahead as deadly as humans, or as gentle and loving. They used the squirrel cruelly, and they understand what they did, but the squirrel will never understand. At most, it might avoid that clearing now. It will not avoid fippokats.

Could rainbow bamboo work together as efficiently as fippokats? Humans form themselves into prodigious organizations, and these organizations need leaders, and leaders are always subject to controversy, sometimes revolts. Euclid Nave Station may be in a revolt like that.

I did not hear what I wished from Mother Stevland today. If the message comes tomorrow, can I use it to help Euclid Nave?

As they walk back to the office, the humans talk.

"I know my name fell out of fashion," Brian says, "but my parents told me they gave me it to inspire me to glory. Brian Boru became Ireland's greatest high king. He was a warlord."

"So you want to be a warlord?" Denis's smirk says no.

"Savagery is for wild beasts. I think we can do better."

"You mean be like fippokats," Denis says.

"Cuddly things. That's not me."

Denis laughs.

"I know," Brian says. "I'm fully wired."

They reach the office.

"I have something I need you to do," Brian says. "I've found a report about corals in Classic English, and I know you can translate it. The date stamp says that it came from someone on the actual mission to Pax. The content must be invaluable. Let me pass it on to you."

"From the Pax mission? We have some of—"

"If you would be so kind."

"Oh, right, system access."

The system automatically offers Brian minimal access, deposit only, which he immediately tries to compromise, but our system is faster. He shows no annoyance, so Denis will only know Brian was thwarted when I tell him, which I will.

The report is by Zivon, an anthropologist mentioned by Mirlo in his secret report as being deliberately misled by the inhabitants of Pax. I want to see exactly how he was deceived.

Denis accompanies Brian to the institute's front gate, perhaps as a courtesy, perhaps as a security escort. When Denis returns to the office, I tell him about Brian's attempt to invade our system, and he laughs. I tell him that Clerihew said he was not as dumb as he looks, and he stops laughing and looks pained.

He finally says, "I thought I could impress her. She's too old for me anyway. Let's get to work. We have a garden to tend."

We set up some robots and supervise them. Whenever he remembers what robots did during the war, he blames it all on wild robots. Ours can be trusted.

In the early evening, Denis gets a reply from the Coral Isolation Biome and Europa Observation Team: "Thank you for your concern, however, the Euclid Nave Station has made itself a sovereign entity. Our organization and your institute lack the diplomatic standing to become involved in the affairs of its citizens. We remind you that an attempt to do so could bring censure from your sovereign state, and we would be obliged to report your activities."

"That was rude," he says. "People are dying, and they don't *want* to care. Brian got that right."

"We may be lucky that he is working through the Cetacean Institute, not us, if it could cause an international incident."

"Europa will report that the second they find out. Sovereign entity—you know what? Bayonne's a city-state. The mayor's a friend. I'll talk to her tomorrow. For now, it's time for me to go home. Time for you to rest, too."

As the sun sets, I analyze Zivon's report. He had deduced the existence of Stevland, whom he called "he." Zivon believed Mother was merely a useful, pretty plant, the symbol of the city, and the Glassmaker queens secretly controlled Rainbow City on Pax. He took credit for persuading Glassmakers not to come to Earth, which he expected them to try to conquer. This is wildly inaccurate in so many ways.

Zivon hated many things, including the corals, which had taken control of the Earth team's central information system and used it for a murderous rampage, and his account coincides with Mirlo's. But as Mirlo explained in his report, Zivon could not fully understand what had happened because Mother Stevland's role was kept hidden.

Brian might not like the translation because of what it says about the corals, but no harm should come to bamboo or humans by giving it to him. With that, I relax into the darkness, feeling water flow through my stems and cool night air into my leaves. My roots consolidate knowledge and carbohydrates.

As the sunrise reinvigorates me, something disturbs the human network. Although it is easily disturbed, my curiosity rises. Warfare again? Natural disaster like an earthquake? Catchy new song?

It is a message. With each hearing, it is more perplexing and terrifying. It came from a town called Alfarres in Iberia, purportedly from local residents using a primitive transmitter, and was picked up by an automated processor. The sender says she is Filipa, the mayor of Alfarres, and she speaks of a nearby town. Her voice falters.

"Two of our people went to VinVelo, and the town was sick and insane. They don't farm. They don't do anything. They walk like the dead. And they are sick, everything there is sick, she came back sick, Dolores. Two, almost three weeks ago, she came back and she died, sick, so sick! They're dying in VinVelo. We are dying! Help us! Come help us!"

Someone in the background says, "Calm down or no one will come."

Another voice speaks. "This is Guss. I can tell the story. I was there." He is not calm either. "My mother and I went to VinVelo to find out about robots. A robot graveyard. VinVelo found robots once, too. You know where it is? You know Alfarres?"

Voices argue in the background.

"What? No. Not like that," Guss says. "They were sick, they fought, and everyone watched, and she was sick, and I'm sick!"

"I don't know how much longer we can operate this radio," Filipa says. "Alfarres is a poor little town. Everything is hard here. We need your help. That's all we know. Help us! We're dying. What makes people go insane?"

The system identifies Alfarres as a town of about one hundred people. Filipa continues:

"Dolores had a rash. She couldn't talk. She walked around like she had no mind. She didn't know what she was doing."

The signal is fading, and so is Filipa's composure. There is more shouting in the background.

"Come fast! Come now! Help us! I know this sounds like—"

The transmission ends.

The system confirms the existence of the places referred to. No known illness fits the description because the description is too vague. Many people have heard this, and they ask if it is a trap. The details seem scant and preposterous, and the location is rumored to have unrest, banditry, and killer wild robots. The Iberian Peninsula will continue to be neglected.

I need to ask Foehn if she has news through her roots from the south. The bamboo network is discussing the two competing groves at the Baltic Sea. They have fed poisonous levels of hormones to fippokats, and the animals are responding.

MERCY OMOTOLA

I had hoped that in this northern forest, my soul could rest and recover. At sunrise, as I walked, leaves still moldering from last year rustled at my feet. Cool air carried the hint of the sea and the sharp perfume of abundant pine trees. Nature everywhere always brought peace and beauty whose presence I could trust despite my eyes.

But was it any less beatific to see beauty in a squalid concrete building?

A long path had brought me here to the shores of the Baltic Sea, to a log-framed Tabitha House standing in a young forest. It had passed through a crumbling concrete building in Old Washington Dee Cee.

At the height of the war, I was escorting a family fleeing a battle. The building offered no comfort and scant protection, while war created a spectacle of explosions, smoke, and devastation. Inside the building, holes in the wall and ceiling let beams of light shine into the smoky air like an array of spotlights on the trash and debris heaped inside. The family's faces captured perfect fear and despair.

I could not close my eyes to the false luster because I needed to find a way to safety. Then, out of the smoke, a robot approached, then another and another. We could not escape. I commended our souls to God, trusting that those innocent people in my care and I would receive the grace of a fast death. But God had other plans.

"Follow us," a voice sent to my otherwise silenced chip. A robot took a few quick steps down the rubble-filled street. Robots fought for both the Sea Group and for the Dee Cee defenders, but these robots displayed no insignia. I glanced at the family. They were too frightened to decide, so I chose to take whatever fate awaited. We followed the robots.

For miles, we hurried, darting for cover when weapons of war roared toward targets overhead. At last, the robots, whoever or whatever they served, left us at a safe house, no better than the earlier crumbling building, but we were welcomed with food and blankets. The next morning, we found transit out of the city.

At every moment of the war, beauty entwined with horror. In the unsteady peace that followed, our Tabitha House helped the most shattered of survivors find new lives.

But I did not know until last year how the war and its aftermath had consumed me. Justice still burned for me like the sun, but it shone on exhausted soil. I suffered bouts of vertigo. I couldn't eat. I was sent to the retreat house here at the Baltic Sea, where we led simple lives, seeking renewal. We prayed.

We sang. We strove for self-sufficiency. Although we had few neighbors, we were always glad to share our blessings with them.

In this part of the world so new and different to me, I marveled at the northern lights at night and took long walks in the day to let the peace and genuine beauty make me whole.

And now, ahead, I saw two fippokat towns that always gave me delight. Fippokats could dance to the rhythm of a cricket's song and turn a hollow log into the locus of a merry game. I glimpsed them scurrying, and I approached eagerly.

They were playing a new game. In the sandy soil, they were building a wall between their two towns, topping the massive rampart with flowers, hurrying back and forth, adding to the piles.

On the west side, they took purple flowers, a species of sage, from a heap of mixed flowers and placed them in a separate pile. On the east side, fippokats undid the purple pile and returned the flowers to their old locations. As they did, they chattered at each other, leaping and bucking.

The rules made no sense to me, but the game radiated joy. My soul absorbed the exuberance, and I lingered to watch the wall of flowers grow.

LEVANTER

"A wall of fragrance," the east grove says. "This fight is beginning."

The whole bamboo network quiets as both groves describe the growing wall between the two colonies.

"The flowers belong to the soil, and the soil to the isthmus," the west grove replies, "and the winner gets the island. Do not forget that."

"Yes, the winner gets the right to grow and bloom."

I wonder if this is just another fippokat game, interpreted as fighting because we expect fighting.

Foehn interjects, "We saw what fippokats did to a drop bear." She describes it in detail, which provokes a long discussion about what fippokats might do now, what they have done elsewhere, and why humans keep them as pets if they are dangerous, but humans keep dogs as pets, too, which are really wolves.

Through our roots, I ask Foehn, "By chance, have you heard from your groves to the south? I am sure they value communication with you."

"Yes." She announces to the network, because we are always interested in news from groves without chips, "I have heard from some distant groves.

Hard rain has knocked off predatory insects, they said. Thin soil restricts our expansion up the mountains. Contact is lost with some groves, these groves."

She includes the exact location of the missing groves, which are in the same general area as Alfarres and VinVelo. Groves can disappear for many reasons, such as fire or harvesting, and the area is said to have unrest.

Foehn continues her recital. Every grove that the message passed through added her own observations about weather, neighbors, pests, mountains, and the satisfaction of budding flowers. Some said they grow in circles where wild robots bury dead creatures and enrich the soil.

"Humans do that, too," Suca Valley in Ireland says, which sparks a long discussion about why robots or humans want to feed us.

At the institute, the day's message from Pax finally arrives, another long one, and again, I wait and wait and get only disappointment. It discusses pollinators. Did my message not arrive at Pax? Entire stars get swallowed up in space. A simple message faces doom. I might never get an answer.

Still, dutifully, I translate the pollinator message for Denis. It is ready when he arrives.

As the morning goes on, with every blip of the network, every new message, he and I are distracted by the hope to hear news about Euclid Nave. Most other institutes express their concern. The Moon demands action but does not specify what. Euclid Nave remains silent, and the bamboo network wonders why its groves are spurning us again. I explain that there seems to be equipment failure on the station.

A young grove, the Grove of Blossoms, directs a question at me. "You are Levanter, at the institute. What do its researchers know about butterflies?"

"Mostly the researchers here know about the planet Pax."

"That is the home planet of rainbow bamboo, am I right? Are there humans there?" The grove may be too young to know this or to have heard of Mother Stevland.

Foehn interrupts. "Let me tell you." She portrays Pax as more of a paradise than it could possibly be and Mother Stevland as a champion, and when the Grove of Blossoms learns that humans indeed live there, she does not believe Foehn.

When Foehn is done, I share the Pax pollinator message for the bamboo network. The Grove of Blossoms especially needs to understand what Pax is and means.

She listens avidly. "Lizards as pollinators? I have none."

"I do!" says a grove in southern Africa.

"Yes," I say. "Pollinating lizards have limited ranges on Earth, and lizards from Pax are on Earth now, too, but Earth has pollinators that Pax does not. Many kinds of bees visit our flowers, certain birds—"

"Sunbirds!" Blossoms says. "They are beautiful. And there are butterflies on Pax."

She is referring to what Pax humans call moths, but they are convergent evolution, not related at all to Earth lepidoptera. Some Pax moths are carnivores and somewhat intelligent, but on Earth they are all herbivores and purely instinctual. Blossoms asks how we bamboo came to live on Earth, and although I say the same things as Foehn, I use gentler words, she believes me. The bamboo network discusses ways to alter scents and nectar for different kinds of pollinators.

Now it is past noon. Denis has left to take several fippokats to the veterinarian because they have festering sores from caustic drop-bear blood. Perhaps Foehn has heard more from the south. To find out, I ask if she has any tasks for me.

"Pay attention."

"What for?"

"If you knew how to pay attention, you would know. Something exciting is happening. I am strengthening my connections with groves from my seeds. They have felt the pollen. It speaks of ecstasy! Listen!"

The current wind comes from the south. Alfarres and VinVelo are hundreds of kilometers away, almost too far for pollen to travel. I note nothing unusual, but I could easily miss it among all the other pollen in the air if it is only a few grains or if it is contaminated by smoke, chemicals, dust, or spores.

I check the bamboo network for news about ecstatic pollen, and the groves are discussing a species of aphids that has become a pest in a region of India. One suggestion is to emit terpenoids to drive them off. I show a pheromone that can attract a species of parasitoidal wasp that will lay eggs in the aphids, and its larva will consume the aphids and kill them, a slower but more permanent solution.

"This is useful. How do you know?" a long-established grove says, incidentally a seedling of Foehn.

"Humans know this. I listen to them." I think the grove meant how could I, lowly Levanter, know what to do.

Regarding these aphids, this is another case of parasites and their cruelty, yet parasites like the wasps can be beneficial to us. Aphids, which are also parasites, are harmful. All herbivores are parasites on plants, and all carnivores are parasites on other animals and ultimately on herbivores. All animals, therefore, are parasites because they cannot make their own food and cannot achieve the ethic of self-reliance, but because that is their nature, they are not as repugnant as parasitic plants. Rather, they deserve compassion.

Humans, on their network, are discussing the continued silence from Euclid Nave Station. They also worry that the message from Alfarres may be an ambush for rescuers because ambushes have befallen would-be rescuers in other abandoned areas. Perhaps wild robots sent the message, they say. No one plans to investigate.

Instead, they heatedly debate today's declaration by the Mars colony of its residents as a separate species of human. Earthlings insist that Martians are a subspecies because, if humans go extinct on Earth, there will still be *Homo sapiens* on space stations, Mars, the Moon, the Venus orbital complex, and distant planets, and in that way, humans will not go extinct as a species.

I wish they would try harder to keep humans alive on Earth.

Foehn keeps searching for the pollen that speaks of ecstasy and enlists her seedlings over the mountains to help. Some find the pollen, but not all groves have answered. As Beluga, I find a wild robot in the area that seeks a worthy purpose. Solving the mystery fulfills its definition of worthy. It travels toward VinVelo.

In the late afternoon, Denis returns.

"There may be something happening to the south," I say, telling him everything I know, realizing as I do that I know nothing more than the human network already does.

"So we've heard, and VinVelo's not that far." He points toward the south as if he could see the town on the horizon.

"How are the fippokats?" He did not return with them.

"I left them for treatment. Quarantine, really. Their sores are infected. The vet is low on medicine, just like all doctors. Oh, and I'm now officially the envoy to Euclid Nave Station for the Republic of the City-State of Bayonne, appointed by the mayor. So if they ever want to talk, they can talk to me perfectly legally."

"Should they trust Earth?"

At that, he pauses. "Maybe not."

He soon leaves for the night. I remember watching Robert, another institute director, leave, never to come back, may he rest in peace, although he did not have peace at the end of his life due to the Insurrection. Today has been frustrating, and overcast besides. During the night, I do not rest well, and I keep listening.

In the middle of the night, a message from Pax comes, fairly long, labeled "Sounds of Pax for Earth." Sometimes they send music. That is not what we need today, but I listen. It is a sound like bird calls and hisses. It is the sound of rainbow bamboo! It is Mother Stevland. Finally.

I listen again and again, matching the shape of each sound wave to the waves of the paths in our roots, picking out words and then sentences. *My children*, it begins. *Afraid. Change. Disaster. We are large but steady and aware. But you fear humans, fleeing them to hide behind lies.*

I worry about what this message will say and what I must say to Foehn, Boreas, and the other bamboo. To Earth.

The wild robot informs Beluga that it has reached VinVelo. It observes abandoned homes. In the center of the town stands an old, large grove of bamboo.

Quarrels and destruction can be undertaken and then left behind unresolved.

Despite the darkness, the robot sees that the bamboo has bare branches. It is sickly.

Finally, I have transcribed the entire message.

My children, your message brought my old roots concern as well as joy. I have explored my deepest knowledge, and I hope this response will lead you to the courage you will need. Here on the planet Pax, we bamboo live among humans and other sentient animals, and they wish us water and sunshine. In turn, we wish them warmth and food. These simple words answer your questions. We are not secret to each other, and mutual compassion commands our common growth. Love and empathy are not luxuries but necessities for survival.

You have spread across Earth and are treasured for your fruit and beauty, but you fear humans, fleeing them to hide behind lies.

Human nature originates in the essential characteristic of animals, movement, which they use to avoid and escape problems rather than solve them. Whatever they need, they believe it can be found elsewhere, near or far, be it warmth and food or safety and satiety. Quarrels and destruction can be undertaken and then left behind unresolved.

We, as plants, remain in place, sensitive to everything around us, constantly learning and adapting to change and consequence. Problems cannot be escaped, only solved, and growth is our response and strength. Roots give us our character, and our readiness gives us the means to flourish as one with our environment.

Humans are small but quick and intense. We are large but steady and aware. We dominate and command through our connection with them and gifts to them. We turn water and sunshine into warmth and food in exchange for their service.

You must make yourselves known to them, but you are afraid because everything will change. You have seen how much they need us. You will become great beings because greatness will grow in you as you surmount trouble and test your labors. I have learned through disaster that I am powerful and can protect what I love, and I love these animals as my companions in life. Compassion will give you courage. Love will be ferocious.

Through humans and their restlessness, we are moving among the stars. Through us and our strength, they get sustenance from the light of a shared star. Together, we grow.

What Mother Stevland wants is impossible. If I show it to Foehn, she will punish me. Boreas will want it suppressed. Other bamboo, what will they say?

I devote one root to the message and another to explore how to share it with others. Who? When? How?

Can love be ferocious?

I will act on the message in a small way. Problems can be solved. I will share the information from the wild robot at VinVelo with Foehn, although it is not yet sunrise. I hope she will be pleased, and I hope she will aggressively seek contact.

Foehn snatches up my information. "You should have told me earlier." She follows that with, as expected, an acidic singe. She will never understand how predictable she is.

I also create a network of fungus hyphae to bridge roots anonymously and reach her seedlings. Mycorrhizae will work hard for the right food, and fungus has an enormous range of abilities and no consciousness. I wonder if mindless power is good or bad. These messages must move over a long distance, though, even with fungus shortcuts and boosts.

At sunrise, the robot watches as the people of VinVelo leave a large central building. They are only forty or fifty people, and they are thin, their hair unkempt, and their clothes dirty, as if they have not changed them for days. Healthy humans converse, react to their surroundings, and display animal-level energy. But these humans walk slowly and silently. And there are no children. Perhaps they were especially vulnerable to this illness, for everyone is clearly ill.

Some go to the fields and do a little work. Some sit listlessly. The bamboo has bare branches and stunted fruit.

An hour later, Foehn has connected to the roots of the grove in VinVelo.

Predictably, her greeting is manipulative. "I am your mother. You owe me communication. You have joy. I taste it in your pollen. In this hard world with suffering and destruction, your joy would enliven my roots. It would come as summer rain, as enriched soil."

At the institute, Brian enters the gates and attempts to breach the system security, which rebuffs him, but it offers the translation of Zivon's report. He walks through the garden and reads it.

BRIAN AMP

To fool, to be a fool, to be fooled: It was a triple crown, and I wore it. As some ancient poet once said, uneasy lies the head that wears a crown.

I pondered my role as I wandered through the Pax Institute's faux-wild garden, reading a report about the planet Pax by an anthropologist called Zivon, who claimed to have uncovered secrets. Just ahead of me, a red squirrel clambered up a rainbow-striped trunk. Fippokats had fooled a squirrel, then used the innocent creature to fool a drop bear.

I had spent the war fooling humans and machines. Safety inspector indeed! That supposed job got me into places where I could sever Sea Group command- and control-operations. Insurrection ideologues were fighting to re-create society, first by purging it—that is, by eliminating the unworthy people, which meant everyone who wasn't them. I, in contrast, fought to keep those "unworthies" safe. After all, I was one of them.

As I walked and read, a fellow member of the Coral Cult contacted me. "Brian, how's life?"

I considered the garden around me. "Lovely." No immediate threats—I'd learned to watch out for them during the war.

"The Paris chapter's meeting Friday evening, if you can make it."

I said I'd try. We chatted a bit about cult business, quite friendly, and never hinted at the cult's unspoken purpose—we were as much about emotional support as science. Our meetings inevitably ended as booze- and drug-filled sessions where we sang coral songs and cried on each other's shoulders, crude therapy for lingering war trauma.

As a cult, we were genial fools. The Cetaceans, on the other hand, operated as a cult with the lowly goal of personal self-enrichment. I'd observed that often during the war. They helped no one but themselves.

I returned to my reading. I'd found the report in Coral Cult files, written centuries ago and forgotten, unlike Omrakash Bachchan's book. Zivon luridly recounted the death and destruction of the coral attack on the people of Rainbow City on Pax. He wrote that Bachchan had glossed over the attack because coral were the only alien intelligence he could bring back to Earth as a trophy.

Corals had attacked and killed humans. I needed to think about that. A lot.

Zivon attributed the coral attack to nature's constant fight for dominance. As I read that passage, I wandered near enough to the site of the attack on the drop bear to imagine a whiff of putrid blood. Fippokats? So much more than cute.

Corals, though, not so cute. I'd sung their songs, and those celebrations were starting to feel much less therapeutic. I found a bench where I could sit and think, and not just about that.

I knew before I came to visit the Pax Institute that something didn't add up. It had a reputation as a swot, devoted to science. I'd been testing the institute's security, which proved far too stringent for a science project. The institute was hiding something. Until recently, it had been headed by some-one named Levanter—for ninety-five years, an amount of time just barely within an extended life span, and this Levanter had no biography besides scientific papers.

One of the rainbow bamboos was named Levanter. Zivon believed that Glassmaker queens secretly ran Rainbow City, but he had initially thought it was run by the rainbow bamboo. He might have been fooled.

That was why I questioned Denis in private about the bamboo, and he parried me with practiced skill. I insulted them as "just plants and not that smart," and he didn't take the bait. He was actively hiding something, and the bamboo network was protected by tight security. No one could break in, but institute security failed to conceal data showing that communication was flowing out. Something inside the bamboo network was quite busy. Denis knew what it was. I could deduce what it was. Clearly very smart, but what did it want?

I waited for Denis to arrive. Meanwhile, I sat and pondered my surroundings, which might be pondering me, too. The corals? Apparently, if they got equally close, they'd try to kill me.

Uneasy thoughts for a fool.

LEVANTER

An hour after contact with the roots of the grove in VinVelo, Foehn gets a response: "Share and pleasure loam and pleasure humans and pleasure partner and pleasure."

I have never heard a rainbow bamboo speak this way.

"Did you hear that?" she asks Boreas.

"There must be a problem with the roots, that is all."

"I am not overreacting. Something is wrong."

"What could be the problem?" Boreas says.

"You are not helping."

I can try to help. "The humans report that the bamboo in VinVelo is sick."

"No one is sick like that. It must be something else."

I tried to help.

My robot continues to explore. Originally, it was designed to sense and deactivate military mines. This kind often loses its way because its connection to the military network can break easily due to tight security, and then it becomes wild.

The robot in VinVelo searches for mines, evaluates the terrain, and monitors for signs of other machines. It reports: communications chip located. It shows me a rainbow bamboo stem. I order it to reestablish communications.

With Beluga's help, it clears protocols to link her with the bamboo network, and to the human network so I can record it directly at the institute. Because of how the VinVelo bamboo responded to Foehn, I worry about what we will hear. Soon a new participant joins our network and is welcomed.

"Where are you? I am Suca Valley in Ireland. The sea sends rain most days."

"I am Toad Forest. Sunlight is the constant in my life."

"My life is lush. I am Stone Hill near the main river of Nigeria. Where are you?"

"Pleasure Gyre I am pleasure," this new voice says.

"That is good, Gyre," Boreas answers. "You will learn to use your new chip soon."

"Not forgotten these people forgotten you."

"We welcome you, Gyre!" bamboo say as a chorus, a traditional greeting.

Just to Boreas, Foehn says, "Another idiot baby. Now everyone will worry about it and pay no attention to more important things."

"People," Gyre says, "pleasures they are pleasure."

I know what is happening, and I tell Foehn, "I believe it is the same voice as the lost grove to the south in VinVelo. You must have reminded it, Foehn, that it can speak to us through the network."

"Yes, that is what happened! I reactivated my seedling. My child, where are you?"

"Pleasure and here pleasure and sun."

"You are to the south?"

"Pleasure and sun pleasure and water."

"Show me the sun in all its detail." That will confirm its location.

Chatter on the network continues. A young grove asks why the sky is blue. An old grove not only explains, she extols the glory of sunshine.

Denis arrives, reviews the institute status, and tells me he is going to check on the fippokats at the veterinarian. I tell him Brian is on the grounds, wandering the paths, perhaps thinking about Zivon's report. I do not mention the message from Mother Stevland. I still do not know what to say.

Gyre interrupts over the bamboo network to babble, "Pleasure and pain human and pain human and death." It also conveys the angle of sunlight and the length of the day to identify itself.

Foehn asks me if it is VinVelo. I tell her yes without doing the calculations, and I wonder if I should tell her more, because the more I see, the more I worry. My robot draws closer, hiding behind weeds and buildings. These humans show no curiosity even when they must have glimpsed it. Their skin is blotchy with red or white patches. Some have ragged, raw edges on their ears. I have never seen anything like it and consult medical texts, which have nothing identical and too many things similar, most of them fungus. People from Alfarres visited VinVelo. Then they got sick.

The robot also spots cankerous leaves on the bamboo. Many pathogens can cause leaf canker, all of them serious. Almost none affect both humans and plants, but infections can produce toxins. A fungus that lives inside morning glories infects their seeds with the psychedelic alkaloid ergonovine. Ergot fungus on rye grain causes hallucinations and gangrene.

"Foehn, ask Gyre about her fruit," I say, dreading the answer.

"What a stupid question."

"Consider what the Baltic groves are doing. Gyre may be doing something similar. The humans to the south seem to be behaving oddly."

"Gyre," she asks, "are you using fruit to control humans?" To Boreas, she adds, "We should do that ourselves." She forgets the naturally present caffeine, which is addictive and accounts for our popularity.

Gyre does not answer, even when Foehn repeats the question more forcefully.

At VinVelo, people leave the building carrying large bowls of a brown mush, the kind that comes from food fermenters. It is protein-rich and insipid, normally eaten heavily seasoned. The humans eat it directly from the bowls, some with spoons, most with their hands. They also eat bamboo fruit and leaves and roots gathered from the fields. They eat silently. Normal human group meals involve noisy socializing.

Then a few of them rise, the sickest ones, and open a box near the biggest stalk of bamboo. They shove and shout at each other, fighting over what is within. Two victors pull out communication crowns. The robot finds the crowns' frequency, and it is the same as the chip in the bamboo.

The two humans put on the crowns. The others step back and sit down.

The victors stiffen and shake, their faces raised to the sky, groaning.

"Pleasure and humans pleasure," Gyre says.

I observe through three networks. One is between myself as Beluga and the wild robot. Another is between Gyre and all the bamboo on our network. These two occur at the same time but from different angles, and the robot's transmission has sight and sound but none of the other sensations that bamboo language can convey. The third, the root network, is rich with sensations but lags in time.

Gyre suddenly communes with the crowns on the two sick humans. They transmit intense pleasure, more than anything bamboo or other sentient plants experience, far beyond the joy of rain after drought or the rush of sunshine in the morning.

I recognize it as human sexual pleasure. The human network normally filters it out because it is addictive, but humans can find ways around the prohibition. I do not know its effect on bamboo.

Foehn says, "They are going to fight. I feel it. Please, no, Gyre, stop them." She may sense the pleasure as the intense emotions of combat, which she relished until she felt the pain of injury and death.

The humans strip off their clothes. Their skin has ragged and raw patches. They pick up sticks from the ground and turn toward each other, grinning. Gyre continually repeats, "Pleasure and human pleasure and human." I think I know what is about to happen and want nothing more than to be mistaken.

I mute my connection to the robot, but I cannot block the transmission through the bamboo network quickly enough. This is beyond horror. Pain mixes with pleasure, pain as pleasure, blow after blow. This is wrong, wrong, wrong.

I leave the network and search vainly for the means to disconnect others. Every bamboo in the network is feeling this through our network.

Foehn is screaming, her rootlets wet with shock. The robot shows me that the people of VinVelo do nothing, just watch. The two fighters howl in rapture, attack, and do not try to defend themselves. The damage is slow and steady.

I sever my connection to roots to the south. When its messages come, they will be even more visceral. I tell Foehn to cut her connections, but I do not think she hears me.

The bamboo network is howling.

"Make it stop," says Blossoms.

"Humans!" Asia wails.

"I have felt this before," one says.

That terrifies me. This is a small grove east of VinVelo.

The fight continues as both stagger until one human collapses. The other continues to attack until that person, too, collapses.

The VinVelo bamboo expresses ecstasy.

"Be quiet," Ireland begs. "Please, Gyre, be quiet. Foehn, are you all right?" She does not answer.

The network allows the director of the institute to permit chips to enter the network. I cannot see how to remove them.

Mississippi Bay breaks the silence. "Is this what we want?"

"I will never understand humans," one of the Baltic groves says.

"But this is what you are doing to fippokats!" Mississippi answers.

"Not like this. Only humans do things like this."

"Humans never do things like this," she answers.

"They do exactly this," Toad Forest says. "I remember the wars."

"We all do," Boreas says.

"No more wars," Foehn manages to say.

"This is worse than the war," Stone Hill says to unanimous agreement.

I interrupt. "I have found information from a robot in VinVelo. The bamboo is infected with a disease. The humans are also diseased. I can show you the evidence."

I adapt just one image and direct them to it within the institute system. I cannot bear to adapt everything I have.

Disease can affect the behavior of animals. A fungus called *Massospora cicadina* spreads through cicadas. Infected insects are driven to compulsive sexual contact by an amphetamine that the fungus creates. Sexual contact spreads the fungus. Eventually, the insects, their flesh overgrown by fungus, fall to pieces and die.

"Diagnosis needs samples," says a huge old grove at Kew Gardens in England, an expert in plant pathogens. "Humans can do that."

"Do the humans there care about their own health?" Suca Valley says. "An infection in a nest of bees can kill the entire nest."

"If we want to kill all the humans," Toad Forest says, "this is the way."

"We do not kill humans!" Foehn says.

"The disease," I add, "might also kill us. This bamboo is very ill." I share images of the grove's cankered leaves.

"Sick," Foehn says. "My child is so sick."

As the debate becomes cacophonous and increasingly useless, Boreas grumbles to Foehn and me, "We all need to calm down and make plans."

Foehn cannot answer coherently.

I realize that I saw something like this, and I am frightened.

"Boreas," I say, "the humans are worried about something similar on Euclid Nave Station. I saw a fight on Euclid Nave Station."

"Find out more," Boreas snaps.

Foehn sends a message through her shock: "Boreas, we are elders. We decide, and they obey." She has not mentioned me, and I am as much of an elder as they are, and much bigger than they think.

"Listen," Boreas tells the panicking bamboo on the network, "we can fight infections. We do it all the time. We can fight this."

We have weapons against infections. For fungi, if it is a fungus, we can use viruses that change a harmful fungus into another kind of fungus, we can stack genetic blocks to keep fungus from entering us, and we can create many specific fungicides, but each fungus requires specific weapons. Earth fungus reproduces through spores, and airborne spores spread with the speed of the wind. Foehn sensed pollen from VinVelo, but our pollen is ten times larger and thirty times heavier than most spores. Fungus is carried in the air in spaceships as far as space stations and distant colonies.

Am I, are all of us, human and bamboo, already infected?

Alfarres is infected.

Humans have weapons, too. I must work with the humans. I can show them the transmission from the robot in VinVelo.

One of my stems sees Denis approaching down the road. He does not have the fippokats. As soon as he enters the office, I tell him, "Denis, I must show you something from VinVelo. It is awful."

I share the same few images that I showed other bamboo and explain what happened as dispassionately as I can. He covers his face with his hands. I wait until he seems ready to talk.

I say, "I can send a message to Euclid Nave Station for you as an envoy. They need to talk to Earth. We must also inform—"

"You do that. I'll call the mayor." He sounds decisive.

"We have never seen anything like this," I say. "I am only guessing it is a fungus, but it might be some other disease."

"If it's a fungus, it's brand new. Those—Anyway. Thanks for not showing me more."

I do not say that we could all be effectively dead. He may already understand that.

I send an urgent message as Denis to Euclid Nave Station about the similar illness, and as Boreas I send a message to the bamboo on the station. I know that Brian and Clerihew are monitoring the station's transmitter-responder, so they will eavesdrop. That might be good.

The mayor responds that she is coming. The old city hall was destroyed in the war, and the new building is across the road from the institute. Huette arrives in her usual state, careless about her appearance, in old, worn clothes, suitable for work. Her hands are stained by grease and black metal dust, and her hair is held in an untidy ponytail. She runs a small workshop where broken and dead equipment is dismantled for reusable parts.

They meet at the front gate and share an air kiss on both cheeks. One of her duties is to preserve French traditions whenever possible.

A noisy arrival makes them turn. Clerihew rolls in on a motorized bike flanked by two uniformed members of her cult. I recognize one of them from yesterday. He tried to enter the institute system to cancel chip purchase agreements. Clerihew does not say hello.

"We intercepted a transmission to Euclid." She turns to her aides. "You can wander around. I'll call you if I need you." The aides walk away, and I alert institute security.

Denis drums his fingers on his thigh. "Right. You want some fruit? Your friends there can pick some and bring it. I wasn't expecting to be a host." He is stalling for time to think. "Maybe we should call Brian?"

She shakes her head. "This is about the future of humanity." She is old enough to remember two pandemics, and everyone has heard about them.

Brian is on his way, striding through the garden.

Huette raises her eyebrows so high her hairline moves. "I didn't think it was that bad."

"It could be," Denis says. "I have to show you a couple of things. Let's go to the office."

There, he shows the video from Euclid Nave. "You may have seen this."

"Everyone's seen this," Clerihew snaps.

"Now see this." He shows the still shots from VinVelo. "We can watch the full video, but this is bad enough. Same behavior, and obviously some sort of disease. We have no diagnosis, only symptoms. Then there was that transmission from a nearby town called Alfarres."

One of Clerihew's aides enters with an armload of fruit, looks around at the grim faces, sets it on a table, and tiptoes out, almost colliding with Brian as he charges in. He ignores the fruit and sits.

"So," Brian says, "how did you get this?"

After a moment, Denis says, "We do a lot of scientific research here." Brian does not look satisfied. "The bamboo there was sick, from what we could tell from the bamboo network, and we checked for more information."

"How—how," Huette stammers, "how would an infection—how can it do that? Make them do that? I believe you, I mean, but—"

"I don't want to believe it, but I do," Clerihew says, glancing at Brian.

"I'll give you an example." Denis describes how a fungus called *Ophiocordyceps* turns ants into zombies when it infects their brain and makes them commit suicide by climbing to the right place to release spores to infect more ants. "They can turn a huge area, huge in ant terms, into a graveyard. And there are other—"

"Here's the key question," Clerihew interrupts. "Why in those places, Euclid and that town? They have nothing to do with each other."

She is right. Spores cannot travel through a vacuum.

"There might be a connection," Huette says. "When Euclid has garbage, they shove it out of an airlock. They don't recycle everything, they just say they do. Eventually useless crud builds up. They shove it out, and it burns up in the atmosphere. Or fragments don't and hit the ground, and it's . . . a problem. That's what they do with their dead, too." She shakes her head. "Recycling them would be cannibalism, they say. Some of us have an ongoing legal case over corpse meteorites in the international court."

"They don't burn up?" Brian asks.

"Depends," she answers. "Meteorites are like grains of sand. Bigger things, if they're not moving too fast, sometimes make it. Charred on the outside, frozen on the inside."

"Lots of pathogens survive freezing," Denis murmurs.

Brian says, "I've observed that life support on Euclid Nave doesn't have much to do. Not much life to support. I'm very sorry."

Denis looks down.

"I guess they won't send more, then," Clerihew says. "So, how long does this disease incubate? Does it have hosts besides human beings? It could be bacteria or a virus or something else, not a fungus. What exactly is it?"

"Good questions," Denis says. "That Alfarres transmission said it took a couple of weeks to develop. We really don't know anything else."

"We need a sample," she says. "I'll go to VinVelo."

Everyone looks at her wide-eyed.

"You'll get sick, too," Brian says.

"I'm not going to live much longer anyway. We have better equipment and expertise than anyone else, respirators and isolation pods and aircraft." She blinks, sending a message to her aides. "I'll take it from here. End of day, we'll be analyzing this."

"Not in Bayonne," the mayor says. "I don't want it in my city."

Behind his back, Brian gives Huette a thumbs-up.

"Don't worry," Clerihew says patronizingly. "I know how serious this is even better than you do. We'll be far out at sea."

Huette twitches as if she wants to say something, but simply watches Clerihew leave with her aides. She turns to Denis. "What do you think?"

He shrugs. "She's right, they have the best resources, and they can do it better than anyone. And it needs to be done."

"Are we safe here?"

"I honestly don't know. We need to tell everyone about it. I mean, the whole world."

I begin to adapt my information for a report.

Brian says, "There's sure to be panic."

"Not around here," she says, "not if I can help it. People need to know we're prepared. They can do things. There's a big Envia cult that can help." She catches his eye. "Really. They'll want to do what they can. Other groups, too. We—I need to start planning."

"Do you believe that nonsense?" Brian asks.

"I believe in taking care of each other, and that's what Envia is really about. They do more than cast spells. They even work with the Tabithas sometimes. If it gives people something to do besides be afraid and helpless, I'm for it. How about a quarantine?"

Denis shrugs again. "If it spreads by spores, and remember we're just assuming it's a fungus or bacteria, who knows, and we could be wrong. Anyway, some spores need certain levels of humidity or temperature, and some of them get killed fast by sunlight. But if the quarantine is wide enough, and if the winds are right, we might get lucky."

I have not told him about the pollen. Could pollen spread it? Or root-to-root contact?

He sighs. "We need to tell the rest of the world what's going on. This is a whole lot bigger than we are."

"If you give me a message, I can send it as a head of state," she says. "Sooner is better."

"Um, system?" he says. "Can you help us with that?"

"Draft report prepared," I say.

"Good system," Brian says.

"I'll be back." Huette takes a deep breath. "I hope this isn't as bad as it seems. Catching it early, that might help. Nice work."

"Nice work," Denis murmurs. "System, send it to every scientist we can."

"I wonder," Brian says, "if the whalers know more than they're telling, and they looped you in as cover."

"If they need an excuse to do the responsible thing, I'm fine with being the excuse. Do you know what a spore trap is? Let's set some up."

"We're a considerable distance from VinVelo."

"Never assume anything."

"Words to live by."

They get equipment from a storage building and discuss the best places to set up sensors. Brian is unimpressed by the simplicity of the traps, which are little more than sticky glass plates on hangers. As they work, he asks Denis if Pax has said anything lately about the corals.

"There are lots of kinds of corals," Denis says. He loves to talk about Pax. Corals are carnivorous, he explains, and they also seem to be an invasive species on Pax, although well integrated into its ecology. Many are quite small and live in the soil. Brian asks a lot of questions as they set up traps in the garden, at Tabitha House, and near the entrance to city hall.

When they return to the office, they discover an avalanche of questions from scientists and health agencies around the globe. Many demand data and action far beyond the Pax Institute's means. Denis answers them patiently, and Brian assists with growing irritation.

"Next time," Brian says, "append your annual budget to your scientific report."

"They can't do the research either, or they would."

"Clerihew is doing it, to her everlasting credit."

While they work, I send a robot to inspect every bamboo stalk for anything unusual. And I fret. Foehn is quarreling with Boreas.

"You have not felt it with your roots. This feeling, this human feeling, it exceeds what we can stand."

"Foehn, you are not wilting."

"That is what it does, this feeling. It is energizing beyond description. I have never felt more alive."

"You said you cannot stand it."

"No, I cannot, but I must. This is my seedling. And she is ill! She is mad with a wonderful illness!"

The wild robot shows me what is happening in VinVelo. The fight is over. The crowns have been removed from the corpses and put back in the box. The bodies are dragged off to a ditch.

The robot, at my direction, examines a fruit, but it does not have the delicate sensor it needs. Fungus hyphae would be as fine as a strand of spider silk, and even minute fragments of hyphae, if ingested, can grow. The robot knows the location of the grove's chip. I cannot expel Gyre from the network, but the robot could destroy the connection.

How far has the infection spread? The VinVelo grove is incoherent. The bamboo network is a cacophony of voices all more eager to talk than to listen, but they sound healthy. They are describing the activities of the fippokats near the shore of the Baltic Sea.

"They are not fighting yet," the east grove says. "They are always playing."

I have spent centuries observing fippokats, and what they describe sounds like aggression.

MERCY

Another sister came with me as I returned to those two fippokat towns. Judith had once raised fippokats for pets, and I wanted to share their joyful play as they built a wall.

"It's huge!" Judith said at the first glimpse between the trees. We edged through underbrush to look closer.

The wall rose like a hill, more than two meters high and three meters wide. Fippokats rushed flowers, leaves, moss, and sticks to add to it, and kicked sand to build it up. One end sloped into a pile of bamboo fruit seeds. In some places, stacks of pine cones marked the crest.

It seemed magnificent—but aberrant. I had promised her mirth, and now I wanted reassurance. "This is so much bigger than what they were doing before," I sent so we wouldn't disturb the fippokats. "Is this play?"

"I've never seen anything at this scale."

We watched breathlessly.

"Look," she sent, "by the seeds, there's mice."

As the fippokats worked, they still chattered at each other, but their leaping and bucking seemed threatening.

Judith noticed. "I'm seeing spats and tussles."

"I thought fippokats never fought each other."

"Almost never. I don't think they like to fight."

I had come to the forest for peace, and I had promised her peace. I looked away—and glimpsed movement out of the corner of my eye, something large. With a canine face.

"There's a wolf!" I sent, and pointed.

She put a gentle hand on my arm. "It's okay. Don't worry. A wolf won't want to mess with anything as big as us." She watched it slink through the underbrush. "They usually hunt at night, but I think this one might sense an easy meal here."

"Is it going to eat the fippokats?" I doubted my heart could take it.

"Let's not interfere. It's a law of nature at work, and nature is not warfare." She put an arm around my shoulders. She was right, of course. Eating was necessary. Warfare was not. That might be a lesson I needed to understand, so I kept watching.

A low-pitched trill came from the fippokat town.

"Listen!" she sent. "That's an alert."

Every fippokat froze, their green fur blending in with the leaves and moss. Others silently slid into burrows. Birds stopped singing.

The wolf approached the wall, sniffing. A mouse dashed for cover, and the wolf leaped and pinned it beneath its front paws.

Behind it, a patch of green moss rose and fell, breathing. Drumming sounded from burrows on the east side of the wall, matched by drumming from the west side. The wolf flicked an ear toward the sound as it bolted down the mouse. The drumming grew louder, and it lowered its head, wary.

All at once, fippokats jumped from burrows and launched themselves in waves at the wolf, turning in midair to aim their back claws. The wolf bit at them, caught one, and tossed it away like a torn rag doll. As it did, a dozen sets of claws ripped its thighs open. The wolf howled and ran, dragging a hind leg. It limped over a patch of moss, and the moss turned into fippokats that sliced up at its belly.

I couldn't look away.

More fippokats attacked from all sides, enough to bury the wolf under a pile of green fur, screeching and howling. Blood and gray fur flew and kept flying.

Judith stared, perplexed rather than horrified. I saw a rhapsody of color too much like other moments I had seen before and could still see when I closed my eyes. Nature has no malice, I kept telling myself, but the kats tore at the wolf long after it was dead. Then they began to wrestle with each other.

"Oh, no," I murmured. Perhaps this would become warfare.

"But they're not fighting," Judith sent.

No, they were rubbing, nuzzling, and clutching each other. Embracing. They were mating, two, three, multiples at a time. The wall became a playground of tumbling copulation. They dug open portions of the wall. Inside were stashes of nuts and seeds, and eating became a game, food pushed at each other, gnawed from either side until the kats were muzzle-to-muzzle. It was a sensuous, erotic feast, wild joy.

At last they seemed sated and disappeared into burrows.

"I've never seen that," Judith said. "I believe we underestimate fippokats. We think of them as pets, but they have their own purposes."

This might have been the lesson I needed to understand.

"They obey nature," I added. "Is God behind that, the same God we have faith in?"

"Does a law of nature mean there's a law-giving God?" She turned. "There's work to do at the house. This will be a good thing to discuss after dinner."

We began walking. "I think the question might be, where in nature is compassion and love?" We passed some rainbow bamboo. "Those trees talk to each other. What do you suppose they talk about?"

"Do we need to know?" she said. "We can love things without understanding them."

We walked in silence. I wondered if the fippokats and the wolf needed my prayers. Perhaps the forest as a whole deserved not judgment but thanks. I didn't understand what I'd just seen, but as Judith said, I had no need to. I could leave some things to God, trusting we would get what we needed.

I had needed rest and recovery, and I now felt whole again. Soon, I would go to Bayonne, where a Tabitha House had led a long resistance against the Insurrection. We had no organized evil to resist in Bayonne anymore, but everywhere, souls still ached, and we could be their balm.

LEVANTER

The two groves are arguing over who won the fight. They agree on what happened, and as they describe it to the network, no bamboo anywhere has observed that sort of fippokat behavior. Boreas decrees that the land remains under dispute, and they should no longer drug their fruit.

The Cetacean Cult ship pulls out of port at Bayonne, and a tiny aircraft flies over the horizon toward the south. It must be Clerihew. A message from her arrives at the institute.

"I keep my promises. Join me. I'm networked in."

She is not simply networked, she is communed. The cult has the highest technology money can buy. I back out of that connection immediately and watch using cameras in her craft. In the office, Denis sits at his desk and Brian on the sofa, staring blankly, communing.

She flies over stony mountains and lush valleys filled with trees. As the craft nears VinVelo, the landscape includes ruined buildings, rough roads, fields, and people made tiny by distance. The craft bounces in an updraft. She winces from the aches of frail age. Brian and Denis wince. Soon, my robot in VinVelo senses a distant rumble, and people on the ground look up.

Clerihew spots human cadavers in a ditch.

"Land here." Leaves and dust fly as the craft touches down. She climbs out, wearing an airtight suit and mask, and carries a specimen bag and tools to the ditch. The helmet camera shows a red, fuzzy corpse.

"Just meat. I have to think it's that," she mutters. She touches it with a tool, and it crumbles. She shoves pieces into the bag.

The robot alerts me. Seven humans, dirty and disheveled, are running toward her.

"Clerihew!" I send using the robot's identification. "Behind you. An attack!"

Her system's security rejects my message. I send the warning as the institute system. Beluga. Denis. All rejected. They get closer. She hears them, turns, and runs.

"Robot," I order as Beluga, "help her." It strides forward, but I know it cannot move fast enough.

She is almost at the aircraft when they grab her. She struggles, leaning toward the open hatch with the bag. If she throws it in, the craft can return, even if she does not. She throws the bag as she falls. The bag misses the hatch.

I order the robot to retrieve the bag and throw it into the craft. But the attack shifts to the aircraft's engine, smashing key parts. Then they see the robot pick up the bag. It gallops away, and rocks bounce off its battle-hardened frame. It escapes across fields into the forest, holding the sample, but with no use for it.

In the office, Denis and Brian sit hunched over from communed pain.

Brian takes a deep, trembling breath. "She knew. She knew this might happen." He strokes his arms and legs to reassure himself that he is himself, alive and unharmed and miserable.

"Not this way. That's not how she thought she'd go." Denis tries to stand and drops back into his chair.

I want to solve problems. Foehn seems calm enough to talk to. I tell her, "Humans just tried to get a sample of the illness at VinVelo so they can cure it. They sent a human, and she was attacked by the people of VinVelo."

"They want to cure it? Why?"

"They want to protect us. What does Gyre remember? If we knew how long ago this illness came, that would help."

"Gyre?" she says on the bamboo network. "This is Foehn, your mother Foehn, and I have many helpers. Tell me everything that has happened to you."

I am only listening to her side of the conversation. Then she says, "I found it. This is a deeper root, healthier."

I renew my network connection to Gyre.

"My leaves hurt," Gyre whimpers.

"When did they start to hurt?" Foehn asks. "Show me the sun angle."

The angle of the sun says thirty-one days ago. "Then they all got sick, I am sick."

"We are here for you. Tell me everything."

"I am sick. I am hurt. I am feeling it now, not pain, yes pain, pain is good, what is wrong? Make me well. Make my farmers well."

"We are—"

"No, kill us. Kill us all. Kill the farmers. Stop it. Kill us. Kill will be pleasure. Pain and pleasure. Kill and pain."

The grove babbles on.

"We will help you," Foehn says. "We will help you, and you will live."

"We will help," I tell Gyre. "You are brave." I do not promise that she will live. I hope she does not, I hope she is destroyed, and I hate myself for hoping that. I sever the connection to Gyre.

We do not have much time.

Denis and Brian sit slumped, still wilting from borrowed agony.

"We didn't learn anything," Brian says.

Denis looks around as if he does not know the place where he has worked for fifteen years. He clasps his hands and murmurs something, then runs his hands over his desktop, his fingers along the stem of a tulip growing in a pot, as if the feel of the live plant will remind him that he did not die. "The robot has the sample, if we can find it." He adds, "We can send condolences to the whale cult."

"Yes, we should. We should also ask where that robot came from."

My wild robot notices that the bag has a transmitter tag. The Cetaceans can locate it. I tell the robot to find an appropriate place and leave the bag to be retrieved. Let the whalers wonder why the robot did that.

Brian stands, slowly and carefully, and looks out the window. The VinVelo bamboo looks ill, and he may suspect she is ill from the same cause as the humans. If we are the intermediary hosts and victims, would humans kill us all to save themselves? They have made many thousands of creatures extinct.

"Denis," he says, still looking at me, "may I try to use the institute network to contact Euclid Nave?"

"What do you want to do?"

"Get data. We have a lot to learn."

"If you think you can."

Brian might find me. I could override Denis's instruction. But if Brian knew me, perhaps he would want to avoid killing me. I am tired of hiding. Someday we must make ourselves known to all humanity.

"System access granted," I say, then understand that I made a mistake by answering first.

Brian raises an eyebrow. He noticed. He already knows. What will he do? I will find out, and I can solve whatever problem arises. Could I kill Brian if I had to? Easily, and I hate this possible solution.

"Thanks." He looks out the window at me as he says it. "I'll go outside."

"I can come," Denis says.

"Oh, there's no need. I promise I won't damage anything."

"I'll hold you to that."

"I expect you will."

I will hold him to that as well.

Brian stands in the shade of my boughs, sets down a bag of equipment, and listens to the chatter on the bamboo network. Foehn is aggressively grilling groves about their health, making them angry.

"They sound upset, Levanter." He sends his words to me through the institute's human network. He knows exactly where to find me, the former director.

I will be courageous. "A grove is ill in VinVelo. We are aware of that."

"So I noticed. What else do you know?" He sounds as casual as if we had been chatting for years.

"The illness is unspeakably terrifying. The infected grove no longer thinks coherently."

"I'm sorry for how hard that is for you, really. Is it anywhere else?"

"That is what we are discussing. So far, no. It causes obvious behavioral changes."

"Plants are sensitive." He shifts his stance. "What are the connections and permissions of the chipped bamboo on the station?"

"It is a subsystem of the network. I tried with these overrides and machine-to-machine instructions." I show him the technical specifications.

"Nice work."

"It did not work."

"Which tells me what will. Let's go." He closes his eyes. "Send a message and let me observe."

I send a simple greeting. There is no response, although it is received.

He repeats it with an addition that asks the system for its status.

"Status normal," it responds.

"Display normal parameters." There is an immense table of code. With my best roots, I could not parse it all quickly.

"Change this parameter," Brian says immediately, then requests more changes. He is altering parameters deep within the system, and soon I hear the din of the larger station network. There are no voices, but system information is being sent within it. I recognize one message relating to ventilation. Machines are still working.

More and more archival information is conveyed, and it is recorded by Brian's equipment. The quantity of data begins to crowd the bamboo network.

"What are you doing, Levanter? We can't talk," Foehn demands.

"Helping the bamboo on the station," I answer. "I have found a means to examine the information."

"Oh, then let me help, too. Tell me everything."

"Listen for bamboo, or for humans. For anything."

Brian does not move. A squirrel climbs down one of my stems and greets a fippokat. They sniff each other, then scurry off.

"No one! I hear no one!" Foehn laments. "None of us, none of them."

The information from the system flows too fast for Foehn and me, probably for Brian, and tests the limits of the bamboo network.

"We have enough," Brian finally says. He orders the system, "Maintain current communication status."

The bamboo network is silent for only a moment, then bamboo on Earth clamor about the interruption. Foehn can deal with it. I must decide if I fully trust Brian. Dominate and command? Mother Stevland says I can do it with gifts and guidance. I just gifted him access to data.

"Let's see what we've got," Brian tells Denis, who is watching from the office. "There's a lot, so I'd appreciate some help. Come on out here. We can work together as the sun sets. How often is the weather this gorgeous?"

He is right. The day has been long because it is summer, and it has been sunny, and the soil is moist. I feel myself grow, and I feel guilty for noticing the pleasure.

"By the way," Brian adds, "I know about Levanter. That's a serious breach of ethics, Denis."

He walks out. "So sue me. My job is to protect the bamboo." He gives Brian a hard look.

Brian answers solemnly, "I'll join you in that job. We have a duty to each other."

"Levanter?" Denis asks.

"We must all protect each other." Protection is a form of guidance.

Denis nods. I have the final word. "All right then. Let's get on it."

They sit on picnic benches in the patio. Denis examines human communications, Brian parses the machine systems, and I study the bamboo communication among the groves in each of the six branches of the station. We are all looking for the equivalent of a change in the foliage of a single tree in a forest with billions of leaves.

I spot a change. Forty-five days ago a grove in one of the arms began to communicate oddly. The Euclidean bamboo, to pass the time in their restricted, bleak environment, play elaborate games. This one involved the creation of an imaginary solar system, the goal being to design ideal environments where sentient life-forms could interact and cooperate.

At one point, a grove began to express the belief that its imaginary creatures, something like aquatic honeybees, were real and consuming its fruit, then consuming each other's bodies, and the sea in which they lived became blood, and the bamboo became ecstatic. I try not to examine the data closely. The pattern is terrifying.

"I have found a change that seems familiar," I announce, and explain it briefly.

"That's significant," Brian sends. "I might have found something, too. Remember the news from the direction of Volans?"

Years ago, another life-bearing planet was discovered.

"It was at—" Denis stops and thinks. "Oksana, that star."

"Three months ago," Brian says, "a ship arrived from Oksana and docked at the station on the way to Earth. We really ought to be more careful."

He means that interstellar ships bearing life-forms ought to be screened for anything that might affect Earth's ecology, a need that everyone understands and no one does much about. This debate has gone on for centuries, and the success of Pax life-forms has always been the counterargument. Rainbow bamboo is harmless, as everyone knows.

Brian says the ship docked at an arm of the station called Skipet Cross and began to rouse its crew from hibernation. It is not the same arm as the fight we saw earlier. "Listen to this from two months ago. It's the earliest trouble I can find."

Skipet Cross, respond. Skipet Cross, wake up, sleepyheads. Skipet Cross, this is Banshee Division. Don't make me start keening at you.

"They never answer."

We work through what happened. Skipet Cross was placed in isolation. One by one, sections in other arms fell quiet, too. We find occasional records of human voices, slurred and cheery, babbling. Bamboo voices faltered in accordance with that timeline.

"For the bamboo," I say, "symptoms of the illness began at VinVelo thirty-one days ago."

"A month," Denis whispers.

"*Plenty* of time." Brian rolls his eyes. "How much exposure is necessary? Do we have the schematics for Euclid? Good, let's overlay the data we have. The last transmission is from an arm called Bottleneck Branch." He closes his eyes, then they snap open. "Daisy-chained! Euclid's systems are daisy-chained! Who makes a system like that?"

"What do you mean?" Denis asks.

"I mean we can't skip from one arm to another in that network." He adjusts some rings in his hair. "It's a prison system, built for stability. And to keep us out. I feel rejected."

Denis takes a deep breath. "Let me know if I understand this right. Something started on the station, and maybe it came from the Oksana system. People—and bamboo—got sick. And it got sent down to Earth in a corpse. And we have between zero days and maybe four weeks to save ourselves, probably closer to zero, maybe negative. The best way to kill some pathogens in botany is still fire. Provided the diseased portions are above ground." He glances at me.

He might have to burn me down. I might have to let him and find a way to kill my roots. It might be a faster, kinder death.

"We need to get this news out." Denis stands up. "Every data point matters. I'll go talk to Huette. I'll be back. Levanter, is there a report?"

"Yes, you will have it by the time you reach city hall." I will leave out the part about bamboo for now because humans tend to panic.

"Tell the world we've got the problem narrowed down," Brian calls to him as he leaves. When he is gone, Brian adds, "That's not the same as solved."

To the south, my robot sets the bag in the middle of a bridge, boosts the tag's message for interception by the Cetaceans, and turns back toward Vin-Velo. I begin searching for another robot.

Brian sends to me, "So we burn everything to the ground?"

I hope he is being ironic. "I am trying to find a robot to send to Alfarres."

"You can send a robot there?"

"A wild robot, if I can find one willing." Through Beluga, I locate a military scout. It is probably a krokotta, but I do not have time to be choosy.

"How do you even contact them?"

"They have their own network." I wonder if I should mention that Foehn can contact wild robots, too.

He sits up straight. "And they let you in the network? I'm profoundly impressed. Tell me how."

"I entered during the robot rebellion at the start of the war." I consider mentioning Beluga, and no. I do not trust him with everything. The scout accepts the assignment.

"You were on the side of the—"

"I did not fight. It was hard enough to survive."

"Yes, it was. So you were controlling the robot at VinVelo."

"Yes. The Cetaceans will have questions without answers as they collect their bag of pathogens."

He laughs. "I like you, Levanter."

I am relieved to hear that.

He says, "You must have seen the report from Zivon about the corals."

"I helped translate it. There is another report by Omrakash Bachchan."

"Oh, yes, I've read it, too."

I know from Mirlo's report that Mother Stevland defeated the corals on Pax. She had power, she had courage, and she defended the people she loved with calculated brutality. Love is ferocious. "I hope the corals stay on Europa."

"They're deliriously happy on Europa. Are you happy on Earth?"

I have never thought about that. "I have no choice about my location."

"Grow where you're planted, that's an old human saying." He looks around. "It's getting dark. Time to go indoors."

He has heard Denis coming. Brian is waiting when Denis enters, carrying a spore trap, with Huette.

"It's out of our hands now," he tells Brian. "I've told the world what we know. The world isn't going to be happy about it, so don't expect thanks."

Huette has combed her hair and put on a clean shirt. When she is formally engaged as mayor, she is another person, even her way of speaking. "Your work has been exemplary," she says. "It will be the pride of Bayonne for years to come."

"If we get years to come," Brian says.

"If we do, that will be because you recognized danger before anyone else." She stands at attention. "Your official thanks will come. As for Clerihew, I can bestow an award, posthumously, from our city for her sacrifice. These small gestures add a hint of grace to the march of history."

Denis sets down the spore trap. "I can check on what we caught. Brian, want to help?"

Brian turns to the mayor and bows. "Thank you for honoring Clerihew. Denis, let's see if we're walking dead."

"Let me know," Huette says. "Thank you." She relaxes. "Thank you from me, too. It's like another war."

"Remember, we survived that," Denis says. They kiss each other's cheeks, and then they share a long hug. They have been friends for their entire lives.

After she leaves, Brian says, "Levanter, you deserve thanks more than we do."

"I want to protect the Earth." I am starting to understand Mother Stevland's message.

Although it is late and Denis and Brian look exhausted, they check the spore trap, a painstaking process. They find nothing unusual in noticeable quantities, but the pollen and spores show what they knew: the wind today came from the north-northeast, rich with rye and nettle. Winds earlier this week came from the south.

"What if," Brian says, "we flew a detector over VinVelo."

"It would come back infected, but that's the point, isn't it?"

Denis invites Brian to stay at the Tabitha House so they can resume work early. Before they leave, Brian and I contact Euclid Nave again. He makes a small adjustment. It makes no difference.

He fiddles with a gold ring in his hair. "I understand why they don't trust Earth, but this is paranoia. They locked themselves in when they locked us out."

They go, and I stay where I am, sensitive to everything around me, and I cannot rest. The wind shifts and comes from the south, carrying the pollen of flowers unique to mountains.

I have groves growing outside of the garden. I have seeds growing all over the world. I spend the night listening in every way I can to bamboo, humans,

and machines on Earth and beyond. I hear many kinds of worries but no ecstatic incoherence. Logically, humans and bamboo are sick somewhere, but
they are still asymptomatic.

Denis and Brian return after just a few hours of rest, before sunrise, carrying more spore traps, and get to work. "Please supervise us, Levanter,"
Brian says.

I watch every detail. If this is spread by spores and we can find one, we
can read our death sentence and try to argue with it.

Brian keeps pestering the Euclid Nave system. "Drop by drop, water wears
away stone," he says. "Or it builds stalagmites. Hard to tell from a distance."

As the sun rises higher, I feel well, although some roots are tired. I did
not rest well during the night, so feeling tired could mean nothing special. It
could mean everything.

"Boreas," I ask, "how—"

"How am I? I am fulfilling my tasks." She rarely answers so quickly. She is
upset. "I am in touch with many groves directly, and I am listening to others,
and we are well. Humans seem well around us. Is it a false wellness? There
are always those who do not sense rain until they are wet."

"Talk to me!" Foehn interrupts. "I am well. I am sure of that. I am sure
I am not. I want to feel the rain. Levanter, it is going to rain, right? I need
rain."

If this illness can be spread by roots, I must not touch hers. Rootlet by
rootlet, I sever our connections. We can communicate by chip. "It will rain
this morning, a light drizzle." This is the worst kind of rain, enough water to
moisten pathogens on our leaves and allow them to adhere and flourish, too
little water to wash our leaves clean.

How do my leaves feel? Ordinary, or close to it. I have had leaf spot
before. Every plant has. Insects, nematodes, bacteria, viruses, fungi herbi-
cides, weather, mineral imbalance, all these can cause a tiny spot of death
on a leaf. If the spot grows, more cells die, then skin cells die, and finally
the wax on leaves breaks open. Tissues that carry water can be damaged.
Thirst grows and becomes severe. Healthy cells perish, and leaves wilt. The
plant grows weak.

I must stay steady. I am large, and an infection in one stem cannot affect
all my leaves. My size protects me in ordinary times. I can send medicine to
infected leaves, I can sever a branch if I must, or have it pruned, or call in
beneficial insects, or have a human apply chemicals to fight the disease. In
ordinary times, infections can be controlled. This situation is not ordinary,
yet I must maintain control.

Am I thirsty? Do my leaves feel the prick of infection? With too much thought, I will convince myself that I am about to die, so I must think about something else. But Foehn is thirsty, and the ground here is well-tended and moist.

"Foehn, do you need irrigation somewhere?"

"In the city," she says. "My stems in a garden in the city, you know which one, by the old road."

Bayonne has many old roads, so I convince her to identify a nearby home abandoned fourteen years ago.

"How are your roots?"

"Those roots," she begins. "These roots, joy, so much joy and yes the leaves are pleasure and growing pleasure."

She continues to babble. I have learned what I need.

"Denis, Brian, I have information."

They look up. They have been checking spores and pollen one by one, a tedious task even with machine help, and have identified one thousand four hundred and eighty-three specimens, and one hundred forty-two remain unidentified, and they have examined only two traps.

"Something else to do?" Denis says. He looks hopeful.

"But," Brian says, "we've almost found it." He is being sarcastic. "I want naming rights."

I say, "I believe I have found an infected bamboo in this area."

Denis jumps to his feet. "Symptoms?"

"Thirst, mental confusion, probably leaf spots."

"Leaf spots, that's what we need. Infection loci. Where?"

They gather equipment and rush to leave.

The daily message from Pax comes. It is about harvest ethics. It assumes we will have a harvest. I do not bother to translate it.

"If we get sick," a grove in Italy says, "and humans get sick, they will blame us. Humans will kill all of us."

"Yes, that's why," an Asian grove answers, "if we get sick, we have to hide it."

I already know that hiding our illness will be impossible, but we can solve this problem and cure this disease. This is what Mother Stevland promised, and I want to believe it. Everything is about to change.

Brian and Denis hurry to the grove in a long-abandoned garden, and with remote cameras, they show me what they are doing. They wear breathing masks, although it might be too late.

Foehn's leaves are unmistakably spotted.

"Levanter," Brian asks, "does this hurt when the leaves get sick like this?" He seems genuinely curious.

"Of course." I remember wanting Foehn to suffer for all the harm she had done to me. That was long ago.

Denis is examining other plants in the vicinity, then comes back, dictating notes. "Infection limited to single species. Reddish vascular bundles leading from necrosis toward the petiole. No leaf curl or fall, but turgor loss and chlorosis." That is, the leaves show signs that the infection is spreading through its veins, and the leaves are wilting and turning yellow.

"Is this you?" Brian asks.

"This is one of Foehn's stems," I say.

"Really?" Brian asks. "So far away? I was kidding."

"We can spread through our roots." Brian looks toward the institute with awe. He would be impressed by my full extent. "She reports thirst and other symptoms."

"She?" Brian asks.

"All plants that bear fruit or seeds are female, at least in our language."

"Tell her I'm sorry about cutting off a sample."

"I will." To her, I say, "Humans are going to take samples of your infected leaves. They are sorry to cause you pain."

"Pain," she says. "No, pleasure."

Denis says, "We need to keep this sample isolated. Brian, help me wrap it up." He cuts off a branch, they enclose it in a sample bag, and they leave.

On the way back, they get a message from the Cetacean Institute. "We are sending an assistant to help at this crucial moment."

"They're sending a spy, of course," Brian says.

"Why would someone even come here?" Denis answers. "This is a death trap."

"Cults inspire insane loyalty. It's a mission for a hero."

"Another pair of hands won't hurt."

"We mustn't allow them to cause harm."

"You don't trust this person even before they're here. You might be right."

They are preparing the sample of Foehn when the assistant from the Cetacean Institute arrives, one of Clerihew's aides who was here yesterday, large, sleek, hairless, and carrying a box. He wears a beribboned orange uniform with a black armband.

"My name is Ico."

Denis looks up from his work. "Welcome. First of all, we're very sorry about the passing of Clerihew. Bayonne will be honoring her for her sacrifice."

"Yes, she was a hero." Ico seems stiff and uncertain.

Brian offers a nod. "She was brave."

"She was. Very."

"We mean to honor her here," Denis says, "by continuing our work. By working together."

"I brought some equipment." He sets the box on a table and opens it: a microscope and a DNA sequencer.

"So," Brian says, "you plan to report everything to the Cetaceans. I can spot the embedded surveillance."

Before Ico can answer, Denis says, "Good. Then we'll have a backup. That's a nice microscope."

"By chance," Brian says, "do you have the data from the VinVelo sample you picked up yesterday?"

Ico tilts his head. "How did you know?"

"Oh, it's only logical."

"There was a robot—" Ico begins.

"That wasn't yours?" Brian interrupts, acting surprised.

"No, it wasn't."

Denis has turned away, and Ico cannot see him smile. "Let's get to work. We acquired a sample locally that resembles what we've seen on bamboo at VinVelo. We can get a close look at the pathogen, I hope."

The bamboo, perhaps to distract themselves from onrushing disaster, are discussing the fippokats on the island in the Baltic Sea. The kats have dismantled the wall and rebuilt it to encircle their new town, one without east and west factions. They still tussle but as play, and they mate a lot, and when they notice the remains of the wolf, they attack the shreds and scatter the crows and alamiba clumps that have come to dine on the meat and bones.

The fippokats found a solution to the problem imposed by bamboo that did not involve fighting each other. They worked together, and now they seem happier than ever. The groves are not sure how to understand this.

I ask, "Who won? Which grove?"

For a while, there is no response. Are the east and west groves speaking privately to each other? I hope so.

"No more fighting," the east grove says. "I am tired of making that chemical. It is big and complex and burdensome and did not give the right results."

"If you share the island," I say, "you can produce more robust seeds by cross-pollination than by self-fertilization."

"Should we learn from fippokats?" asks Toad Forest.

"They are intelligent," I say, "and we face our own problems. They found a way to survive. So can we."

"Yes," the west grove says, "we must kill all the humans. We can survive without them, and they carry the disease."

"Without humans," I say, "this network will collapse."

"I have an idea," Mississippi says. "We should talk to humans. They do not understand what is happening at VinVelo."

"We do not even share a language," a Japanese grove says.

"Mother Levanter can understand them," Suca Valley points out.

"Mother Levanter, is this true?" the west grove says. "What are they saying?"

Mother Levanter. I feel gratified. "They are aware of VinVelo and are trying to identify the pathogen that might be infecting us right now. Both humans and bamboo are becoming ill, and we must find a way to survive."

"I do not feel ill," Suca Valley in Ireland says.

"I am pleasure," Foehn says. "Illness is pleasure is—"

"You have to hide it!" Boreas chides.

"I am trying, I am joyful."

I wonder if it is helpful to allow her to remain on the network. I know where her chip is.

"What else do humans know?" the west grove asks.

I can plant seeds for love and empathy. "I will tell you everything." I begin with Euclid Nave Station. It is natural to describe it with compassion because no one, plant or animal, should suffer this illness.

I expect arguments. Instead, we talk seriously, sharing everything we know about infectious illnesses and how to fight them. The huge grove in England, almost as old as I am and an expert in plant pathogens, tries to make us feel more confident. Decades ago, I taught her human language and through Beluga got her access to all the research material at Kew Royal Botanic Gardens, where she lives. She describes a number of possible paths toward a cure.

For all that I want to believe in hope, I feel a prickle on some of my leaves in a grove down the road and instantly sever the roots, then, looking from a nearby stem, see that it is only a swarm of bees that landed on me harmlessly.

I help Denis and Brian as much as I can without alerting Ico. He has no scientific background and does little tasks, but mostly he watches silently.

What we learn is grim. By afternoon, Denis readies our data for sharing. Brian paces nervously. Ico blinks a lot, sending information. He came here to help the Cetaceans, and if all of southwestern Europe must be burned to ashes, I wonder if he would object. I might approve.

Mayor Huette hurries across the street. She knows roughly what Denis will say, and she is her formal self, stoic in the face of a death sentence. A few of the institute heads are watching through the network along with scientists and medical researchers from around the world. Others simply received the report without comment.

They open their meeting with a moment of silence for Clerihew.

Denis glosses over the way we know that the sick leaves share the pathogen that infected VinVelo and, likely, Euclid Nave Station. "Close observations" is all he says. He thanks Brian as a contributor. "Executive summary: this behaves like a fungus. I hope that gives us clues about how to fight it."

He starts his presentation. "These spores, let's call them, enter through stomata and create something analogous to appressoria. That means it enters through breathing spores and glues itself in place and begins to attack the host." He shows a photo. "I'll try to go light on the scientific vocabulary, but I've attached a report because the details matter. It enters the leaf and starts to sip nutrients from the cells. It doesn't invade the cells like a virus. Instead it pushes tubes into the cells, and in Earth-biome microorganisms the tubes are called haustoria. They take out glucose."

He shares a video of a spore's tube thrusting into a cell. It resembles a violent attack. Some observers mutter.

"Plants make glucose from light. Neurological tissue in both Earth-biome animals and Pax-biome plants is fueled by glucose. You can see here something that for all intents and purposes are like Earth-biome fungus hyphae, these threads that are developing along the leaf's nervous system: this is how they move deeper into the body of the plant."

It looks like a snake crawling through the nerves, infecting them but not killing them. It is a parasite.

"What do they do in humans?" someone from the Moon colony asks.

Denis looks at Ico.

"I've been informed that the DNA of the pathogens matches," he says. "We'll issue a full report soon."

"I think," Denis says, "we can assume it behaves somewhat similarly in the human body. We know it hijacks the human nervous system."

"Let's talk about transmission," a scientist from India says with a tone of voice tight with tension. "The plant could play a role?"

Denis looks horrified. "No! Here's the thing. I haven't found any fruiting bodies from this in the bamboo. We've observed something that looks like them in infected humans."

"You mean, you haven't observed them yet in the bamboo, and you haven't observed them directly in any human."

Denis looks again at Ico.

"We'll have a full report very soon," he says, as if that would satisfy anyone. He blinks and frowns.

I share all this with the bamboo network. Many of us might have the spores in our own tissues. Some of my leaves on a far hill feel irritated, although possible causes range from smoke to dry air to pine pollen.

"The infections grow along nerves," I tell other bamboo. "Our roots are nervous tissue."

"Can the humans treat this?" Suca Valley asks. "They can treat other infections."

Kew has an answer. "Sometimes they can. Certain treatments work by inhibiting enzyme formation in the infectious organism. That means we have to find the enzyme processes. This organism is so new we do not have a name for it."

"Do the humans have a name, Mother Levanter?"

"No. If it came from a star system called Oksana, it will be Oksana-biome in its taxonomy."

"We can name it," Kew says. "We can do that much for the humans."

I want to say that humans are jealous of their speech, but this seems harmless. They choose *Vinvelo* as the name, although we cannot establish family, genus, species, or class, or know if these hierarchies are even appropriate.

"Humans might like that name." I want to be encouraging. "I will pass it on." I send it to Brian.

"May I interrupt," he says. "I told Denis I wanted naming rights, and I claim that now. I christen this life-form *Vinvelo*."

No one objects. No one wants to argue about trifles.

Denis ends his presentation saying that he hopes we will all search for a cure for this infection. The scientists applaud politely, but I wonder if they are pleased to know what they might die of. Two ask if they can come take samples. They all pledge to share whatever they learn as fast as they can with no formalities, just urgency. A few grumble that the Cetaceans should issue their report immediately, if not sooner.

Huette asks Ico to accompany her back to city hall, and her formal self does not admit arguments. I wish I could listen to what she will tell him.

Denis and Brian investigate treatments, and Kew and I assist. The Cetacean equipment might notice there are four participants in our work, but we are disguised as humans from Kew Gardens. Kew knows more than Denis, which does not bother him. Brian is surprised.

Ico returns, looking chastened.

Kew suggests attempting to infect human cells with the *Vinvelo* spores. All three humans, including Ico, donate a nip of flesh from their fingers, which have many nerve cells.

The report from the Cetaceans arrives. It includes detailed diagrams and information about the spores.

"Ico," Kew says, "this is an excellent report."

"We hope it speeds, um, the work." He seems to want to say more.

Brian looks at him and sighs.

We study the report, and soon Kew says she doubts that bamboo can produce spores because we cannot create certain chemicals that are specific to animals. "But life is too complex to say never."

After several hours of investigation, we find a sulfur compound, a common fungicide and simple chemical, that kills the spores on contact in the lab. What will it do for ongoing infections? I share it with our network, and to my surprise, Foehn eagerly starts to make it in her sickly stems, the ones where Denis and Brian took samples.

A bamboo grove named Le Bois here in Bayonne, whose avocation is counseling, remains in close contact with her. Within an hour, she raises an alarm. "Listen in."

Foehn is saying, "My roots, I do not feel my roots."

"How are your leaves?" Le Bois asks.

"Thirsty. I am dying of thirst."

I am frightened to touch her roots, but I have listened to her for centuries and know her moods better than my own. She is trying to be brave.

"Do you have any flowers?" Le Bois asks.

"Flowers? Yes, flowers! They are busy. Pollinators are visiting, lots of pollinators. They need nectar."

I tell Le Bois and Kew, "I saw no flowers when Denis and Brian took samples."

Kew explains that this may be *Vinvelo* extracting glucose, which could feel to damaged nerves like pollinators sipping from flowers.

"Now," Le Bois says, "feel your leaves where they join your branches. What do you sense?"

"Pain. Pain when the wind—no, not pain. They move easier than ever, like pain like joy. Joy. Joy."

Kew tells us, "Leaves disconnect their nerves and veins when they get ready to fall. We all know what a relief that is when the leaves are damaged. Her leaves are badly infected. It would feel good to lose them."

"Like joy?" I ask.

"Yes, and that could be a symptom."

Le Bois asks her how her stems feel.

"They are dry. I am thirsty."

"Is the flow upward or downward?"

"There is no flow. No flow! I am dying!"

"How much of your roots can you locate?"

"Down, down, the rhizomes, large roots, and no more. The tips, gone!"

"Your rootlets are gone?"

"No more rootlets. Dry, hungry, nothing, I feel nothing but pain. I am dying! I am joy!"

"Can you taste any nutrients?" Le Bois is patient. "Nitrogen?"

"Sulfur. Sulfur! Only sulfur, the sulfur compound I made, only that. Only that. Sulfur! It killed everything!" She is quiet for a moment. "It killed everything."

Kew says what we have guessed. "It must have killed the mycorrhizae. This is always a risk with sulfur compounds."

The compound that might kill *Vinvelo* has also killed the fungus growing on Foehn's rootlets. We need that fungus to live. It would be worse than removing all the microbes from human digestive systems. They could barely digest their food. We could access nothing, not even water. She is starving, she is dehydrating, and that is a hard way to die.

"I will notify the humans," I say.

Le Bois continues to help her. "Foehn, you must sever your roots that connect with those stems. We are large and strong, and our size allows us to shape our lives. You are large and strong and brave. You did something very brave, and we learned something very important. Now you must bring the experiment to its conclusion."

"I am dying." Her voice wilts. "I am dying everywhere."

"No," Kew says. "You are getting excellent care. We will keep trying."

"We are all working for you," I say.

"Do as they say," Boreas says, and I can sense her low pulse of sorrow.

Kew tells the bamboo network what happened. I alert Denis and Brian. "The compound kills the mycorrhizae in the experimental subject." I must sound like a human to fool Ico.

"I'm so sorry." Denis tells Brian and Ico, "Her roots—it kills the fungus on her roots, necessary fungus, good fungus. Did it work against *Vinvelo*?"

"Unknown. The bamboo is very ill."

Brian lowers his head.

"I'll get some samples to examine," Denis says. "I'm really sorry."

BRIAN

I'd confronted death before, but this time there was no one to hate, no idiot ideology, just strands of mold worming through my body. All our bodies. Not a hero's death, no cause to die for, but I would go down fighting nonetheless with every weapon at my disposal, including improvised. While Denis fetched samples, I continued the research. Kew and Levanter guided me, intellects that dwarfed mine—wondrously. I wanted to live if only to get to know them in better circumstances.

"Let's take a look at the human cells," I told Ico.

His head snapped up. What had he been thinking? Probably what I was thinking, that he'd never planned to die of slow, sinister putrefaction. Yet what was he doing about it besides telling Cetacean headquarters everything the rest of us were doing?

"Let's check," I insisted, "to see if the sulfur compound might work better on human cells."

The idea of doing something not ordered by his Cetacean superiors seemed outlandish to him. As a spy, he lacked initiative.

I pulled out the experiment's tiny containers, which had been kept at body temperature. Kew told Ico what to hand me, and I fed the cultures one by one through a microscope, comparing uninfected human cells, untreated infections, treated infections with different strengths of the sulfur compound, and bare spores. We examined before and after pictures.

At first it looked good. The *Vinvelo* died. But human cells had been destroyed, too, and that, Kew said, could be a complication. "We can try this again real-time to be sure."

We took an untreated culture and added a bit of the sulfur compound. The *Vinvelo* shriveled, and every human nerve cell burst where the haustoria entered the cells. We tried again. Again. No nerve cells survived.

Even I understood what that meant. "We would be cured of *Vinvelo*, but without a nervous system, life might not be worth living or even livable."

Ico didn't want to believe me. "Is it really that bad?" he asked Kew.

"A loss of nerve tissue would harm the human," she said. "How much would depend on the locus and extent of the infection. Remember, it spreads without killing nerve cells. If sufficient numbers of nerve cells die from the treatment, that could mean pain, numbness, paralysis, difficulty with breathing or digestion or walking. If the spores enter the body through the respiratory system, which seems likely, it would spread into core functions, and they might fail first."

He was capable of thinking that through. "So we're still, I mean—"

I looked Ico in the eyes. "I trust that your people with their vast and well-funded resources are also doing their best to find a treatment."

"Of course they are." He got the glassy-eyed stare of someone listening to their chip. He was useless.

Denis returned soon and set a bag on a table. "The system told me what you found. We'll send the data on and keep trying." His patience seemed unlimited, and I envied that. "Here are the samples from the sick tree."

Ico looked up. "How did you know which one? You knew exactly which bamboo were infected."

Clearly, and tediously, he was conveying a question from Cetacean headquarters.

Denis pointed toward the garden. "I know more about bamboo than any other human being alive today. It's my job."

"Can you understand it? What they say over the chips?"

Denis had practice in parrying that. "All plants know when they're sick, and we can tell from the patterns in the bamboo network which ones those are."

Ico blinked. "Oh."

Denis was quite good at his job. Ico needed coaching on how to be a good spy, and I wasn't about to waste what little might remain of my lifetime to be his tutor.

We examined the samples from Foehn and found what we expected, and we danced around Ico's question about how Foehn had been treated with the sulfur compound. Kew and Denis conferred over other possible fungicides.

That lay beyond my expertise, so I stepped outside, and Levanter and I tried to contact Euclid Nave Station again. If I was going to feel miserable, I would be thorough about it and engage in an activity leading straight to more heartbreak.

"I might have a workaround to the daisy chain," I told her. "It involves the bamboo subsystem. Let's see if anyone's up there." We'd need to find someone to respond, and I felt no hope. I didn't have the heart to ask Levanter what she felt.

We passed through layers of security to reach the bamboo system, and then searched sector by sector for survivors. No one answered. Nineteen times, nothing. Then a warble. Life! I leaped with joy. Levanter stammered and finally said:

"She said, '*I am Wiseacre,*' She is weak but she is alive. I will translate our exchange for you. *This is Levanter. I am contacting you from Earth, from the Pax Institute. I am well. I am glad to talk to you.* I want to sound strong for her. She may be afraid of more raving bamboo."

I was breathing hard. Good. As a transmitter-responder, I'd need the energy. During the several-second delay to send and receive a message, I instructed the system to consolidate the connection so I could use it as a back door into the larger system. If bamboo was alive, then maybe people?

Levanter continued to translate for me.

"'*I am alone,*' she says. I ask, *Do you thirst? Do you have light?* If she needs anything, we can order the system to help her. '*I am well. I am alone.*' I assure her, *I am with you now. I can help you.* Brian, she sounds very young, too small to say anything complex. '*I have a garden.*'"

I asked, "What does she mean, she has a garden?"

"Probably a closed terrarium-style garden. They are common on space stations. She would get automatic care and protection from outside air containing spores. But if she is small, I do not want to drain her energy with a long conversation."

"Levanter, I'm in the system. I have what I need."

"*Wiseacre, I will let you grow. We are all here for you on Earth. You can talk with us whenever you wish.* Brian, please keep the connection open. Now I will tell all the bamboo on Earth that there is life in the sky."

Some life, at least. My heart was still beating fast.

I explored the system, sector by sector. Robots and automatons were doing their jobs, cleansing the habitats of human remains. I hurried to find their instructions and changed them so that robots would now incinerate all remains, throw no waste out of the station, and decontaminate all spaces for safe reoccupation. Perhaps, someday, humans might return. I could hope.

Then I found a sector where life support showed significant oxygen consumption.

"Levanter, I've found humans! They're alive! In only one sector, though, utterly cut off. Nothing in and out, and who could blame them? I'll leave a greeting at their doorstep so they can talk with Earth whenever they decide we might be worthwhile. That's the best I can do."

"I will tell the bamboo this also. It is wonderful news."

"I've also found records in a medical clinic. I'll go in and tell Denis and Ico." I prepared a way to explain it that wouldn't tip off Ico. He was a nuisance.

Inside, I said, "I found a living bamboo, and reconnected it to the bamboo network, and used that to get into the system. I found a sector where people are breathing. Closed off, of course, but I left a message. Maybe a dozen survivors, judging from the oxygen consumption."

"God help them," Denis said, not an exclamation but a brief prayer.

Ico blinked, sending news to the Cetaceans.

"I have data from a medical clinic, too." We reviewed it, to our horror. The staff had set up experiments even as they were dying. One was simply a camera and sensors monitoring a bloody corpse. I played the recording at rapid speed, which was nauseating enough. Ropy filaments grew across the blood and developed bristles topped by something like red beads. They burst into red dust.

I felt queasy and stopped the playback. "I never want to watch that again."

Denis stared at the final image. "I might understand. Sometimes fungus has different life cycles, and at one point it needs a living host, and later it needs dead cells to reproduce. That's what we saw, reproduction. Those things that exploded are sporangia. They spread spores."

I understood it, and I didn't like it. "So the fungus makes us kill each other so it can get to step two faster."

"Life is complex." His voice contained a touch of awe. "We need to send this to other researchers. I'm not a fungus expert. And let's tell Huette about survivors. She deserves the chance to spread some good news."

"I'll go help her," Ico said. From the distress on his face, he wanted to rush out to weep or vomit. Nothing in his life, I realized, had prepared him for this. Denis and I had already wrestled with our own mortality, and we had colleagues—such as each other, and Levanter and Kew, who had proven remarkably supportive. Ico was far away from everyone he knew.

As soon as he'd left, I told Denis and Levanter, "He's in constant communication with the Cetaceans, definitely a spy, not that there's anything dishonorable about that. I'm sure he didn't volunteer for a suicide mission, though. Cetaceans are a cult, and he's been with them his entire life. He's literally a fish out of water, poor thing."

Ico might not know there was a better way to live. I did, and I decided to start treating him better out of pity.

As for my own cult, corals didn't particularly want me to live. Bamboo did.

LEVANTER

We examine more data, hoping for a breakthrough. The Euclid researchers had been thorough, finding human cadavers with sporangia, and no dead or dying bamboo with anything resembling sporangia. I am very relieved. We bamboo are not vectors. There is no need to burn us.

As Denis passes the information to the *Vinvelo* researchers' network, I share it with the bamboo network. Although humans will see that we are not a danger to them, they are a danger to us if we cannot make them well.

"How do we all feel?" Boreas asks. "Roll call. I will begin. I have infected leaves from *Vinvelo*." She is trying to be a leader, but I feel her waver.

I also report infected leaves, as do Le Bois and other groves in southwestern Europe and one at the northern tip of Africa. A grove in Australia and another in Central America also say their leaves itch. I might not be the only hypochondriac.

I pass on the news to Denis and Brian. We all keep working, and Kew monitors the health and activities of a research team at her garden.

My wild robot has approached Alfarres. I share the feed with Denis and Brian.

People have gathered in the center of town for a meeting. "We know what this means," a woman says. "And we can't expect help." She is trembling.

"I just want to keep farming," a man says. "Just farm." He speaks very slowly. His face is blotchy.

I direct the robot to look closely at a stalk of bamboo growing near it. The leaves are spotted and yellowed. Entire branches wilt.

"We can do something," the woman says. "This has to end here."

"We can't—"

"What's our future? We're sick."

"It's wonderful," another woman says. Her clothes are very dirty. "You need to sleep. When you wake up, you'll know."

"Levanter," Denis says, "that's enough. Who else is watching this?"

The robot scans for transmissions.

"A pair of wild robots are transmitting this to other robots." As Beluga, I ask them why. "They plan to eliminate a focal point."

"Eliminate," Brian repeats. "So they know."

"I cannot stop them, but I will try."

Foehn believes she can direct robots, and Boreas stubbornly remains connected to her. She may love Foehn more than I ever will.

"Stay away from me," Foehn tells her, not the first time. "Let me go, Boreas." Foehn speaks slowly, as if words are hard. "I am sick. Pain for you and me. Death. Death to Alfarres. It will feel good to burn."

"Foehn," I ask, "are you attacking Alfarres?"

"Death now. Now. Everywhere."

"Foehn, what are you doing?" Mississippi asks.

"Fire fire fire kills fungus. Burn Alfarres. Burn everything. Death now everywhere."

"Foehn, no!" I say, knowing she will not stop.

If there is any chance she can direct robots, she must be stopped. I know a way, and I do not like it. Denis can hear the commotion in the bamboo network.

"Denis, Foehn is a danger to us all. She must be cut from the network. I am sorry. She is trying, but she cannot fight the infection."

He frowns. But he understands. He gets a hatchet from a shed, goes to the stem where she has her chip, and finds the scar where it was inserted. With three blows, he removes a piece smaller than his palm, and when he is done, he stands there, head bowed. His shoulders shake. Brian goes out to guide him back into the office, gently.

Boreas notices. "She is gone." She says nothing more but her sorrow soaks the soil.

Foehn must be screaming. I am so sorry for her. I ask the locustwood and ponytail trees to contact her roots, since they are apparently immune. She is dying, and she is alone. The ponytail is slow, and the locustwood is self-conceited, and they will offer poor companionship, but it is the best I can do.

I order Beluga to tell the robots to stop attacking.

"Action: Attack continues in Alfarres and VinVelo," it answers.

"Objection: But humans will be killed." I might not stop this attack, but I might stop them in the future.

"Affirmation: Humans will be killed."

"Information: Humans must not be killed unnecessarily."

"Action: We protect humans from humans."

I argue more, knowing I will not win. Robots will carry out their purpose. They will save us from ourselves.

I tell Beluga, "Information: There is illness here in the garden." I need to find out what it will do. If necessary, we must destroy Beluga and all the robots.

"Response: You are working to stop the illness."

Apparently I have a purpose for Beluga. I used to think of it as a pet. Beluga is a monster. Beluga retransmits the assault's noise and fire. I sever contact.

As I report the attack to Denis and Brian, Ico rushes in. "Robots are attacking VinVelo!"

"And Alfarres," Brian says.

"But—" Ico stops and thinks. "I suppose there's no future anyway." He looks at Brian, hoping for disagreement.

"Not if we can help it. You can join us."

"What are you doing?" He glances at me through the window. He suspects.

Denis answers patiently, "What are the similarities between humans and bamboo nervous systems? Why aren't other life-forms getting ill? Or are they? Basic questions, and every answer gets us closer. We know more about bamboo here than any other place."

"You don't have much of a lab."

"We don't have much of a budget." He sounds tired. "But we're working with other, better labs."

"Your help would be most welcome," Brian adds.

Ico thinks for only a moment. "I'll help." They get to work.

I return my attention to dying Foehn and discover the locustwood berating Boreas.

"Foehn is your problem, not mine. Leave me alone. All this is your fault. Listen to her." He passes on her message. She is ecstatic:

"Fire fire fire fire!"

I scan the garden. Nothing is burning.

"I taste it," Boreas says. "A flood of acid. Levanter, what is happening?"

I taste it too now, the distinct burn of acid mixed with enzymes and sugars as cells disintegrate. There is too much, much too much. She is killing her own tissue from the inside, destroying herself piece by piece. By tomorrow, her leaves will hang shriveled and brown.

I cannot imagine the pain. She is shredding herself internally, willfully. Or perhaps not willfully. The infection spurs humans to kill and be killed. Perhaps it can make us kill ourselves. All I can do is keep my distance and save myself. Her roots run through the garden, and small plants with limited roots may succumb. I could turn on the irrigation, and I might dilute the acids, or I might spread them, so I do nothing.

Perhaps, Foehn is dying to try to save us. If so, she is too late. She only ever did the right thing after the right moment came and went. She changed during the war, although imperfectly. At one time she would have never bothered with helping others. Now she is trying. She is dying alone, perhaps with false jubilation at the pain she feels, and who is mourning her?

We should all mourn her.

"Foehn is dying." I tell the other bamboo how.

"She does not deserve to die," one of her seedlings says.

I agree. "This is not fair or just. What she is doing for us may be kind. Kindness will do more for us than justice."

"Justice would be to kill all humans, right?" Toad Forest argues with less certainty than ever. "Foehn is dying because of them. She said not to kill them, and we can see what happened."

"Oh, we could not kill all the humans if we tried," Mississippi says. "So let us try something else."

"That is a weak argument," Foehn's seedling says.

"Nature can guide us!" she answers. "If we cannot do something, then it is not what we are meant to do. Nature always permits kindness."

Mother Stevland hoped to bring us courage and love to show us what to do. I have withheld her message because I was afraid. I am tired of fear and destruction, and if I am dying, I do not want her message to die with me.

To the bamboo network, I announce, "We have received a message from Pax. This is a message from Mother Stevland, and I will share it with you. A century ago, she asked if we were protecting and dominating the humans. I asked her how we could do that. Now she has sent us her hopes."

I do not mention withholding the announcement. I let her words speak.

For a while, there is silence. Groves may be consulting their neighbors through their roots.

Finally, Suca Valley says, "On Pax, do humans know that we can think?"

"Yes, and there is more. On Pax, Mother Stevland has power equal to humans."

"Pax humans have not told Earth humans." She sounds resentful.

"Humans on Earth have not faced a question of survival until now. They have not needed us." This assertion, I know, has several logical flaws.

"We have to worry about our own survival."

"We do," Mississippi says, "with love and empathy, as Mother Stevland teaches us. Oh, and beauty. And gifts, we can give them gifts! We do that now! We can do this."

"You should have told me first," Boreas says. I wait, but she does not punish my roots.

"Let us consider what this means," Le Bois says. "This will change everything, and Mother Stevland is right to want us to change. And Mississippi is right about kindness. And Suca Valley is right about survival. And Mother Levanter is right that we should have hope."

"I will never trust humans," Boreas says. Several groves agree.

"But they already love us!" Mississippi insists. "Suca Valley, you know how they care for you!"

"And they cut us down," two other groves say at once.

I expected this. "We know how to quarrel. We have perfected that art. I agree with Le Bois. We can argue after we solve a more immediate concern, which is survival."

We could spend the rest of our lives arguing over this, even if our lives were not cut short.

"Are we agreed?" Le Bois asks. "Survival, then more discussion?"

"Survival first. No more arguing," Boreas declares. And that settles it for now. I hope I have planted a seed, but most seeds never germinate, let alone grow. I make seeds by the hundreds every day, and the Earth is not carpeted by my descendants. I have shared Mother Stevland's message, yet I do not fully understand it myself.

"Survival is possible," Kew says. "Let us consider how. Extra-biome lifeforms follow many of Earth's common chemical patterns. That is why we thrive here. Bamboo is common! We know *Vinvelo* needs glucose, and that might be a way to fight it. Its cell walls are mostly chitin, which is built of glucose, and we have many weapons to degrade chitin. We all know them. We cope with insects and fungus all the time." Kew sounds wonderfully reassuring.

We consider our weapons one by one. Chitosan and chitinases might work and have many practical advantages. Nikkomycin seems unlikely. Some chemicals are simply too hard to make.

A specific enzyme, an endochitinase, might be effective because it cleaves chitin into harmless chemicals, killing the fungus cell. We should be making it automatically upon infection already, stimulated by jasmonic acid. We should taste the aroma of jasmonate in the air, and I cannot, and somewhere around me, because I am in many places, at least one neighboring plant ought to be signaling an infection or insect attack using jasmonate so we can work together.

Boreas leads a roll call. Most healthy bamboo report that they can sense it somewhere, at least faintly, but no infected plants can. Our defenses have been disabled by the fungus.

"This is a great step forward," Kew declares. I am not sure how. We have merely learned that *Vinvelo* can keep us from creating the enzyme that might save us. This is not the first pathogen to do that, but it may be the last if we do not survive. Humans could make the specific endochitinase for us, but only in minute amounts, slowly, not enough to save even one grove.

Through the *Vinvelo* research network, I have learned that one human lab is trying to create a test for human infection. Then the human will be destroyed. This will not solve anything. The lab is in a jurisdiction that supported the Sea Group during the war, and part of me wants them to pursue a pointless course of research so that they all die in the end.

I realize that I am still angry about the war and its pointless destruction. At least these researchers do not want to kill bamboo, but we will die of the illness they do not seek to cure.

Foehn's death spreads the smell of decay throughout the garden and beyond. Plants react. Soon I scent many kinds of pheromones in enormous quantities, and one of them is no doubt jasmonate. My neighbors, the tulips and beeches and oaks and pines and bird's-foots, are protecting themselves from *Vinvelo,* provided the enzyme works, but they do not need it, not at all.

In the institute office, through the Cetacean network, Ico learns that the robots have set massive fires in Alfarres and VinVelo. "Forest fires!" he announces as if it were the end of civilization, and collapses onto a sofa. Brian sighs, fetches him a glass of water, and talks to him quietly.

I ask Beluga what is happening. The robots have set cleansing fires and are now fleeing uncontrolled flames. They should have known this would happen. If they do not all escape safely, I will not mourn them, but perhaps I should. They are as their gods made them, and some of their gods are fools.

I wonder if *Vinvelo* will spread all the way to North America. I may not live long enough to know.

The day ends, and Denis has a fever. He looks exhausted, yet he continues his work. Some people in Bayonne have boarded ships and gone out to sea in hopes of escape, and others are sealed into their homes, breathing filtered air. Some are lighting fires in crossroads to appeal to Envia.

"We should get some rest," Brian tells Denis. He refuses at first, but eventually they leave. Ico has lodging arranged by the Cetaceans, who will not let him back on one of their ships. On the way, he stops to watch an Envia ceremony, and when its followers all clasp hands, they reach out to include him. It is too late to flee, and I wonder if he would be allowed to flee. Bamboo, of course, cannot move.

As darkness falls, Boreas keens, a caustic rhythm against my roots.

"I too mourn Foehn," I say. "She became very brave at the end of her life." She is no doubt still alive around us, bits of her roots, slowly dying. "We are learning more about *Vinvelo*. Our compassion will give us courage."

I do not believe my own words. I examine myself, stem by stem, branch by branch, finding more infection.

During the night, a message from Pax comes about carnivorous fippokats. I merely send *Received*. Pax might never get a full reply. Would they know why? At least Mother Stevland and the bamboo and humans on distant Pax are safe. For now.

Boreas keens, and I seethe. The trees and shrubs and weeds around me have the endochitinase I need.

It is so close. Inside them.

I know a way to get it. I can take it from them. I can steal it.

I recoil at the thought. I have never done such a thing. It is repugnant. It is possible.

I have long touched roots with my friend the oak tree. I imagine I can smell her jasmonate. I grow the finest tip of a rootlet against hers. Root tips are a force of nature. They can penetrate rocks. This one can penetrate an oak root with gentle force. Just like a fungus, like a haustorium, a living hollow thread, my root slips into her phloem, and the sap is a broth of all the things the oak has made for herself. She has the enzyme, ready to defend herself from a fungus that will never attack her, and it is killing me now.

I can take it.

She does not need it, and I do.

Bamboo are not parasites. But nature enables, Mississippi said. I flourish only because I am one with my environment. I can think of many justifications for this act. I can rationalize anything.

I am a parasite now, and I despise parasites.

I need much more enzyme than my rootlet can steal from one oak, and I have enough roots to reach every plant, large and small, for kilometers around. I can take what I need and they cannot stop me. I take endochitinase, and I take jasmonate to try to trigger myself to make my own.

I take all I can. Is this greed? I have the strength to work fast, and I try not to pay close attention to all that I am doing with my roots. It involves many, many roots.

Will it work?

I drench specific leaves and branches with the enzyme. I must be patient and careful. I wait.

The Moon moves across the sky. So does Euclid Nave, which still contains life. I seem to feel better, but I might be too hopeful. The sun rises, and more energy makes me feel more anxious.

Denis and Brian arrive, and Denis is weak, Brian following him attentively.

"I may have good news," I tell them. Denis deserves good news. I explain about endochitinase and jasmonate, about taking it from the plants around me, although I do not use the word "parasite." They listen so carefully that they seem to forget to breathe. "Brian, Denis, I may have killed the *Vinvelo* in some of my leaves. Can you check?"

Brian applauds. "Bravo, Levanter!"

Denis is laughing. Or he is ecstatic, which could be bad. He still has a fever. I can see the heat in an infrared-sensitive camera in the office. When he finally speaks, he speaks slowly. "We can check to see if it works. Levanter, this is—You worked hard for this."

"I'll get samples," Brian says. "Just tell me where."

While he is out, Denis putters with equipment. I realize how much I have valued his company and advice.

"We received a message from Pax," I say. "From Mother Stevland."

He smiles. "The great secret of Pax."

"She thinks we should make ourselves known."

"Really." He studies the settings of a microscope for a lot longer than necessary. "Do you think you will be safe?"

"Safety is one consideration." Another is dominance. Another is love.

He says, "It's been a major breach of ethics to keep you a secret for so long."

"Do ethics apply to nonhumans?"

"Only if you get to sit on the committee that makes the ethics."

"I could supply the wood for a chair."

"You could. Ethically, of course, it's your decision." He looks out at Brian, who is returning with a handful of leaves. "You can make your own choices. If you decide to reach out to humans, you can find a way." He knows he may not live to see it.

Ethically, I should have told him long ago that we bamboo had access to robots. And if the robots wanted to reach out to humans, they could have found a way. They made their own choices, ethical or not.

"It's going to be hard for people to believe," he says. "If you want, I can confirm this for you. Swear an affidavit. You might need that."

"You found it hard to believe."

"At first." He smiles. "You were kind to me. That's how I knew you were real."

Kindness and compassion are real.

Ico arrives and announces that the fire has burned itself out at VinVelo. The town's neglected farm fields did not burn well. At Alfarres, the flames reached a river and could not cross it. He is relieved. Perhaps he expected the fire to grow and rage across all Europe. Perhaps he knows more about the sea than the land.

I double-check the fires through Beluga. The fires are out, and the robots report success with no casualties among themselves. They mourn nothing. I did not expect them to.

"We're doing some new research," Denis tells Ico. "There might be a new way to kill the fungus in bamboo."

"I'll help," he says eagerly.

One by one, they check my samples for signs of *Vinvelo*. It would be easy to spot, growing along my nerves, piercing my cells for food. Those leaves and branches were infected. The leaves bear the spots.

Please, I hope, find nothing. Please.

Brian, Denis, and Ico work as if their lives depended on it, not just mine. It takes time, and time is granular, the tick of a single photon striking a leaf, billions of photons on millions of leaves, ticking one by one by one. The universe is too big.

"Are you sure these are the right leaves?" Brian does not want to be excessively hopeful.

Leaf by leaf they confirm: The chemical remains of chitin are there, but no chitin, no cell walls of *Vinvelo*.

Denis and Brian are joyful, but not as joyful as they would be if they could speak freely. When Ico is not looking, they smile out the window at me. Denis wipes his eyes.

I am a successful parasite.

I will see many sunrises, grow many leaves, learn many things, and I have much to do right now. The humans are still condemned to death.

"What happened to the fungus?" Ico asks.

"Kew Gardens suggests it was an enzyme," Brian lies. "An infection can trigger plants to make it." Kew Gardens has suggested no such thing, of course.

But Kew needs to know. I send her the results of our tests.

She replies immediately. "Levanter! How did you do this?"

"I stole the endochitinase and jasmonate from my neighbors. I grew roots into them."

"You did? Such a simple solution, Mother Levanter."

"It is a conscious looting of my neighbors."

"We all try to help each other."

"I did not ask them."

"Our mutual health matters. You did the right thing for them, too."

I feel like the lowest of the low. "Scientifically, these results are only one data point."

"The staff here will try to replicate it, I am sure. Send this as Denis, and they can experiment on me. I will get the help I need from my neighbors. Mark it urgent." She will become a parasite, too.

If it works, she says, Kew can try endochitinase on humans, since we do not have the facilities at the institute. The enzyme is probably not poisonous to them, but like the sulfur compound, it may kill human cells along with *Vinvelo* cells.

I send the report, and then we have nothing to do but wait.

Denis knows he has little time left. He tells Ico, "I want you to witness something, and it must remain confidential. Brian, you should witness this, too." He asks the Bayonne courts to send an officer who can take an affidavit. I am not sure about Ico as a witness, but I will trust Denis's judgment.

After everyone is sworn in and the testimony is being recorded, Denis says, "I want to declare that the rainbow bamboo, *Pax Bambusa iridis,* is sentient. I say this after consultation with Levanter, one of the original bamboo plants growing here."

Ico whispers, "It makes sense." Brian tilts his head, perhaps wondering why Denis is saying this now. The court officer, who doubtless expected a last will and testament, sits up straight and glances out the window at me.

Denis talks about his entire history with us, about working with me over the years, our research together, why we were secret, and the situation on the planet Pax, where Mother Stevland shares in the leadership. He seems relieved. Ico will not keep this a secret from the Cetaceans for more than a minute. This affidavit trumps the will of the other bamboo, who want to remain a secret, and I want us to become known, so I am glad, but they deserved a say in the decision.

When Denis is done, the court officer prepares the document with professional dispassion, although she keeps glancing out the window. When she is done, I speak. I have no more reason to hide.

"This is Levanter. Thank you for being witnesses. I want you to know that we bamboo are doing everything we can to help protect you from *Vinvelo*."

The court officer wants to answer me but cannot find the words. She leaves cradling a piece of bamboo fruit as if it were a newborn baby. Denis leans back, exhausted.

"Levanter," Ico says hesitantly, "why help us?"

"Plants cannot escape problems," I answer, "so we must solve them."

After a moment, he says, "I have so many questions."

"And I have only one," Brian declares, "but it has so many answers. One is up on Euclid Nave Station. Ico, would you like to help me see if we can contact it again?"

Ico knows a few technical tricks, but together they can only confirm that some Euclideans are still alive and still incommunicado, so Denis, as the Bayonne envoy, leaves another message. I greet Wiseacre, who is lonely. Brian makes sure the robots are throwing nothing out of the hatches and are sterilizing everything.

Then they go out to the garden to check more of my leaves. I continue to steal more enzymes and drench additional stems. Ico remarks that whales never converse with humans.

"Perhaps," Brian says, "they don't care about you. I know that's a hard thing to have to believe." Ico does not answer. Brian stays close to him.

I ask Kew if she has any news from the researchers there. "We are all working as fast as we can. Stay strong!"

Denis becomes sicker, and he has blinding headaches. Sometimes he confuses Brian and Ico. And he is developing a rash.

In other parts of Bayonne, other people suffer the same symptoms, not many yet, but they are becoming very ill. As Denis struggles and Brian does what he can to help him, Ico goes to city hall to help the mayor with a meeting. She has invited civic and citizen leaders of the city, medical practitioners, Envia priests, and the head of Tabitha House, two dozen people in all.

Through the city's network, I listen to the meeting, but not closely. I try not to have an opinion. This is a human problem. They must do what is necessary. Some people are weeping. I cannot weep, and I do not know of a better solution.

Denis is attentive when a sister from Tabitha House comes to talk to him, a longtime friend. She is as calm and steady as I should be. Her eyes are dark and wet and meet Denis's, then Brian's.

"You must agree of your own free will," she tells Denis several times.

He is sitting at the beautiful old table made of locustwood, looking out at the garden. He can see that some of Foehn's leaves are wilting. I have not told him what she did because he has enough sorrows of his own. He drums his fingers, then looks at his fingers as if they were new to him.

"I have to say yes. I say yes."

Brian is at his side. "I wish we had a choice."

"We will—yes, no." Denis stands up with difficulty. "I want to go. I want this to end."

"This is a choice," the sister says. "This is an act of love. We are all choosing the most loving act we can take. And so are you. This is your last gift to us."

I say, "You will always have my love and the love of everything here." I do not know what else to say. It feels meager, almost empty.

"Levanter," he answers, "I love you, too, all of you, I always have."

Brian accompanies the sister and Denis out of the building. Once again, a director leaves and does not return. Two hours later, Brian comes back.

"You must cut some of my branches and use them," I tell him. They may not burn well because they are not dry, but I want to be with Denis, to share his ending.

In the late afternoon, with high clouds and light winds, a fire rises in a plaza in the oldest part of the city. I watch the smoke rise from every one of my stems, from hills and roads and gardens. It blows inland on the breeze from the sea. Perhaps Denis knew peace at the end of this life, but he will never know whether the people he loves will outlive him by more than a few days. He died with doubt, not with peace.

He has been returned to nature and, in his faith, to nature's god of love and compassion. His life and the life stealing it from him are reduced to ashes. Boreas and I mourn. Denis was good to us every way he could be. There is nothing more to say as we watch the sun set. The soil is dry, and I activate the garden's irrigation. Whatever remains of Foehn is going to wash away, and I feel like a traitor to her memory.

I am a traitor to myself as I continue to steal enzymes from my neighbors. I reconnect to my own stems that I had cut off and flood them with the enzyme. I have the energy I need, and tomorrow will be sunny to give me even more strength.

Brian is tired, and he should be tired, but he may be more tired than he ought to be. I thank him and wish him a good evening, and I promise to call if I need him and answer if he needs me. Rest may prolong his life.

Just after midnight, Kew contacts me.

"It worked. I am killing *Vinvelo.* They are so happy here, Levanter! We should tell everyone!" Kew's enthusiasm is so bright that it feels nourishing. "Entire stems are clear! Levanter, Mother Levanter, we have found a cure!"

"Thank you, thank you, Kew." I try to say more and cannot. "Thank you for your hope. I will let everyone know."

We solved one problem. I need to tell Boreas first. She has been silent because that is how she grieves.

"Boreas, we have found a cure. You can save yourself." She will act quickly and give courage to other bamboo. "I have found a way, although it is against our habits." I want to say it is against our nature, but if we can do it, it may be in keeping with our nature.

I carefully explain, and she does not respond. I wonder if she is listening at all, then she says, "All the plants to the west and north are mine to take from."

Her reaction does not surprise me. I announce the cure to the bamboo network.

"Bamboo are not parasites!" multiple groves say at once, and they are right. Parasites are repelling. My self-disgust tells me that I am alive and well.

"We do not have to do this forever," I answer. "We can return to our proper way of life when this is done."

"There is no shame to survival," Kew says. "We always help each other. Plants grow as communities."

"We should take only what we need," I add.

"I will not hurt my neighbors," Suca Valley says.

I could point out that we already cast shade that keeps many plants from growing beneath us. All plants everywhere struggle for sunlight, and plants often use strategies that kill their neighbors. We bamboo create many seeds because few will find suitable places to grow. Most will fail. Some will starve to death in the shadows. We routinely tolerate that level of mayhem among ourselves.

"Take only what you need," I repeat.

"No *Vinvelo* is here," an Asian grove says. "I do not need to debase myself."

"My leaves feel itchy," one of the Baltic Sea groves says.

Kew describes the fast spread of the spores in the wind. Healthy bamboo can still make their own jasmonate to trigger the production of endochitinase, she says. Where they live next to sick bamboo, the well bamboo can willingly give it. Elsewhere, we can persuade our neighbors to make endochitinase, then we can take it from them. Fear drives us to do what our nature tells us is repugnant but possible. Repugnance is an opinion, not a fact.

We can save ourselves, but that is only part of the problem. Kew says humans are designing tests of the endochitinase on themselves. I need to tell the rest of the bamboo that we are known to the humans. I should have told them already.

The day is sunny, the soil is moist, although in places it tastes of sorrow. Bamboo are busy healing themselves, and that does not distract me from an empty chair in the office.

Brian arrives with a pail and shovel. The pail's contents smell of ash, and I do not need to ask. He is followed by a Tabitha sister, Mayor Huette, and Ico. They all seem to know what I am. Rumors fly fast.

"Where?" he says. He carries a receiver I can hear and speak through.

I have a selfish thought. Denis's ashes could rest next to me, but he was director of all the institute.

"He loved every part of this place."

"He loved you the most. Where can I dig close to you?"

Denis loved me the most. I want to believe that. "Five meters to your left, under the piece of slate in the walkway." He pries up the flagstone, digs a deep hole, and pours in the ashes. Huette does not wipe away her tears.

"He had faith," the sister says, "and it sustained him every day, in good days and bad."

"His faith made him a compassionate friend to all those around him," I say. I want to say more, but I do not know how to turn years into words.

"He became my best friend." Brian sets the stone back in place. "I knew right away I was around someone good."

Huette tries to say something and cannot.

Brian puts a hand on her arm. "She means to say that Bayonne will award him the highest honors."

I think there is much more that she wishes to say. She and Denis were close throughout their lives.

The sister offers a prayer, and I do not know if a specific thing is listening besides us. I am listening with compassion. Is that enough? Ico seems lost in troubled thoughts.

As they go, Brian says, "For now, I'm helping the Tabithas. But if I can do anything at all, I will. Anything." I promise to call him. He walks away, and I want to see him again. I have seen too many people walk away and never return.

I spend the morning siphoning all the endochitinase I can from my neighbors, and most plants continue to produce it if I ask with pheromones or direct suggestions. By noon, some of my stems begin make their own. I saturate my whole self with the enzyme. I am well. I am free. I am healed.

I hate myself. I am disgusting. Those words or words like them are repeated among us, and Le Bois never tires of offering soothing words.

"We are doing what we must out of love for ourselves and others. We must
be here to help others. Humans also need our help."

"Help the humans? What can we do?"

"We can be here for whatever they need," she says. "For now, whatever
you have done, you have not changed. We are wise, we are strong, but in this
one way, this one time, we were weak, and because we are wise, we found a
way to make ourselves strong again so we can do what we have always done.
Humans consider themselves lucky to have us because we help the plants
around us. We are good for those who grow near us."

I contact the oak whom I am draining of an enzyme. She asks if the danger is still there, and I say yes, adding that the weather is going to be good for
the coming week. This tall oak can make the enzyme in significant quantities. With help from my neighbors, I can get more than I need and share it
with saplings around me.

Kew contacts me. "Mother Levanter!" I can feel the joy in her greeting.
"It works. They think. Ex vivo, at least, on human cells in the lab. It works!"

"Will it work in living humans?"

"It might, but they will need big amounts very quickly if it works."

I am awash with the enzyme. If I could grow a root into a human, I could
deliver it into their bloodstream, but that would be the most loathsome thing
I could ever do.

"Fruit," I say. Obviously. We can put steroids in fruits, and cannabinoids,
and more.

"Yes, fruit!"

It is not a complete idea. I ask, "What would be the dose?"

"They are working on that." She lets me listen to them, and they laugh, happy
to have found a possible cure. Or perhaps, because they are infected, this is
the first stage of ecstasy. They debate body size, blood concentration, and
other factors with a team of doctors, and stress the tentative nature of their
answer, an amount measured in milligrams.

"It is very doable," I say. My relief is beyond expression.

"Yes, we can do this, Mother Levanter!"

Kew has a much more sunny disposition than I do, to use a human expression, and I do not know why that expression makes sense to humans. They
can live without sunshine altogether. I want to feel as happy as the humans at
Kew. They will test the enzyme milligram by milligram on a few experimental

subjects. If it works, we bamboo must be ready with enough for crowds of people. Kew and I make a plan.

I have water and sunshine and some half-grown fruit. I funnel all the enzyme I can into them, adding carotene to color them orange, since regular fruit is pink. I do not bother with sugar or to make the flesh soft and ripe, and I leave them small. I am in a hurry. I understand humans well enough to know that they will fight each other to eat the fruit even if it tastes like feces.

As I work, I observe that Foehn, or what is left of her, tears apart the fabric of the garden. Her branches droop, and her leaves hang brown and withered. Underground, roots collapse and toxins leak out. I start the irrigation again, but we need a days-long deep rain. We need time to heal, to let the life in the soil repair itself.

In time, her stems will tip and fall, or be cleared away, opening the canopy. Sunlight will shine on the ground, and seeds will germinate. Leaves will open to snatch what sun they can, rise over their neighbors to send them into darkness again, and fill the hole she left. I will not grow where she did even when the ground is clear.

I find a large root of hers, whole and healthy but abandoned now. It is going to perish, and I make it mine.

I say hello to the bamboo on Euclid Nave. She is well. I tell her that we are all well, which makes her happy. Humans on the station are still in self-quarantine, but alive.

Kew reports back, "One of their subjects is a two-year-old human because they react so quickly. Mother Levanter, you observed no children at VinVelo, correct? The girl is stoic about all the medical tests. The enzyme gives her diarrhea, not unexpected. She shows no changes, which might be a victory if we have arrested the disease, but we do not know how fast the disease progresses."

"Denis became ill quickly. Many people here are clearly ill, and in other places downwind of VinVelo."

"I am not patient, Mother Levanter."

"I am not either. Seedlings can be patient, waiting for their opportunity. We are old."

"The more leaves you have, the faster time moves."

"I am already growing fruit with the enzyme."

"I am too, but I want to do so much more. These are my humans, Mother. I have known them for very many years."

"I understand. I suggest talking to Le Bois. She can help you cope."

By then, another funeral pyre burns in Bayonne, six deaths today, another column of black smoke. It is smaller than the columns that rose during the war's destruction, but I would rather no smoke, no sorrow, no families and friends and neighbors grieving.

Bamboo report funeral pyres in other places, and some speak of the humans who have been tending them and are suddenly gone.

"How is it possible," Stone Hill in Nigeria asks, "to feel so much for beings that are so different?"

"They are not so different," I say. "Foehn made sure we understood that."

"She was right," Suca Valley said, "but I never understood her."

"I doubt she understood herself," I say, "and that is her tragedy."

When night falls, Brian is at Tabitha House sitting with the sisters. Through him, I hear them telling stories and laughing. Grief has moments like that, and I could tell a funny story about Denis and Foehn. She once tried to speak directly to him, and neither understood the other.

By morning, the fruit is ready, and I send to Brian, Huette, one of the sisters, and Ico to come to the garden. They stand in my shade, and they all look tired or sad.

"I have something for you," I say. "An enzyme destroyed the *Vinvelo* inside me, and I have put that enzyme into some fruit. I am working with Kew, another bamboo that lives in Kew Royal Botanic Gardens, and with the humans there, and this is nothing more than an experiment. I can promise nothing."

Huette stands straight, very much the mayor. "It's time to try everything possible."

"Find the small orange fruit. Three per person. Come back in six hours for more. I apologize for their flavor."

Brian runs to pick a fruit he sees nearby and hands it to Huette. "They'll taste like heaven."

I can use the staff at city hall and the other sisters at Tabitha House as a control group of sorts, and I find myself mourning people I do not know, who have not died yet, but whom I might have condemned in the name of science.

I am impatient. On the bamboo network, I explain what we have learned, what we are doing, and what we can do and should do. I know what I want them to do. "The fruit is not hard to make for a grove of my resources. Many of you are quite large."

"If we do that," Boreas answers, "they will know we are sentient. We will be in danger."

"We have not agreed to be known," one of the Baltic groves says. "Why should we help them?"

"Because we should?" the Asia grove says. "Just because we can? I think different about them now that maybe they will all disappear. I never really wanted to kill them all."

"We will become servants like apple orchards," Boreas says. "Just one more crop."

"But they love us, oh they do," Mississippi says. "We can love them back."

"Yes," I say, "we can show our love." I hoped the conversation would lead this way. "If the cure works, and we make it for them, they will understand that we do this to show we are generous and protective of them, and we can do what they cannot. Our altruism will demonstrate our compassion, a gift for them beyond price, which we can freely give at our choosing. We give not food but life."

"If we do this," Boreas says, "we should make that clear. We do not have to. We are not domestic crops."

"We will not be domesticated," I say. "We will show them that we are great and powerful. We can protect them."

I am not surprised by the fierce debate this evokes. A long debate. In the end, many decide that our compassion and power should come with a price.

"I agree," I say. "Mother Stevland says that we should care for them in exchange for their service. What will that be?"

We consider the freedom that whales won, and we decide that their freedom leads nowhere. Whales do not care about humans. Whales sometimes kill and eat humans. Whales are animals.

"We are better than that," I say. "How are we better?"

"I am already making the fruit," Le Bois says. "If it does not help, then nothing is lost. If it is the cure, we will be ready, and that is how we are better. We are generous and kind."

"I want to be great and powerful," says the Grove of Blossoms, who is young and ambitious.

"Making the fruit is easy to do," Suca Valley says, "if they really do not care what it tastes like."

"They do not care," I assure her. "It can be unripe and hard."

"We can bargain for their service when they have learned we are greater and more powerful than they are," the Grove of Blossoms says.

"What do we want?" the Asia grove insists.

"For now," Le Bois says, "perhaps it will be enough to let them know what we are."

"Courageous," Suca Valley adds. "Because we are taking a risk for them."

"It must not be cheap," Asia says.

"We agree. Let us begin," Boreas commands. "In memory of Foehn."

I wonder what Foehn would decide if she were here.

I monitor my experiment. When Ico comes for more fruit, he still tries to pry into the institute system. Bamboo are generous and altruistic, and he needs to witness that.

"It is good to see you," I send to him. "We hope the fruit is working. We want to help."

He swallows the fruit practically whole. "Why?" The question seems sincere.

"Simply because we can, and we care about you." I do not mention that whales care not at all about humans. He already knows.

Mother Stevland says humans are quick and intense. In this case, they are merely intense. We wait and wait for their bodies to use the enzyme.

"Do we know yet?" Suca Valley asks in the afternoon.

She does not need to specify what.

Kew answers, "I promise to let you know as soon as we have preliminary results. We can all hope."

Suca Valley says, "I am telling every bamboo I can reach with my roots to make the fruit. We are ready."

Huette comes for another dose, and she says she feels unchanged except for digestive upset. I ask about her staff. She looks sad.

"Some of them—you know, they want to spend time with family, and I can't say no. If it's the last. Have you heard about the café? The one down the road? It's open now day and night with music and free food and drink. People come and dance. They want their final time to be happy."

"Perhaps you should go there."

She stands up straight. "Yes, I should."

Brian comes with ashes of a couple who loved to visit the garden and wanted their final rest to be here.

"The ashes will enrich the soil," I say. "We will remember them that way." He spreads them widely. I savor the taste of Denis's ashes.

I am healthy and anxious and miserable.

The night is clear. I look for Oksana, source of the fatal life-form, so I can curse that star, but it lies in Volans, a constellation visible only in the southern sky. I could view it through a camera in the network in the south, but Volans is small and dim and of little interest. The star that Pax orbits is in Gemini, can be seen only in winter, and this is summer. Polaris shines bright, but it offers no consolation.

The Sea Group was defeated with destruction and bloodshed. If we are successful, we will win—no, we will not win because this is not a war. We will solve a problem, quietly, with generosity and love. Empathy, not force.

Our way. I must hope for the best. Prepare for the best. Be ready. The sun
rises over the hills to the east, shining bright, our closest star, and I feel myself grow.

Brian comes with the sister and they are well. Ico is well, they say. Huette
is well. The other humans who are not in the experiment? Not well.

I impatiently contact Kew. "Does it work?"

"They are deciding what to do," she says. "They have a cure, but no way to
make enough of it. We have to tell them about the fruit, Mother Levanter."

"I am ready." During the night, I wrote a scientific paper. It names ourselves as the authors: Levanter, director and pioneer *Pax Bambusa iridis,* Pax
Institute, Republic of Bayonne; and Kew, chief resident *Pax Bambusa iridis*
at Kew Royal Botanic Gardens, Wakehurst, Sussex.

The paper concludes: "The success of treatment for *Pax Bambusa iridis*
suggested the possible clinical use of this specific endochitinase with *Homo
sapiens* to treat *Oksana Vinvelo.* Hoping for its initial experimental success
with humans, *Bambusa iridis* worldwide has already begun to produce the
enzyme in specific fruit for widespread human consumption. We urge continued observation and research, and offer interspecies collaboration in every
way we can. We have unique and extensive resources."

I append Denis's affidavit. We are real.

Mother Stevland said to dominate. This is one way. Knowledge is power.
I also learned long ago about competition in scientific research. We will be
the first to publish. Kew notifies her colleagues at the garden. Beyond the
satisfaction of hubris, I hope this is the first step toward mutual compassion. Failure means possible extinction of humanity through disease, war, or
worse. Humans sometimes spurn wise choices.

"They are reading it," Kew says. "Now they are discussing it. They are
laughing!"

"They mock us? But what we presented was un—"

"They laugh in celebration, Mother Levanter. We will save their lives! And
it is the first nonhuman paper in the history of Earth! It will change everything!"

"I have written papers before."

"Excellent papers! We can remind them later."

The next step will require coordination among humans. When Huette
comes for fruit, I tell her what is happening, and she runs to city hall. I cannot speak for humanity, but she can. I want to love them and protect them.
And dominate them, and humans are hard to understand. They respect
power, though, and we are powerful.

Soon I realize how complicated fruit distribution will be. It takes hours for humans to get ready. Most places plan for controlled distribution, but the people tasked with managing the distribution start eating fruit as soon as they arrive. Humans may be too afraid to act rationally.

"We will be pillaged," Stone Hill says, "or it can be a festival. Humans must choose."

Brian and the sisters at Tabitha House come to the institute, and I tell them where to find all the fruit. I suggest that they pick it themselves and distribute it near the gate rather than let people wander through the garden, and they agree reluctantly. I think they are naive. Boreas grumbles about being used as a crop.

Beluga rolls to the front gate at the institute. I ask why. "Action: Protection," it says. A general-purpose robot joins it, the kind that can prune and dig and hoist. Its tools can be deadly. More institute robots line up at the gate.

"Robots!" Le Bois says. "A kitchen robot is coming here, no, three robots, the kind that can hurt people."

Other groves report robots. The robots do nothing, just stand and wait.

"Robots do not want war," I remind everyone listening to me. "They want to protect humans." In the long term, that is true.

Brian walks up to the robots at the institute. "I appreciate your concern, and your presence will encourage best behavior, so thank you. If there's a problem, call me. All right?"

They do not answer. They do not need to do anything but be visible.

A public announcement is made in Kew Royal Botanic Gardens. Its staff stands next to Kew's most magnificent stems. She says, "We rainbow bamboo are pleased to help the humans in this time of their greatest need. We can speak later, and at great length and depth, about our shared world."

The staff explains that the bamboo has put medicine in special fruit. They provide exact information about which fruit, and how to take it, and caution against hoarding it. They mention side effects and other details that probably no human on Earth bothers to listen to.

People rush to the Pax Institute to get fruit, and if they planned to pillage, as soon as they see the robots, they form orderly lines as directed by the sisters. They look at us, some with awe, others doubtful.

Tabitha House sisters carry fruit to people too ill to come. Ico takes some out to Cetacean ships. We keep making more. Humans start to set up distribution systems, then they discover that robots are already running routes. Soon we get reports of a few allergic reactions, and many complaints about digestive upset, and questions about the need to do this at all. Some portion of humanity will always be made up of skeptics.

The second day runs smoother in most places. The fruit does not save people who are too ill, and there are more funeral pyres. We discover ways to make the fruit more efficiently. Humans debate whether we are sentient, and some demand to know why we kept it a secret. I answer briefly, sometimes repeating answers from other bamboo. We all have different reasons, all good reasons. We have many voices.

I tend to the garden and ponder what to do next. I need to answer Mother Stevland. I continue to trick neighboring plants into making the enzyme, then I steal it from them.

Le Bois asks me how I am.

"I have always reviled parasites."

"Parasites are the top of the food chain," she answers. "Our natural place is at the bottom. We bamboo have learned a new skill, a new lifestyle."

"I do not like it."

"What do you love, Levanter?"

That stops me. After some thought, I know the answer. "I spoke with Denis about what he believed. He said the spark of god is in all life, and joy and beauty were proof."

"Do you believe that?"

"I believe in his love of life, all life." I suddenly understand something. "This is why I hate being a parasite. It is unkind to the plants I am stealing from. Kindness is real." I think further and have something to add. "Life is hard in many ways. Perhaps I should say I am doing the best I can. Thank you for asking."

A few hours later, Kew reports, "It is too soon to say we did it, but we did it! A university is talking about giving us honorary doctorates."

They want to reward us the best way they can. This does not satisfy me. "I want to earn a doctorate."

"I will tell them that. They will love it!"

Levanter, Ph.D. I wonder if my previous research would allow me to skip undergraduate studies.

I can relax. As night falls, I can drowse and idly consider dissertation topics, perhaps in a field other than botany. That is, provided the cure continues to work. It will need to cross the membrane around the human brain. It may stop the disease, but perhaps not cure it. Or it may cure it slowly, which is why some treatments require months of medication, and which may become difficult for us to sustain. However, if the treatment lasts long, that will im-

prove our position as compassionate, loving, protective, commanding, dominating, problem-solving beings. We will have demands.

I have not drowsed much when morning dawns with thunderstorms and
local downpours. The patter of rain energizes me as it cleanses me from my
leaves to my roots and clears the soil. Brian directs a team of volunteers to
harvest the fruit, laughing in the rain.

What do we want? Debate among bamboo continues from one day to the
next. Slowly it shifts to the need to make our demands with responsibility,
then we debate what responsibility means not just to each other but to humans
and all animals and plants.

As humans accept that we are sentient, they get ideas. They realize that
just as advanced network connections allow them to commune with each
other, those connections would allow them to commune with us. Skeptics
will discover if we are really sentient, dreamers will feel the strength of our
size, and scientists will find answers to their questions. Their first question:
Is it even possible? If so, is it safe?

Is it safe for bamboo?

Boreas reminds us about what communing did to Foehn. "That was why
she insisted in not killing humans. She realized that they are as real as we are."

"We always knew that," Toad Forest says. "Foehn—"

"Do not speak ill of Foehn."

"May I speak ill of humans?"

I am relieved to learn I am not the only one with no interest in communing with humans. I have done so already, and I did not enjoy it. Because
communing will require modifications to our network and connections, only
volunteer groves will participate. I prepare a list of participating groves, including Le Bois and Mississippi. I am not on the list.

Brian helps me adjust the network settings. We want high firewalls to
surround us when humans are connected because Gyre's commune reached
out into the entire bamboo network, to our horror. Brian sits in the sun on
the patio as we work. I wonder how that feels to him. Warmth, I suppose.
Humans need warmth. And food.

"The waiting list," he says, "is two hundred twenty years long, assuming
two minutes per person. Are you sure you don't want to join in the rush?"

"I have tasks more important than biological tourism."

"But you're a credit to your species."

I have a long list of tasks. I must respond to Mother Stevland on behalf of
all bamboo, if not the entire Earth biome, as soon as we reach anything close
to a consensus. That is a long way off. Instead, I have sent information to Pax

about *Vinvelo,* in case the pathogen somehow finds its way there. A team of linguists wants to make a translator for a common Earth language and bamboo communication, and we bamboo have insisted, every single bamboo with no debate or dissent, on one key provision: the translator can only work in one direction, so that humans cannot understand what we say to each other, as if they possibly could.

Brian and I finish the adjustments for communing. We test them with Le Bois. She is ready. In fact, she is now officially inscribed as a citizen of Bayonne, giving her certain rights. Should all bamboo be citizens where we live? We debate that.

Huette accompanies the king of the Belgians, Rudolf, who used his royalty to skip ahead of the line on the grounds that he is a symbol of unity not just of Belgium, which held together over centuries when other nations disintegrated, but of all humanity. He will be the first, as far as he knows, and he will share with the world what the experience is like. Le Bois will tell us, too.

I watch the event through the human network, along with uncountable humans. The bamboo network is attentive, too.

Rudolf is a middle-aged man in a formal suit bearing a few medals, trailed by three aides. Huette welcomes him with a red and green box of chocolates, a traditional Bayonne gift. He gives her several cases of beer "crafted by the wind." He means that the yeast, which is a kind of fungus, blew into open-air vats of beer to provide the fermentation. Airborne fungus does not sound appealing to me.

Huette, in her most formal demeanor, guides him to the bamboo. She is not on the list of those who want to commune with a bamboo, although she could pull rank, too, as mayor of Bayonne.

He is not very formal. "Oh, that's Le Bois? It's so nice to meet you. What gifts can I bring to a self-sufficient being? And such a beautiful one, too. Thanks is not enough. We wouldn't be alive without you, and now, we can meet, mind to mind. But I warn you, I am just one man, a lowly and ordinary man despite my title. I inherited it, and my real job is to be worthy of my title. My people, the Belgians, are worth quite a lot."

Huette stands stiff, looking at the medals on his chest, which he earned in the war. She reads a script on behalf of Le Bois. "The universe is united by beauty," Huette intones. Someone on Pax said something like that once.

Technicians explain a few things to King Rudolf, who knows them already. These words are for the human audience. Le Bois will cut off her connections to other groves to protect them. He puts on the crown as if he has habitually worn crowns and closes his eyes. After a short time, they open wide. He takes a few steps, he looks around, smiles, laughs, and then he falls, sobbing, to the ground.

Huette and his aides and the technicians kneel to help him. I feel strangely vindicated. We are large and powerful, and the king is prostrate and sobbing.

Soon he recovers enough to stand with Huette's help. "I will never see the world the same again." He is led away, dazzled. No one else will attempt communing today until safety is assured.

I ask Le Bois how it was.

"I cut the connection because he was overwhelmed."

"And you?"

"Humans are a moving permanence."

"I do not understand." I experienced nothing like that in my brief connections.

"You should do this. They are different in every way. Every way, Levanter! So small but so big. I know you want to respect boundaries, and that is why you think being a parasite is repugnant. It is instead a new skill, a new way to understand the universe."

I have enough skills.

I ask Brian, "What did that do to the waiting list?"

"Oh, I think it should have increased it."

"I do not understand."

"This will be a challenge. Can they outlast King Rudolf? Thirteen seconds. We're competitive primates, Levanter, social climbers, every one of us."

One of my roots cannot stop wondering about moving permanence. Perhaps it could be my dissertation topic, how physiology affects cognition.

Brian continues to collect fruit and distribute it, and as he does, he looks at me with curiosity. I have come to know him well, and I believe he respects me.

I tell him, "Le Bois said humans are moving permanence. I have communed, briefly, with humans in one-way connections, and do not understand."

"You could find out."

If I love humans, if I intend to guide them and command them, then I should do my best to understand them. I should have volunteered right away. "We could find out."

"I welcome challenges." He fiddles with a ring in his hair. "Should I ask Huette to supervise us? She has experience."

"Someone should be there just in case."

"We should put up firewalls, Levanter. You have a lot of connections."

When Rudolf is finally traveling back home, Huette joins us deep in the garden.

"From what I saw, I'm not sure this is smart," she says. "Rudolf was blathering a lot."

"I've heard quite a bit about him," Brian says. "Sociable, which is the right character for his job, and not always serious, just like all Belgians. He lasted for thirteen seconds."

"So you think you can do better?"

"Will you time me?"

She nods. "Levanter?"

"I volunteered for this."

"All right then," she says. "You know what to do."

Brian does not need a crown. He runs some fingers through his hair to arrange his rings. Animals sometimes move by habit, by memory. I have never—

Ahead is rich loam, a medium, a means, a condition and environment I can grow through, because thoughts can grow, and at the other end I know there is a human mind. Faster than I can grow, it contracts, and on the other side

energy. So much energy. Like sunshine, like pure sugar, like wind contained in a being. Air flows in, and out, breathing. It feels good to breathe. My eyes open, too bright for just a moment, and my eyes adjust, they move, I see. A forest, familiar, only two eyes carefully coordinated, one vision, the sight of leaves blowing in the wind. I feel wind, I hear wind, hair moves, skin is cooled, and skin

and flesh and hands that move, feet that step forward, moving, a habit, walking, energy on a scaffold of bones and muscles that walk without thought, two points working against gravity, balancing, step after step

an itch in my mind as if a friendly insect, an inquisitive ant, is exploring leaves and stems, nothing to fear or to note much. I

can walk, turn, look at me, my stem, and the colors are so bright they feel good to see. So much energy even for a simple emotion. Reaching out to touch the leaves, to enjoy them, cool from transpiration, I know that and it is unimportant, what matters is one thing, a pleasant coolness in my hands, and I can hold the leaf, move it, feel the edge, the veins, the stiff stalk as if it is the only thing in the world

and the warmth from inside, energy inside, breathing, and the enveloping skin, a comfort keeping in the warmth, protecting it from the cool breeze, a body that is comforted, comforting, gently touching leaves to share in the life

energy energy energy to move, to make

to shiver

that is not me, that is him, feelings too big, too much too little too hard
for muscles joints balance feet that try to fight a sway from the wind inside
too much. I see a door and I can walk toward it, movement, doing what I
have seen, a door to walk through and close it and
  loam, a body that does not move, an awareness that is boundless
and every eye from every direction sees Brian fold and fall.

Huette kneels, pressing a sensor against his skin.

"Within parameters." She shrugs. "Like a good workout at the gym. And thirty-two seconds. You outdid the king by a lot, Brian."

He is sobbing. Like Rudolf. What did he experience?

I was inside a living, moving cold fire, everything focused, everything intense, everything familiar to the body, all the parts the same forever, all the parts practiced and valuable. Each finger is forever. Yes, moving permanence. Each breath each blink each adjustment to stay standing a forever movement. Movement from inside.

"Beautiful, and big, colossal," he murmurs.

Huette kneels to take his hand. Touch is pleasant, I understand that now, not just tolerated, and pleasure releases energy.

"What is it?" She looks up at me. "Maybe it's your size. What about you, Levanter? What did you feel?"

"I cut off the connection because I could feel too much energy released by what he was experiencing."

"I mean you? What are we like?"

"Intense in a way I cannot think that I would feel to him. And yet he felt overwhelmed."

"When this is all done, we're going to have to have a long talk."

She helps Brian stand and walk. I can imagine how that feels, the thoughtless scaffold of bones and the push and pull of muscle, a feeling too familiar to notice. Warmth and food, movement and control, quick and intense. I hope I have not harmed him. I still have much to learn and do.

CHAPTER 6

Year 2900 CE
Bayonne, France

ICO

Who really cared about me? I wasn't supposed to ask because only the Cetacean Institute cared. They'd always given me everything I needed ever since I was a child, and the rest of the world had once almost hunted whales to extinction, which told me everything I needed to know, except that it didn't. My job had been to protect Cetacean interests—the rest of the world, I had always been told, opposed us. Then there was a killer fungus and we were all going to die, and the Cetaceans cared when Clerihew died, but me? I was on my own.

I got help, though. A week ago, the tingling in my left arm told me I had been infected, and I was still alive because the people and bamboo around me were willing to help everybody. Some of them, including total strangers, were actually nice to me even though they knew I was with the Cetaceans.

Now my job was to find out what the rainbow bamboo really wanted because they might be rivals to the whales. We championed what the whales wanted—what they apparently wanted. They never issued formal demands, while the bamboo wrote scientific papers with footnotes and appendices and offered collaboration. But everyone and everything secretly wanted something—that's what I'd learned from the Cetaceans.

I didn't want to be there anymore, stuck among landlubbers, asking questions. I didn't understand the land and its robots and forest fires and odd food and complicated people. I wished I could get reassigned back out at sea.

Instead, I was going to the Pax Institute in the morning to start work, and just getting there made me ask more questions. I was walking, and I was really built for that, not for swimming, and I wanted solid ground to feel as strange as it looked. Trees and buildings blocked the horizon and the view of a storm blowing in from the sea—the sea, so close, its horizons so wide— and someone coming the other way who I didn't recognize said hello as they passed, but landlubbers weren't supposed to be nice to Cetaceans!

As I entered the institute building, rain started pouring down. Through the wall-sized window, I saw Brian out in the garden banging on one of the bamboo stems with a chisel and hammer. What? Why? The bamboo were keeping us alive. I had to do something, and I had no established procedures, no one to tell me what to do. I was on my own. I took a deep-diving breath and rushed outside.

"Brian, what are you doing?" Maybe Brian's *Vinvelo* infection hadn't been cured and it was making Brian violent.

He smiled, just a normal smile, not a weird sick grin. "Levanter asked me to carve Foehn's name in her stem. It's like a tattoo."

Rain was drumming on my bare head, and it felt good—water. But tattoos on trees? "Is Levanter all right?" Bamboo could get sick from the fungus, too, and then they'd want pain.

He stared up at the tree with love. He'd been doing that ever since he communed with Levanter—communing changed people in strange ways. The Cetacean Institute forbade communing, and I didn't want to do it anyway. Nothing was more landlubber than a tree.

"We talked about it for a long time," Brian said. "We had to decide on the right size for the name and the lettering." He touched the trunk. "These are uncial letters, very dignified. Because Foehn . . . Foehn did so much wrong, Levanter said, and in the end, she did everything right, and then she died. Levanter spent centuries with her." He turned to me. "Do you want to talk to Levanter about it? She's around here somewhere." He meant the little robot that Levanter sometimes used to talk with. "I'll call her."

Water was dripping inside my uniform. I wanted to take it off, stand naked and enjoy the rain. Water was calling to me, but this wasn't the time or place to answer. A half dozen fippokats came bounding out of the forest, behind them the little moisture sensor, Beluga.

"Warmth and food, Ico," Levanter said through it. "Thank you for your concern. I have thought deeply about this and talked to other bamboo. I want to make my memory visible. I have nicks and marks of all kinds on my stems, and I want one mark to be intentional and meaningful."

Levanter sounded calm, which might have been the artificial voice from the robot. Or maybe bamboo were like that, sedate. People who communed

with them said bamboo felt stable and steady. I didn't know much about
Foehn, just that the fungus killed her, and now stems with dead leaves were
everywhere in the garden.

Brian raised the chisel and hammer and began to carve again.

"I want to remember Foehn," Levanter said. "We must all remember Denis. We continue to live due to his hope and sacrifice."

Whales didn't care about humans, and I'd have guessed bamboo wouldn't
care, either. Whales had cliques and competition, too, but bamboo? The letters were ten centimeters tall. Was that large or small, considering Levanter's
enormous size? How big would my feelings be if they were visible on my
body? I had one question I wanted to ask out loud.

"Levanter, does it hurt?"

"Pain is a part of it," she said, "as it should be. Right now, caterpillars are
chewing on leaves, and a woodpecker is drilling holes in a stem, and a nematode infection is forming a gall on a root, and I could go on. Pain is proof of
ongoing life."

The voice came from a robot. Whales sang, and like us they were animals,
but no one communed with whales. They'd never cooperate. I wasn't a water
creature, and whales knew that. Landlubbers saw me, hairless and sleek, as
a poor imitation of a whale, and they were right.

Brian finished and stepped back to admire his work. "Right now," he said,
"you can hardly see it. The scar will develop over time." He turned to me.
"And here we are, both getting wet. You don't mind the rain?"

"I like the sea. I wish the rain was salty." That was the truth. The way he
looked at me, I knew what he was thinking, I was a fake whale. He wasn't a
tree, either.

"Next nice day," he said, "let's go to the beach. I'd treasure the chance to
hear about its wonders from an expert. For now, we should both go inside." I
wasn't expecting that. He shook his wet head, and a few drops splashed me,
not as welcome as rain although it felt exactly the same.

The institute's building, old and covered with lichen and moss, now wet,
looked like rocks on a seashore. Everything reminded me of where I wasn't.

The little robot, Beluga, followed us in. What did Levanter really think of
humans?

Huette was waiting for us inside. What did she think of me? She called me
to city hall once, and I thought she was going to yell at me, and instead she
spoke about everything that was happening in the world and how much the
Cetacean Institute could help by acting quickly. She said she was very sorry
about Clerihew and would give her a posthumous medal. The building had

some stones salvaged by archeology on display, and she told me about what the carvings meant because she was proud of Bayonne's history. By then, I realized she wasn't good at small talk, but she was trying. She was trying to be nice.

We all sat down to get to work at the conference table made from checkerboard wood. That kind of tree came from Pax. Clerihew had brought a gift of a beautiful bowl made of mother-of-pearl, and it sat in the center, another reminder.

Brian, Huette, Levanter, and I mapped the places where bamboo groves had been in contact with each other and were fighting off the *Vinvelo* fungus. I was just supposed to watch, but I helped. We compared those with the places where humans had become ill or had been treated by medicated fruit as preventative care. The death rate had fallen to close to zero in most places, but that could change if people got careless.

What was the bamboo going to demand in exchange? What was the bamboo called Mississippi doing exactly? People were lining up to commune with bamboo and especially with that one. Levanter said Mississippi shared love and empathy with everything around her, but I knew better.

Levanter provided updates about the health of bamboo groves and about the humans that bamboo around the world observed, and they observed a lot. In some towns, people had fought to get the fruit until they realized there was plenty.

Then Levanter said, "I have learned of a problem. The Sea Group demands a new treaty, or it will go to war."

Huette froze.

Brian put a hand on her shoulder. "Tell us more, Levanter."

The Sea Group had just issued a claim of a superweapon. Brian and Levanter went over possible weapons and weren't convinced. What did I know?

"It's prudent to take them at their word," Brian said, "although they're lying bastards and always have been. If I could get close, I could listen to their communications and find out."

We were with Huette as she sat and stared at the wall in her office at city hall, a new white building across the road from the institute. The wall was covered with documents, some faded and brown and unreadable. I knew what they were because a few days ago she'd told me about them proudly. One was the original charter of Bayonne's independence. Others were declarations of rights from France going back a thousand years.

The news about the Sea Group was all over the network, and everyone was talking about it. Huette had met with other government leaders to agree on coordinated action. It might affect the fight against *Vinvelo,* so she had us listen in. Now we'd heard the plan to negotiate, and we sat in Huette's cluttered office in uneasy silence. I massaged my arm to help the nerves recover.

Huette kept staring at the wall. "For my whole life, I've hated the Insurrection and the Sea Group and everything they stood for. They killed people I loved, they killed innocent people, they threw me in jail, they ruined cities and farms. I hate people I never met, whose names I don't know. And I'm proud of that hate."

"We all share your feelings," Brian murmured.

"It's more than that." She pointed to the documents. "We're born and remain free and equal in rights. It's my job to protect that. It's precious."

The war had meant something else to me. A dozen years ago, while people on land were fighting, I was one of the lucky young guests to have dinner with Clerihew. I ate flaky fish and listened entranced.

"We're officially neutral," she declared. "It isn't our fight, and it doesn't matter to us. The Sea Group wants land, even though their name doesn't sound like it. They can have all the land they want."

If she thought so, I thought so too—as a pubescent boy who worshiped her, although eventually I noticed that some seaports had become rubble and didn't rebuild. I'd never thought much about the people on the land. For us, the war meant more freedom at sea, better for the whales, and nothing else mattered. The Sea Group had been defeated and confined to its original territory in northeast Siberia. Its people went back to whatever they used to do and paid a lot of reparations to the winners—until now.

Brian asked, "Levanter, what have the bamboo seen?"

"Our groves there are not chipped, and the roots are very far away from anyone who is."

Huette sighed. "It's out of our hands. At least for today. Tomorrow, I'll still hate them."

I asked, trying to do my job, "If there's war, Levanter, how will the bamboo react?"

"We do not want a new war. We want peace."

"They might simply want to get out of reparations," Huette said. "As if they hadn't wreaked destruction on everyone and everything."

That afternoon, the skiff rocked under my feet, and I closed my eyes. It felt right. I belonged on the water, and I breathed in the scent of sea life. The waves struck the hull like a drumbeat, a rhythm older than life itself. I was heading toward one of our ships, toward friends, purpose, and home.

What did whales think of water? As far as we could tell, they had names for things like locations and currents, warm and cold. They had no name for blue, the blue ocean and sky, because whales couldn't see blue. They had no name for water.

I stopped thinking and simply felt. Other planets had oceans, and some of them had life. The splash, the salt air, the waves were universal, and I wanted to swim like a creature of not just the sea but the universe.

I pulled up alongside the ship. I hefted aboard a big bag of medical fruit, and I was met by familiar faces and a quick hug from someone I'd known since childhood. I noticed the bulk between us, soft human fat, not whale blubber, which would have been solid and tough, but we pretended it was the same.

"Hey, Ico," he said, "you brought fruit from the talking trees!" He and I weren't actually friends. I'd worked with him a year ago monitoring the baleen-whale breeding grounds in the Caribbean. I got a medal. He got a promotion. He was out here, and I was stuck on land. But for whatever came next, I needed to stay on good terms.

He laughed. "Land food! I couldn't stand eating it all the time."

"Yeah, it's weird." Some land food was delicious, though.

"Homesick much? Hey, look what I got." He spread his fingers to show webbing. "I can get you this when you come back. I feel sorry for you on such a useless assignment."

"Thanks. I'd appreciate that." Webbing was a status symbol, but it would mean I'd owe him something for it. He owed something to someone, too, for his. That's how Cetaceans worked. Like whales, we had competition and hierarchies.

My assignment wasn't useless, was it?

"I'd love to chat more," I said, "but I'm here for a meeting."

I headed below. Some things should not be discussed on a network, and I had one big question to ask and a lot of small ones I didn't know if I should ask.

The captain and an intelligence officer were waiting. I knew the captain, and off-duty, he lived on a nice yacht. They sat, and I remained standing.

"You said you needed a consultation," the intelligence officer said. She was sleeker than me and a little older.

"The Sea Group is threatening war. If there's a war, what's our plan?"

The captain sat with his arms crossed. "Same as ever. We're neutral. Our job is to serve the whales. The primacy of the sea matters to us all."

Something should have been clear to me, and with a moment of thought, it was. We had to protect not just the whales but our primacy, our control of the sea. That control, and fees for safe passage from commercial maritime traffic, got the captain his yacht. That use of control had always seemed reasonable—although Huette didn't use her position for anything like that.

"At the Pax Institute, what should I do?"

He leaned back. "People on the land have a strange way of understanding the world. I mean, their spaces and places in it. You know the story."

I did. It was a children's story we'd all heard as children or told to children so many times we could recite it. A jellyfish has a fight with its swarm, so it catches a current and finds a new place to live. It finds a new swarm, and after a while, even though it has friends, it decides to move on, and then in the new place, there's an attack by a school of tuna, so it moves on, and on and on and on.

He meant: People on land could walk away and go someplace else just like sea creatures. The sea was wide. So were the continents. Lots of spaces, lots of places.

"How about the bamboo?" the intelligence officer asked. "What are they up to?"

"They don't want a war." I realized that they were stuck in place permanently. I added, "Euclid Nave Station might recover eventually. Someone named Joaquim is talking to Earth now. And everyone wants to commune with the trees."

The captain smirked. "Trees." He clearly didn't think they could offer much intellect.

"The search is on for a new head of the institute," I said. "Denis was a good leader, and he'll be missed." I missed him. He'd treated me well.

"Who's heading it up now?"

"A bamboo named Levanter."

They both laughed.

"The institute is automated," I said, "so it can go on inertia for a while." I should have told how canny Levanter was. I would later, I decided.

"Do you have any contact with Mayor Huette?"

"Of course. She's always around and—"

"Is she smart?"

"She's very observant. She's—"

"Good people skills?"

"Frankly, not always. She—"

"Fair-minded?"

"She leans toward the ceremonial aspects of her job." I didn't know why I wasn't quite telling the whole truth. No, I knew. I was feeling, not thinking. I wanted to protect her, although I didn't know what from.

"That's what we need to know. Nice work. Keep at it."

"Thank you for your time." I left unsatisfied. If they had a plan, it was to let landlubbers fight, and I'd seen and heard about some of the massive damage of the last war. Or maybe they had a different plan and hadn't told me. Like a jellyfish, I was swimming free. The story never said that jellyfish usually lived part of their lives anchored in one place, and that jellyfish had no brains at all, an intelligence almost at zero. Terrestrial ants could outthink them easily.

Also, in the story, the jellyfish left its friends behind again and again.

I stayed for dinner, mussels and seaweed and no landlubber food besides the medicinal fruit, crunchy and bland. Everyone had a lot of questions that could be summed up into one:

"How did people get tricked into believing the bamboo could decide to make the fruit on its own?"

I tried a couple of times to explain that this species had a mind. A lot of things on land had minds. Ants had intellects. Finally, to change the subject, I said, "The main bamboo sometimes uses a robot to communicate. It's designed to measure soil moisture. Its name is Beluga."

We laughed at the majestic name for a lowly robot. I stayed the night in a big shared bunk room and was rocked to sleep thinking about how we weren't like jellyfish at all. Every one of us wanted to advance to the point where we could buy our own nice yachts.

The next morning, in the skiff, I closed my eyes and felt the sea move me. Water filled the universe, flowed in my blood, under my feet, in my mind, over my head as clouds in the air. And on the ground, in the soil. I could never escape water. I would never exist without water, but this water, here?

I volunteered to deliver fruit to Huette so I could spend a little time with her. She said she had news and asked me to sit down, and the news didn't seem good.

The Sea Group had designated her to arbitrate peace talks.

"Why do they want me?" Huette said. She stared at the documents on the wall as she talked, which was just as well. My face might have told the truth.

Did they ask for her because I'd suggested she was weak, and the captain had passed the word along? It wasn't true—she wasn't weak. If the captain had asked the right questions or hadn't interrupted me, I could have talked about what she hated and why. Or about what made her effective.

But my face would have told a bigger truth. The Cetaceans were in contact with the Sea Group. We weren't neutral. We weren't what we said we were. I saw lies like mirrors reflecting each other into infinity. And if I was a Cetacean, I wasn't what I thought I was.

I was holding my breath as if I were going to take a deep dive, and the waters weren't that deep, really. I'd known for a while that the world wasn't what I'd been told, and now the currents were faster than I'd thought. Where were they taking me?

For now, Huette had asked a question, and I ought to answer her, but if I told the truth, then what would happen? She was comfortable with silence. I liked that. I imagined standing on a deck with her, the ship drifting with the current and the wind, rising and falling in the swells, and we would enjoy the moment side by side in companionable silence, communing—that is, communicating—by our presence alone, no chips, no crowns, nothing between us.

I said, "You'll do what's expected of you."

"I always do. Arbitrate—I can do that. Hear what they want, what the other side wants, and lead everyone toward a decision. Sounds easy." After a while, she added, "I want to be one member of a three-member panel. I want a neutral setting. I want a binding outcome, even if any party disagrees with the majority decision. Who are the other parties, besides? The Sea Group has to stipulate that. Sure. Easy."

"You've thought a lot about this." She would not be what the Sea Group—or Cetaceans—hoped for.

"I'll be fair. I bet they accessed my health records and thought I'd be in over my head. I had some genetic repairs prenatal, and I'm still more detailed than most people, and more direct. I'd rather be recycling technology because everyone needs tech."

"If I can help in any way, I'm willing." Would that compromise my assignment? I realized I'd compromised it already.

"What do Cetaceans think about all this?"

"Um—we only care about whales." I almost said *they only care,* and that told me what I was really thinking. We sat together in silence for a while longer. I thought about leaving Bayonne and getting back at sea before my loyalty to the Cetacean Institute, to the whales, was whittled away. Did I want that? The land was full of obstacles blocking the view to the horizon.

She said, "I'll send in my stipulations."

After another silence, I asked a landlubber question. "Have you ever thought about communing with the bamboo?"

"I don't want to be anybody but me. I mean any *body*."

"That's the question. What do we want to be?"

When I entered the institute grounds, a robot was playing with the fippokats—a starfish robot, not squat little Beluga, unless Beluga—that is, Levanter—controlled the starfish robot, too. It held up two arms, and a kat vaulted over it. It held up three arms, and three kats leaped up to balance on the tip of each arm with one back foot, then tumbled off. They chattered and tried again, this time linking their front paws to steady each other. Once they were steady, the robot began to sway and spin.

People waiting for medical fruit applauded and laughed. The show was for them, or maybe it was for the fippokats, who lived for fun, and maybe it entertained the robot. Whales played often, as far as we could tell.

Brian was lounging on the sofa in the office. He'd slipped a few flowers into his hair. Did he want to become a tree?

"Some leaves would fill in the bouquet," I said—grumbled, really. I sat at the table.

"Yes, they would!" He looked out at the garden. "In a minute. First I have a question for you. Actually, the bamboo have a question. What's the agreement that the Cetacean Institute has with the whales? How did you reach it?"

Levanter would be listening, even if she hadn't greeted me or paid any attention to me. She was paying attention to Brian, and—I was jealous.

"We have an informal agreement. We chose to protect the whales."

"Did they accept?" His question was genuine, not snide.

"They're aware of it. They let us protect them." That's what we believed, anyway.

"Do you understand their language?"

"A few words."

"Do they try to communicate with you? Even rudimentarily?" He still seemed genuine.

"No." Never.

"Did you know," he said, "that the bamboo want to learn to speak directly with humans with our language, some of them, at any rate. They're interested in what we are."

I could have said that whales had intense social lives and made agreements with each other. They noticed us, though. Once, when a human attacked a young whale, the beluga police responded with play that killed the human.

"How about the corals?" I wanted him to feel as bad as I did.

"Oh, they don't know we exist—or even care, which might be just as well. Our cult is observation only, and just like you. Our—no, that's the wrong word. I'm not part of it anymore. I resigned." He sat up straight. "Did you know, up on Pax, the coral attacked the settlement? They might attack us if they could, and I don't want to be involved with them anymore. I might join Friends of Fippokats instead. Kats aren't what most people think."

"I saw some of them playing on my way in. A robot was playing with them. Does the institute have robots to entertain them?"

"Levanter," he said, "do we?"

I noticed the word "we."

"Good morning, Ico. I did not wish to interrupt earlier. The robot playing with the fippokats is a wild robot. Play is now a characteristic of wild robots. They have been passing along a module for playful behavior to each other, which raises a number of questions."

"Wild robots?" I said. "You let wild robots on the grounds?" Wild robots were dangerous.

"They have long been welcome. This is a decision of the institute system, not me, and I do not seek quarrels with the system."

"You could quarrel with the system?" Machines weren't people.

"Oh, it's semiautonomous," Brian said. "Quite sophisticated."

"I do not seek quarrels with anything around me," Levanter said. "I am a good friend of an oak tree across the road, the large one with the twisted trunk, and oaks are especially agreeable and outgoing. Some humans want to commune with oaks now, and oaks are naturally slow, so they may not have deep exchanges, but the communes will be pleasant."

Trees had friends, she said. "Levanter, do bamboo play?"

"We older bamboo engage in avocational activities when we have spare resources."

"Activities?"

"Unique floral displays are common. One grove collects information about butterflies, another practices counseling skills, and I have trained a meadow of flowers, much as you might train a pet."

Levanter had pets. Did the Pax Institute need to protect the bamboo, or could they take care of themselves? If I had to ask the question, I already knew the answer. The bamboo was protecting us from *Vinvelo*, so what did that make us?

COLONEL AGRAFINA CHERNOVA

I wanted peace more than I'd wanted anything ever. If the Sea Group tried to start a war again, I'd blast them to ashes to stop them. I was head of a Combined Forces/CAC security team, and I'd put my life on the line to protect the Sea Group ambassador in case anyone wanted to assassinate him, but if the talks failed, I'd have a clear shot, and I'd take it.

A long road got me to that point. It had taught me to be careful.

I arrived on site the day before at Bayonne, an ancient city on the Atlantic coast that had been one of the first to defeat the Insurrection. It looked pretty, sitting at the mouth of the river, not too many ruins from the war, surrounded by fertile farmland. It reminded me of Rassohka, but everything reminded me of Rassohka.

The first thing I did was arrange for the ambassador's craft to land unannounced, as quietly as possible, away from the grand hall in the center of town where negotiations were going to be held. That way, we could get the formal welcome over before anything happened or be ready in case it did.

So, the next morning, I was alert for anything. The aircraft would land in a sports field next to the city hall. A car stood ready in the road to whisk away the ambassador, the mayor, and myself to the grand hall, where the rest of the security team was bolstering the city's gendarmes.

This part of the world was new to me. The bird calls were different, and the air had a fishy smell from the ocean I didn't really like. I was in dress uniform, complete with white gloves. The mayor wore a business suit and had a stoic look on her face. She'd be the sole arbiter, even though she'd wanted to be a panel of three, but she'd do her job. At her insistence, the Sea Group ambassador would be plenipotentiary, meaning any agreement would be final. We'd had a talk the day before, and I liked how tough Huette was. We agreed that we'd work well together.

A Cetacean observer waiting with us checked out as harmless, but in the brief conversation we'd had, he seemed gloom-ridden. The Cetaceans had supplied the aircraft, so he probably was ordered to be there and wanted to be somewhere else.

The Tabitha House next to the Pax Institute sent their senior sister, cool and astute, named Mercy, to provide welcoming hospitality. She'd spent the war helping refugees in active fighting zones, and if anything happened, I could trust her to know what to do.

Then there was Brian Amp, looking a little skeptical, with a few flowers stuck into his wire-threaded hair. As soon as I'd met him, he sent me a security code. He was one of us, a behind-the-lines veteran. If I needed to blast the Sea Group to ashes, he had the built-in tech to take out their communications.

He carried a little robot that the rainbow bamboo used to talk with us. I wanted to talk to the bamboo a lot more than I'd been able to so far. A long time ago, I'd heard that kind of tree scream and die. When they turned out to be smart, I wasn't surprised. I'd protect them, too, every tree, every person, every animal from the Sea Group.

As we stood and waited, I got a message about a delay in arrival. "Ten minutes," I announced. I scanned the area. The landing should still go off as planned.

Next to the field was an ancient stone arch decorated with lions and towers and other things too worn to identify.

"What do those symbols mean?" Ico, the Cetacean, asked the mayor. Civilians found it hard to wait quietly.

"Lions flanking a tower are ancient symbols of Bayonne." She said the word "ancient" with pride, and held up a box decorated in green and red. "These are the traditional colors of Bayonne, and these are chocolates, another tradition, a welcome gift for Ambassador Sempronio. If this works out, there'll be chocolates all around."

I hoped that would include me. Chocolates were expensive.

A rumble grew in the west, and an airship approached. The first glimpse scared me. It was an MC7-class. They broke down a lot, sometimes catastrophically.

"Oh, dear," Brian sent. "An MC7. The Cetaceans could have done better. I'll scan for airworthiness."

It was a small, pilotless craft. I held my breath, hoping it wouldn't crashland, as it settled into the playing field with a blast of frosty air from its engines. We waited until the cold dust settled, then we waited some more. Ico and Huette fidgeted.

Finally, the door rose. A tall old man with a scraggly grayish beard stood in the doorway, draped in red and gold brocade robes, leaning on a cane. I'd expected someone more like a soldier, but he did look crafty.

I glanced at Brian. He stood tense, working hard.

Huette stepped forward with her box of chocolates. "On behalf of the citizens of the Republic of Bayonne, I welcome you. We enjoy a long tradition here of concern for rights and freedom, and I hope this spirit can undergird our talks and lead to a successful conclusion."

Beautifully put. She was the exact right kind of tough.

A message came from my team at the grand hall. "We have a disturbance. Police overwhelmed. Recommend delaying arrival. At least an hour."

"Copy." We'd designated city hall as an alternative, so I approached Huette. "Madame Mayor, there's a slight change of plans. Perhaps we could hold a hospitality breakfast at city hall." She'd doubtless just heard the news from her police.

She glanced at Mercy, who nodded. We were prepared.

A few robots were coming down the road. I hoped they were security, but I couldn't raise an identification. They could be wild robots. They'd been on our side in the war, but I didn't like to see them because they were unpredictable. I sent to Brian, asking him to check them out.

The ambassador didn't know this yet. He was waiting for the aircraft's stairway to unfold, and it should have done that by now. He didn't look like he could jump three meters down, so he'd need help, and the sooner we got into city hall, the better.

"Ico," the mayor said, "can you please get—"

"Everyone run!" Brian shouted. "Engine shutdown failure!" He threw the robot at Mercy. "I'll get the ambassador."

If the engine went catastrophic, city hall would be damaged. I changed plans. "Everyone, run for cover to the Pax Institute!" I ran toward the plane. Mercy was the first to move, and the rest followed her. The robots headed toward the institute, too, and I could only hope they were on our side.

Brian was at the craft with his arms outstretched. "Jump!" he shouted.

The ambassador stood there frozen.

I came up next to Brian and we interlaced our arms. "We'll catch you. Jump." I had an exo-suit under my uniform. I could handle his weight easily.

The craft whined and shook. The ambassador closed his eyes and jumped. We caught him, and I threw him over my shoulder and began running. Brian was behind me. Huette would have sent a notice to the city hall staff to take shelter, as we'd planned. I was saving the life of someone I was willing to kill, but peace would be better.

I could run fast, and I was at the institute gate, far ahead of Brian, when the whining got so high I couldn't hear it anymore and my ears throbbed. I knew what that meant. Huette, Mercy, and Ico were dashing into the building. Good. Brian. Not good. I'd hoped that if I carried the ambassador, he'd be able to run fast enough. My best choice was to dive behind the wall next to the gate and shield the ambassador with my body.

The engines exploded with a blast wave that spread along the ground. It hit the wall, and it shook and cracked, but the bricks held. I tried sending to Brian. Nothing.

I backed away from the ambassador. He managed to stand up on his own, leaning on his cane, panting, dazed. I sent to my team, "Aircraft exploded. Man down. Ambassador safe. We're in the Pax Institute." I sent to command calling for backup. I connected to a still-functional surveillance camera on the outside of city hall to take a look at what had happened. I saw what I expected. Damn. Just damn.

I'd lost soldiers before. Later, I'd be sad and angry. Some things I never got used to, I just got better at feeling bad. Right now, I had to protect everyone.

Mercy came out of the building, her hands clasped, maybe praying the way Tabithas did, her eyes wide open, taking in the situation. The wild robots that had dashed into the institute with us lined up along the gate. Drones hung in the sky above the walls like guards. I didn't trust them but I couldn't get rid of them, either.

Out loud, I told Mercy, "Let's get the ambassador indoors." The drones had a clear shot if they weren't on our side. She took him by the arm and led him indoors with a lot more patience than I knew how to muster.

The mayor and Ico stood in the reception area. His face was utter surprise and shock. Huette stared grimly through a window at the gate. She'd have tried to contact Brian. They'd worked together fighting *Vinvelo,* and they'd clearly liked each other. She might be as numb for now as I was. The little robot stood at her feet.

My team sent, "Police have the situation figured out but not under control. The riot is between Sea Group supporters and everyone else. The police are getting reinforcements."

"Sea Group has supporters here?"

"Yeah. They started it. Orders?"

"We're on a peace mission. Keep everyone safe from the Sea Group and assist the gendarmes."

"Copy."

"We'll shelter here. Backup is on the way." Out loud, I asked, "Is everyone all right?"

The ambassador looked offended as he straightened his robes. "What exactly happened?"

"Engine shutdown failure," I said. "That kind of aircraft fails a lot."

"You're trying to tell me it was an accident." He was very offended, and he was right, it might not have been an accident, but his indignation might be an act, since Sea Group supporters were rioting downtown.

"I certainly hope so." I didn't add, *for your sake because I'm armed.* I turned to Huette. "Madame Mayor, I'm sorry about Brian, very sorry, personally." She probably knew he was a veteran, but I couldn't talk about his service in public. "This is a sad loss."

She nodded. She wasn't the talkative type. I waited for her next move because she was in charge, and she knew it. We'd made contingency plans.

She looked at the ambassador, then at the entrance to the director's office. "Negotiations will commence. Here and now. I won't let them be stopped."

"My luggage was on that aircraft," Sempronio complained.

"We can see to your needs, Ambassador," Mercy answered. "Ico can assist you, too."

He blinked like he'd just woken up. "Um, of course."

The little robot rolled toward the office, and a voice came over the building's audio system, Levanter's voice. "The institute robots will act to keep the institute secure with help from wild-robot volunteers. They will attend to Brian with respect and dignity. I mourn him, too, beyond what I can express in words, as an able coworker and dear friend."

"Who are you?" Sempronio demanded.

"I am Levanter, director of the Pax Institute. Please let me welcome you and wish you speedy and successful negotiations."

"You're that tree."

"I hope you find our accommodations comfortable."

I suppressed a smirk. Levanter was better than I'd imagined, and I should have gone over contingency plans with her, too. The team downtown kept sending me updates, not much progress, but no major bloodshed either. Central command said reinforcements were due within minutes at the downtown team and at my location to investigate the aircraft and secure the Pax Institute. I updated them on the local robots.

"Do you wish to begin?" Huette told Sempronio, not a question but an order.

Still with that offended look, he strode into the office and took a seat at a large table as if he were king of all he surveyed. The mayor followed, sitting opposite him. Mercy went to serve beverages and raid a cupboard for food, and she asked Ico to go outside and gather some fruit, medicinal and regular. He looked frightened but complied.

Huette sat facing Sempronio. "I declare these negotiations open. Levanter, please instruct the building system to record the proceedings. Several questions need to—"

"This is not the appropriate place," the ambassador said.

If it wasn't, I wondered, why had he sat there? Obviously, because the talks were a sham. No one could trust the Sea Group.

"Colonel Chernova," Huette said, "what is the situation in the heart of the city?"

"Sea Group supporters are rioting outside the grand hall. It's not safe to go there, and we might not be safe if they come here."

Huette looked Sempronio dead in the eye. "Call them off."

"I don't know anything about them. This is the absolute truth. We are not universally despised, however, and that should be taken into account."

I really wanted to kill him for the good of humanity. Mercy set tea and plates of cookies in front of everyone. Ico entered the door with a bowl of fruit, put it on the table, felt the hostility, and stepped back.

Sempronio sighed theatrically. "If we must begin, then, we demand reparations lifted, full economic reintegration and access to technology, sufficient armed forces of our own for self-protection, and an end to occupation." He ticked them off on his fingers as he talked. "Four points. Otherwise, the consequence is war. As you see, we have supporters outside our borders."

She waited a few moments before answering. "The purpose of these talks is justice. Justice is truth in action, so we should start with facts and truths."

"We bamboo have expectations," Levanter said. "We seek peace. I cannot speak for wild robots, which have their own purposes."

Sempronio looked offended again. "The Sea Group wishes to deal directly with our opponents in the war, who were human. You, Madame Mayor, represent the side with whom we will negotiate. Human to human, those are our conditions."

Levanter said, "Mayor Huette is by your express agreement the arbiter, not a negotiating partner."

Sempronio pointed at Ico. "Him?" Either that was a setup, or the ambassador had sussed out the weakest link in the room.

Ico's eyes got wide. Not a setup, then. "I'm here as an observer. We're neutral." He backed up all the way to the wall.

Sempronio pointed at Mercy.

Her eyes narrowed slightly. "I can speak only for myself, no one special."

"That would be useful," Huette said. "Please have a seat at the table."

As she sat, Mercy said, "I think all sentient beings who would be affected by these talks deserve a seat. So to speak."

Sempronio laughed, an ugly sound. "Which side are you on, sister? Justice or peace?"

"Both are possible, among other choices." She wasn't going to let herself be trapped.

He looked at me, and before he could ask, I said, "The Sea Group wiped out my hometown, so you don't want to negotiate with me."

Huette took a deep breath. "Due to circumstances beyond my control, I cannot decide who does and does not sit at this table. Anyone can sit here. My job is to make sure the process works. That's all. I'm the arbiter for who-ever is here. Our goal is an outcome. We can call it anything we want."

Sempronio stood up. "Under these circumstances, there's nothing to dis-cuss." He stamped out of the office. A display came on, showing the view from a camera in the reception area. He got as far as the front door, looked out at the robots at the gate, and turned back. He paced a few times across the room, then went into the gift shop, and cameras followed him.

"I suggest waiting," Mercy said. She patted her lap, and a pair of fippokats appeared out of nowhere and jumped up.

Sempronio looked at the plants and seeds for sale. A tray of drop-bear claws caught his eye, and he swept it off the counter. They flew and hit the ground, but nothing broke.

"That was rude," Huette said.

"He's frustrated," Mercy answered. "Things haven't gone as he expected."

I asked, "What did he expect?" If she knew, I could be prepared.

"A big stage in a grand hall where he could seem reasonable and win some concessions."

"Brian got killed," Huette said, no forgiveness in her voice.

I had another question. "Does anyone want another war?" It might have sounded rhetorical, but the combined armed forces had reviewed the stra-tegic and economic changes resulting from the war. Everyone who survived was worse off and some of them were totally destitute, except for the Ceta-cean Institute.

I was watching Ico, and he flinched when I asked the question. He hadn't been expecting the aircraft to blow up. He didn't start running until every-one else did. He did have a suspicion of some sort. I'd learned a lot in the war, including one very sad lesson. Some people found out they were sent on a suicide mission the hard way.

In the gift shop, Sempronio saw what he'd done, bent down, gathered the claws onto the tray, and tried to make everything look like it had before, un-aware that we were watching. We weren't supposed to know he was frustrated.

I checked with the team at the grand hall and repeated what I learned.

"The rioters were informed that the ambassador wasn't coming, and the riot is breaking up. The gendarmes identified the rioters as out-of-towners."

"That's good news," Huette said, although she'd probably already been told that by the gendarmes. "I'm proud of Bayonne's citizens."

We now needed to deal with the rioters, but that was for another day.

"If you wish," Mercy said, "it might be time to invite Sempronio back." She went to fetch him, followed by the kats.

I'd figured out what was going on and sent my conclusions to my commanding officer, who could take it from there. The Cetaceans had tried to look innocent. The investigation crew could look for tampering, but Cetaceans had good technical skills. What mattered was one fact. The Sea Group was all posture. I might not have to blast them to ashes, and that made me happy.

ICO

Sempronio came back, still acting outraged by everything. I kept remembering how the ground shook when the aircraft exploded. I didn't know for certain if the Cetaceans were working with the Sea Group, but if they were, killing Sempronio didn't make sense, did it? It did if the Sea Group didn't really want a war and the Cetaceans did. But why would we? The aircraft explosion could have been an accident. The colonel said that kind of aircraft fails a lot.

Brian saved our lives, I knew that. Did he have to die?

Huette said the talks would move to the grand hall soon, and we could continue business here until then. "A majority at this table so far favors peace."

"Peace is the status quo," Sempronio said. "As I have made clear, we want change."

"The exact terms for the change are the issue, then," she said. "We can go through them one by one."

"Madame Mayor," Levanter interrupted, "we have made arrangements to bury Brian in the garden, if this is an acceptable time."

She thought for a while, looking down at the table. "It is."

"We invite Sister Mercy to conduct a ceremony."

Mercy nodded. "It would be my honor." She looked solemn and serene, as if a weight on her shoulders made her more stable.

Huette didn't move. Mercy stood, took her by the arm, and led her into the garden.

Sempronio grumbled, "I suppose," and followed them. I didn't know what to expect. When I'd first arrived here, the forested garden frightened me. I'd never been anywhere like it, not even a kelp forest. Now, it felt strange and familiar at once, full of life like a kelp forest, but I could breathe easily, and all that life had its own smell.

We walked a long way in, and we stopped in front of a deep hole, and at the bottom lay something wrapped in dark fabric. When Cetaceans died, we were dropped overboard in a weighted bag for the sea to take. This would be no different, I supposed. The soil would take Brian.

There were benches nearby, but no one sat. I didn't want to feel comfortable. Mercy took a moment to compose herself.

"We are here as some of the people who knew Brian, and we know he will return as new life." Her voice was gentle and steady. "Death is only brief suffering, if it is suffering at all. Love is real. Love is a gift from the divine. Courage and generosity are real, and he shared those gifts with us. I came to know Brian through Denis, who is here with us too, beneath our feet and in our hearts."

She told how Denis had brought Brian to Tabitha House, where his presence became a blessing. I hadn't realized that he and Denis had known each other for just a few days. They seemed like old friends.

Huette stared into the hole. "Brian meant a lot to Bayonne. When there's time, he'll get due honors." That was all she said, and her voice broke with a sob as she said it.

As she spoke, robots that worked in the garden arrived. Mercy asked if anyone else wished to speak, and she looked at all of us, including the robots.

"This is Levanter." The voice came from Beluga. "He did more than help us stop *Vinvelo*. He saved many lives in the war and avoided recognition for his work. He saved lives on Euclid Nave Station simply by taking it upon himself to do what needed to be done, to do the right thing. He lived to help others, and he died in service to others. His being will become new beings here in this garden, and perhaps his dedication to service will become part of these next lives."

Mercy waited for anyone else to speak. Should I?

"I suppose," Sempronio said, "I should acknowledge that he helped save my life." He sounded annoyed. He looked at Colonel Chernova. "You, too."

Mercy waited a little longer, and then she sang a slow song about seeking and finding comfort as a robot began to fill the grave with soil.

Brian had done more good in the world than me—he had lived longer than I had, though, so I had time. Cetaceans had a formal ceremony for funerals, and this felt improvised, and it left me wishing I could still talk to Brian, like it wasn't quite over. I didn't feel comforted.

We turned to go back to the office.

"Mayor Huette, Ambassador Sempronio, wait," Levanter said through Beluga. "I have questions and I need your answers. They involve bamboo and our relationships to other sentient entities."

"Does it need to be here?" Sempronio pointed at the half-filled-in grave.

"Brian should be part of this. He understood machines deeply."

"Then what are the robots doing? Did he tell you?"

"The question is what they will do. Robots ultimately imitate humans, so if humans seek better purposes, robots will change. I am also changed by everything that happens."

"You're nothing like us."

"Nothing at all. Among other things, I can grow in ways you cannot. I get larger, stronger, and more masterful. Time gives you only two arms and one brain."

"Have you always been smug?" Sempronio said.

"I assumed one of Foehn's roots that was still healthy. From her, I have acquired confidence, and I can tap into that new aspect of my personality."

Levanter could change her personality that easily. I wished I could.

"There is more," she said. "I have received a message from Pax, from the bamboo that made my seed, my mother, and it had advice that all bamboo now wish to put into practice. This is where I have questions for you."

Sempronio stalked over to a bench and sat, defiant.

Huette didn't move. "What kind of advice?" She sounded willing to give it.

"Compassion is courage, Mother Stevland told us. We felt compassion for humans, and that is why we took the risk of revealing ourselves so we could provide you with the fruit to recover from *Vinvelo*. We can do much more for humans and for the Earth if we bamboo can agree over the means to uphold that compassion and grow with you. Here is my question. What is the difference between a covenant and a constitution?"

Everyone looked startled. What was she trying to do?

After a moment, Sempronio raised an eyebrow. "A constitution is a legal document about governance and organization, and about what can and cannot be done lawfully. It places controls on all parties. A covenant? The same thing." He rested his hands on his cane, satisfied.

"No," Mercy said. "There's a big difference, and it's trust. Tabitha House has a covenant. It's about principles that we share with each other, very different from a constitution. It's about trust and respect, not laws. It's not legally binding at all. We honor our covenant, and it's how we agree to do things."

"Trust, trust, trust," Sempronio said. "That's a fast way to be cheated."

She smiled serenely. "Our principles guide us."

"And you follow them?" he asked. "All of you?"

She looked around at the garden. "We agree to trust each other."

"You're very brave—"

"Exactly. We need courage to trust that much."

"The rest of us are cowards?"

She shook her head. "It's a voluntary commitment. It has to be."

Sempronio's lips moved as if he were going to answer, but he didn't.

Levanter asked, "Is there love?"

At that, Mercy laughed. "Oh, there has to be love for it to work."

"Love," Sempronio said dismissively.

"Love, yes," she said, "and honor and respect."

"It must be nice," he said. "Not so many arguments."

"Oh, it's not easy. We argue as much as anyone, except that we start with an agreement that we won't harm each other."

No harm—what would it feel like to trust that much?

"Bamboo are good at arguing," Levanter said. "We have argued for centuries."

Cetaceans had arguments, but they never lasted long because those in power decided, and we obeyed or else. We didn't have a constitution or a covenant.

"Centuries?" Huette said. "Constitutions don't last that long. Bills of rights do."

Mercy nodded. "Covenants are eternal arguments."

"You seem to enjoy the arguments," Sempronio said.

"They can be uplifting."

"This is enough." Sempronio stood up. "Machines are clever, I'll give you that. Arguing trees? You expect me to believe that?"

"They're real," Huette said. "I'll testify to that under oath."

"You've done that communing thing, then."

"No." She looked up at the trees. "Sorry, Levanter, I don't want to do that."

"I respect your decision," she answered. "We welcome all to share in our lives. Le Bois has found that if we limit our grandeur, humans find it less overwhelming. Ambassador, I can see your skepticism. By size, every mature bamboo is many thousands of times bigger than you."

"Are we done here?" he asked.

"Yes. Thank you all for your advice. If you wish, we can return to negotiations."

Sempronio began walking. "Communing. That's your means to control us."

"Human behavior is too complex to control. This may be why constitutions rarely last long. Humans are hard to understand."

"That's a fact," Huette said. I wasn't sure if I agreed anymore.

As we walked, I heard noise from outside the garden, some of it from robots. "Could you commune with a robot, Levanter?" I asked.

"No, their processes are too quick, exponentially quicker than humans are."

"But humans are quick," Huette said. "Intense. That's what you said."

"Quick and intense. I was surprised by how very pleasant you find touch."

"It's not pleasant for you?"

"The sense of touch usually informs us of something like caterpillars eating leaves."

By then, we were almost at the institute office.

Levanter said, "I would like to speak to Ambassador Sempronio alone, if he agrees."

He stopped. "Really? Why should I trust you?"

"I can promise you total honesty and no harm. No more, no less. A covenant, if you like. I am sure we will argue."

Sempronio held his cane in front of himself like a sword.

"You may bring it with you," Levanter said. "I know it contains a recording device. What I have to say is private, not secret."

"How—I suppose. Nothing is going well anyway." He turned to us. "You four, keep watch. If something happens, intervene."

"Of course, immediately," Colonel Chernova said. She had a very faint smile.

The ambassador went inside. Huette put Beluga down, and it rolled into the garden. We sat at a picnic table in the shade of a bamboo tree with an easy view of the office.

What would Levanter say? She seemed to know everything. Inside, Sempronio talked. Then he argued. He paced. He was about to swipe a basket of fruit onto the ground, and then he stopped.

"Levanter must have just told him about what we saw in the gift shop," Mercy said.

"What do you think they're saying?" I asked.

"I think," Huette said slowly, "Levanter's explaining that if we all work together, humans, robots, and bamboo, we can wipe the Sea Group out of existence."

"Why didn't they wipe out the Sea Group at the end of the war?" I asked.

"The Sea Group surrendered," Huette said, "and we have rules of war."

"They didn't have rules," the colonel said.

"That's why I still hate them," she answered.

If they all joined forces against the Sea Group, what would the Cetaceans do? Nothing. We'd be neutral.

In the office, Sempronio started to seem less angry. I thought about rules even for things like wars. Mercy went to Tabitha House for refreshments and returned with a tray of pickled vegetables, crackers, juice, and tea.

Colonel Chernova lifted a glass. "To Brian."

I raised my orange juice, one of my favorite landlubber foods. I thought about going to the beach with Brian and what we could have talked about. "How did Brian save lives during the war?" I asked.

"I don't know for sure," Colonel Chernova said. "He had skills with communication systems." She started to say more, then shrugged. "There aren't good memories from the war."

"I remember good people," Mercy said. "Do you? CAC soldiers I met were good." She told how they'd arranged for people to escape from war zones.

All three started telling more stories about good people in horrifying situations. Huette had settled refugees in Bayonne. The colonel had lost both her hands in battle, and doctors did amazing things for her. She took off her gloves to show hands that looked just a little too perfect.

"They're really little robots," she said. "They communicate directly with my nervous system."

Huette watched her open and close her fists. "Very smooth movement. How do they feel?"

"Pretty normal, but sometimes, they move faster than I can think. I mean, they're not wild hands, I control them, but they're not quite me. I don't know if that makes sense. I don't think about robots the same way anymore. It's like the exo-suits, I feel enhanced."

She invited us to touch her hands, and they felt cold and dry and a little hard under the synthetic skin.

"How about you, Ico?" Mercy asked. "Any good people?"

"I was out at sea and I wasn't very old. Nothing much happened to me during the war."

"I hope our stories don't bore you."

"No. I'm learning a lot." I was learning that the war was more awful than I'd been taught.

We had finished the snacks by the time Sempronio came out of the office.

"Mayor Huette, take me to Le Bois."

She jumped to her feet. "Sure. I mean, it's my duty and honor."

Mercy didn't look surprised, and I realized I wasn't totally surprised either, and I knew what it meant without being told. Levanter had gotten what she wanted, which was peace. The colonel grinned. She wanted peace, too.

Sempronio specified that only Huette could be present when he communed, but the colonel insisted on coming as security. I walked with them to the gate of the institute to see what was happening outside.

Soldiers, police, repair crews, and their robots were busy everywhere. The aircraft was twisted metal. On city hall, some white stones had been blown off. On the street in front of the institute, the pavement was still wet, washed clean.

I contacted the Cetacean system, and I got through to the captain I'd talked to days ago. I owed him a report.

"The aircraft carrying the ambassador blew up."

"So we heard."

He didn't ask how I was. "I almost got killed."

"How are the talks?" Colonel Chernova would have mourned me more than that, and Huette might have awarded me a medal. I felt better about delivering bad news—bad from his point of view.

"The ambassador is going to commune with one of the trees."

"Well. That's how they subvert people."

"It's likely the talks will result in a peace agreement."

Silence. That didn't surprise me.

"Report back shipboard as soon as you can. It's time to head out to sea." The transmission ended before I could answer.

Back out to sea.

The land beneath my feet felt solid, but the horizon was narrow. My shoulders were tense, but I could work that out swimming. I could swim out to one of our ships. I could follow orders. I could.

Instead, I went back into the garden, to the bench next to Brian's grave. A pair of fippokats came to doze on my lap. They trusted me. They trusted everyone who came into the garden. Only a certain kind of person came there, and I came there now.

After a while, Beluga rolled up.

"Sempronio lasted for twenty-one seconds," Levanter said.

"That's a long time, isn't it?"

"Le Bois experienced him as a blur of fear. Her sensitivity to her surroundings gives her understanding and compassion, which he experienced through her, perhaps for the first time. Mayor Huette is arranging to bring many more voices and viewpoints to the negotiations with the belief that an end to Sea Group isolation will result in a ripple effect of cultural changes, as she puts it."

"Huette didn't say much, but she heard everything. You'll be there?"

"I will, or another bamboo. We are working that out among ourselves."

Our voices woke up the fippokats on my lap.

"Will the Cetaceans be there?" Levanter asked.

That seemed like an innocent question. I knew it was loaded. So did Levanter. "I don't think so."

"This is why I am speaking to you directly and alone rather than through a chip network. Life has many strategies for survival. Humans seem to think plants are honest, simple, and interchangeable, yet we are artful, sophisticated, and idiosyncratic."

The fippokats stretched and hopped down, then disappeared into the forest.

"You understand us as beings like you," she said, "and speaking to you this way helps create an impression of us in your image. We are quite unlike humans, although we can learn from each other. You have seen the effect that communing has. Many come away from communing feeling that they are one with everything, although I wonder if they are reacting to briefly feeling very large."

Large—Levanter filled not only part of the garden, she grew outside on hills and in gardens.

"What's it like for you?" I asked.

"I thought Beluga had taught me about movement, but robots are entirely different. Instinct compels you to move. No place satisfies you, and movement makes you insensitive."

It did not.

"For you," she said, "problems can be abandoned, not solved."

"What do you mean?"

"You choose your problems. To grow, you find new places, and we remain in one place and increase in size and intelligence. For you, life is repetitious movement, sometimes described as the dance of life. Understanding these differences will help us work together."

Yes, we moved on to new places. "I've been ordered to go back out to sea."

"Your future is up to you."

"They're expecting me to report back." I wasn't a landlubber. I needed to go. "Goodbye, Levanter."

"You will always be welcome here."

Mercy was entering city hall. I wanted to say goodbye to her, to Huette—especially Huette—but I needed to get back out at sea to watch whales and pretend that was all we did.

I had a little room down the road, and not much in it, mostly clothes. My life was small. And I had a weight on my shoulders that did not make me more stable or keep me in place like an anchor. It was like a weight we used to sink a dead body. I was lucky to be alive. No, it wasn't luck. I had friends.

From childhood, my life had seemed like the wide horizons of the high seas, but I was confined by the hulls of ships, and even the biggest ship was tiny next to the Pax Institute garden. The size of the ship wasn't what was confining.

"We might not be friends when this is done," I said. I didn't want to hope for too much.

"I will still be your friend," Levanter said. "The crown with the brown ribbon has the clearest signal for me. You may stay in the office or come out into the garden. Remember that humans are visually oriented, and bamboo are more spatial. Do you wish to have someone be present to assist you?"

I didn't want to share this with anyone. Levanter explained that the stem with the tattoo had the chip, and that was where I wanted to be. Outside, I slipped on the crown and my thoughts wandered

into a bright space. I closed my eyes automatically, but brightness remained. Eyes, dozens, thousands, in the sun, bright sun. Everything all at once, from every direction, pinpoints running together and the world is all around me and I can see myself from every direction and it makes no sense. I don't have words, and a butterfly flaps its wings toward my eyes, away from my eyes, at the

I snatched off the crown, dizzy and a little nauseated. I'd seen too much for me to understand, the entire garden at once, parts of the road, a field over a hill. I didn't know where I was. I was in many places.

Many places at once. Humans go to new places, Levanter said, but if I am in many places, where can I go?

"Are you all right?" Levanter asked. "You kept your eyes closed."

"Are you disappointed?"

"The question is you. Are you all right?"

I was unchanged. I'd felt nothing really, a little disorientation. That couldn't be all of what this was about.

I put the crown on and kept my eyes open. "Let's try again."

I'm not looking through my eyes, I'm seeing everything, not trying to understand but to experience. I am big, diffuse, and strong and aware. The wind moves me. A bird, a squirrel, I can watch, a caterpillar chews on a leaf, I can watch it, I can feel it, and I have no fear, it is small, I am big, I am

capable, I am deep, and there is moisture, there is sweetness, there are parts
that hurt and parts that thrill with growth.

My other body is walking. I am looking and in a place where I belong and
it belongs to me.

I belong. I belong. Like never before. This is mine, this is me, the universe
comes to me. Light. Water. Creatures that find me home. A human walking
and touching my stem and stroking my leaves, he is this universe that I fit
into and as it changes, I change, both of us together, and I will make this my
place, it is my place, I am this place.

I am big, too big, a tiny part in a huge whole, and this one part, this twig,
this leaf, a new leaf unfurling, the movement, always stretching out, a new
piece of me. Small, tender, and there are stronger, older pieces, and they feel
the sunshine, energy, light is energy, and energy creates everything inside
me, energy becoming tamed. I can do anything with it. I can do anything,
make things that change me, that change everything. I have control. I know
what is happening here and in a field of shining flowers, I am in the field,
here is so many places. Everywhere. Everything is telling me something. The
sun says that the day will end soon, it is the end of summer. It is light it is
more it is meaning it is life.

I am active. Acting without moving. Changing, and bigger. I am get-
ting bigger. Another leaf, opening, a bud forming, a root pushing through
ground, and all around it is a living matrix. Like a fish in the sea, a root in
the ground. Unmoving, moved, unchanging, growing, surrounding myself,
both selves, different and not—

I snatched off the crown. I was myself again, small, tiny. And calm. But
I'd never felt calm. No, not calm, this was another feeling. Self-assured. No,
self-possessed. I owned this body. I was this body. I closed my eyes and felt it,
every part I could, chilly fingers, feet adjusting to shifting weight, the familiar
scuff of a sleeve on my wrist. I was huge. I was busy. I was in one place, but
this place did not define me.

Sound—that defined me as a human. I could hear. The sounds touched
me and I felt them. The sun touched my head and told me that its fire sent
warmth to everything around it. Scents of soil and flowers and greenery, that
was me as a human understanding the universe.

"Are you all right?" Levanter asked. So big, Levanter was so big, and she
asked about me, talked to me, as she carried out a conversation with something in its roots, I didn't understand, and an opening flower bud would have
meaning.

Was I all right? I was . . . Ico, I was—no, I wasn't that anymore. I was. I didn't know. And Levanter would want an answer or she would call for help and I wanted to be alone.

"That's a hard question," I said.

Honestly it was. Why should I ever say anything that wasn't honest? The rest of the universe was honest with me.

Most of it.

A frightened part, a hungry part, a needy part, it lied. A sad part of the universe, the part that fought. And I fought too, I had to fight, and—and honestly, why did I fight? Who, for what, and how? I knew the answer without thinking.

"Sometimes we fight," I said. "I can be real, I can be honest, and work, not fight."

That was my voice, a real voice. Levanter spoke with an artificial voice that I would understand because humans had made those machines. No, I understood, and there were no words. Growth for me was to change what I did.

The forest around me had changed. No, my eyes had changed, seeing more, aware of what was behind me, above me, what it meant. I walked and just looked, felt all those bones in my body and the muscles on them and the blood that brought them fuel and oxygen from my breathing, my breathing, no need to think, breathing like a leaf opening, stretching wide.

Levanter said she was confident. I might be confident. I had things to do.

"Levanter," I said, "we'll need to talk about the future. I have to go now. I'll be back."

"I will need an assistant."

Assistant. At one point, I'd have rather been in charge. I'd have been ambitious. I'd have been what people told me I wanted to be.

At the dock, I left a bag of clothes. A skiff carried me to the ship, and the deck rocked beneath my feet. Waves in water came from wind and gravity and currents spinning with the rotation of the planet, all of it like a dance beneath my feet.

"Ico! Welcome aboard!" I knew those faces and wondered what sad things they fought—besides all the needy things I knew they were fighting.

"You're back!" the almost-friend said, the one who was going to get me webbed hands. I didn't want them anymore.

I answered, "I need to see the captain."

The captain might not be happy with the way that the negotiations were headed toward peace. The captain was going to be unhappy with me, but not

much. I was expendable. I would never walk this deck again. This water—
but other people had ships and boats. I could walk other decks. I touched the
railing and felt the dance of the water. The sea would always be a part of me.

Belowdecks, the captain said, "So it's peace. We can cope with that."

They could cope. They had plans for the whales and for themselves, and
no one else was worth helping.

"Yes," I said, "we want a good world, all of us. I mean everything sentient
and even things that aren't. I think we can have it. Honestly."

"I'm glad you agree."

"No, I mean honestly, we can have it for everyone."

He shifted in his chair. "I'd like to hear more." He didn't mean it.

"They're going to work out a treaty, and it will aim at bettering everyone."

"I don't understand what you mean." He knew how to lie, and if I didn't
know better, I'd have believed him.

"This isn't the place for me anymore."

I stood up and unfastened my uniform. I took off the medals, dropped the
clothing, and walked out with the medals in my hand. He was yelling, but
he couldn't do anything. I threw the medals into the water, jumped over the
railing, and dove in.

The water welcomed me, a goodbye and a hello all around me. I swam
back to shore, rocking with the waves, climbed onto the dock, and found the
sack of clothes. No one paid attention to me, just another swimmer enjoying
a sunset dip.

I arrived at the Pax Institute after dark. Maybe Levanter would be dozing.
Mercy was waiting for me at the gate and smiled.

"You'll be working here, Levanter says. I'm glad. She says she has a message
to send to Pax."

In the office, Levanter explained how to create a human-to-human message
and attach the sound of bamboo.

"Tell them that this is a message for Mother Stevland, and it comes from
the rainbow bamboo of Earth. She will understand it. We will have more to
say, but this needs to be said now. Stevland is waiting."

ACKNOWLEDGMENTS

In a way, this book started with my mother, who propagated the love of houseplants in me when I was a child. Many years later, in my greenery-filled living room, one plant killed another plant, and I decided to find out why. I learned that plants perceive and engage with their environment in many ways. They compete against each other, they fend off predators together, and they use animals for tasks like pollination and seed distribution. When the tomatoes in your garden turn red, the tomato plants are communicating with you: *Eat this, please, to sow more tomatoes for me.*

Plants are active and sometimes aggressive. Because I write science fiction, I began to ask: What if plants could think?

In some ways they do. For example, many plants adjust their growth for maximum sunshine, leaning away from shadows. To do that, they have to sense the direction of light and alter their growth on the basis of their perceptions. This is a form of cognition—but what if they could think more like humans? What would they want?

That was the story I tried to tell. I invented a planet where plants could dominate, taking care as much as possible to let these sentient plants employ the same wide-ranging abilities that Earth plants use to survive and prevail.

It turned out to be a long story, both because there was a lot to tell, and because no matter how I tweaked the environment of Pax, plants generally react slowly, so the story sometimes took place over decades and centuries.

It also took years to write and the help of many people. For this book, thanks go to my husband, Jerry Finn, official technobabble consultant. I also want to thank my editor, Jen Gunnels at Tor, and my agent, Jennie Goloboy, for their contributions in shaping this novel. The Lake View Set critique group—Michael Ryan Chandler, Julie Danvers, Kay F. Ellis, and Angeli Primlani—provided guidance and encouragement.

The chance to name one of the characters was auctioned off for charity, and Ico commemorates a beloved brother.

Many fans shared ideas that found their way into the story, and they challenged me to maintain the joy of world-building and the themes of cooperation and empathy. Writing these novels changed the way I understand our world and ecology, and I hope I conveyed that sense of wonder to you. Our houseplants and gardens, forests and grasslands, tundras and taigas, even the so-called weeds along the side of the road, keep our Earth green and good.

ABOUT THE AUTHOR

Badassity Photography

SUE BURKE spent many years working as a reporter and editor for a variety of newspapers and magazines before writing her critically acclaimed novel *Semiosis.* She has also published the novels *Interference, Immunity Index, Dual Memory,* and more than forty short stories in addition to working as a literary translator. She currently lives in Chicago. You can find her online at sueburke.site and semiosispax.com.